R.L. STINE

graphix PRESENTS:

Goosebumps

SLAPPY'S TALES OF HORROR

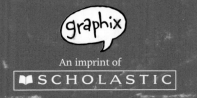

Adapted and illustrated by Dave Roman,
Jamie Tolagson, Gabriel Hernandez, and Ted Naifeh

Color by Jose Garibaldi

graphix

An imprint of
■SCHOLASTIC

The Goosebumps series created by Parachute Press, Inc.

Copyright © 2015 Scholastic Inc.
Illustrations, pages 1–39 © 2007 Jamie Tolagson
Illustrations, pages 41–82, © 2006 Gabriel Hernandez
Illustrations, pages 85–124 © 2007 Ted Naifeh
Cover, illustrations, pages iv, 40, 83–84, 125–172 © 2015 Dave Roman

Based on *A Shocker on Shock Street* © 1995 Scholastic Inc., *The Werewolf of Fever Swamp* © 1993 Scholastic Inc., *Ghost Beach* © 1994 Scholastic Inc., and *Night of the Living Dummy* © 1993 Scholastic Inc.

Library of Congress control number: 2014959511

ISBN 978-0-545-83600-5 (hardcover)
ISBN 978-0-545-83595-4 (paperback)

10 9 8 7 6 5 4 3   16 17 18 19

Printed in China   38
First edition, September 2015

Edited by Adam Rau and Sheila Keenan
Color by Jose Garibaldi
Book design by Phil Falco
Creative Director: David Saylor

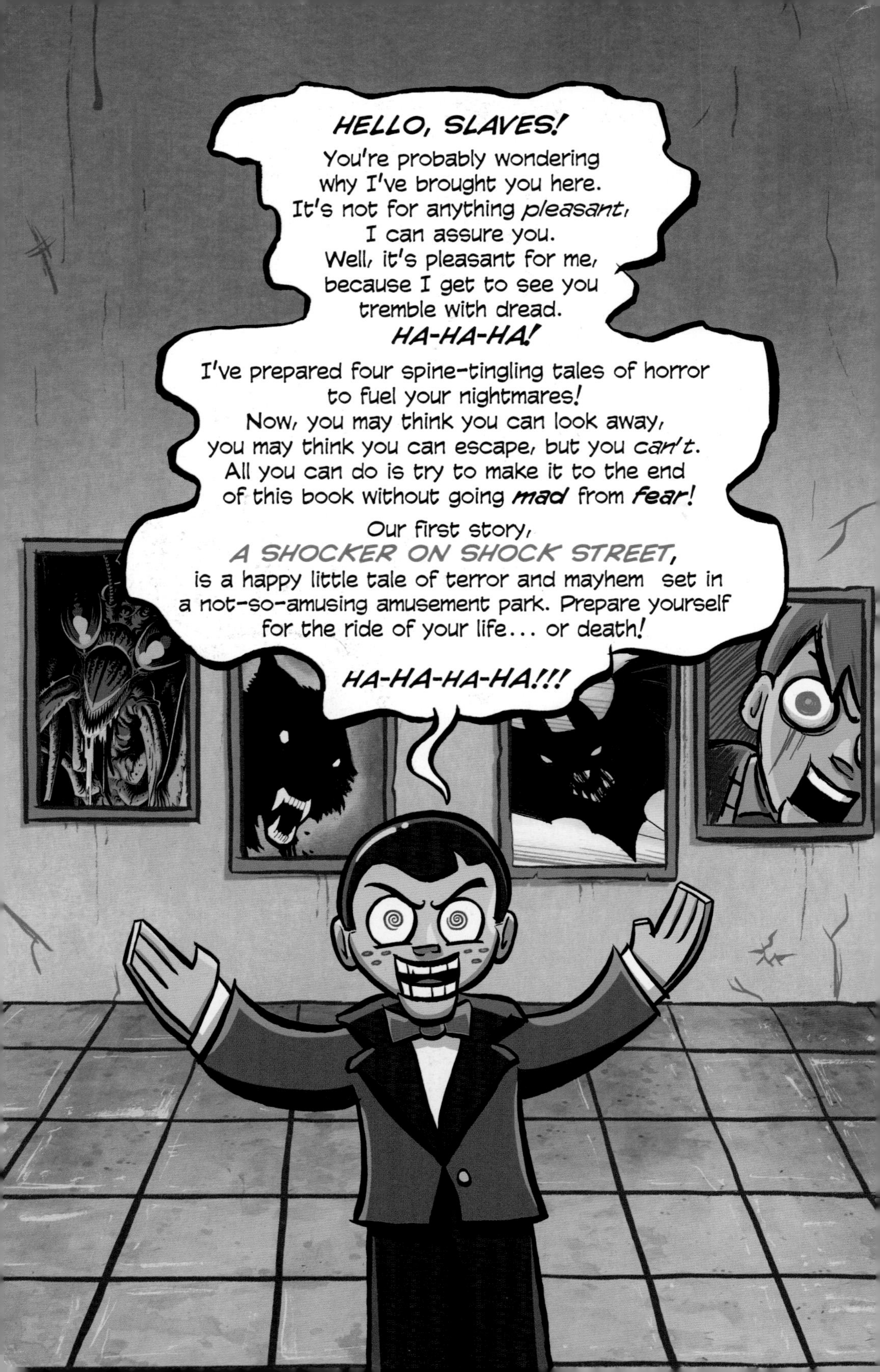
HELLO, SLAVES!
You're probably wondering why I've brought you here. It's not for anything pleasant, I can assure you. Well, it's pleasant for me, because I get to see you tremble with dread.
HA-HA-HA!
I've prepared four spine-tingling tales of horror to fuel your nightmares! Now, you may think you can look away, you may think you can escape, but you can't. All you can do is try to make it to the end of this book without going mad from fear!
Our first story, A SHOCKER ON SHOCK STREET, is a happy little tale of terror and mayhem set in a not-so-amusing amusement park. Prepare yourself for the ride of your life... or death!
HA-HA-HA-HA!!!

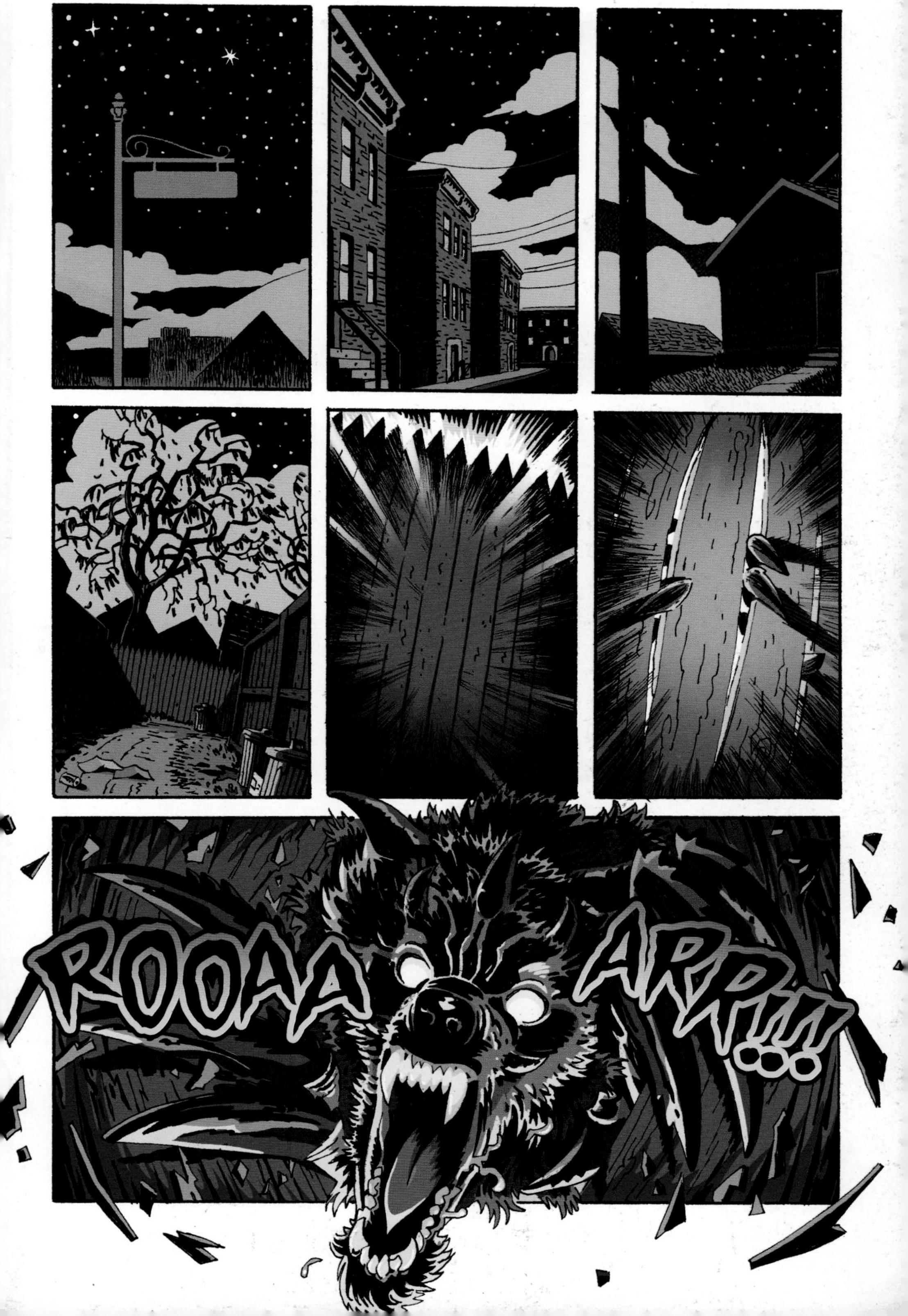
ROOAAARR!!!

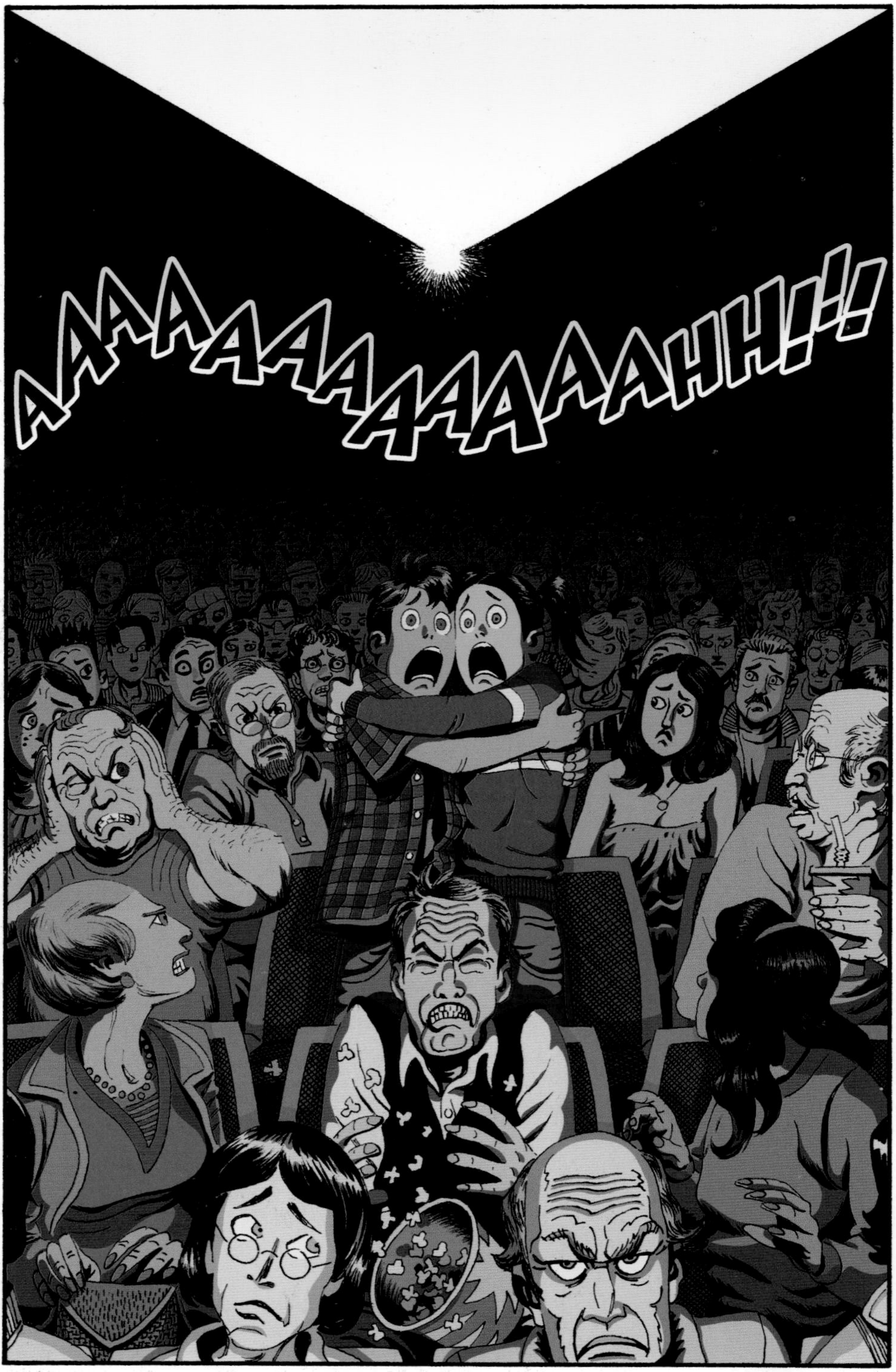
AAAAAAAAAAAAAHH!!!

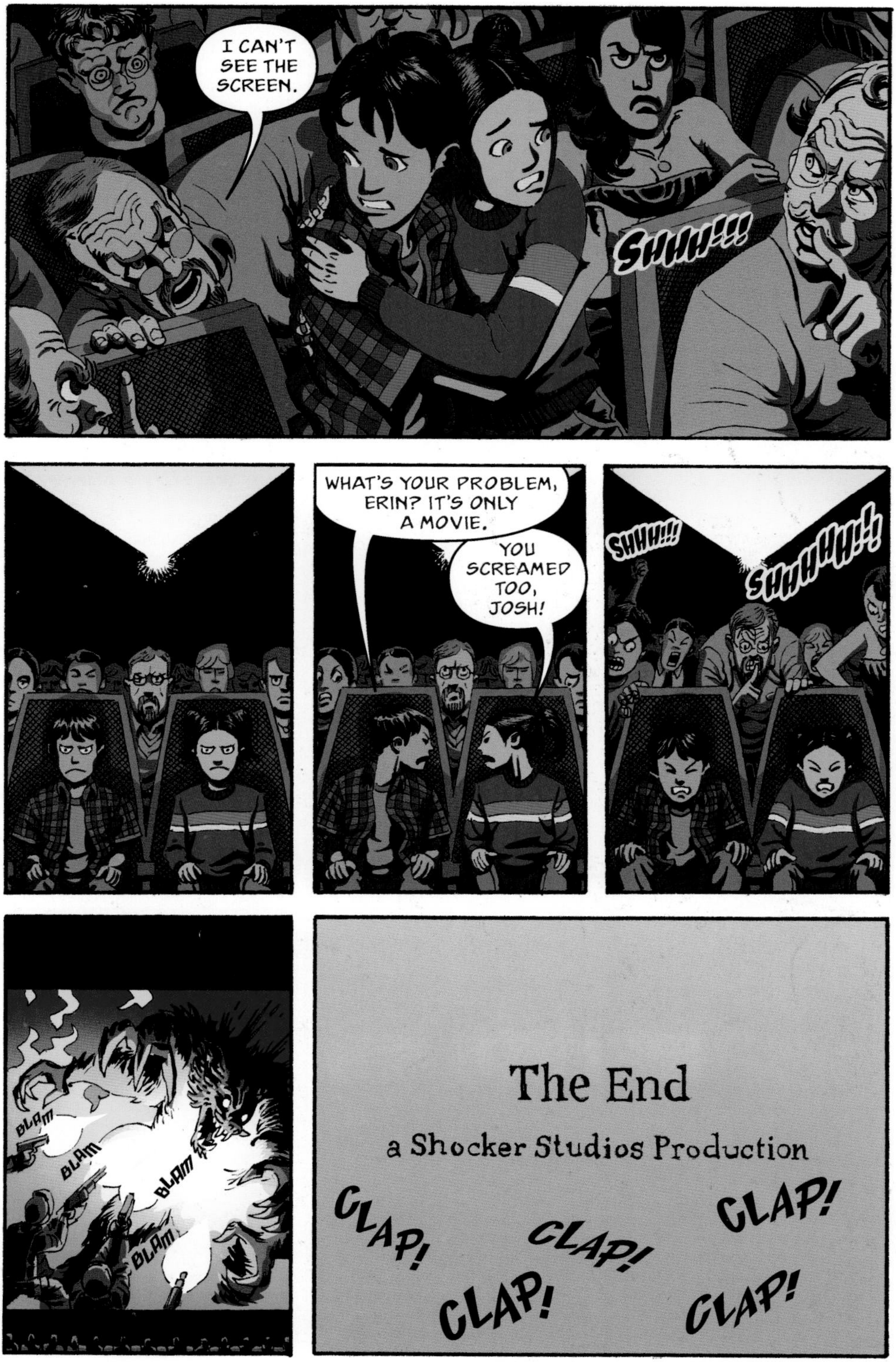
I CAN'T SEE THE SCREEN.
SHHH!!!
WHAT'S YOUR PROBLEM, ERIN? IT'S ONLY A MOVIE.
YOU SCREAMED TOO, JOSH!
SHHH!!!
SHHHHH!!!
BLAM
BLAM
BLAM
BLAM
The End
a Shocker Studios Production
CLAP!
CLAP!
CLAP!
CLAP!
CLAP!

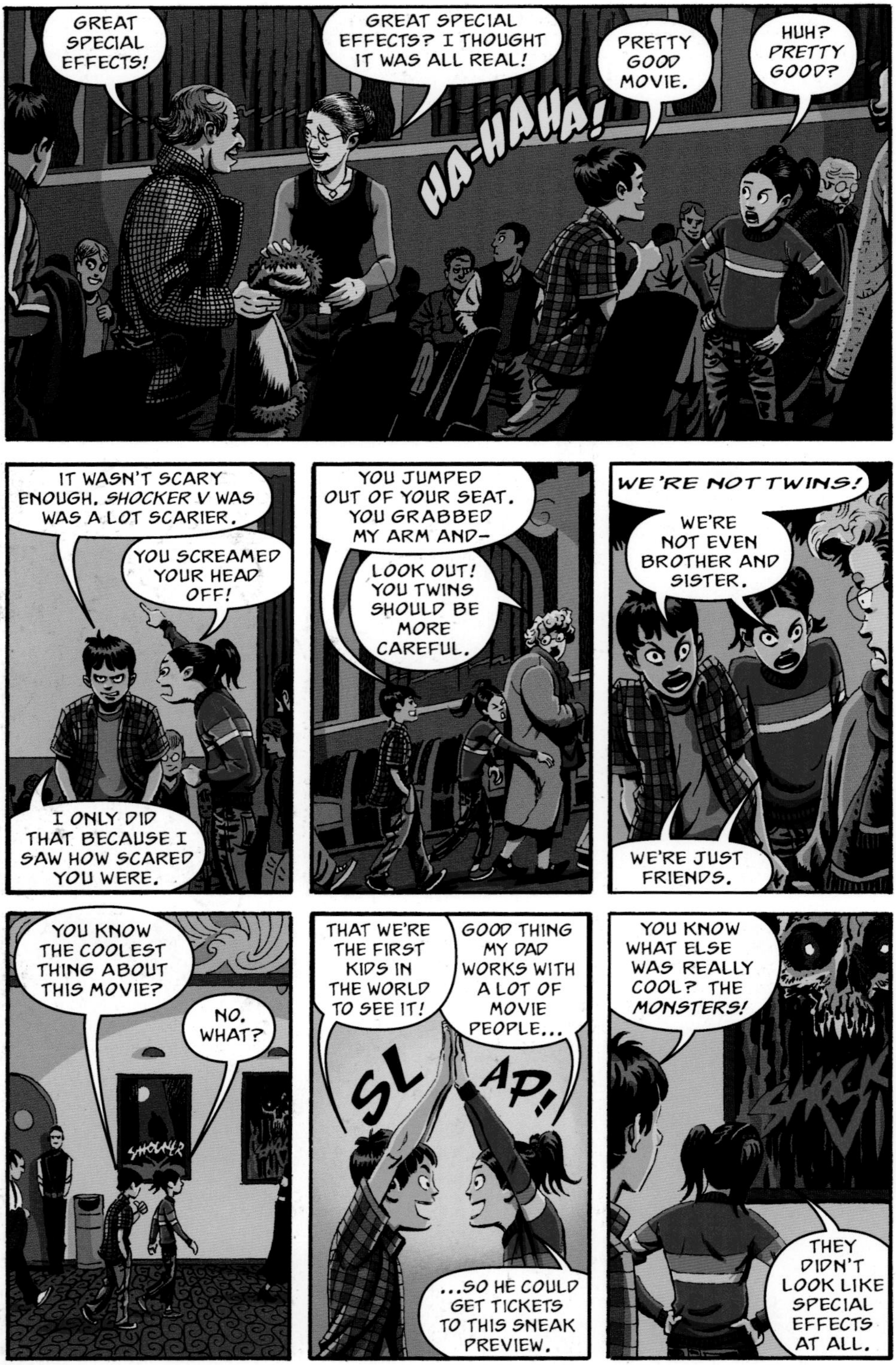
GREAT SPECIAL EFFECTS!
GREAT SPECIAL EFFECTS? I THOUGHT IT WAS ALL REAL!
HA-HAHA!
PRETTY GOOD MOVIE.
HUH? *PRETTY GOOD*?
IT WASN'T SCARY ENOUGH. *SHOCKER V* WAS WAS A LOT SCARIER.
YOU SCREAMED YOUR HEAD OFF!
I ONLY DID THAT BECAUSE I SAW HOW SCARED YOU WERE.
YOU JUMPED OUT OF YOUR SEAT. YOU GRABBED MY ARM AND–
LOOK OUT! YOU TWINS SHOULD BE MORE CAREFUL.
WE'RE NOT TWINS!
WE'RE NOT EVEN BROTHER AND SISTER.
WE'RE JUST FRIENDS.
YOU KNOW THE COOLEST THING ABOUT THIS MOVIE?
NO. WHAT?
THAT WE'RE THE FIRST KIDS IN THE WORLD TO SEE IT!
GOOD THING MY DAD WORKS WITH A LOT OF MOVIE PEOPLE...
SLAP!
...SO HE COULD GET TICKETS TO THIS SNEAK PREVIEW.
YOU KNOW WHAT ELSE WAS REALLY COOL? THE *MONSTERS!*
THEY DIDN'T LOOK LIKE SPECIAL EFFECTS AT ALL.

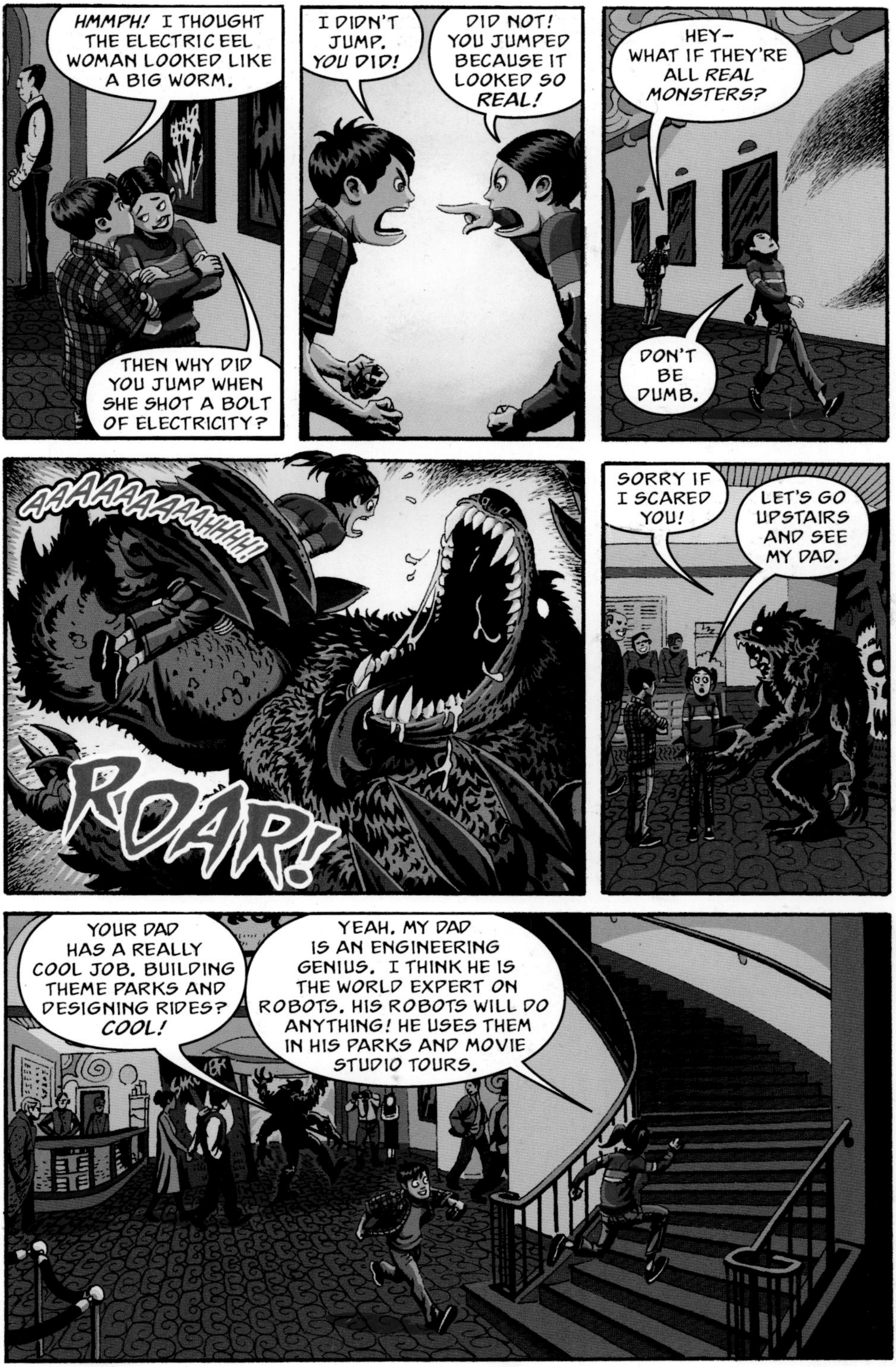
HMMPH! I THOUGHT THE ELECTRIC EEL WOMAN LOOKED LIKE A BIG WORM.
THEN WHY DID YOU JUMP WHEN SHE SHOT A BOLT OF ELECTRICITY?
I DIDN'T JUMP. YOU DID!
DID NOT! YOU JUMPED BECAUSE IT LOOKED SO REAL!
HEY— WHAT IF THEY'RE ALL REAL MONSTERS?
DON'T BE DUMB.
AAAAAAAAAAHHH!
ROAR!
SORRY IF I SCARED YOU!
LET'S GO UPSTAIRS AND SEE MY DAD.
YOUR DAD HAS A REALLY COOL JOB. BUILDING THEME PARKS AND DESIGNING RIDES? COOL!
YEAH. MY DAD IS AN ENGINEERING GENIUS. I THINK HE IS THE WORLD EXPERT ON ROBOTS. HIS ROBOTS WILL DO ANYTHING! HE USES THEM IN HIS PARKS AND MOVIE STUDIO TOURS.

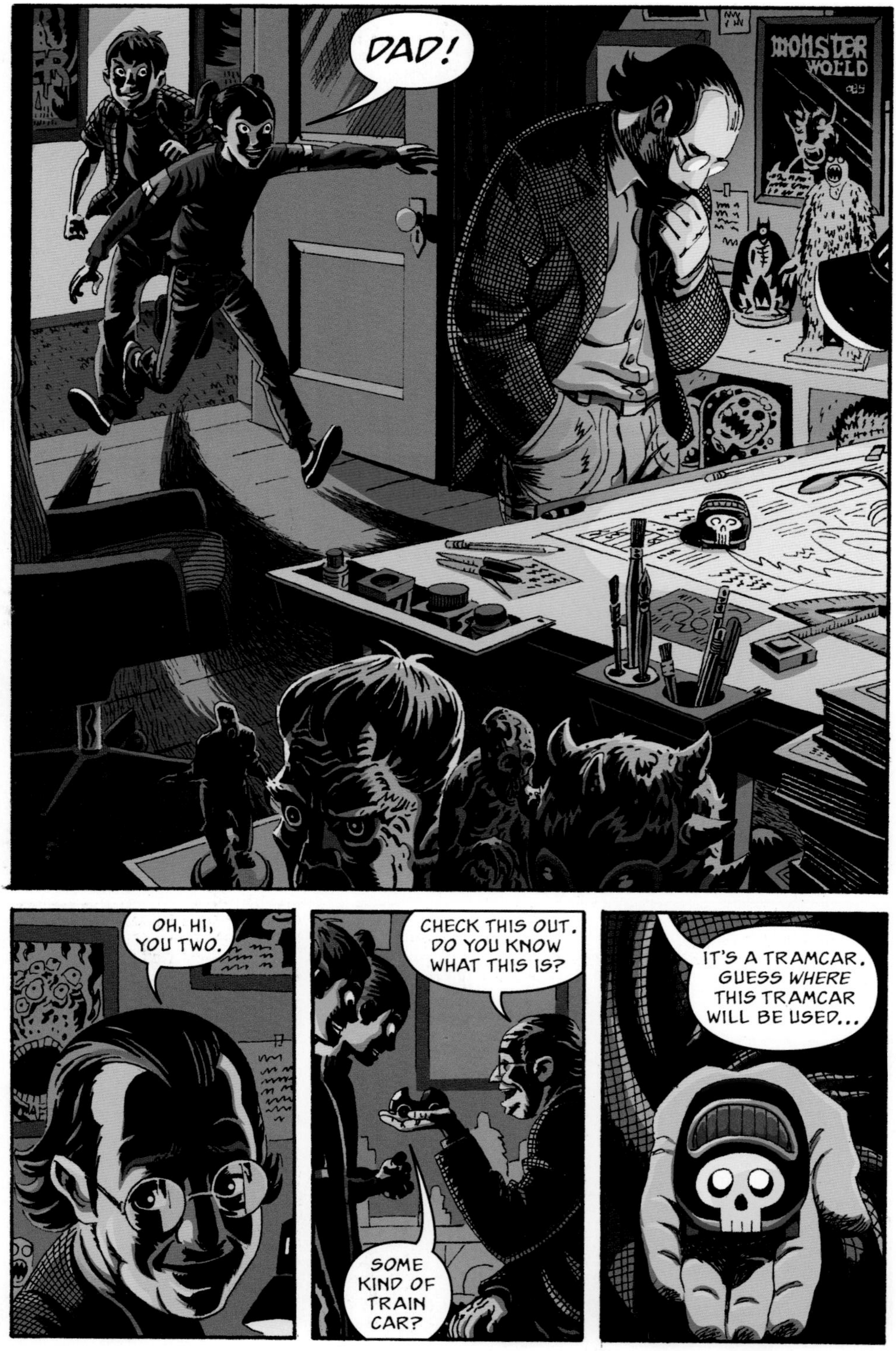
DAD!
MONSTER WORLD
OH, HI, YOU TWO.
CHECK THIS OUT. DO YOU KNOW WHAT THIS IS?
SOME KIND OF TRAIN CAR?
IT'S A TRAMCAR. GUESS WHERE THIS TRAMCAR WILL BE USED...

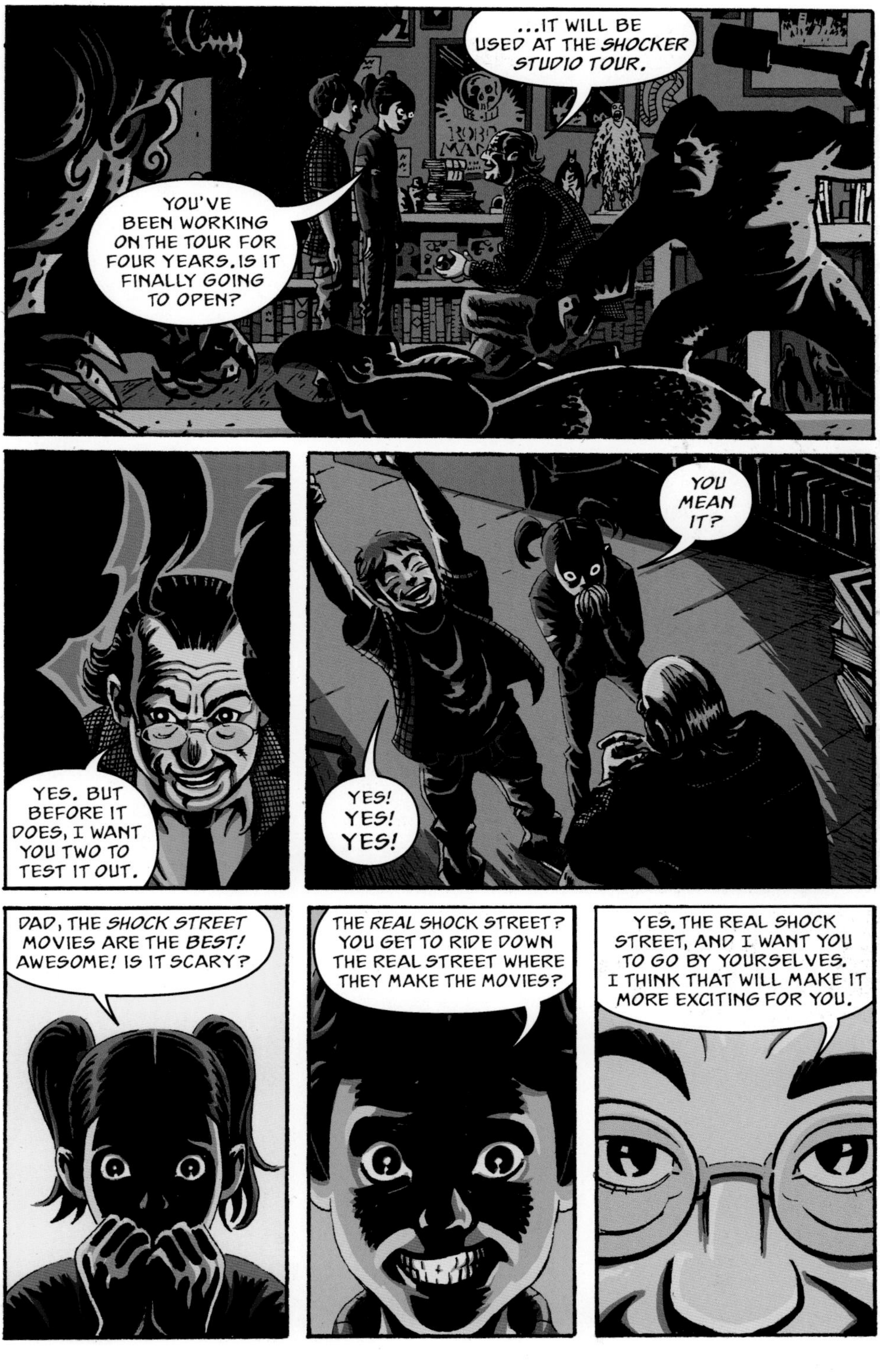
...IT WILL BE USED AT THE SHOCKER STUDIO TOUR.
YOU'VE BEEN WORKING ON THE TOUR FOR FOUR YEARS. IS IT FINALLY GOING TO OPEN?
YES. BUT BEFORE IT DOES, I WANT YOU TWO TO TEST IT OUT.
YOU MEAN IT?
YES! YES! YES!
DAD, THE SHOCK STREET MOVIES ARE THE BEST! AWESOME! IS IT SCARY?
THE REAL SHOCK STREET? YOU GET TO RIDE DOWN THE REAL STREET WHERE THEY MAKE THE MOVIES?
YES. THE REAL SHOCK STREET, AND I WANT YOU TO GO BY YOURSELVES. I THINK THAT WILL MAKE IT MORE EXCITING FOR YOU.

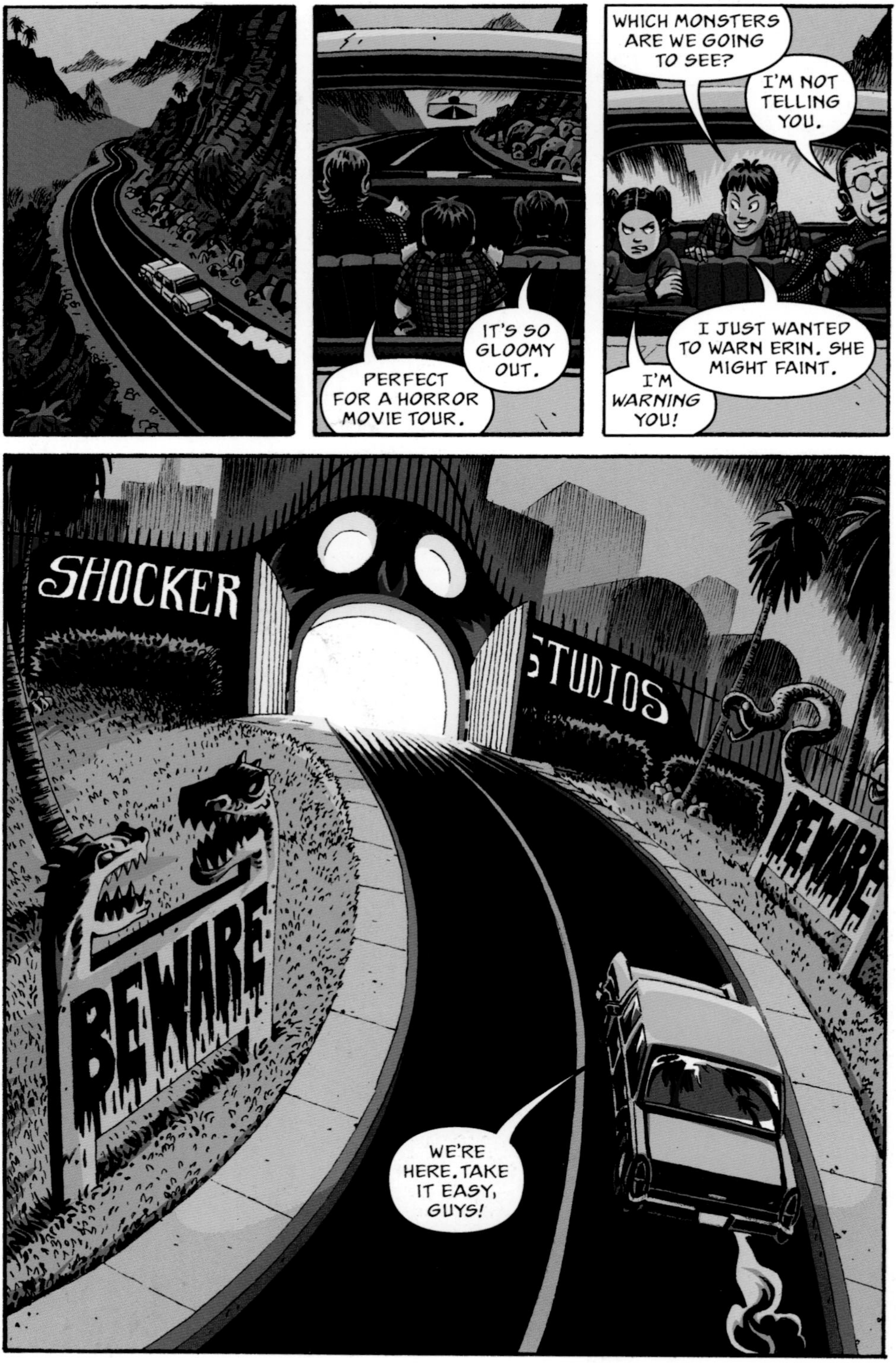
IT'S SO GLOOMY OUT.
PERFECT FOR A HORROR MOVIE TOUR.
WHICH MONSTERS ARE WE GOING TO SEE?
I'M NOT TELLING YOU.
I JUST WANTED TO WARN ERIN. SHE MIGHT FAINT.
I'M WARNING YOU!
SHOCKER
STUDIOS
BEWARE
BEWARE
WE'RE HERE. TAKE IT EASY, GUYS!

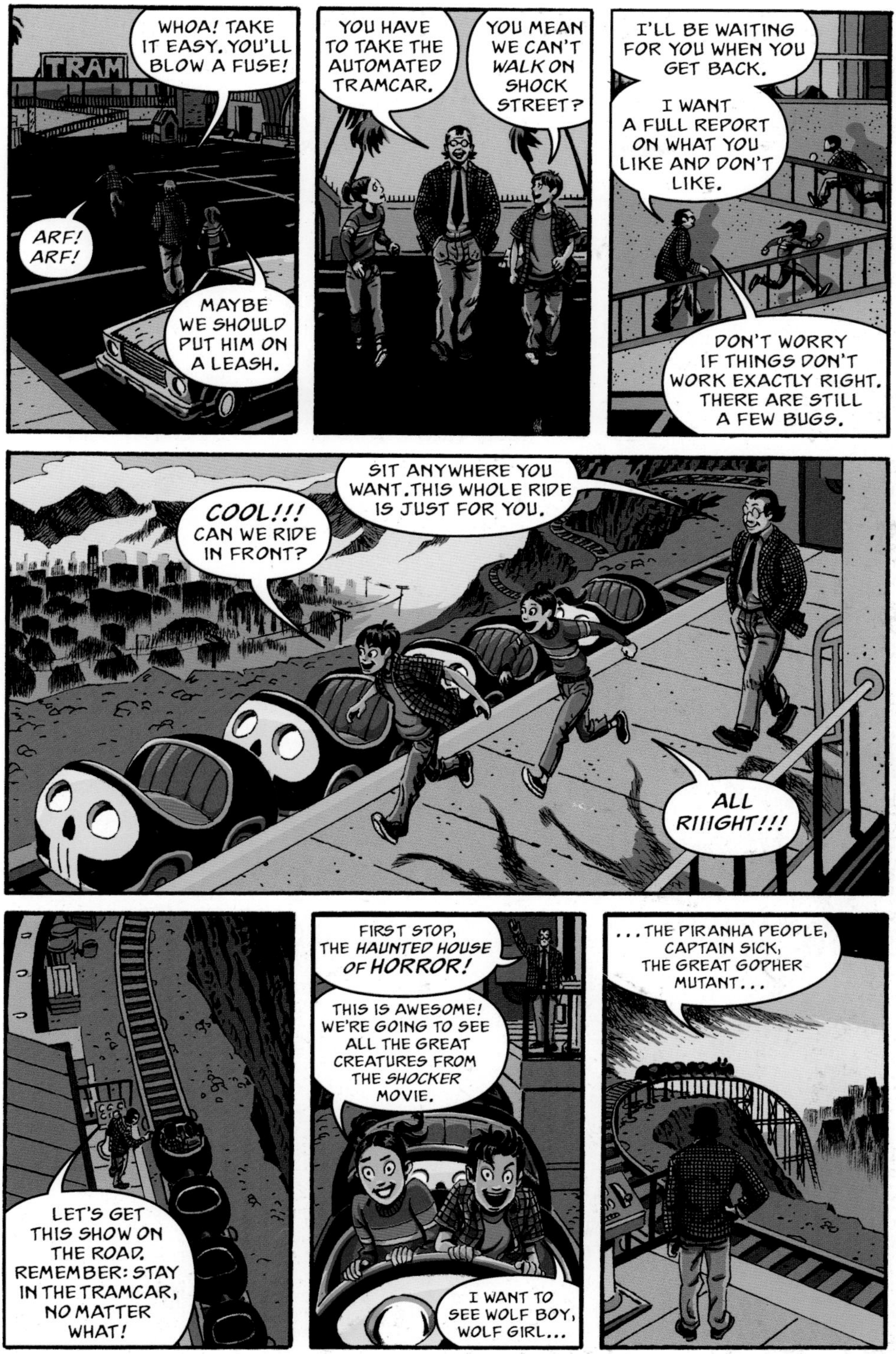
TRAM
WHOA! TAKE IT EASY. YOU'LL BLOW A FUSE!
ARF! ARF!
MAYBE WE SHOULD PUT HIM ON A LEASH.
YOU HAVE TO TAKE THE AUTOMATED TRAMCAR.
YOU MEAN WE CAN'T *WALK* ON SHOCK STREET?
I'LL BE WAITING FOR YOU WHEN YOU GET BACK.
I WANT A FULL REPORT ON WHAT YOU LIKE AND DON'T LIKE.
DON'T WORRY IF THINGS DON'T WORK EXACTLY RIGHT. THERE ARE STILL A FEW BUGS.
COOL!!! CAN WE RIDE IN FRONT?
SIT ANYWHERE YOU WANT. THIS WHOLE RIDE IS JUST FOR YOU.
ALL RIIIGHT!!!
LET'S GET THIS SHOW ON THE ROAD. REMEMBER: STAY IN THE TRAMCAR, NO MATTER WHAT!
FIRST STOP, THE *HAUNTED HOUSE OF HORROR!*
THIS IS AWESOME! WE'RE GOING TO SEE ALL THE GREAT CREATURES FROM THE *SHOCKER* MOVIE.
I WANT TO SEE WOLF BOY, WOLF GIRL...
...THE PIRANHA PEOPLE, CAPTAIN SICK, THE GREAT GOPHER MUTANT...

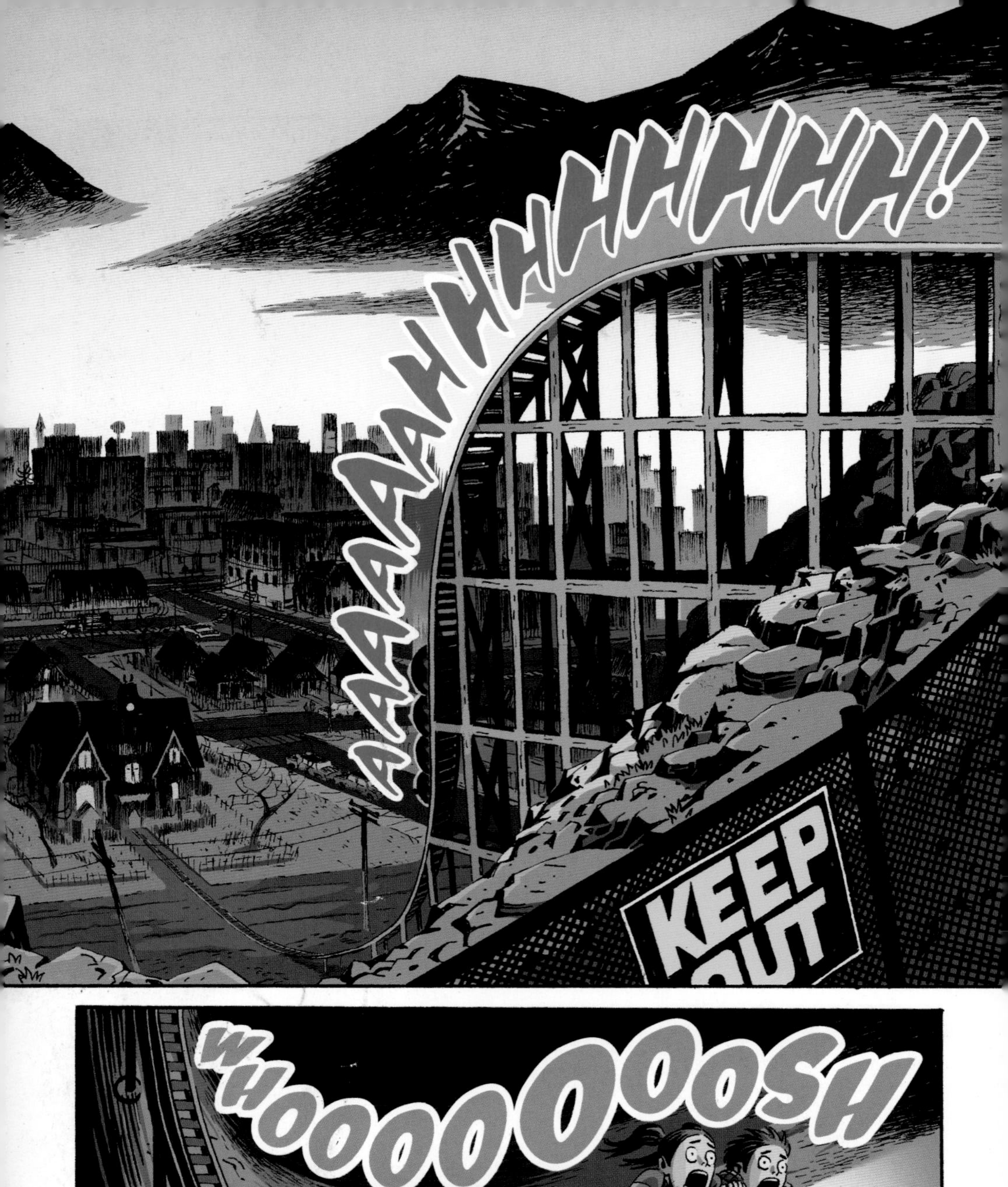
AAAAAHHHHHHHHH!
KEEP
OUT
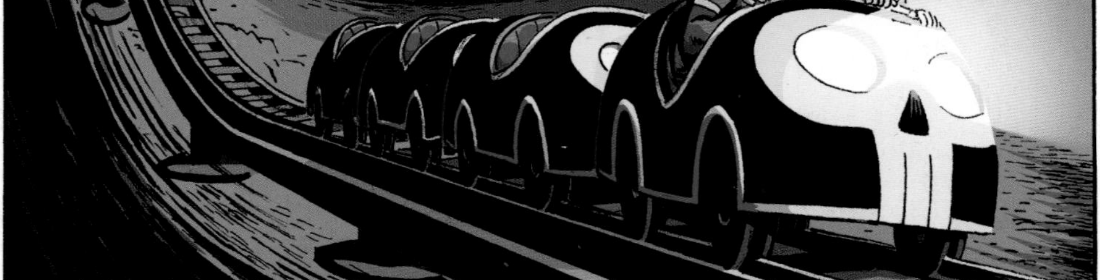
WHOOOOOOOSH

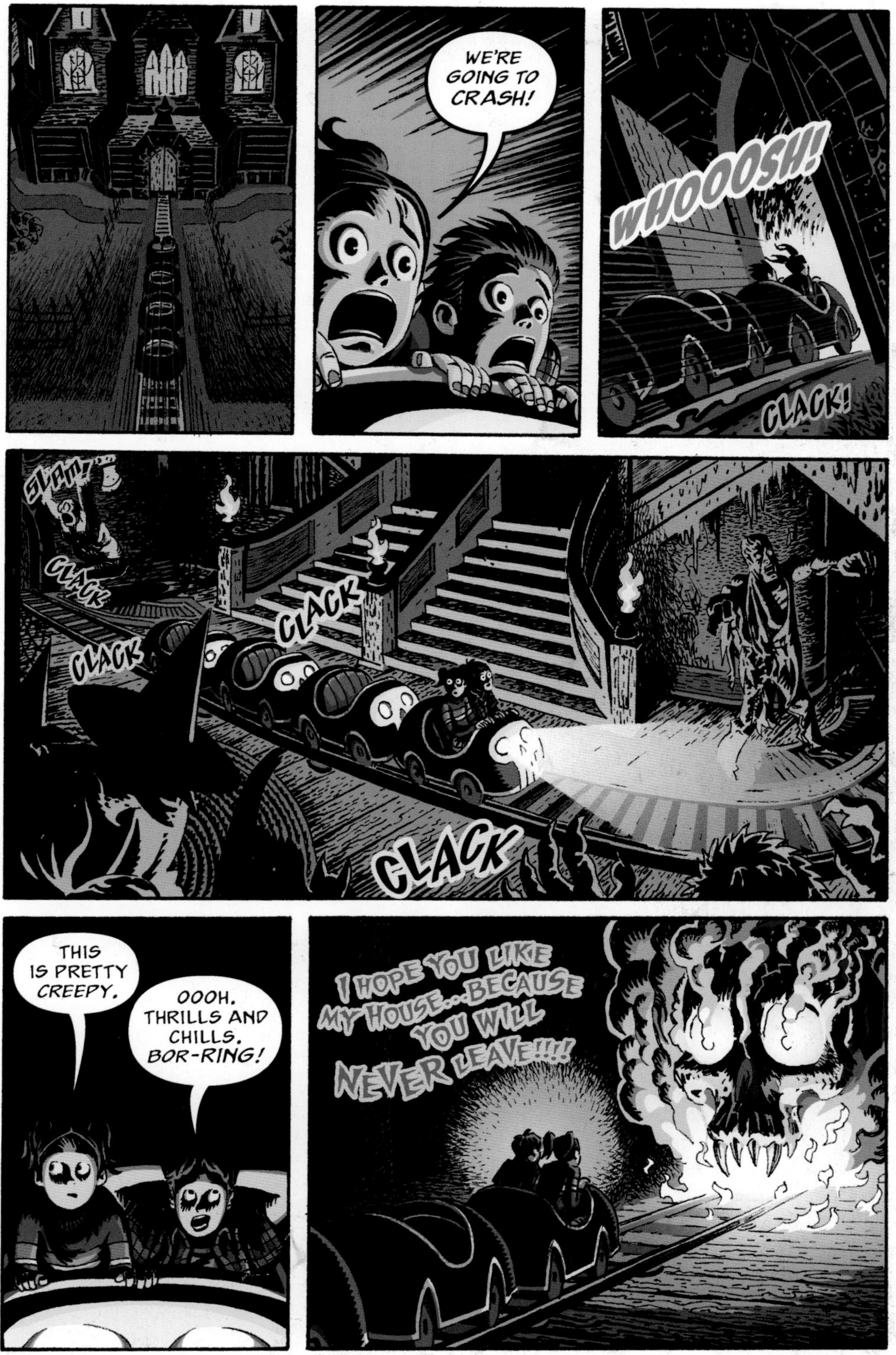
WE'RE GOING TO CRASH!
WHOOOOSH!
CLACK!
SLAM!
CLACK
CLACK
CLACK
CLACK
THIS IS PRETTY CREEPY.
OOOH. THRILLS AND CHILLS. BOR-RING!
I HOPE YOU LIKE MY HOUSE...BECAUSE YOU WILL NEVER LEAVE!!!!

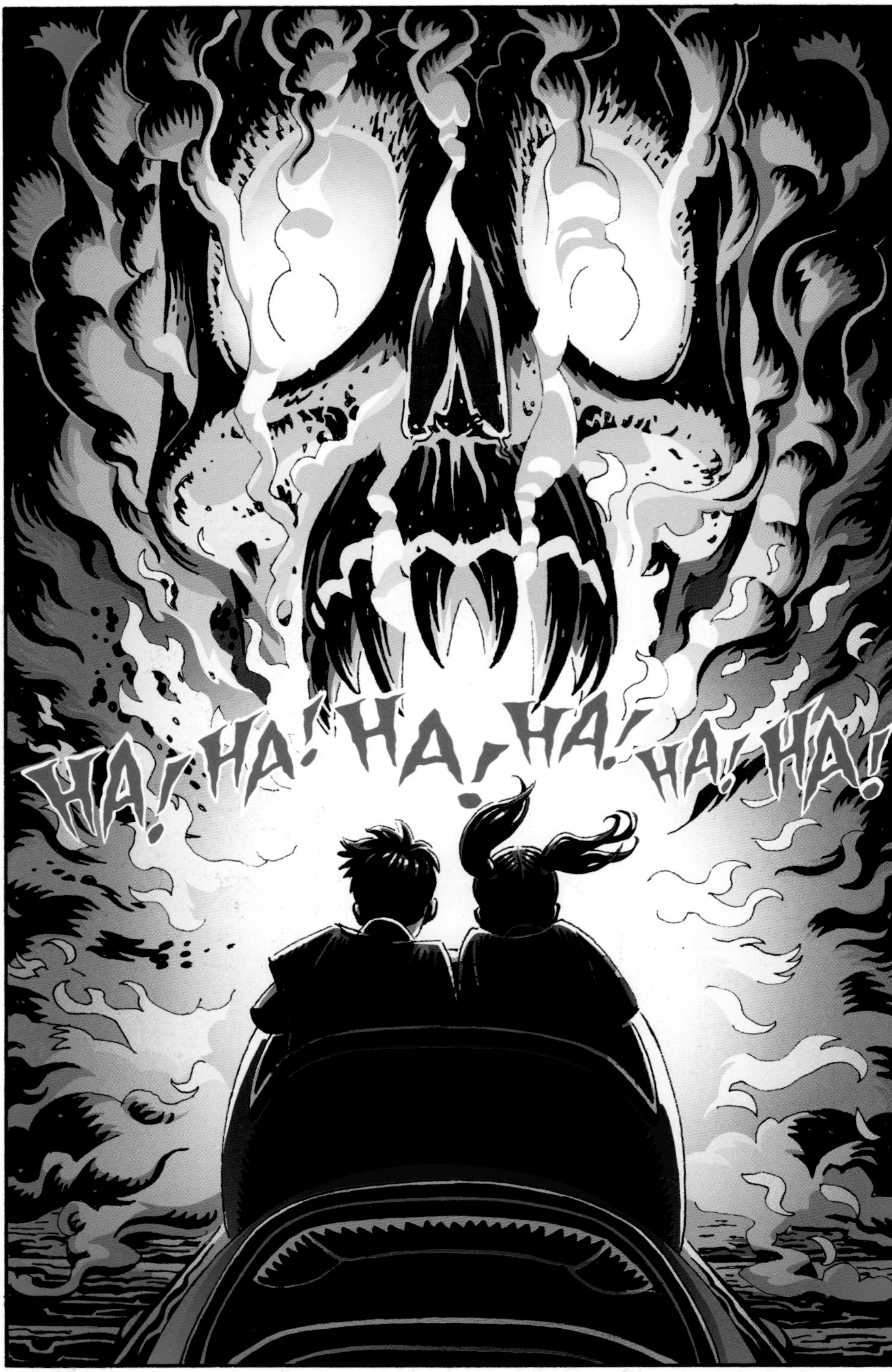
HA! HA! HA! HA! HA! HA!

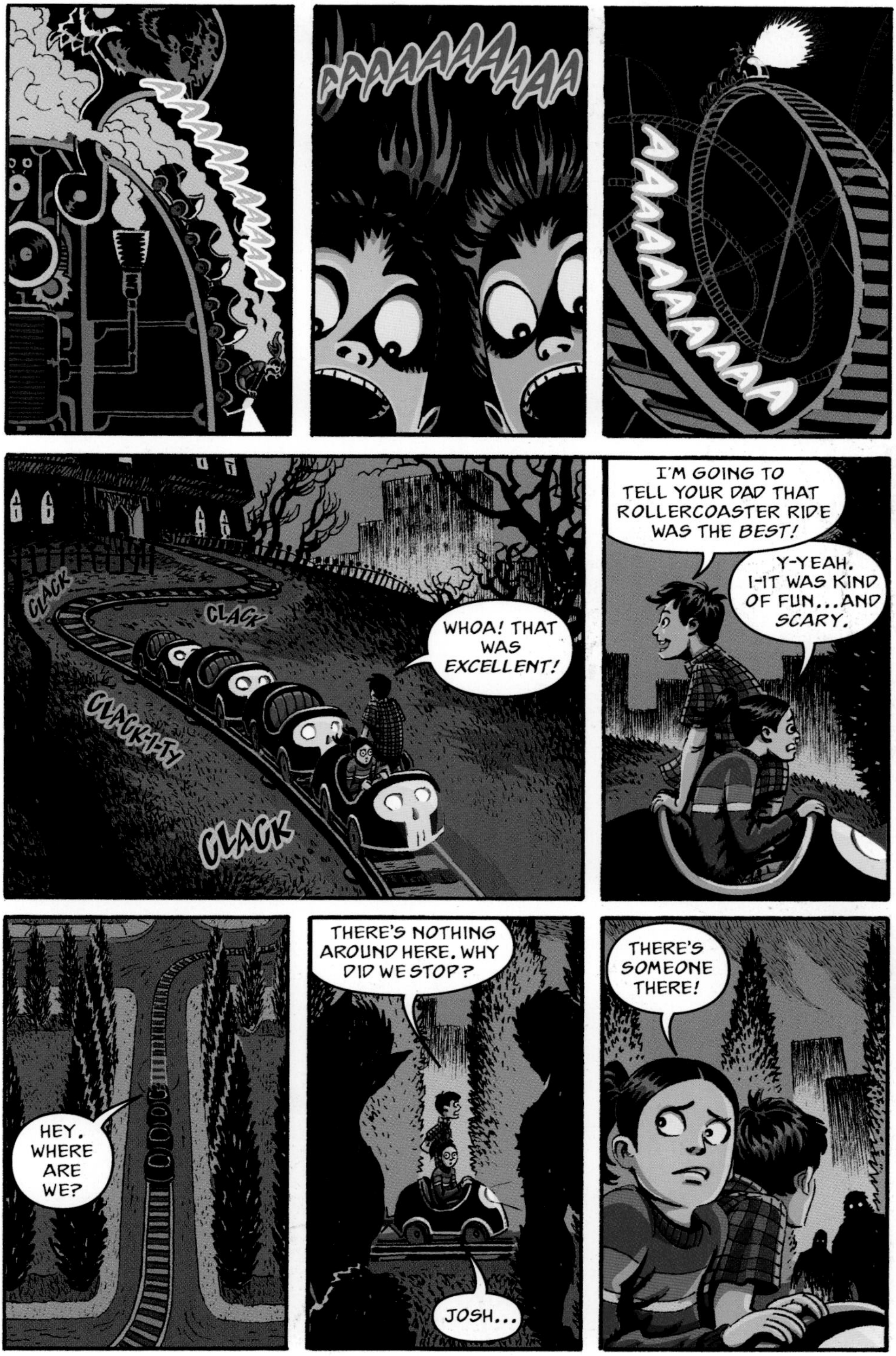
AAAAAAAAAAAA
AAAAAAAAAAA
AAAAAAAAAAAA
WHOA! THAT WAS EXCELLENT!
CLACK
CLACK
CLACK-I-TY
CLACK
I'M GOING TO TELL YOUR DAD THAT ROLLERCOASTER RIDE WAS THE BEST!
Y-YEAH. I-IT WAS KIND OF FUN...AND SCARY.
HEY. WHERE ARE WE?
THERE'S NOTHING AROUND HERE. WHY DID WE STOP?
JOSH...
THERE'S SOMEONE THERE!

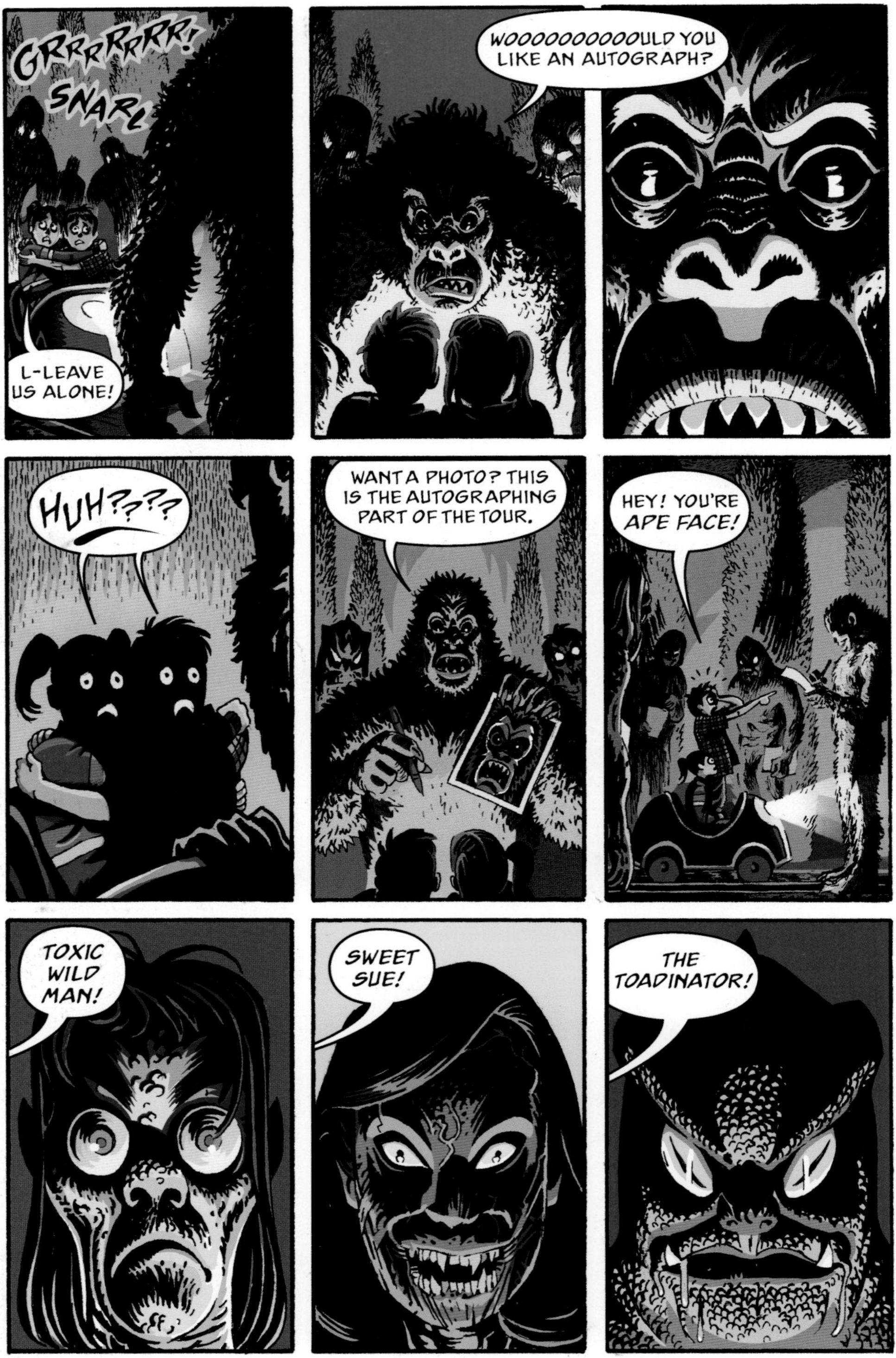
GRRRRRRR!
SNARL
L-LEAVE US ALONE!
WOOOOOOOOOOULD YOU LIKE AN AUTOGRAPH?
HUH????
WANT A PHOTO? THIS IS THE AUTOGRAPHING PART OF THE TOUR.
HEY! YOU'RE APE FACE!
TOXIC WILD MAN!
SWEET SUE!
THE TOADINATOR!

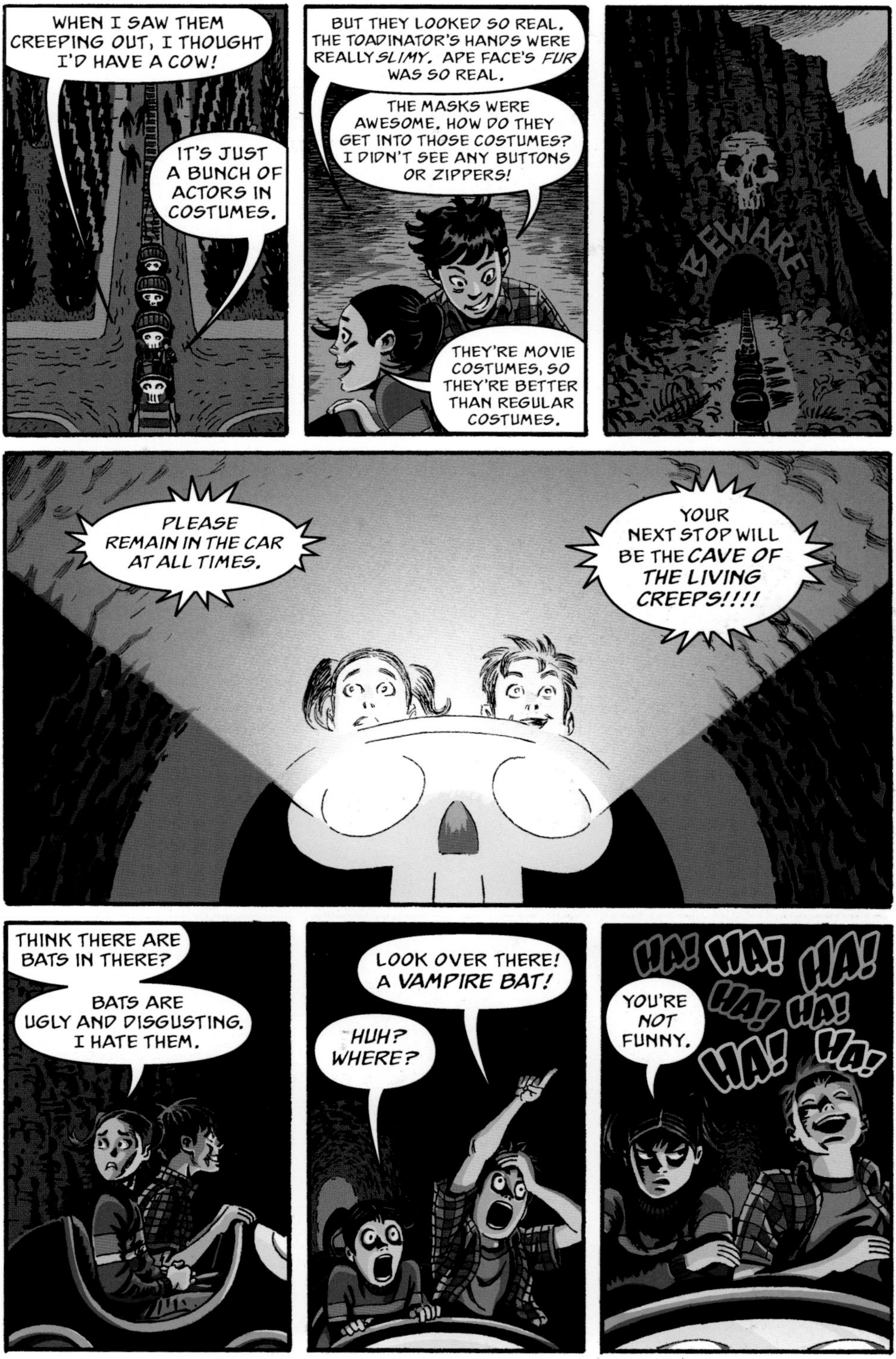
WHEN I SAW THEM CREEPING OUT, I THOUGHT I'D HAVE A COW!
IT'S JUST A BUNCH OF ACTORS IN COSTUMES.
BUT THEY LOOKED SO REAL. THE TOADINATOR'S HANDS WERE REALLY *SLIMY.* APE FACE'S *FUR* WAS SO REAL.
THE MASKS WERE AWESOME. HOW DO THEY GET INTO THOSE COSTUMES? I DIDN'T SEE ANY BUTTONS OR ZIPPERS!
THEY'RE MOVIE COSTUMES, SO THEY'RE BETTER THAN REGULAR COSTUMES.
BEWARE
PLEASE REMAIN IN THE CAR AT ALL TIMES.
YOUR NEXT STOP WILL BE THE *CAVE OF THE LIVING CREEPS!!!!*
THINK THERE ARE BATS IN THERE?
BATS ARE UGLY AND DISGUSTING. I HATE THEM.
LOOK OVER THERE! A *VAMPIRE BAT!*
HUH? WHERE?
HA! HA! HA! HA! HA! HA! HA!
YOU'RE *NOT* FUNNY.

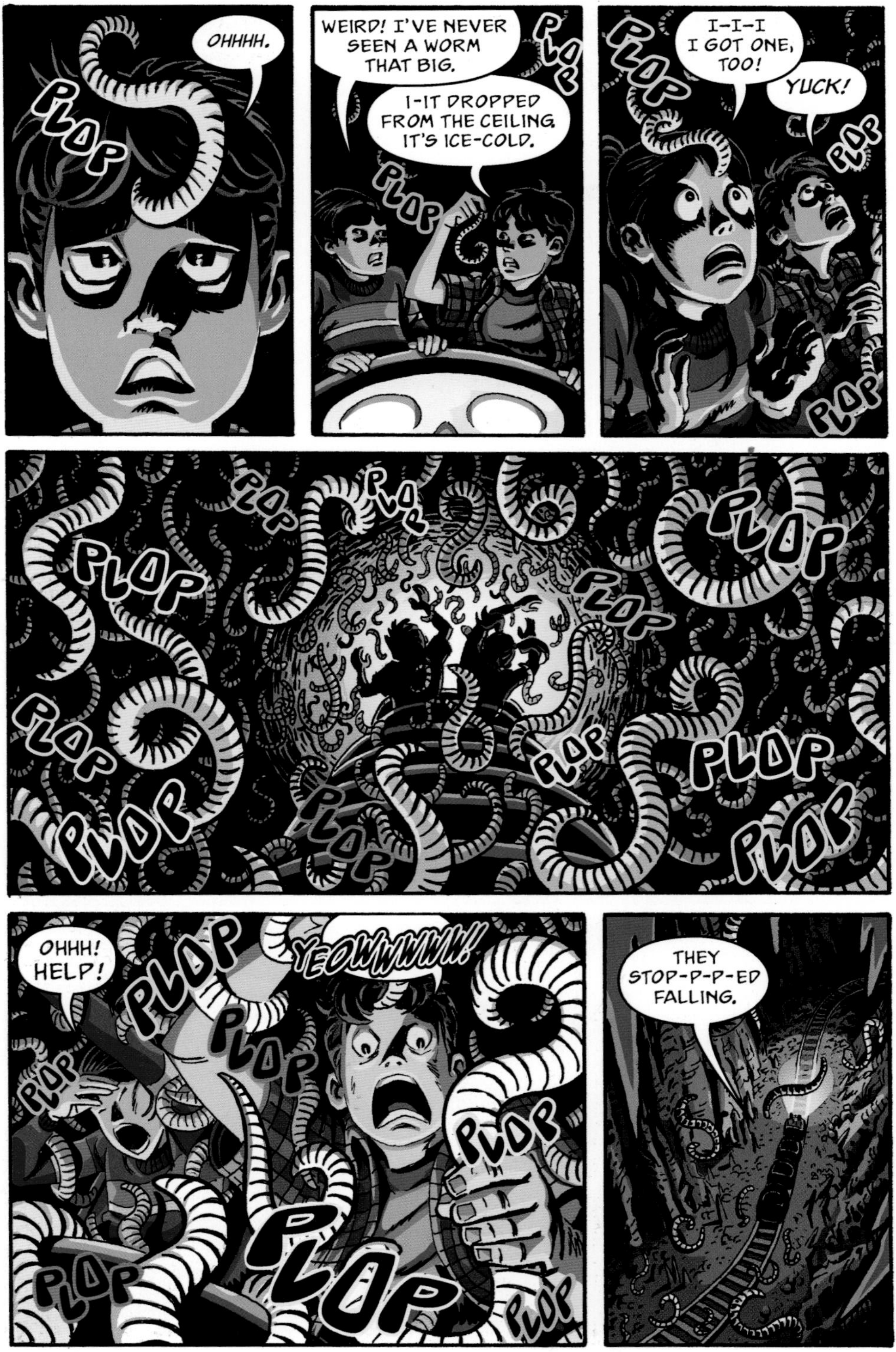
OHHHH.
PLOP
WEIRD! I'VE NEVER SEEN A WORM THAT BIG.
PLOP
I-IT DROPPED FROM THE CEILING. IT'S ICE-COLD.
PLOP
PLOP
I-I-I I GOT ONE, TOO!
YUCK!
PLOP
PLOP
PLOP
PLOP
PLOP
PLOP
PLOP
PLOP
PLOP
PLOP
PLOP
PLOP
PLOP
PLOP
PLOP
OHHH! HELP!
PLOP
YEOWWWWW!
PLOP
PLOP
PLOP
PLOP
PLOP
PLOP
THEY STOP-P-P-ED FALLING.

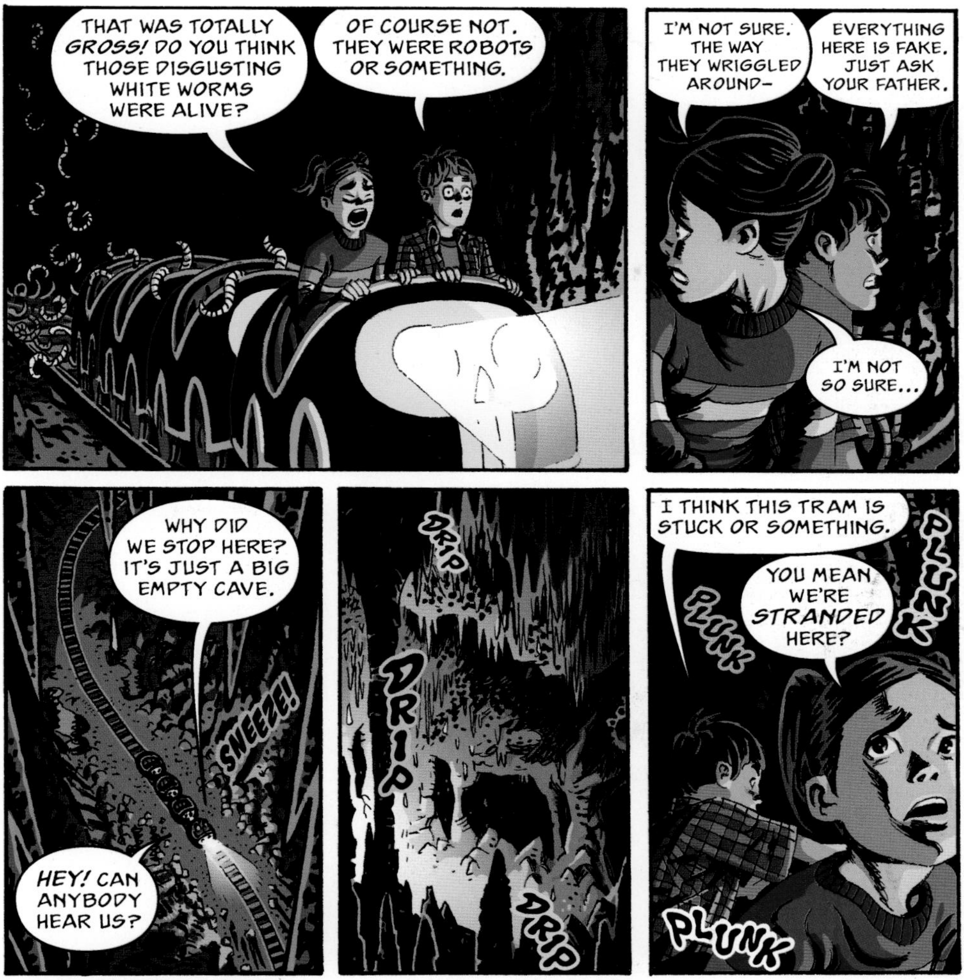
THAT WAS TOTALLY *GROSS!* DO YOU THINK THOSE DISGUSTING WHITE WORMS WERE ALIVE?
OF COURSE NOT. THEY WERE ROBOTS OR SOMETHING.
I'M NOT SURE. THE WAY THEY WRIGGLED AROUND—
EVERYTHING HERE IS FAKE. JUST ASK YOUR FATHER.
I'M NOT SO SURE...
WHY DID WE STOP HERE? IT'S JUST A BIG EMPTY CAVE.
SNEEZE!
HEY! CAN ANYBODY HEAR US?
DRIP
DRIP
DRIP
I THINK THIS TRAM IS STUCK OR SOMETHING.
PLUNK
YOU MEAN WE'RE *STRANDED* HERE?
PLUNK
PLUNK
WE CAN FIND A WAY OUT.
BUT WE'RE NOT SUPPOSED TO LEAVE THE TRAM. GET BACK IN. IF IT SHOULD START UP...
I THINK IT BROKE DOWN.
YOU'D BETTER CLIMB DOWN, WE HAVE TO WALK.
DRIP
WALK? IN THIS CREEPY, DARK CAVE? NO WAY, *JOSH!*
PLUNK
DRIP
PLUNK
DRIP
DRIP
PLUNK

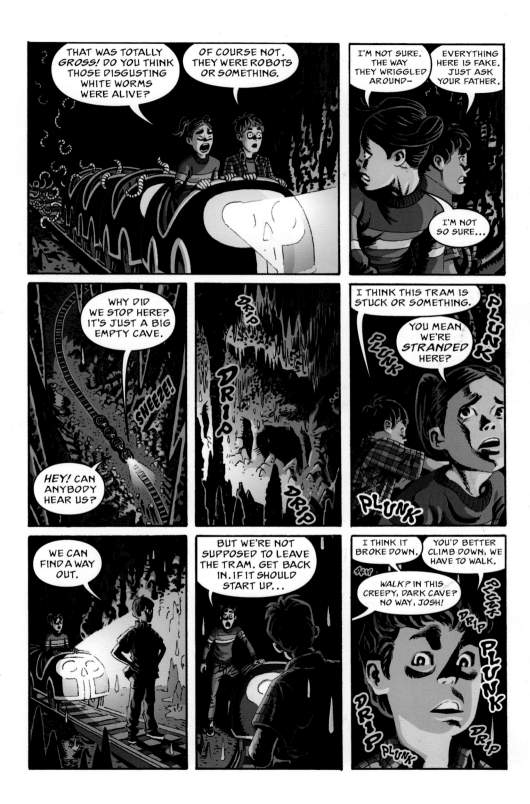

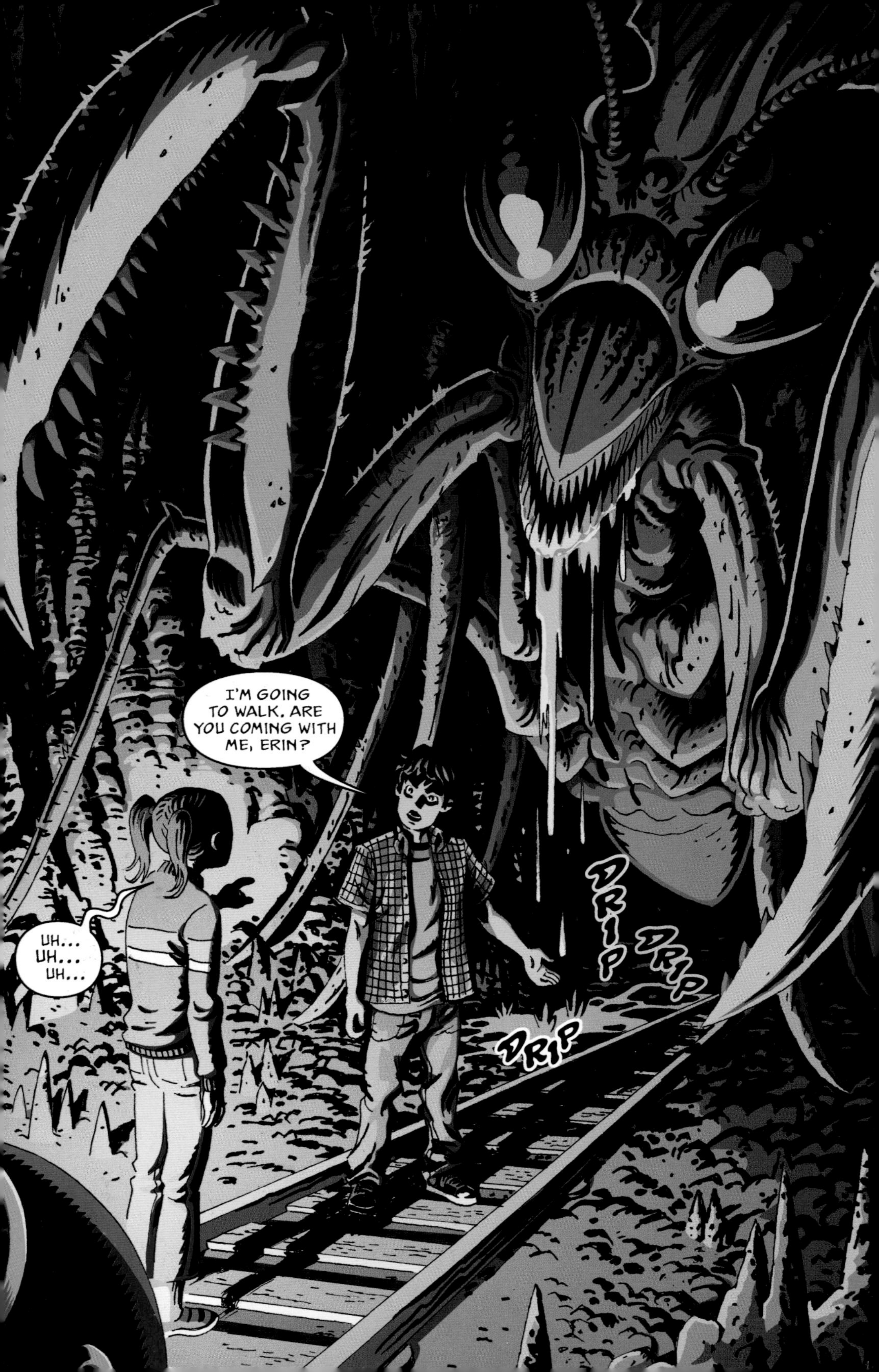
I'M GOING TO WALK. ARE YOU COMING WITH ME, ERIN?
UH... UH... UH...
DRIP
DRIP
DRIP

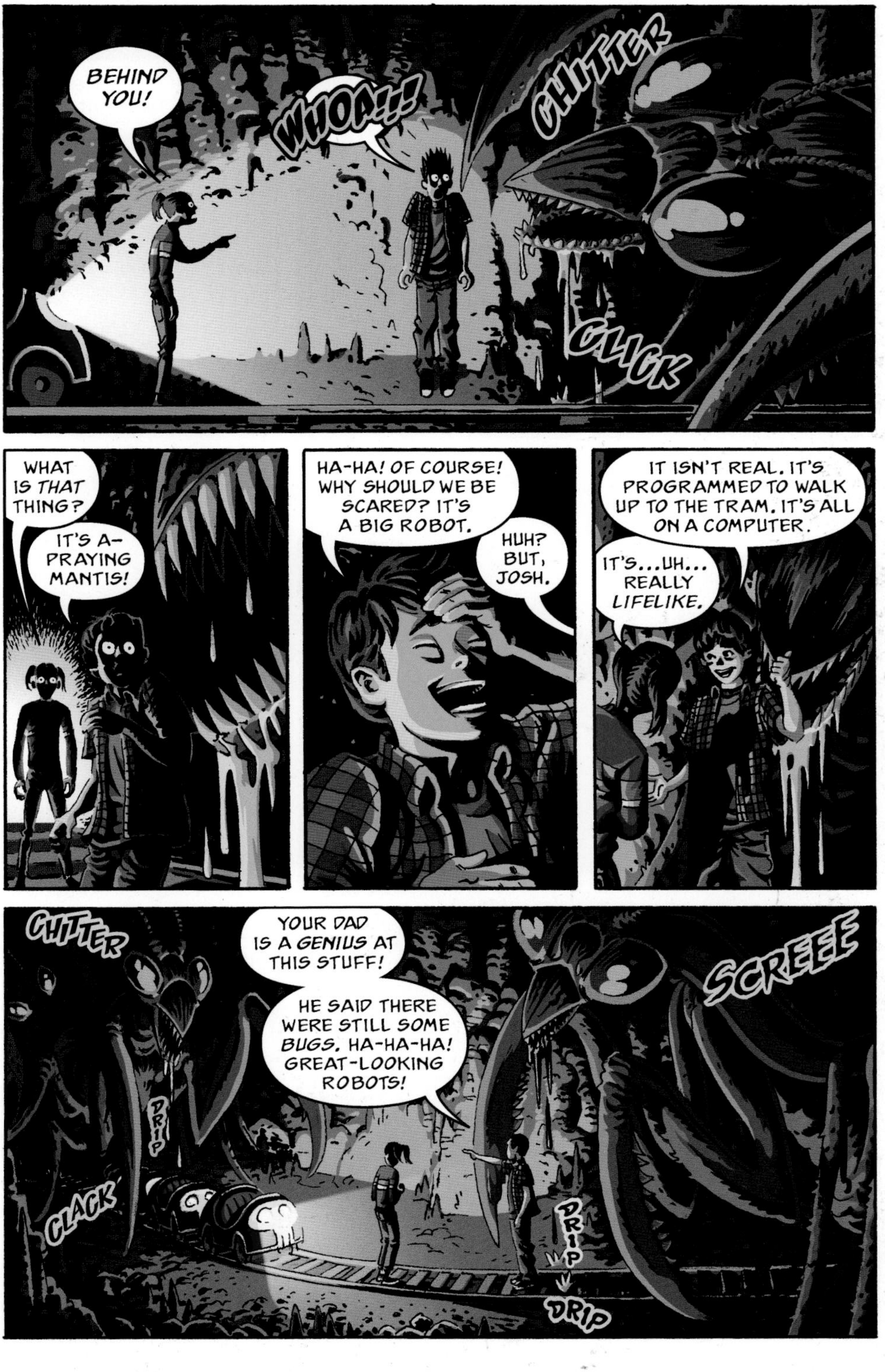
BEHIND YOU!
WHOA!!!
CHITTER
CLICK
WHAT IS *THAT* THING?
IT'S A-PRAYING MANTIS!
HA-HA! OF COURSE! WHY SHOULD WE BE SCARED? IT'S A BIG ROBOT.
HUH? BUT, JOSH.
IT ISN'T REAL. IT'S PROGRAMMED TO WALK UP TO THE TRAM. IT'S ALL ON A COMPUTER.
IT'S...UH... REALLY *LIFELIKE*.
CHITTER
YOUR DAD IS A *GENIUS* AT THIS STUFF!
HE SAID THERE WERE STILL SOME *BUGS*. HA-HA-HA! GREAT-LOOKING ROBOTS!
SCREEE
DRIP
CLACK
DRIP
DRIP

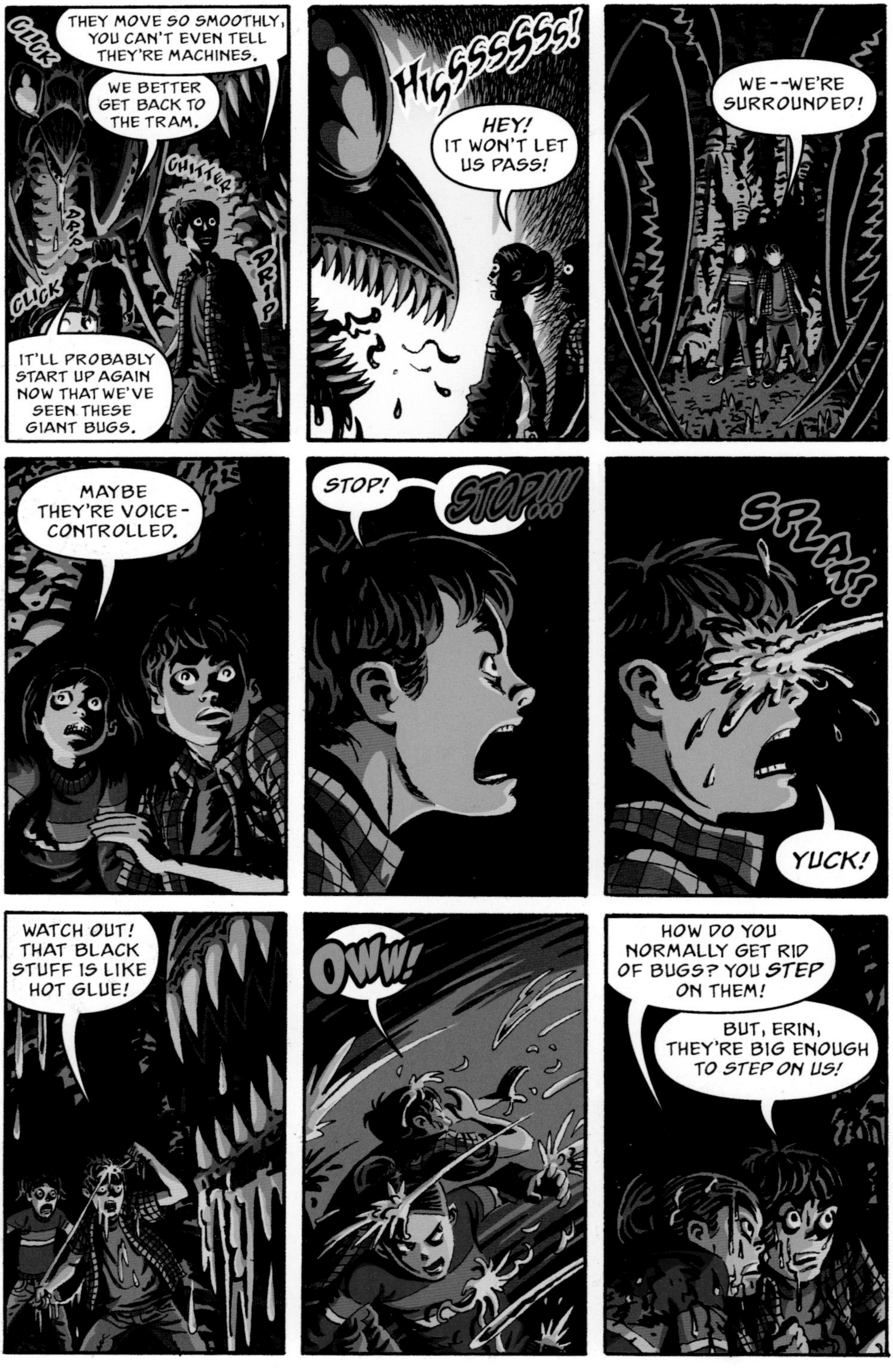
CLICK
THEY MOVE SO SMOOTHLY, YOU CAN'T EVEN TELL THEY'RE MACHINES.
WE BETTER GET BACK TO THE TRAM.
CHITTER
DRIP
DRIP
CLICK
IT'LL PROBABLY START UP AGAIN NOW THAT WE'VE SEEN THESE GIANT BUGS.
HISSSSSSS!
HEY! IT WON'T LET US PASS!
WE--WE'RE SURROUNDED!
MAYBE THEY'RE VOICE-CONTROLLED.
STOP!
STOP!!!
SPLAK!
YUCK!
WATCH OUT! THAT BLACK STUFF IS LIKE HOT GLUE!
OWW!
HOW DO YOU NORMALLY GET RID OF BUGS? YOU STEP ON THEM!
BUT, ERIN, THEY'RE BIG ENOUGH TO STEP ON US!

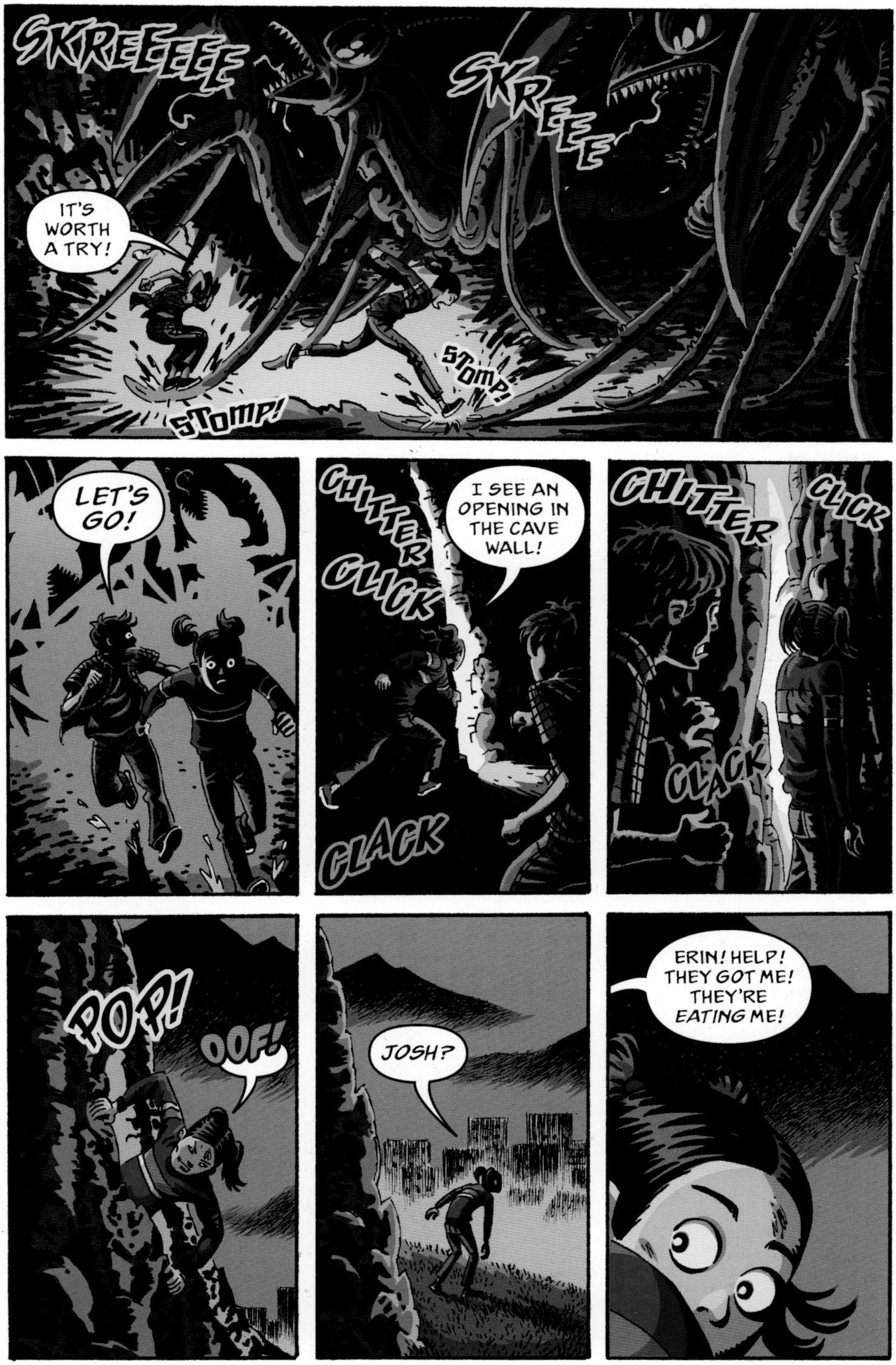
SKREEEEEE
SKREEEE
IT'S WORTH A TRY!
STOMP!
STOMP!
LET'S GO!
CHITTER
CLICK
I SEE AN OPENING IN THE CAVE WALL!
CLACK
CHITTER
CLICK
CLACK
POP!
OOF!
JOSH?
ERIN! HELP! THEY GOT ME! THEY'RE EATING ME!

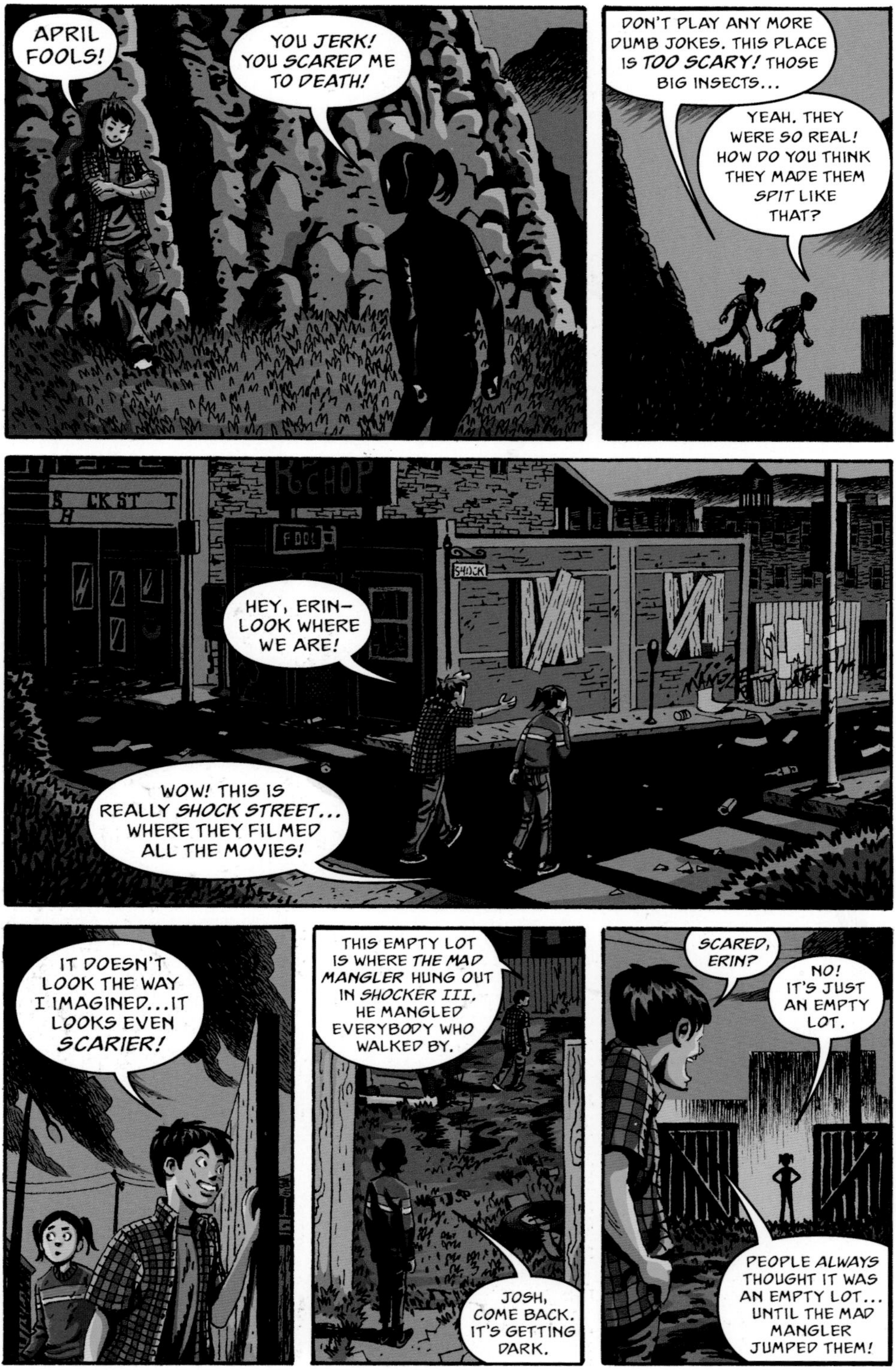
APRIL FOOLS!
YOU JERK! YOU *SCARED* ME TO *DEATH!*
DON'T PLAY ANY MORE DUMB JOKES. THIS PLACE IS *TOO SCARY!* THOSE BIG INSECTS...
YEAH. THEY WERE *SO* REAL! HOW DO YOU THINK THEY MADE THEM *SPIT* LIKE THAT?
HEY, ERIN– LOOK WHERE WE ARE!
WOW! THIS IS REALLY *SHOCK STREET...* WHERE THEY FILMED ALL THE MOVIES!
IT DOESN'T LOOK THE WAY I IMAGINED...IT LOOKS EVEN *SCARIER!*
THIS EMPTY LOT IS WHERE *THE MAD MANGLER* HUNG OUT IN *SHOCKER III.* HE MANGLED EVERYBODY WHO WALKED BY.
JOSH, COME BACK. IT'S GETTING DARK.
SCARED, ERIN?
NO! IT'S JUST AN EMPTY LOT.
PEOPLE *ALWAYS* THOUGHT IT WAS AN EMPTY LOT... UNTIL THE MAD MANGLER JUMPED THEM!

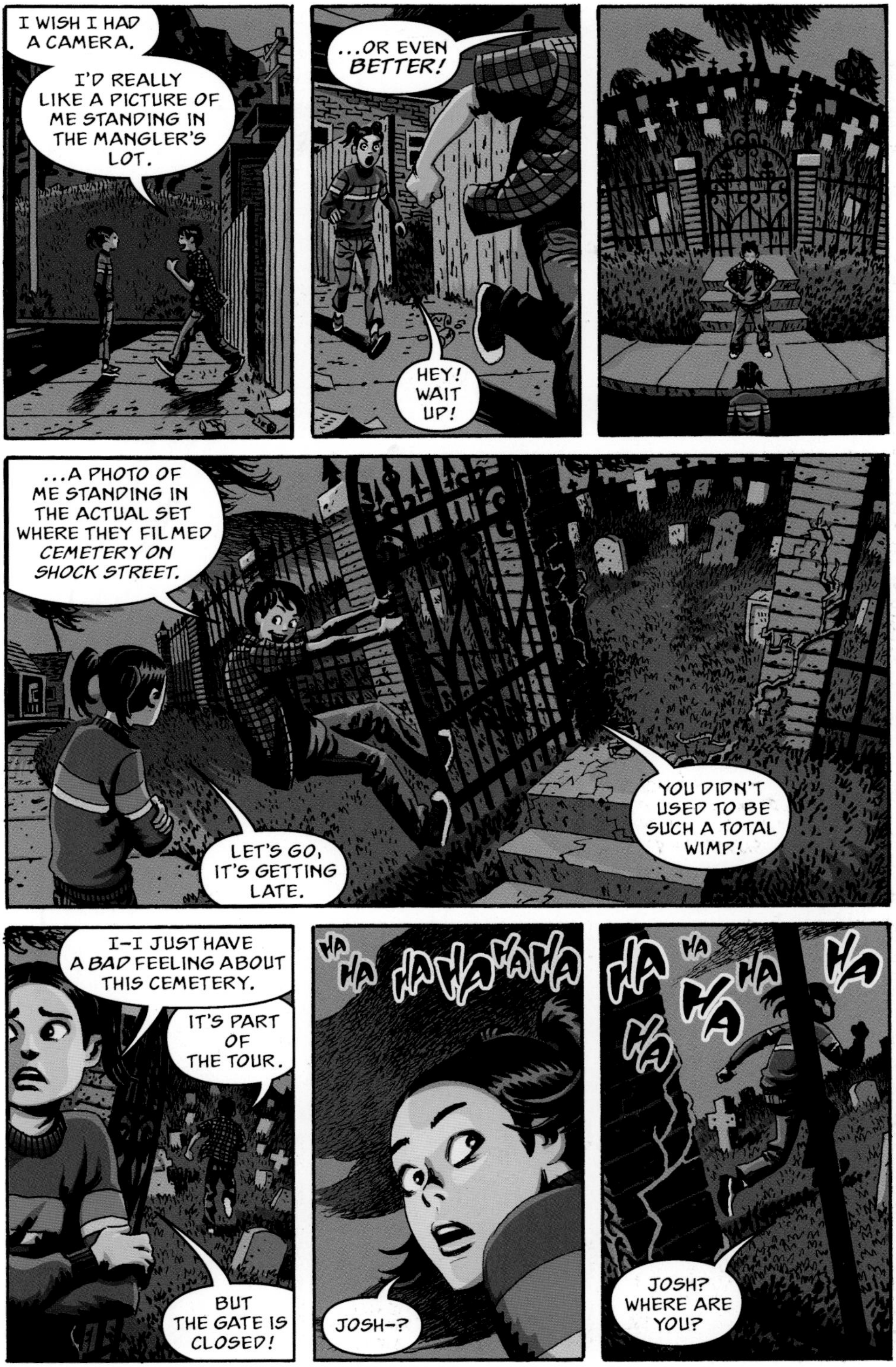
I WISH I HAD A CAMERA.
I'D REALLY LIKE A PICTURE OF ME STANDING IN THE MANGLER'S LOT.
...OR EVEN *BETTER!*
HEY! WAIT UP!
...A PHOTO OF ME STANDING IN THE ACTUAL SET WHERE THEY FILMED *CEMETERY ON SHOCK STREET.*
LET'S GO, IT'S GETTING LATE.
YOU DIDN'T USED TO BE SUCH A TOTAL WIMP!
I-I JUST HAVE A *BAD* FEELING ABOUT THIS CEMETERY.
IT'S PART OF THE TOUR.
BUT THE GATE IS CLOSED!
HA HA HA HA HA HA HA HA
JOSH-?
HA HA HA HA HA HA HA HA
JOSH? WHERE ARE YOU?

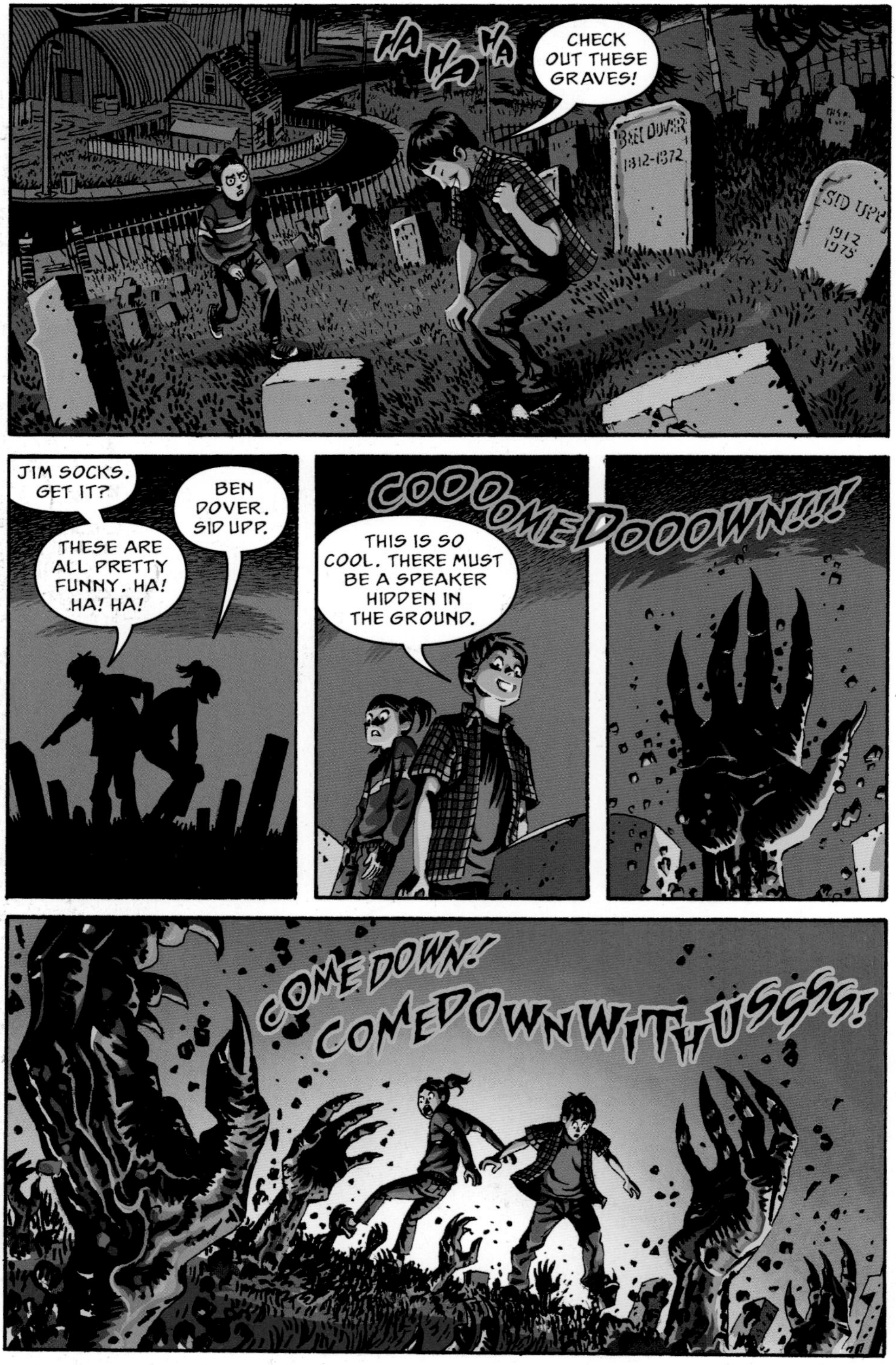
HA HA HA
CHECK OUT THESE GRAVES!
BEN DOVER 1812-1872
SID UPP 1912 1975
JIM SOCKS. GET IT?
THESE ARE ALL PRETTY FUNNY. HA! HA! HA!
BEN DOVER. SID UPP.
COOOOMEDOOOOWN!!!
THIS IS SO COOL. THERE MUST BE A SPEAKER HIDDEN IN THE GROUND.
COMEDOWN! COMEDOWNWITHUSSSS!

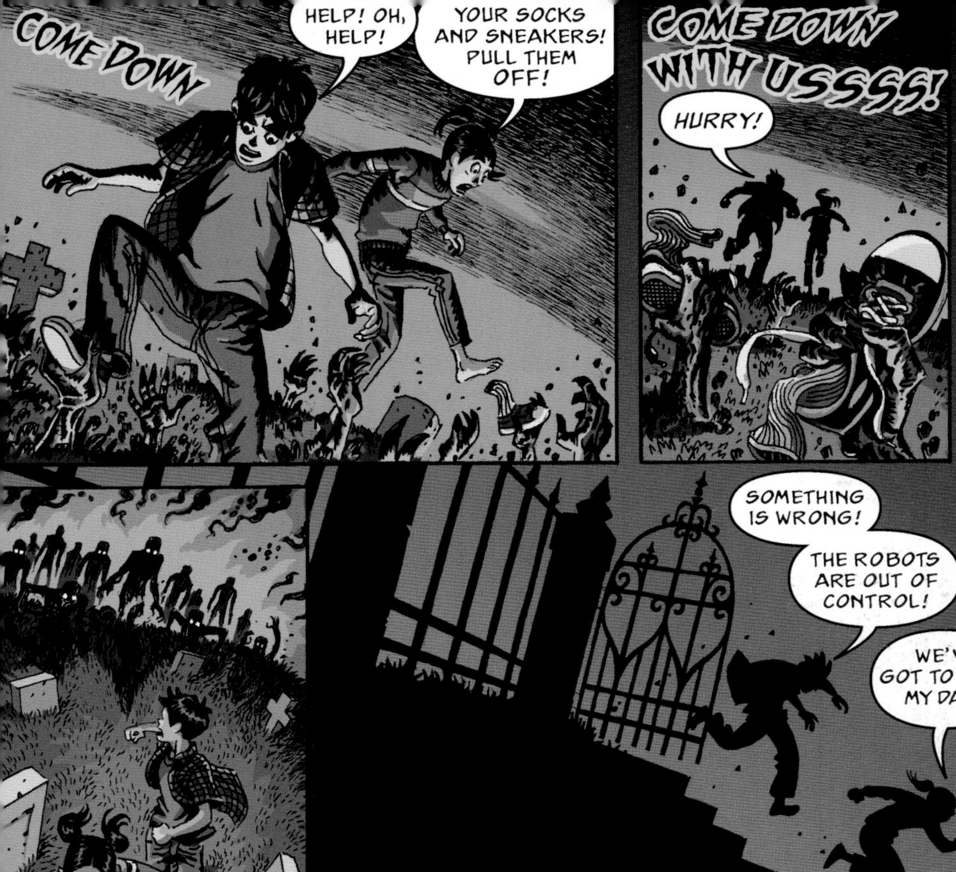
COME DOWN
HELP! OH, HELP!
YOUR SOCKS AND SNEAKERS! PULL THEM OFF!
COME DOWN WITH USSSS!
HURRY!
SOMETHING IS WRONG!
THE ROBOTS ARE OUT OF CONTROL!
WE'VE GOT TO FIND MY DAD!
WE HAVE TO FIND THE TRAM.
CUT THROUGH HERE!
SPLOTCH
SQUELCH
SPLUSH

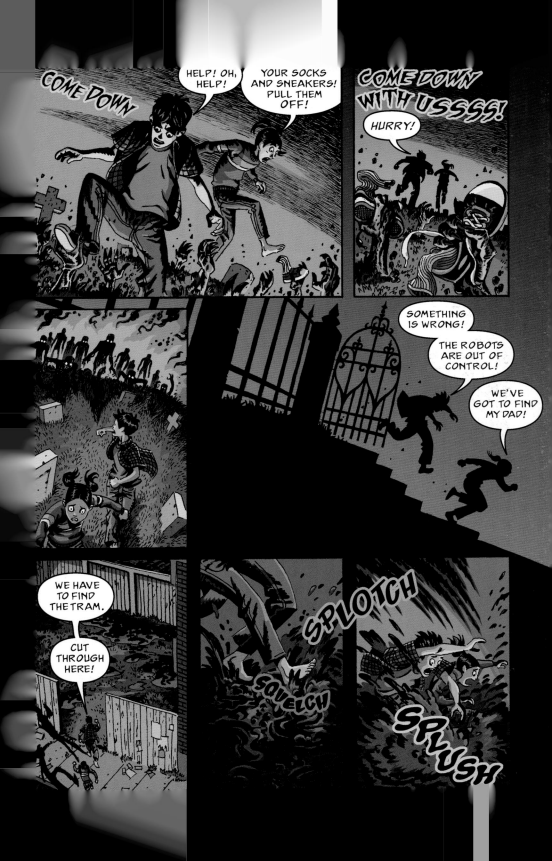

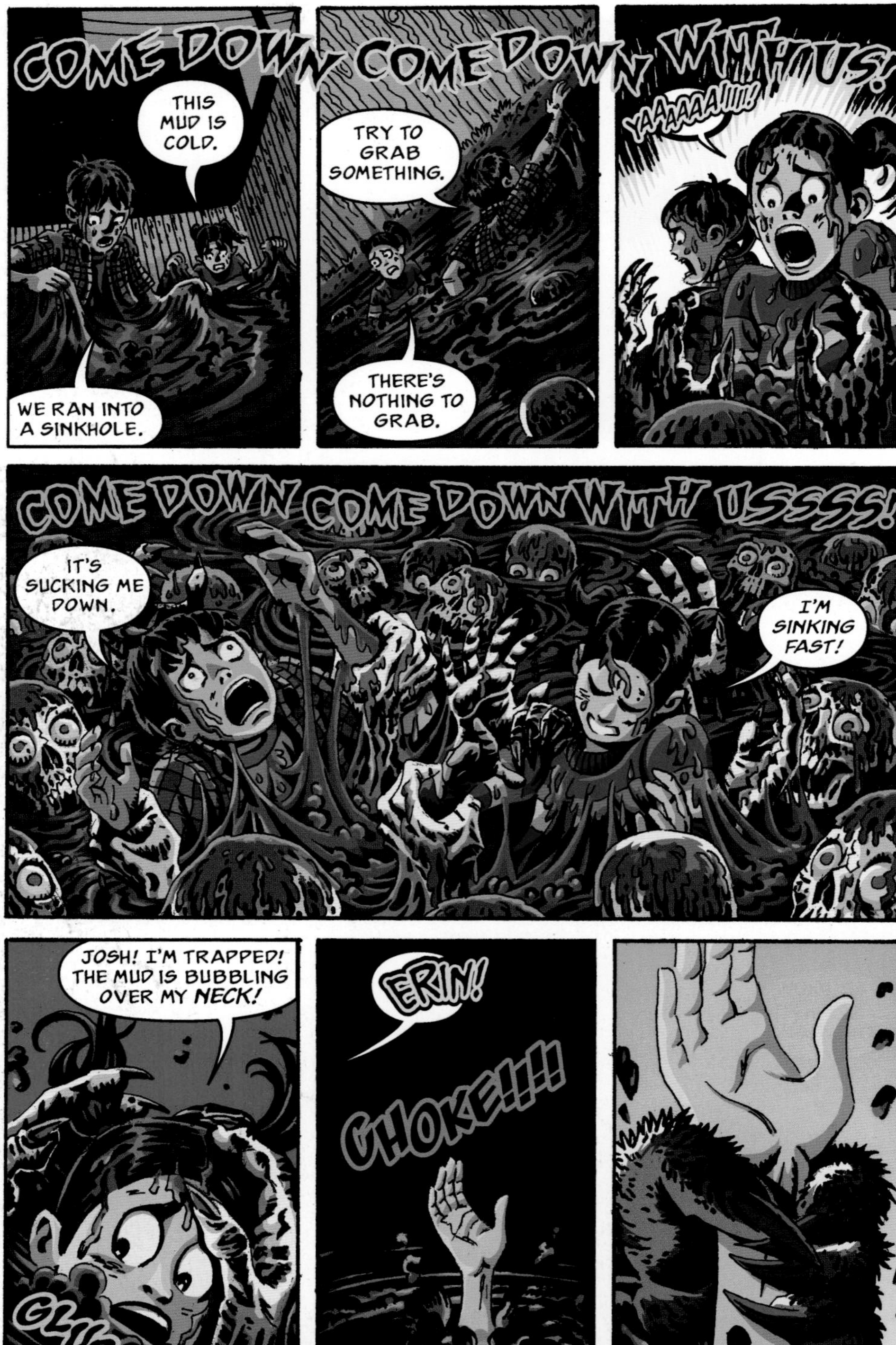
COME DOWN COME DOWN WITH US!
THIS MUD IS COLD.
WE RAN INTO A SINKHOLE.
TRY TO GRAB SOMETHING.
THERE'S NOTHING TO GRAB.
YAAAAAA!!!!!
COME DOWN COME DOWN WITH USSSS!
IT'S SUCKING ME DOWN.
I'M SINKING FAST!
JOSH! I'M TRAPPED! THE MUD IS BUBBLING OVER MY NECK!
GLUB
ERIN!
CHOKE!!!!

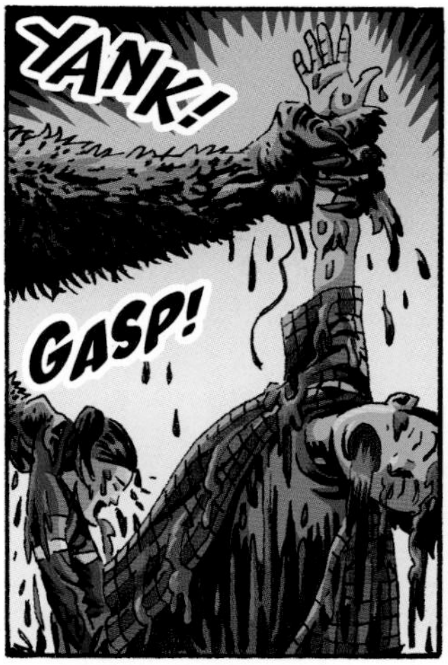
YANK!
GASP!

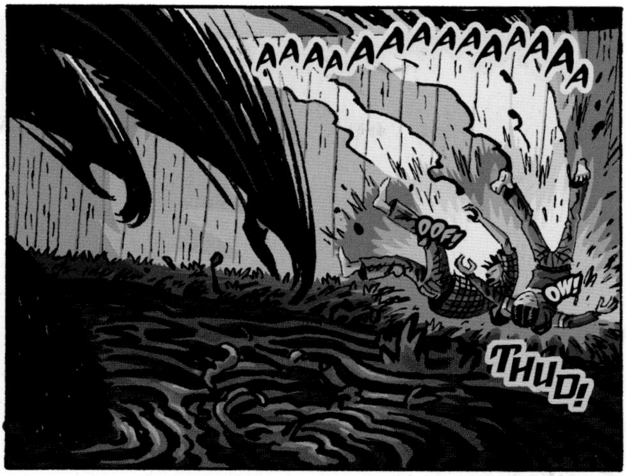
AAAAAAAAAAAAAAA
OOF!
OW!
THUD!

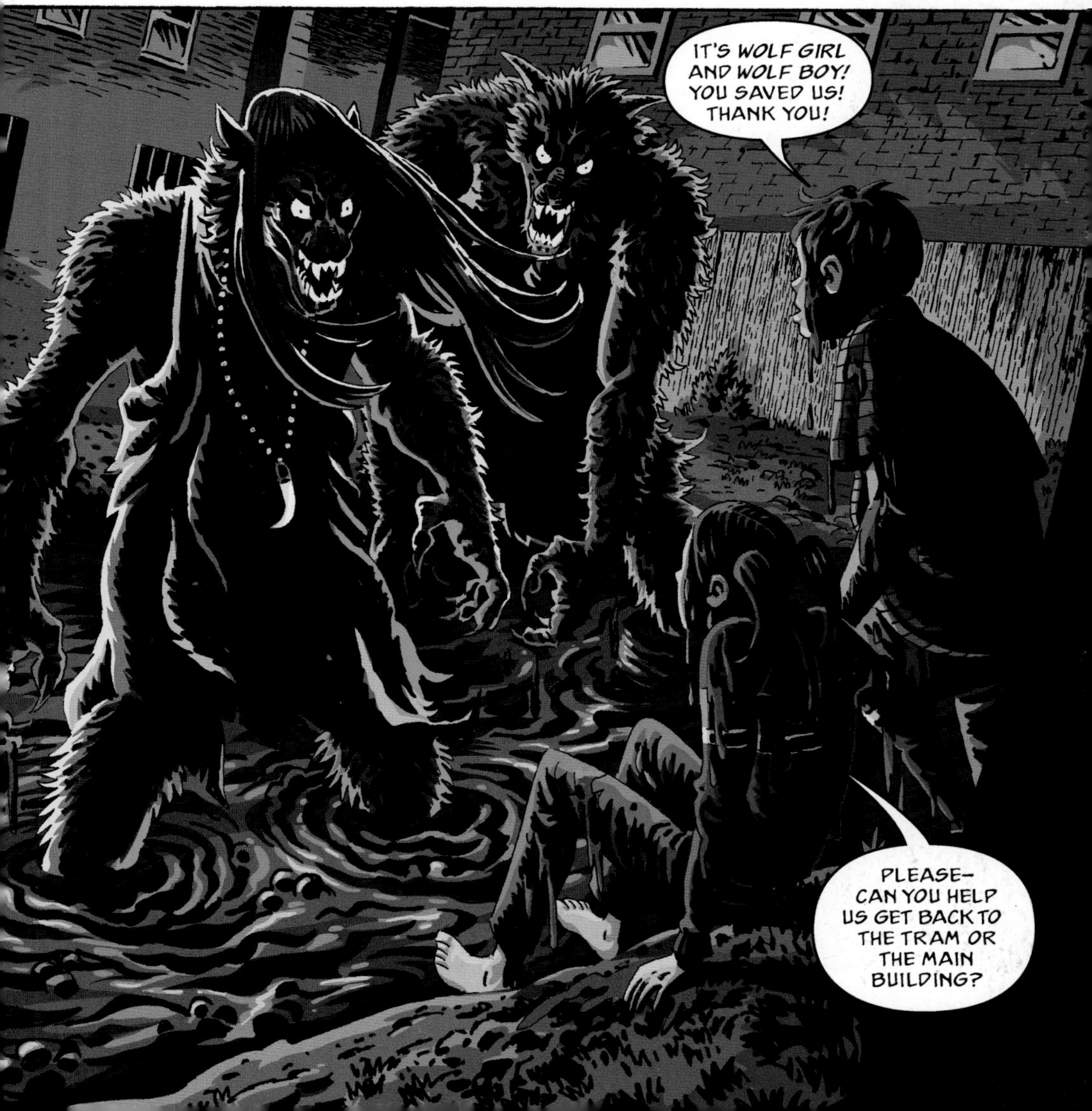
IT'S WOLF GIRL AND WOLF BOY! YOU SAVED US! THANK YOU!
PLEASE— CAN YOU HELP US GET BACK TO THE TRAM OR THE MAIN BUILDING?

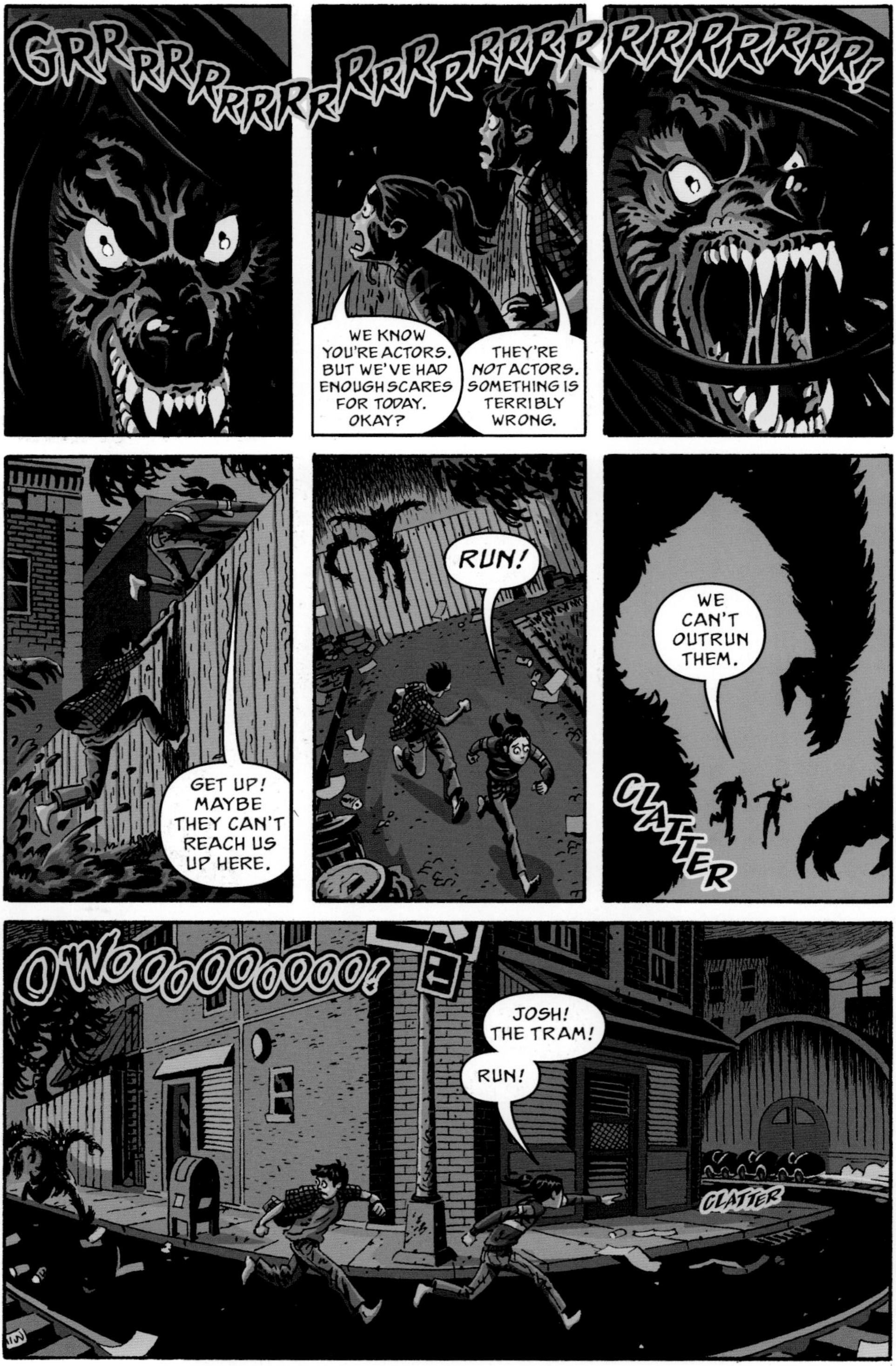
GRRRRRRRRRRRRRRRRRRRRRRRRRRRR!
WE KNOW YOU'RE ACTORS. BUT WE'VE HAD ENOUGH SCARES FOR TODAY. OKAY?
THEY'RE *NOT* ACTORS. SOMETHING IS TERRIBLY WRONG.
GET UP! MAYBE THEY CAN'T REACH US UP HERE.
RUN!
WE CAN'T OUTRUN THEM.
CLATTER
OWOOOOOOOOOO!
JOSH! THE TRAM!
RUN!
CLATTER

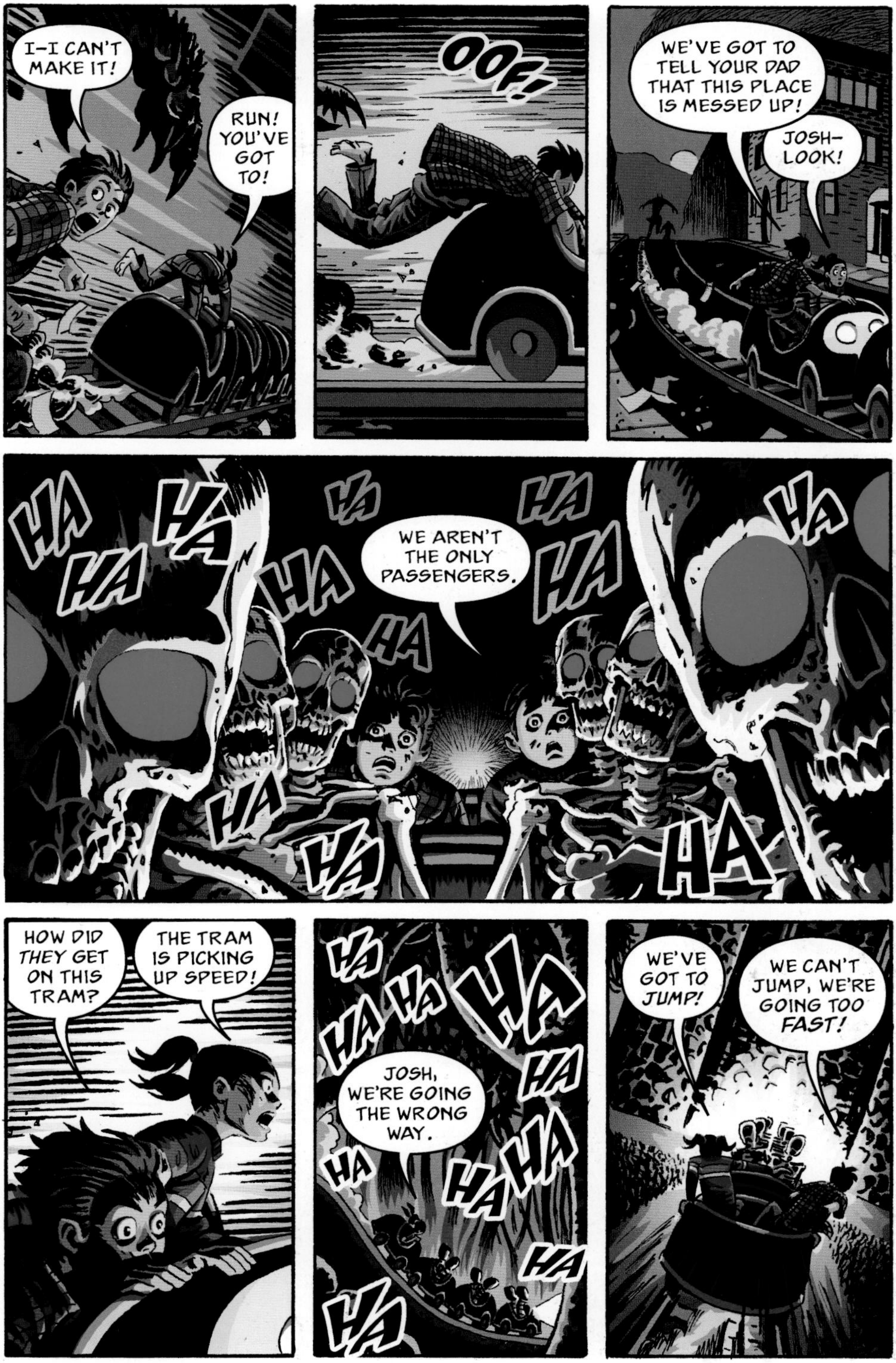
I–I CAN'T MAKE IT!
RUN! YOU'VE GOT TO!
OOF!
WE'VE GOT TO TELL YOUR DAD THAT THIS PLACE IS MESSED UP!
JOSH– LOOK!
HA HA HA HA HA HA HA HA
WE AREN'T THE ONLY PASSENGERS.
HA HA HA HA HA
HA HA HA
HOW DID THEY GET ON THIS TRAM?
THE TRAM IS PICKING UP SPEED!
HA HA HA HA
JOSH, WE'RE GOING THE WRONG WAY.
HA HA HA HA HA HA HA
WE'VE GOT TO JUMP!
WE CAN'T JUMP, WE'RE GOING TOO FAST!

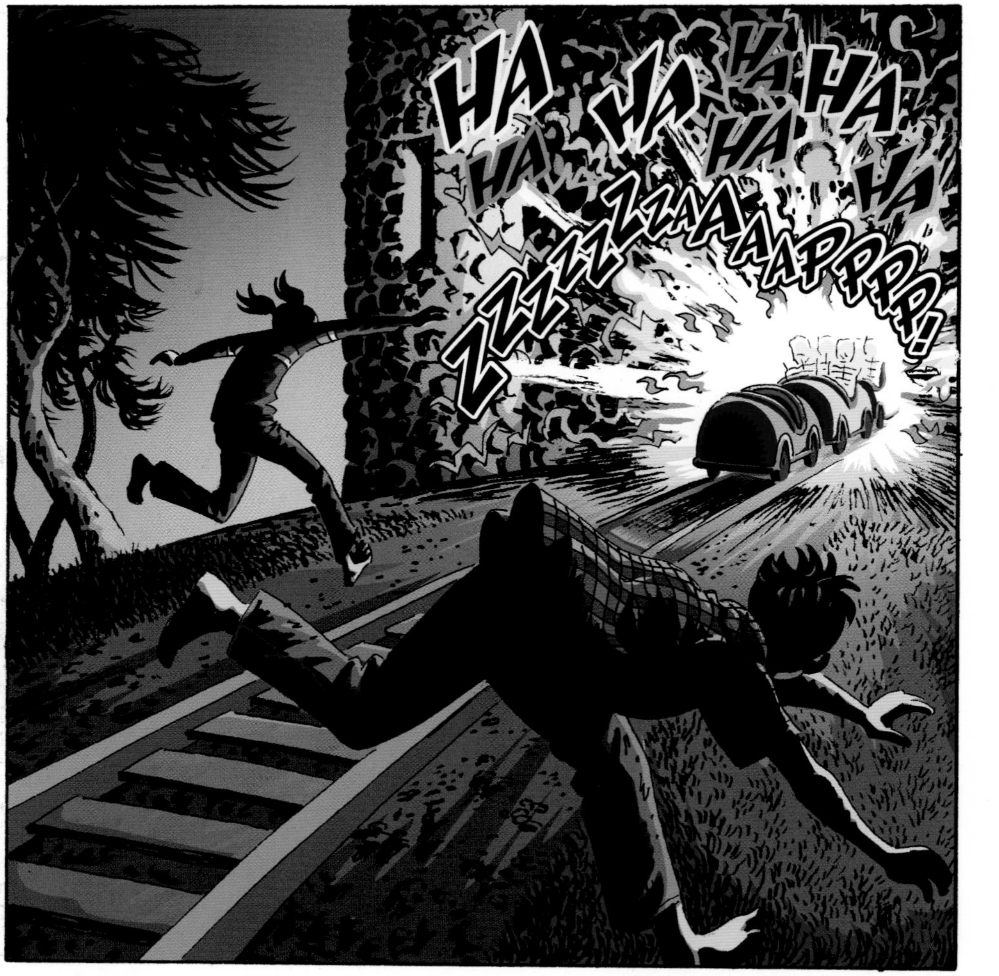
HA HA HA HA HA HA HA
ZZZZZZZAAAAPPPP!

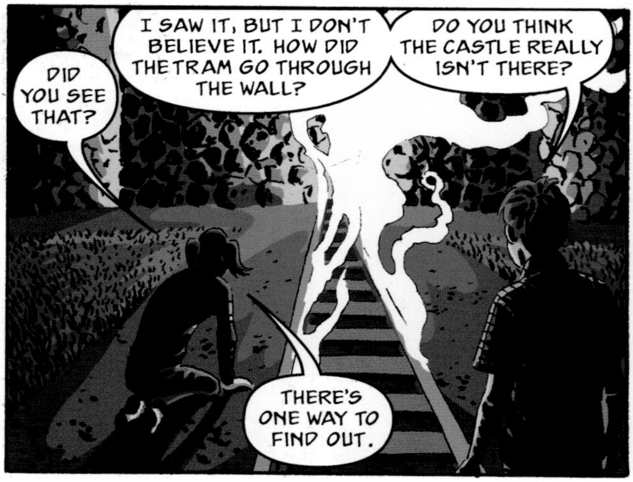
DID YOU SEE THAT?
I SAW IT, BUT I DON'T BELIEVE IT. HOW DID THE TRAM GO THROUGH THE WALL?
DO YOU THINK THE CASTLE REALLY ISN'T THERE?
THERE'S ONE WAY TO FIND OUT.

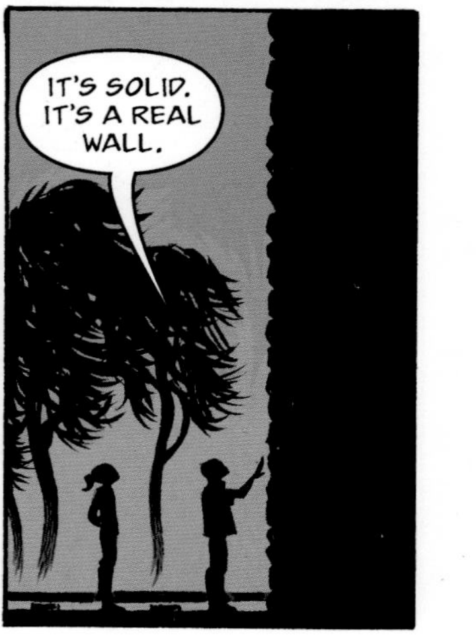
IT'S SOLID. IT'S A REAL WALL.

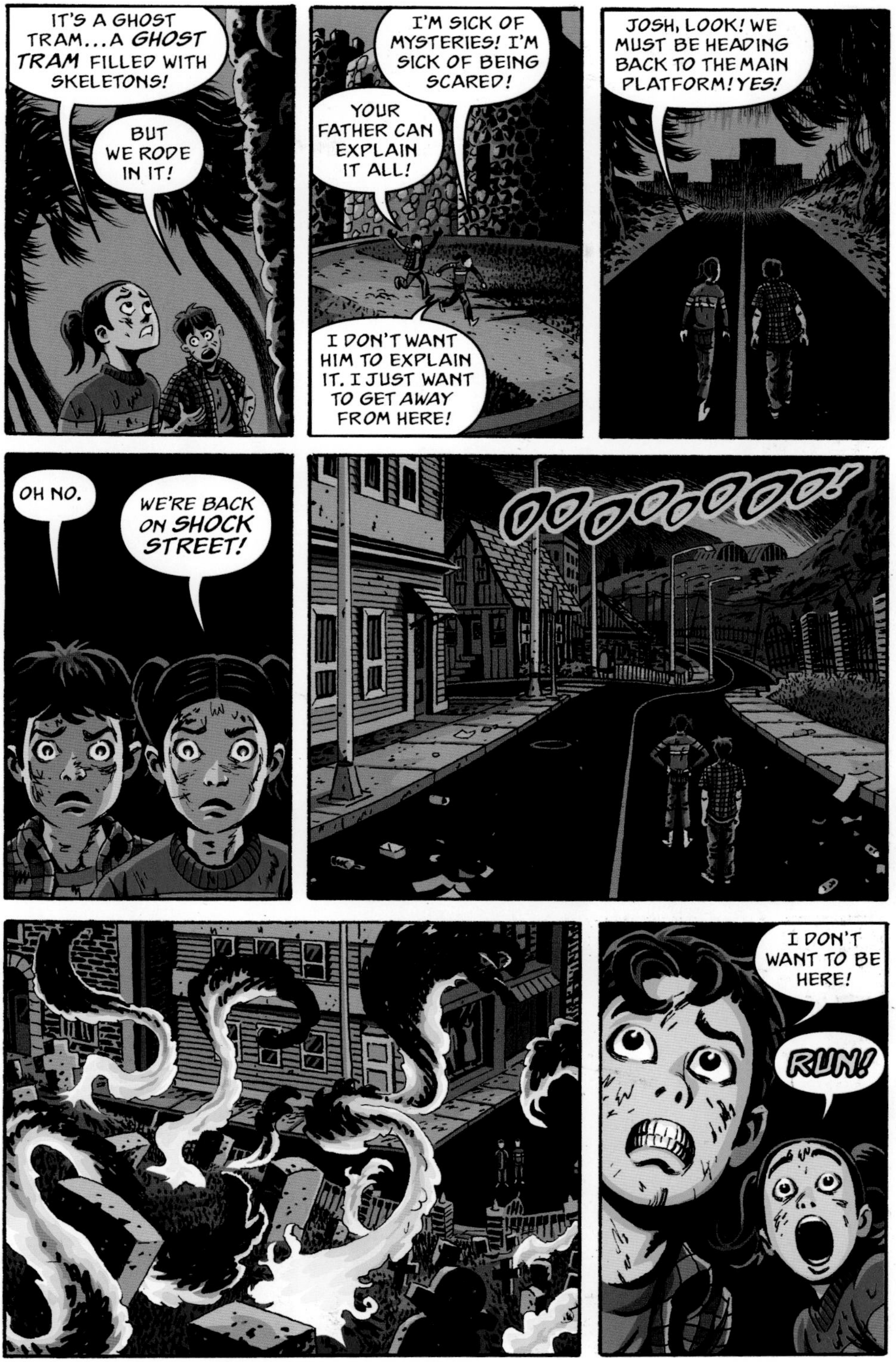
IT'S A GHOST TRAM... A GHOST TRAM FILLED WITH SKELETONS!
BUT WE RODE IN IT!
I'M SICK OF MYSTERIES! I'M SICK OF BEING SCARED!
YOUR FATHER CAN EXPLAIN IT ALL!
I DON'T WANT HIM TO EXPLAIN IT. I JUST WANT TO GET AWAY FROM HERE!
JOSH, LOOK! WE MUST BE HEADING BACK TO THE MAIN PLATFORM! YES!
OH NO.
WE'RE BACK ON SHOCK STREET!
OOOOOOOOOO!
I DON'T WANT TO BE HERE!
RUN!

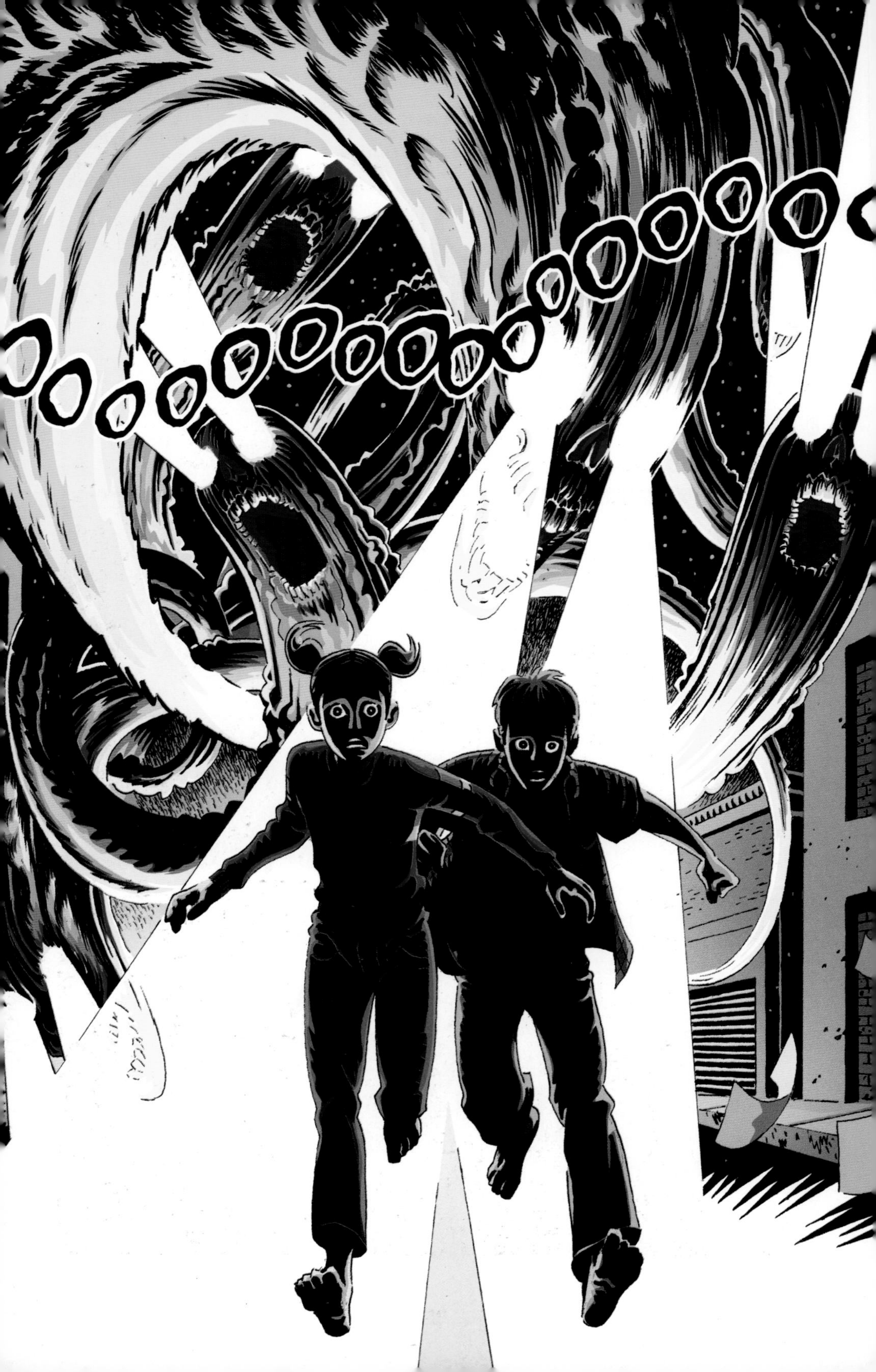

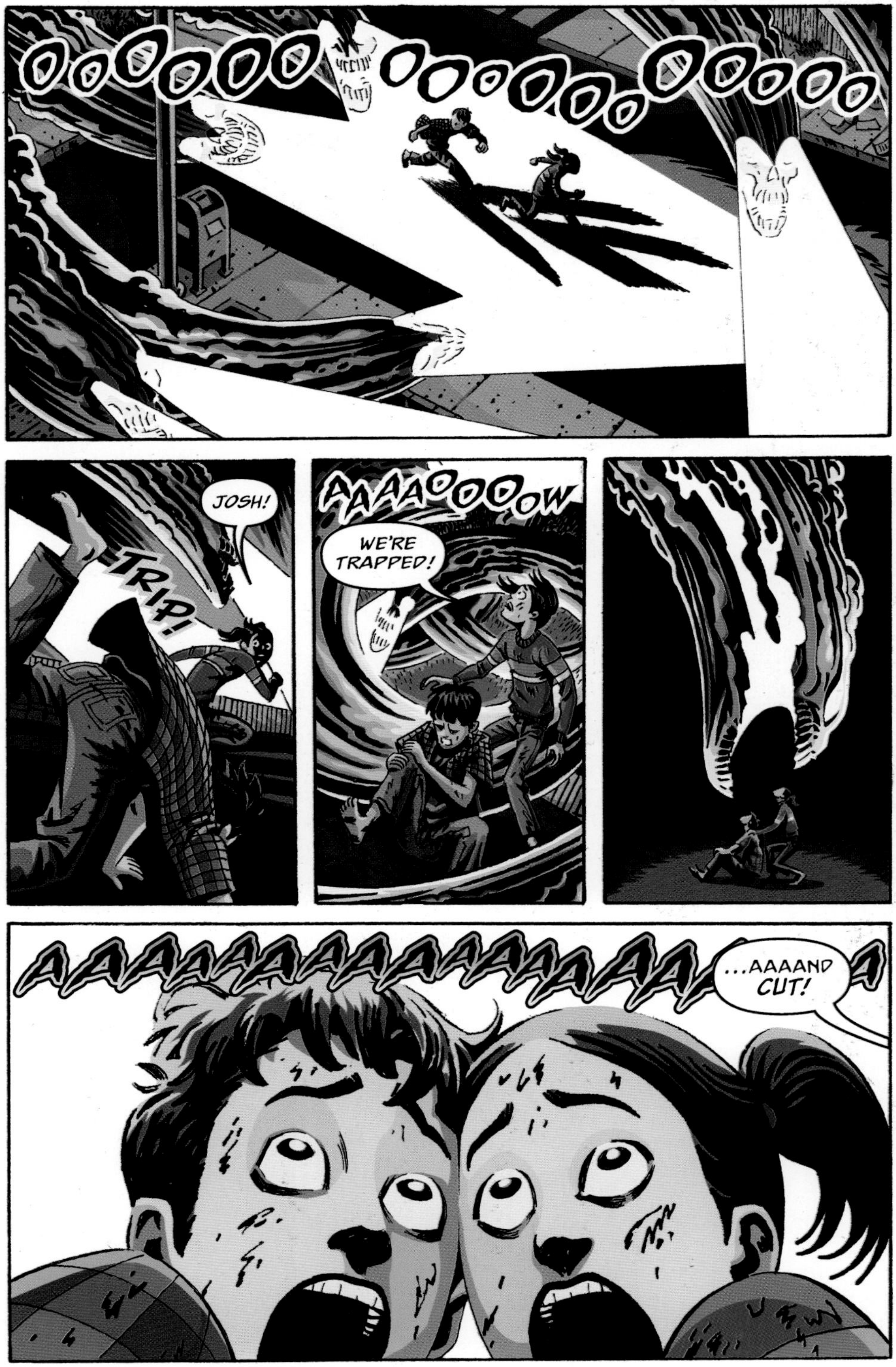
OOOOOO OOOOOOOOOOOO
JOSH!
TRIP!
AAAAOOOOOW
WE'RE TRAPPED!
AAAAAAAAAAAAAAAAA
...AAAAND CUT!

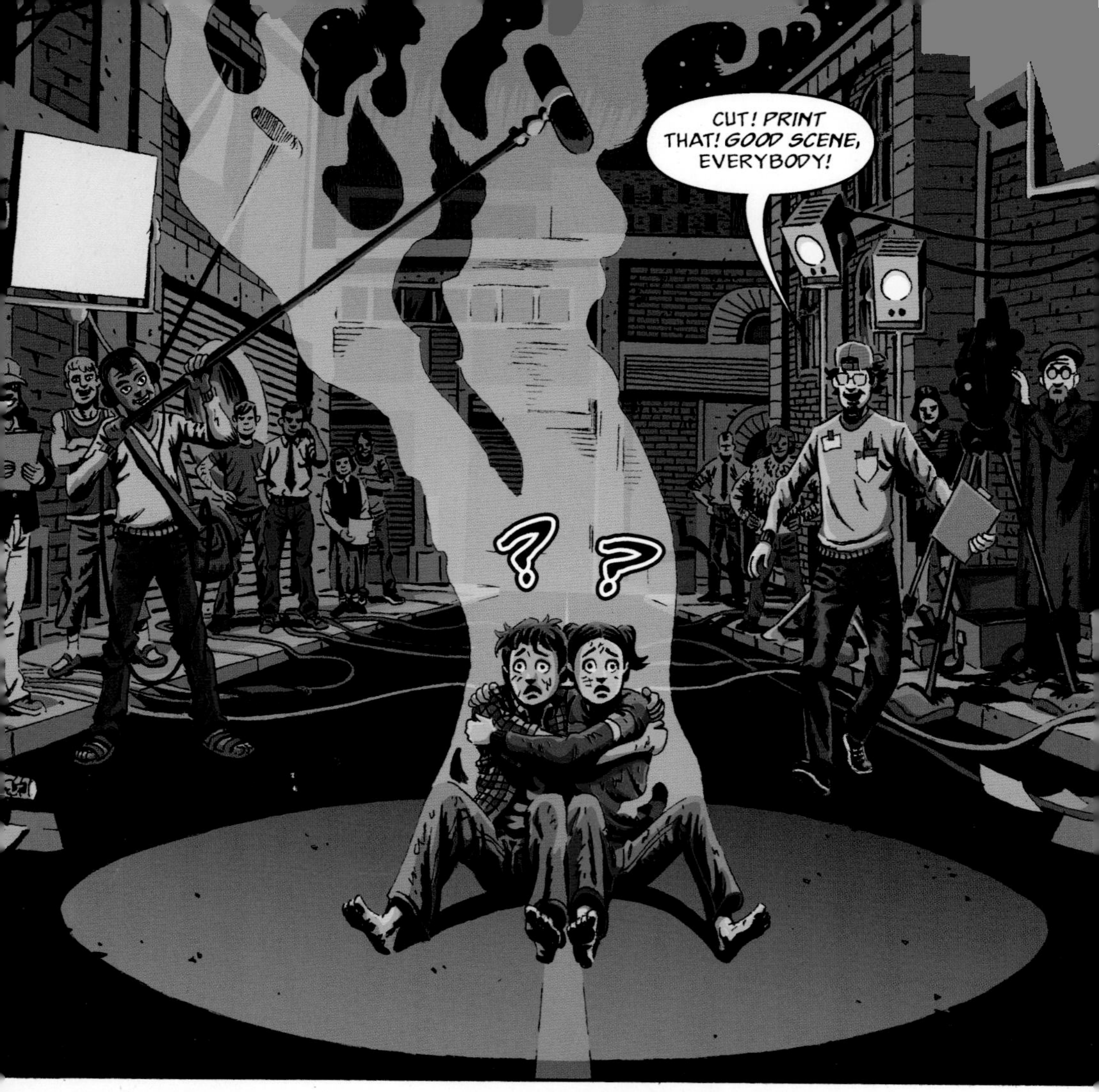
CUT! PRINT THAT! GOOD SCENE, EVERYBODY!
?
?

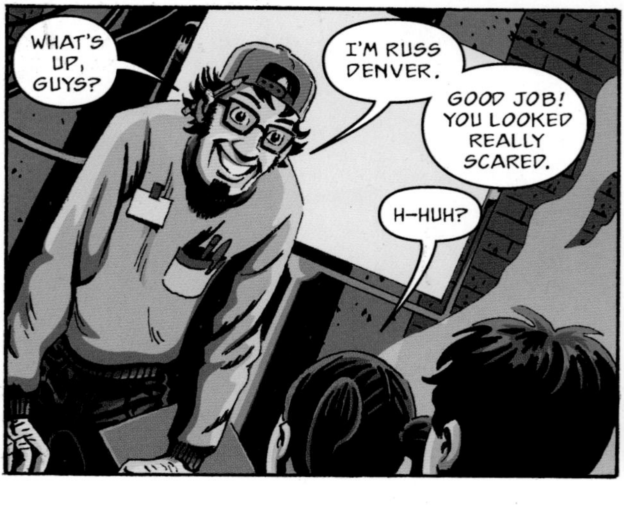
WHAT'S UP, GUYS?
I'M RUSS DENVER.
GOOD JOB! YOU LOOKED REALLY SCARED.
H-HUH?

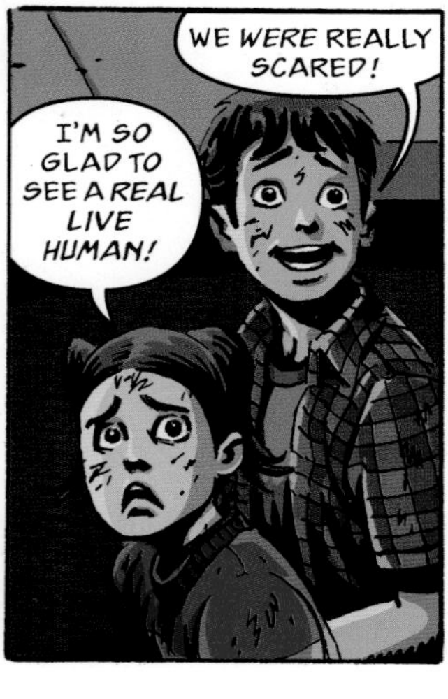
WE WERE REALLY SCARED!
I'M SO GLAD TO SEE A REAL LIVE HUMAN!

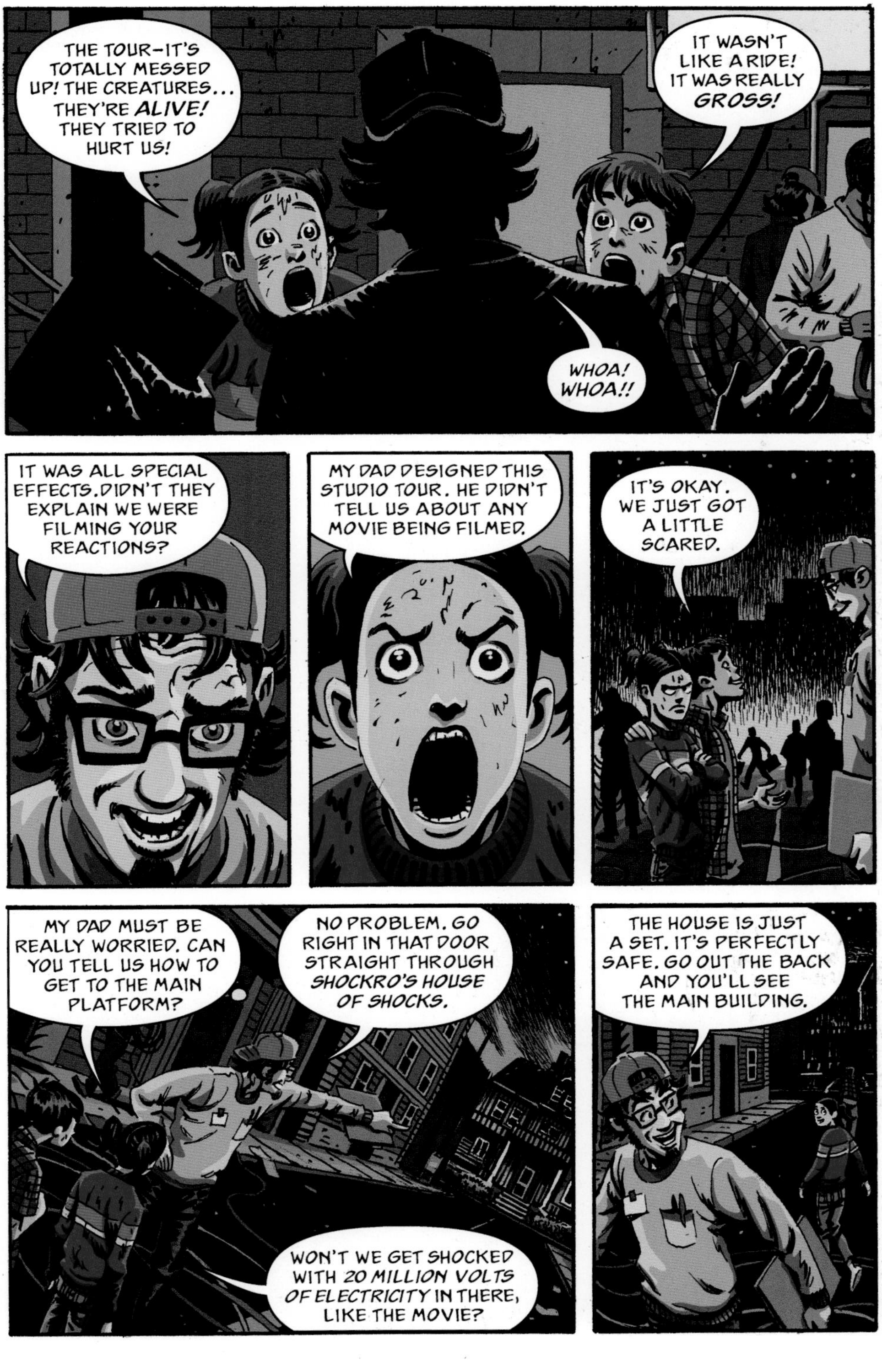
THE TOUR–IT'S TOTALLY MESSED UP! THE CREATURES... THEY'RE *ALIVE!* THEY TRIED TO HURT US!
IT WASN'T LIKE A RIDE! IT WAS REALLY *GROSS!*
WHOA! WHOA!!
IT WAS ALL SPECIAL EFFECTS.DIDN'T THEY EXPLAIN WE WERE FILMING YOUR REACTIONS?
MY DAD DESIGNED THIS STUDIO TOUR. HE DIDN'T TELL US ABOUT ANY MOVIE BEING FILMED.
IT'S OKAY. WE JUST GOT A LITTLE SCARED.
MY DAD MUST BE REALLY WORRIED. CAN YOU TELL US HOW TO GET TO THE MAIN PLATFORM?
NO PROBLEM. GO RIGHT IN THAT DOOR STRAIGHT THROUGH *SHOCKRO'S HOUSE OF SHOCKS.*
WON'T WE GET SHOCKED WITH *20 MILLION VOLTS OF ELECTRICITY* IN THERE, LIKE THE MOVIE?
THE HOUSE IS JUST A SET. IT'S PERFECTLY SAFE. GO OUT THE BACK AND YOU'LL SEE THE MAIN BUILDING.

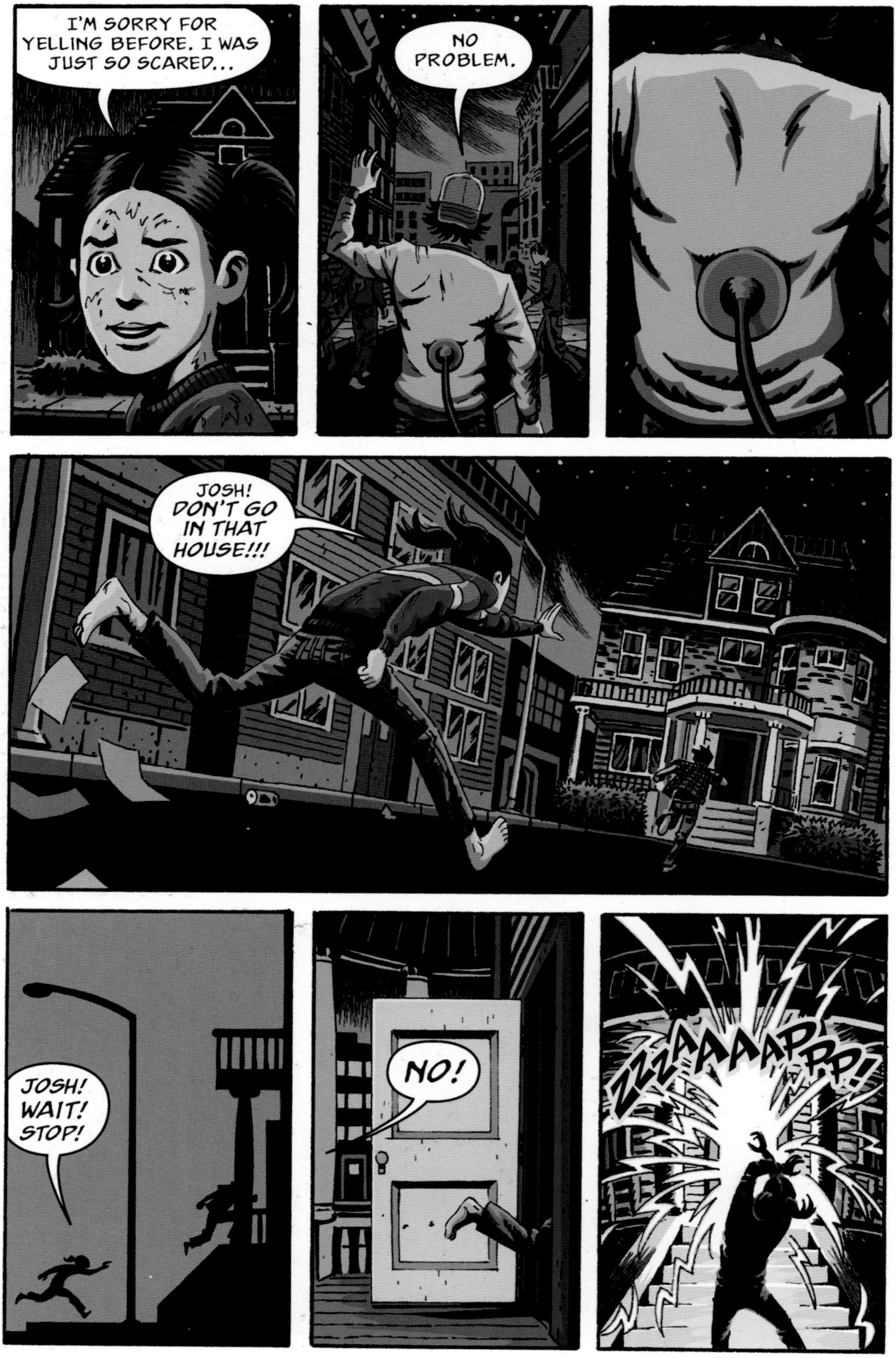
I'M SORRY FOR YELLING BEFORE. I WAS JUST SO SCARED...
NO PROBLEM.
JOSH! DON'T GO IN THAT HOUSE!!!
JOSH! WAIT! STOP!
NO!
ZZZAAAAAPPP!

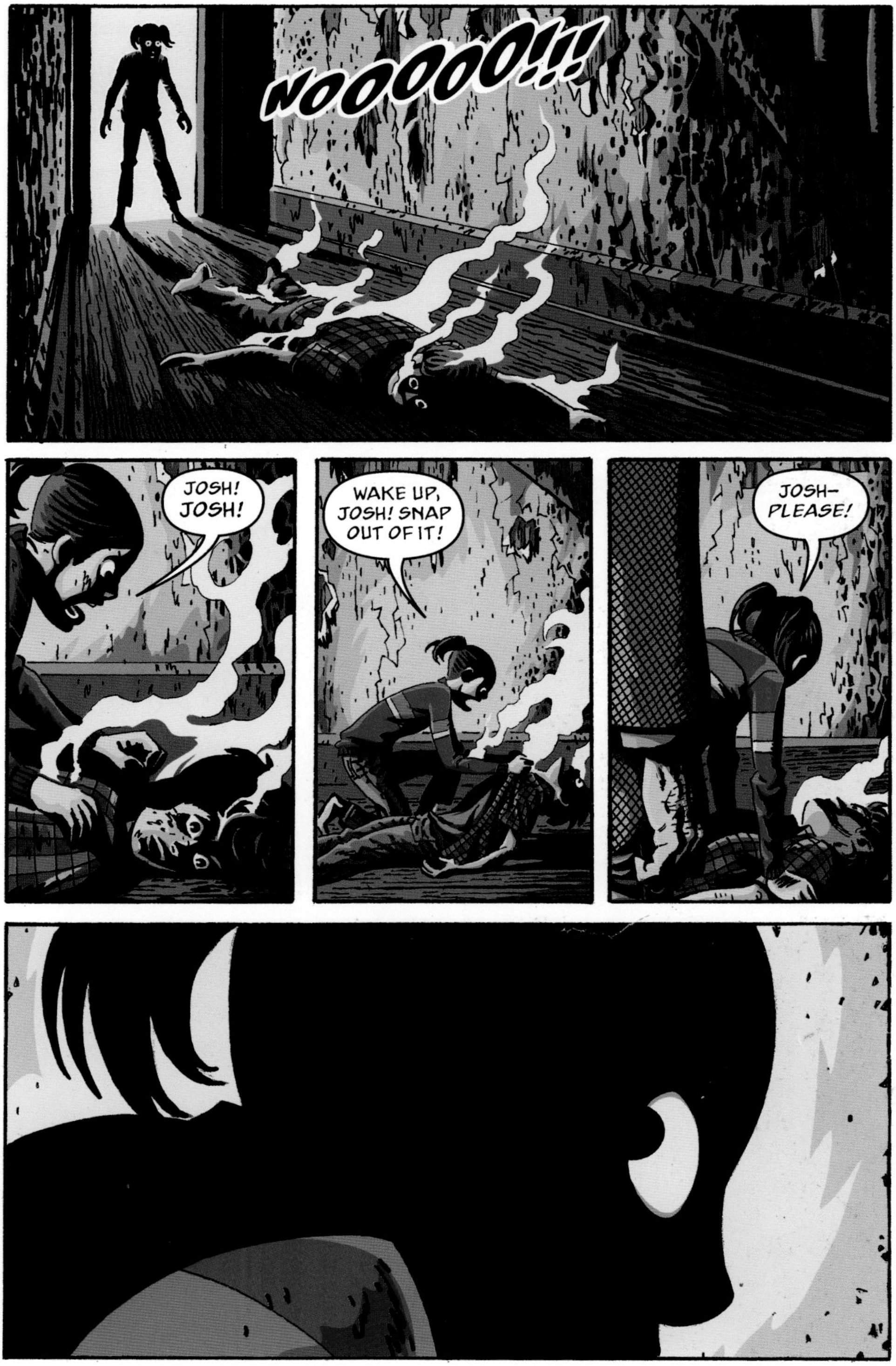
NOOOOO!!!
JOSH! JOSH!
WAKE UP, JOSH! SNAP OUT OF IT!
JOSH— PLEASE!

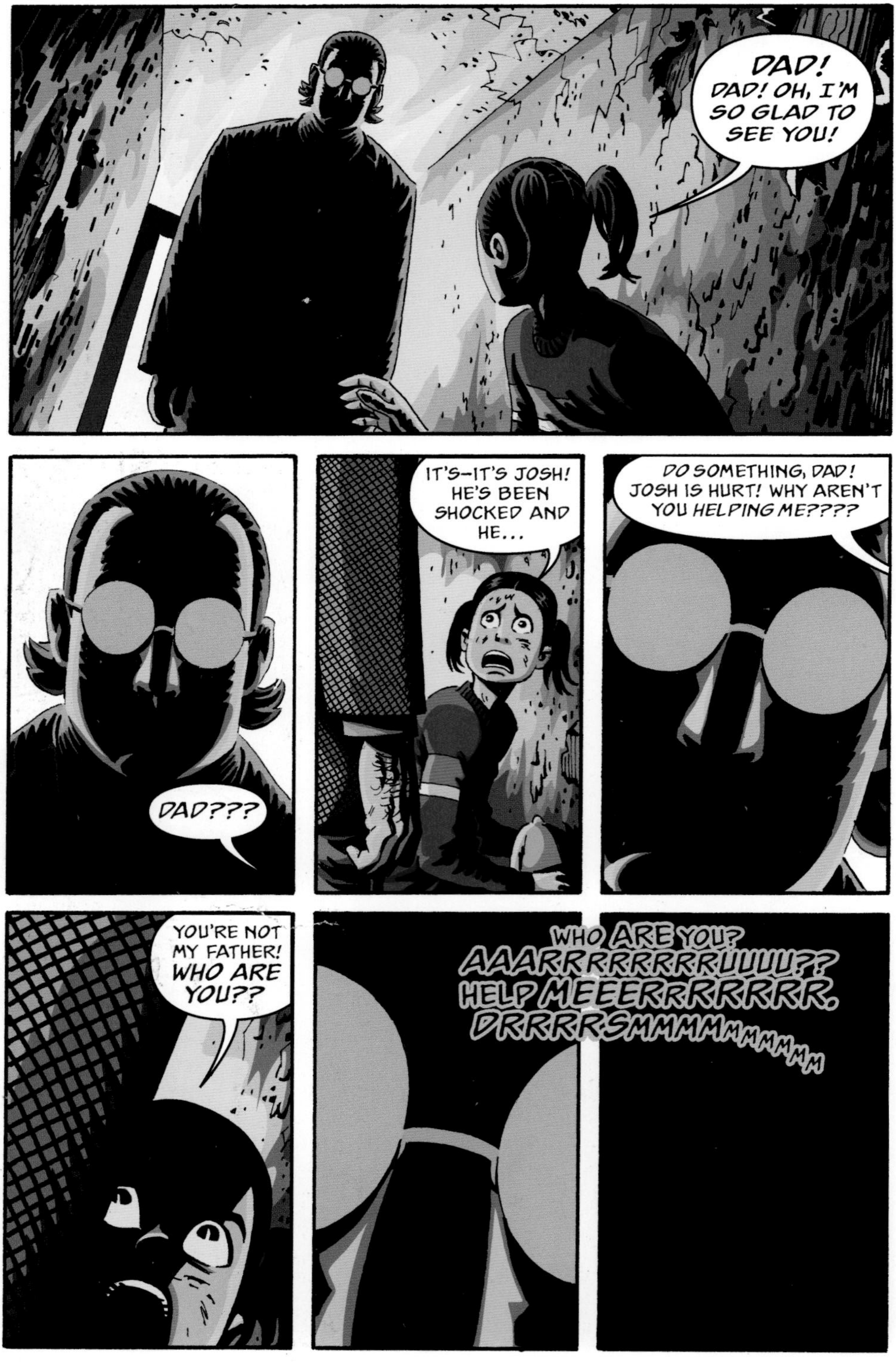
DAD! DAD! OH, I'M SO GLAD TO SEE YOU!
DAD???
IT'S—IT'S JOSH! HE'S BEEN SHOCKED AND HE...
DO SOMETHING, DAD! JOSH IS HURT! WHY AREN'T YOU HELPING ME????
YOU'RE NOT MY FATHER! WHO ARE YOU??
WHO ARE YOU? AAARRRRRRRRUUUU?? HELP MEEERRRRRRR. DRRRRSMMMMMMMMMM

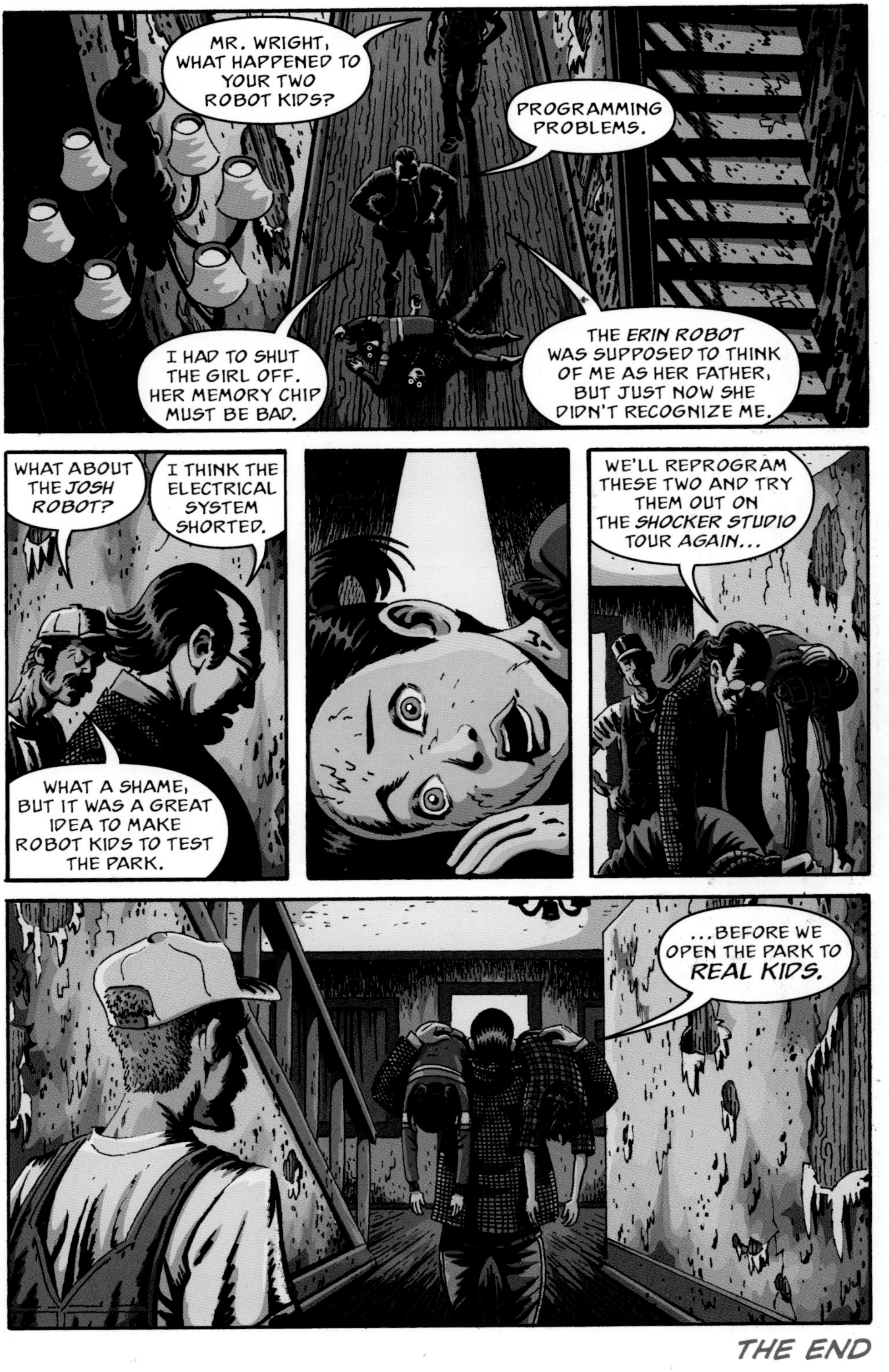
MR. WRIGHT, WHAT HAPPENED TO YOUR TWO ROBOT KIDS?
PROGRAMMING PROBLEMS.
I HAD TO SHUT THE GIRL OFF. HER MEMORY CHIP MUST BE BAD.
THE ERIN ROBOT WAS SUPPOSED TO THINK OF ME AS HER FATHER, BUT JUST NOW SHE DIDN'T RECOGNIZE ME.
WHAT ABOUT THE JOSH ROBOT?
I THINK THE ELECTRICAL SYSTEM SHORTED.
WHAT A SHAME, BUT IT WAS A GREAT IDEA TO MAKE ROBOT KIDS TO TEST THE PARK.
WE'LL REPROGRAM THESE TWO AND TRY THEM OUT ON THE SHOCKER STUDIO TOUR AGAIN...
...BEFORE WE OPEN THE PARK TO REAL KIDS.

THE END

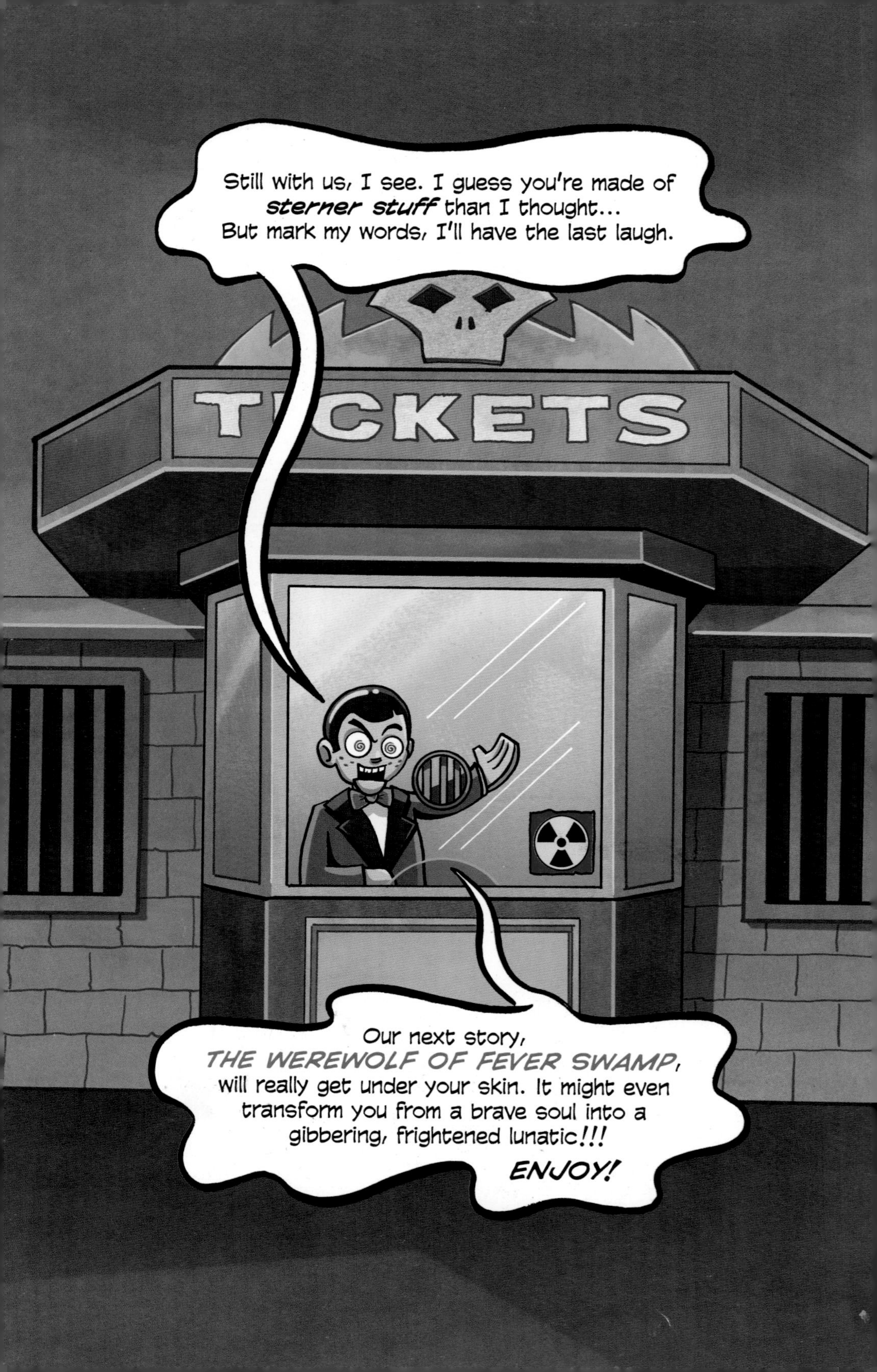

Still with us, I see. I guess you're made of *sterner stuff* than I thought... But mark my words, I'll have the last laugh.
TICKETS
Our next story, *THE WEREWOLF OF FEVER SWAMP*, will really get under your skin. It might even transform you from a brave soul into a gibbering, frightened lunatic!!! *ENJOY!*

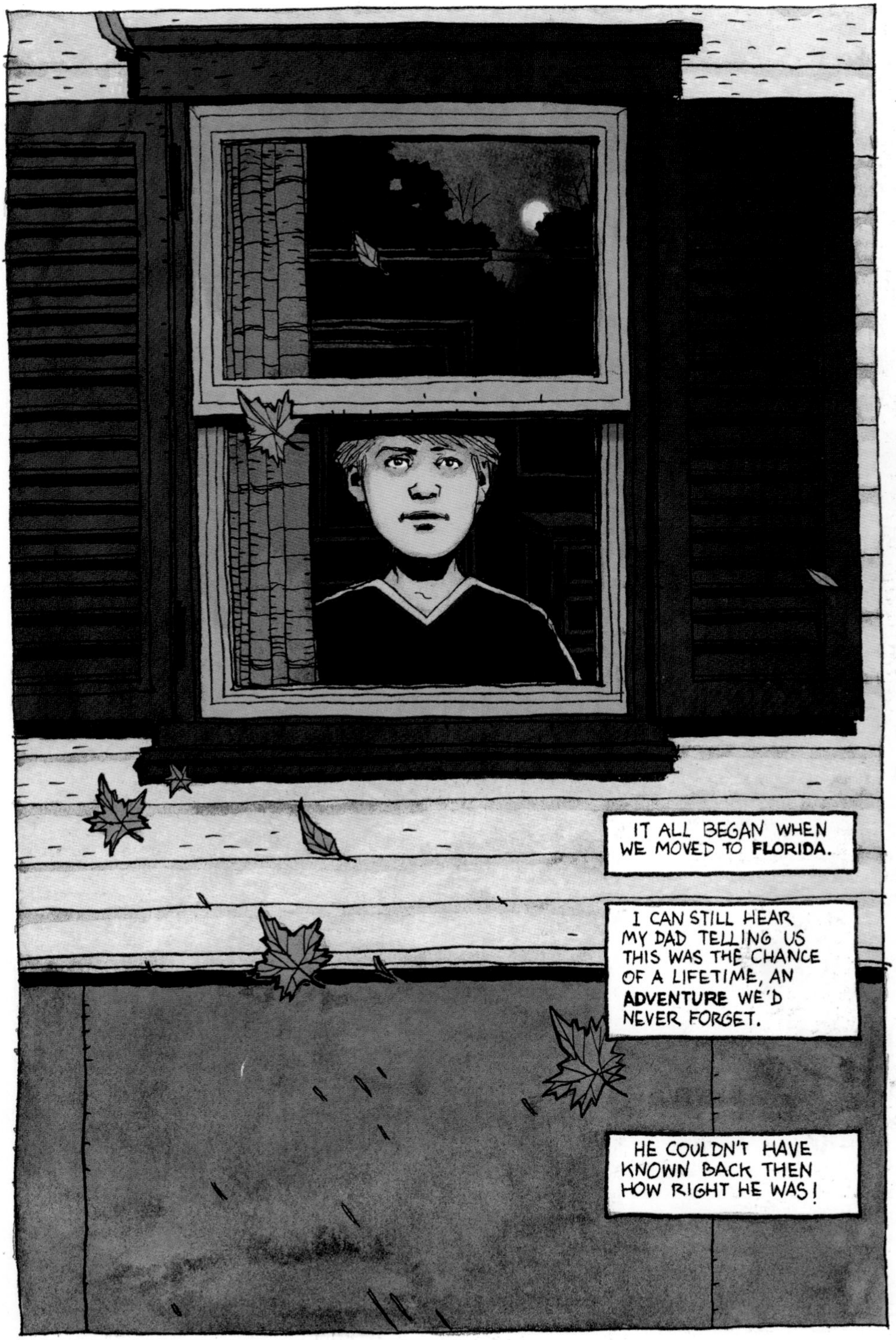
IT ALL BEGAN WHEN WE MOVED TO **FLORIDA**.
I CAN STILL HEAR MY DAD TELLING US THIS WAS THE CHANCE OF A LIFETIME, AN **ADVENTURE** WE'D NEVER FORGET.
HE COULDN'T HAVE KNOWN BACK THEN HOW RIGHT HE WAS!

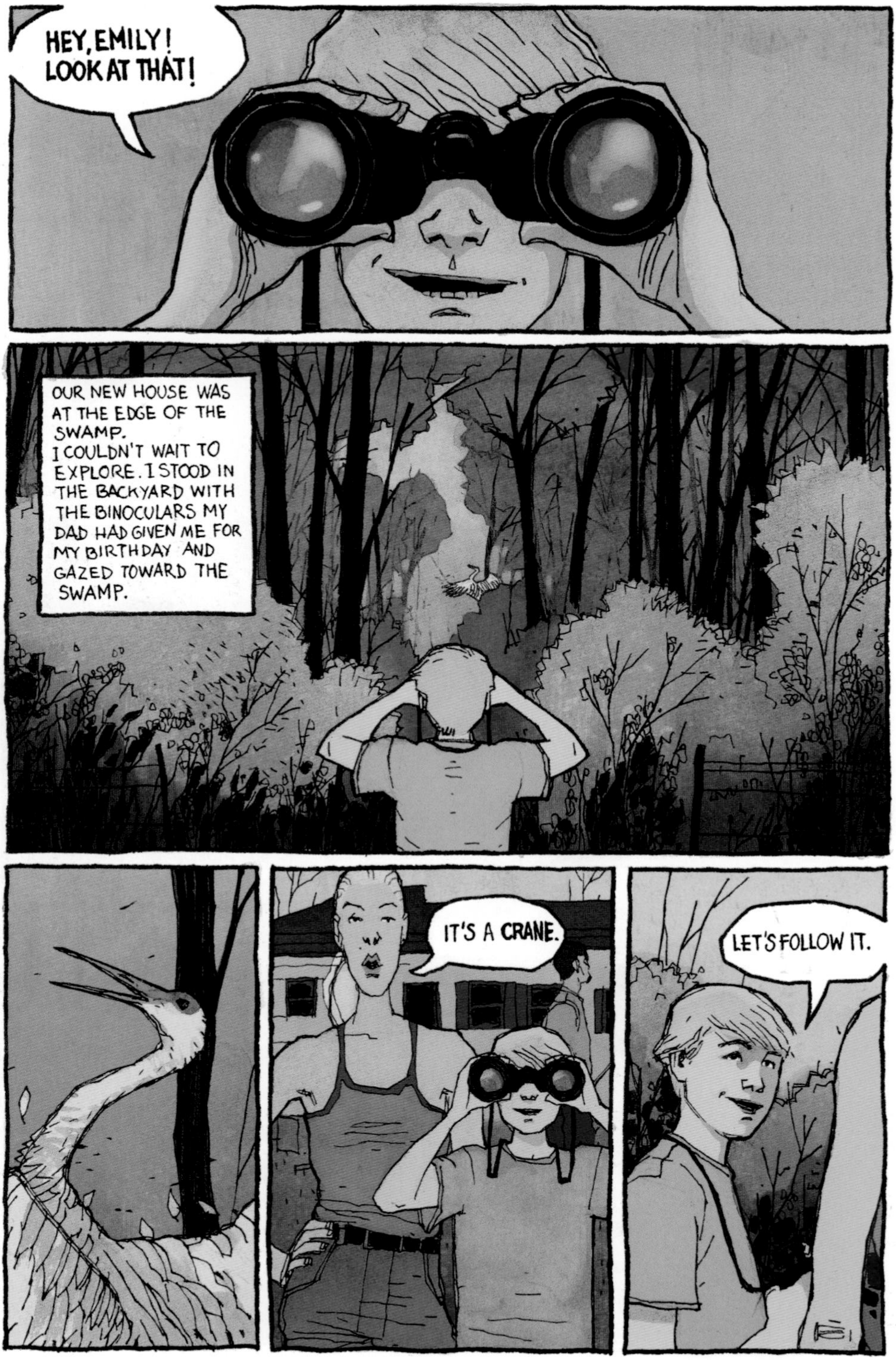
HEY, EMILY! LOOK AT THAT!
OUR NEW HOUSE WAS AT THE EDGE OF THE SWAMP. I COULDN'T WAIT TO EXPLORE. I STOOD IN THE BACKYARD WITH THE BINOCULARS MY DAD HAD GIVEN ME FOR MY BIRTHDAY AND GAZED TOWARD THE SWAMP.
IT'S A CRANE.
LET'S FOLLOW IT.

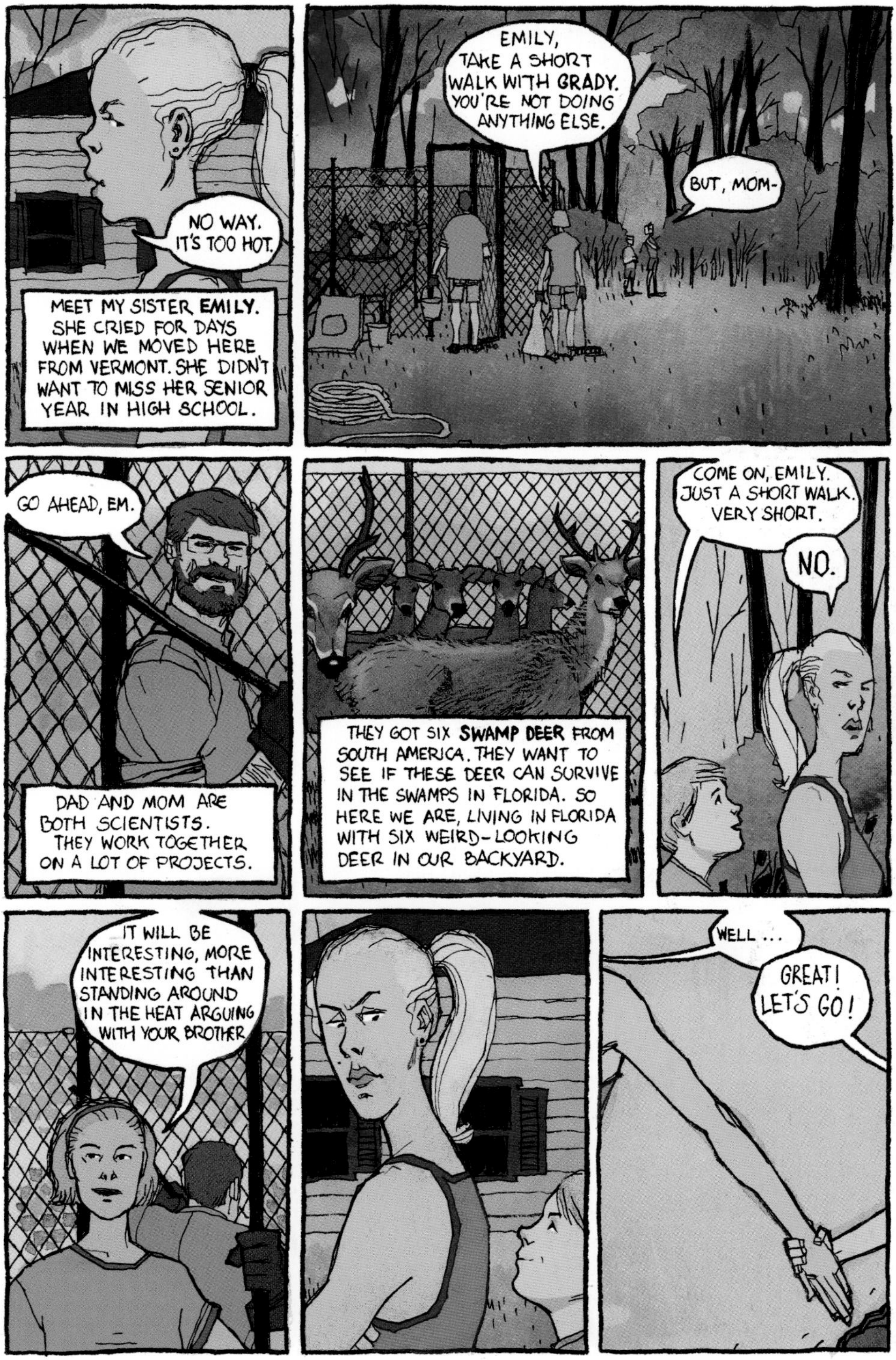
NO WAY. IT'S TOO HOT.
MEET MY SISTER **EMILY**. SHE CRIED FOR DAYS WHEN WE MOVED HERE FROM VERMONT. SHE DIDN'T WANT TO MISS HER SENIOR YEAR IN HIGH SCHOOL.
EMILY, TAKE A SHORT WALK WITH **GRADY**. YOU'RE NOT DOING ANYTHING ELSE.
BUT, MOM-
GO AHEAD, EM.
DAD AND MOM ARE BOTH SCIENTISTS. THEY WORK TOGETHER ON A LOT OF PROJECTS.
THEY GOT SIX **SWAMP DEER** FROM SOUTH AMERICA. THEY WANT TO SEE IF THESE DEER CAN SURVIVE IN THE SWAMPS IN FLORIDA. SO HERE WE ARE, LIVING IN FLORIDA WITH SIX WEIRD-LOOKING DEER IN OUR BACKYARD.
COME ON, EMILY. JUST A SHORT WALK. VERY SHORT.
NO.
IT WILL BE INTERESTING, MORE INTERESTING THAN STANDING AROUND IN THE HEAT ARGUING WITH YOUR BROTHER
WELL ...
GREAT! LET'S GO!

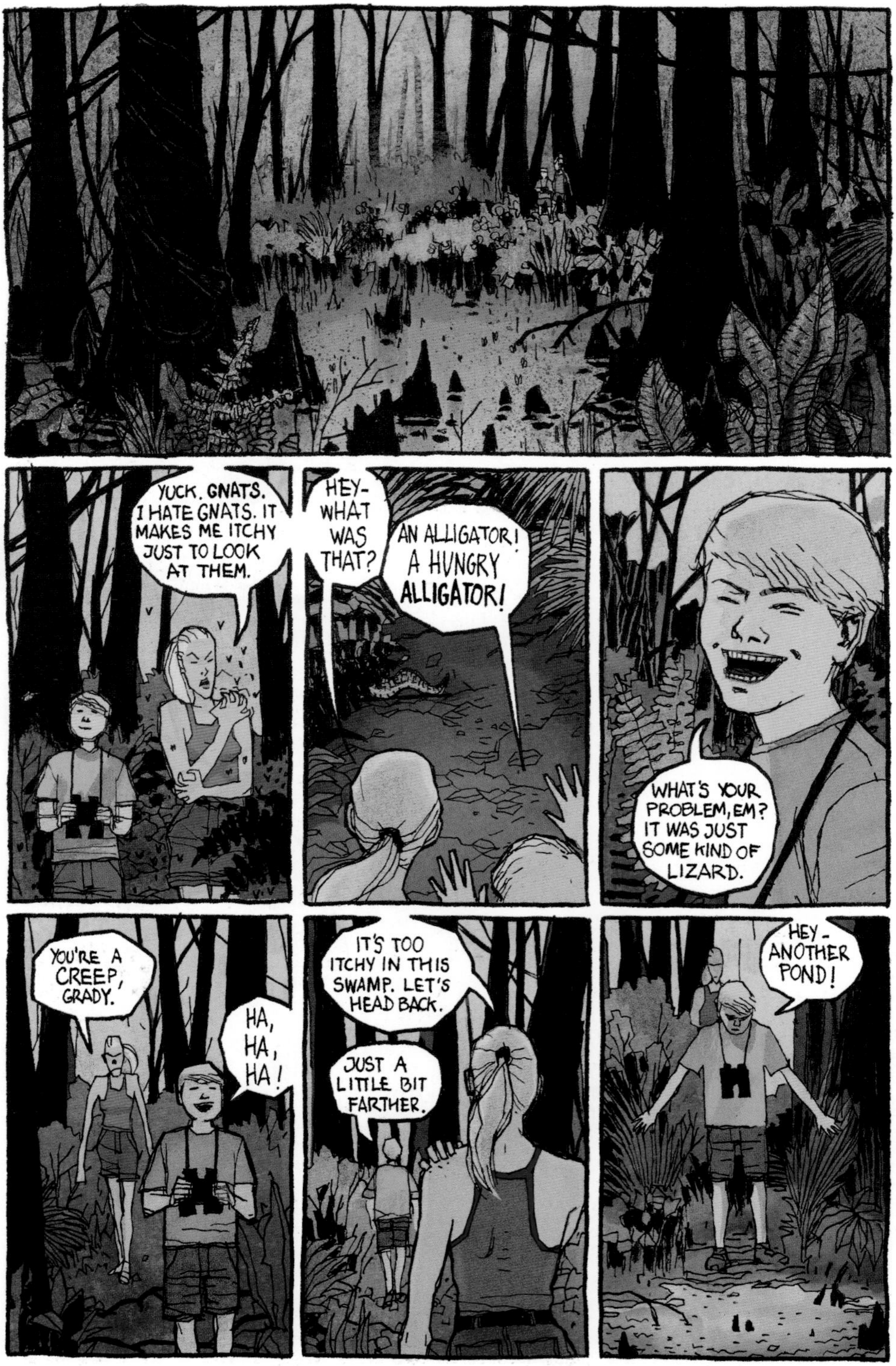
YUCK. GNATS. I HATE GNATS. IT MAKES ME ITCHY JUST TO LOOK AT THEM.
HEY- WHAT WAS THAT?
AN ALLIGATOR! A HUNGRY ALLIGATOR!
WHAT'S YOUR PROBLEM, EM? IT WAS JUST SOME KIND OF LIZARD.
YOU'RE A CREEP, GRADY.
HA, HA, HA!
IT'S TOO ITCHY IN THIS SWAMP. LET'S HEAD BACK.
JUST A LITTLE BIT FARTHER.
HEY- ANOTHER POND!

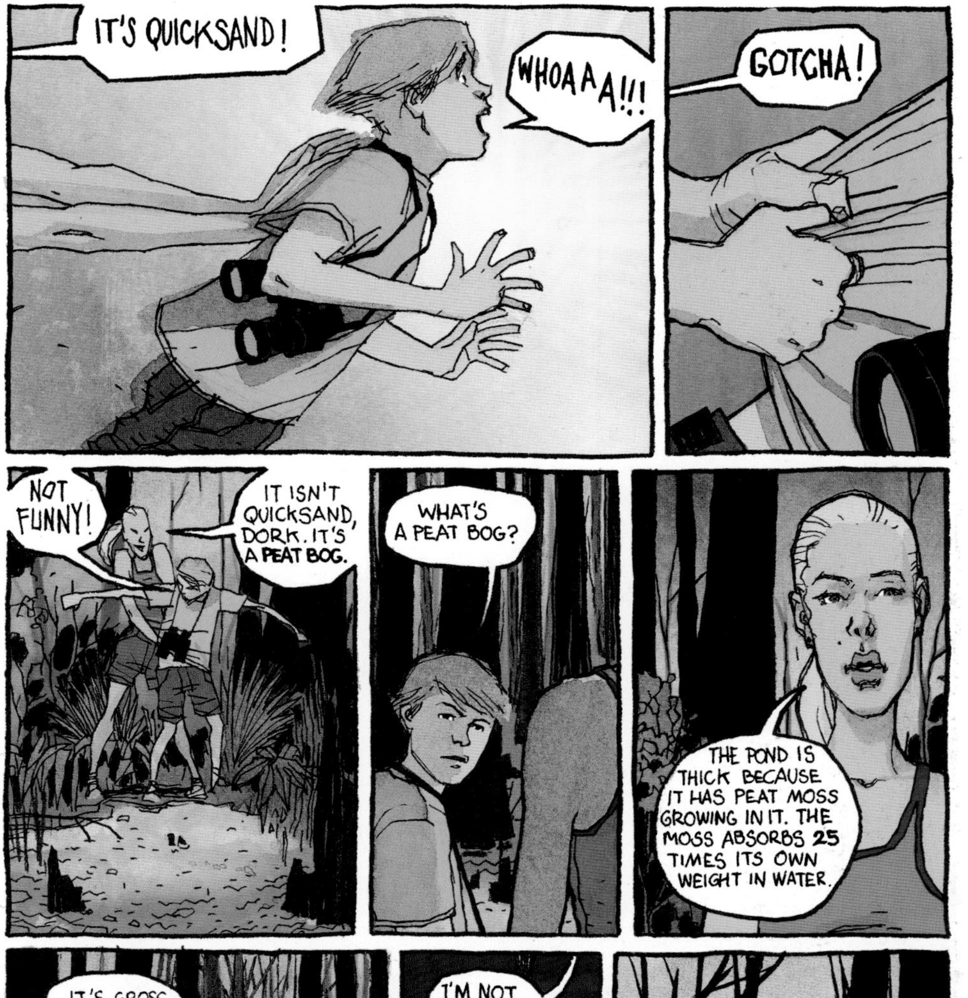
IT'S QUICKSAND!
WHOAAAA!!!
GOTCHA!
NOT FUNNY!
IT ISN'T QUICKSAND, DORK. IT'S A PEAT BOG.
WHAT'S A PEAT BOG?
THE POND IS THICK BECAUSE IT HAS PEAT MOSS GROWING IN IT. THE MOSS ABSORBS 25 TIMES ITS OWN WEIGHT IN WATER.
IT'S GROSS-LOOKING.
DRINK SOME, SEE HOW IT TASTES.
I'M NOT THIRSTY.
BLORP
LET'S GET GOING. I'M REALLY HOT.

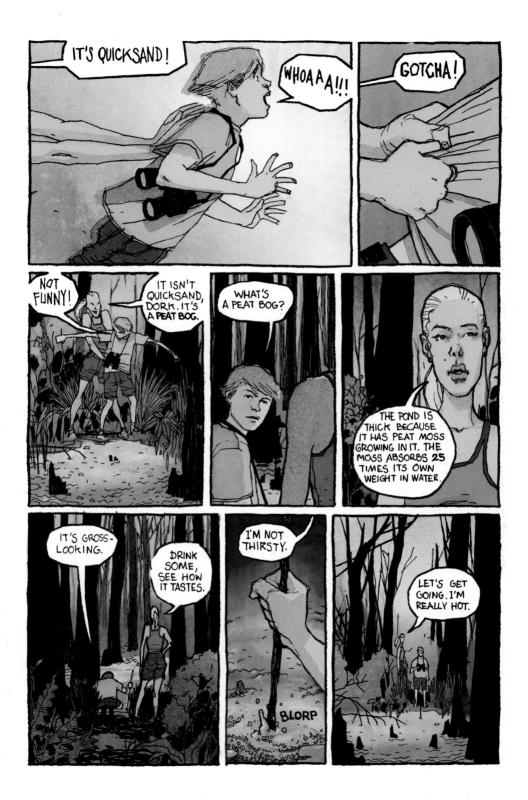

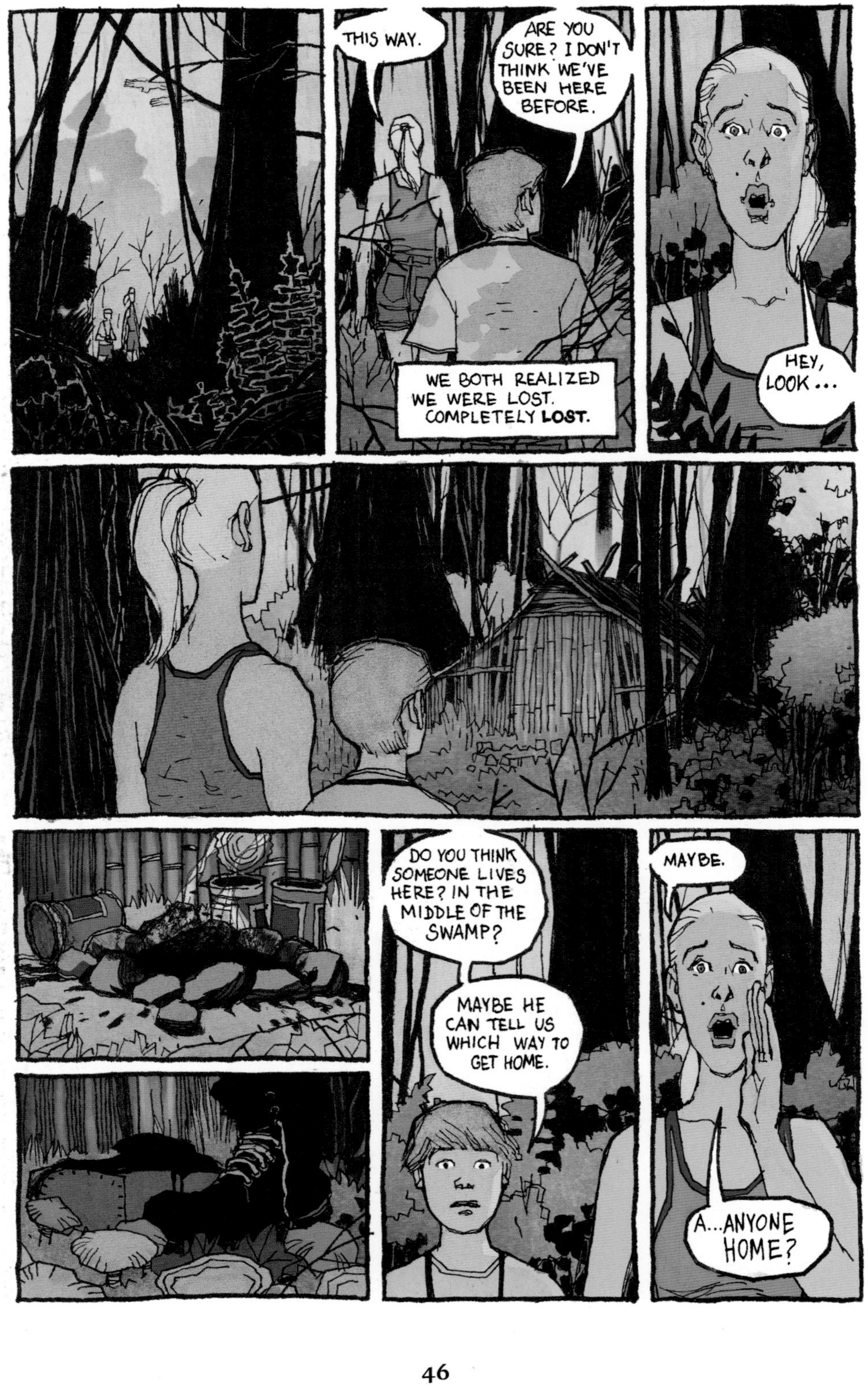
THIS WAY.
ARE YOU SURE? I DON'T THINK WE'VE BEEN HERE BEFORE.
WE BOTH REALIZED WE WERE LOST. COMPLETELY LOST.
HEY, LOOK...
DO YOU THINK SOMEONE LIVES HERE? IN THE MIDDLE OF THE SWAMP?
MAYBE HE CAN TELL US WHICH WAY TO GET HOME.
MAYBE.
A...ANYONE HOME?

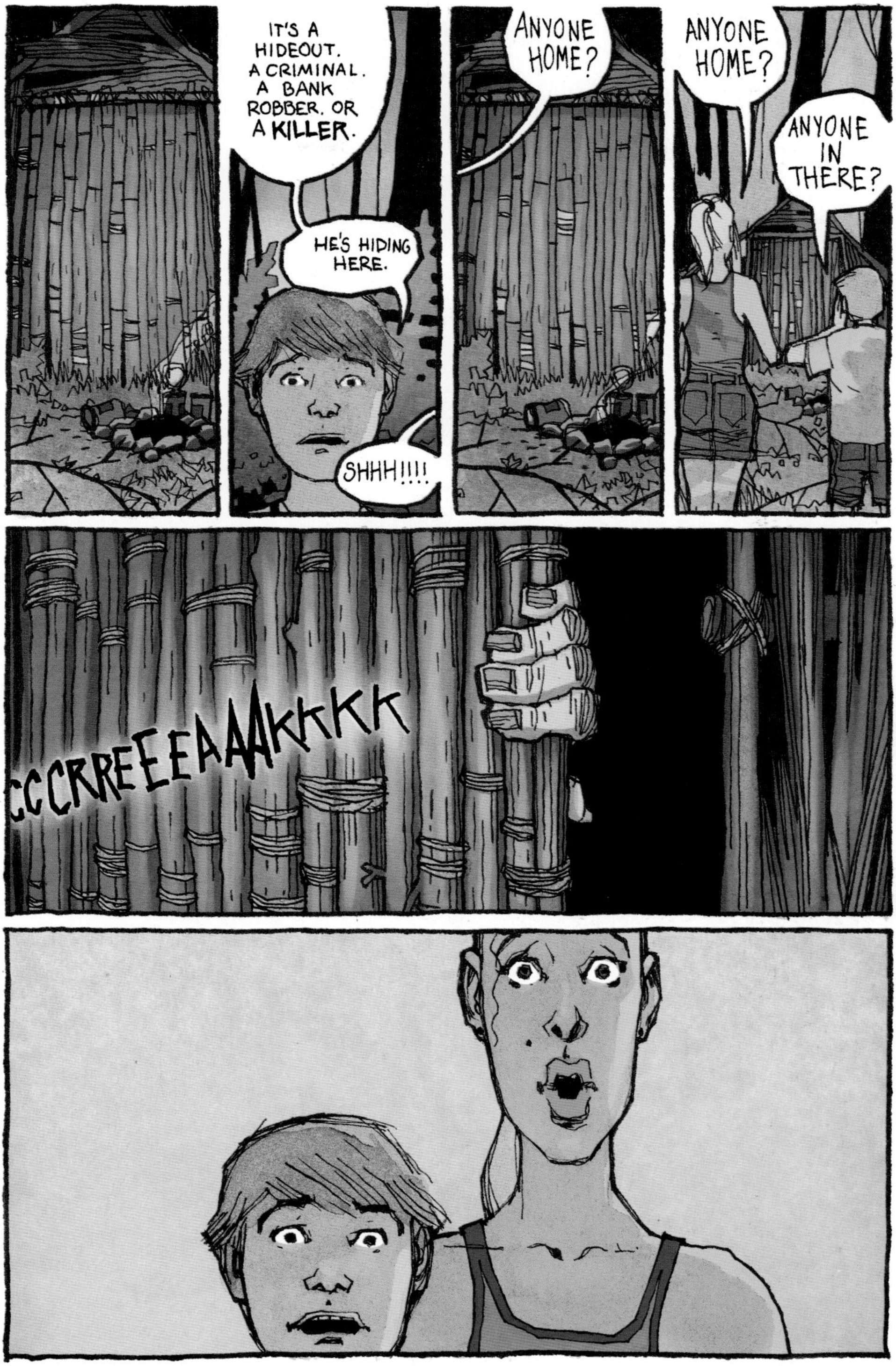
IT'S A HIDEOUT. A CRIMINAL. A BANK ROBBER. OR A KILLER.
HE'S HIDING HERE.
SHHH!!!!
ANYONE HOME?
ANYONE HOME?
ANYONE IN THERE?
CCCRREEEAAAKKKK

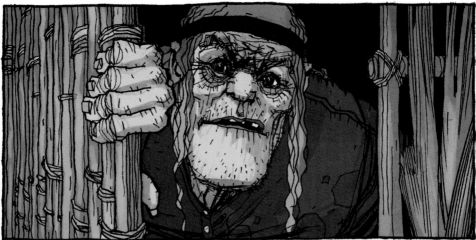

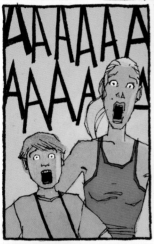

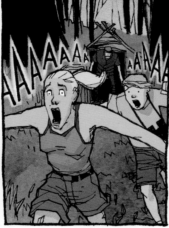

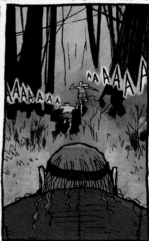

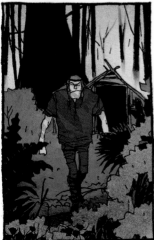

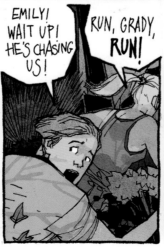

AAAAAA
AAAAA
AAAAAAAA
AAAAAA
AAAAAAA
AAAAA
EMILY! WAIT UP! HE'S CHASING US!
RUN, GRADY, RUN!
HEY, THIS LOOKS FAMILIAR. LET'S GO!

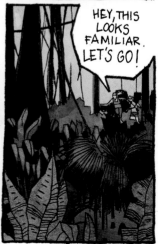

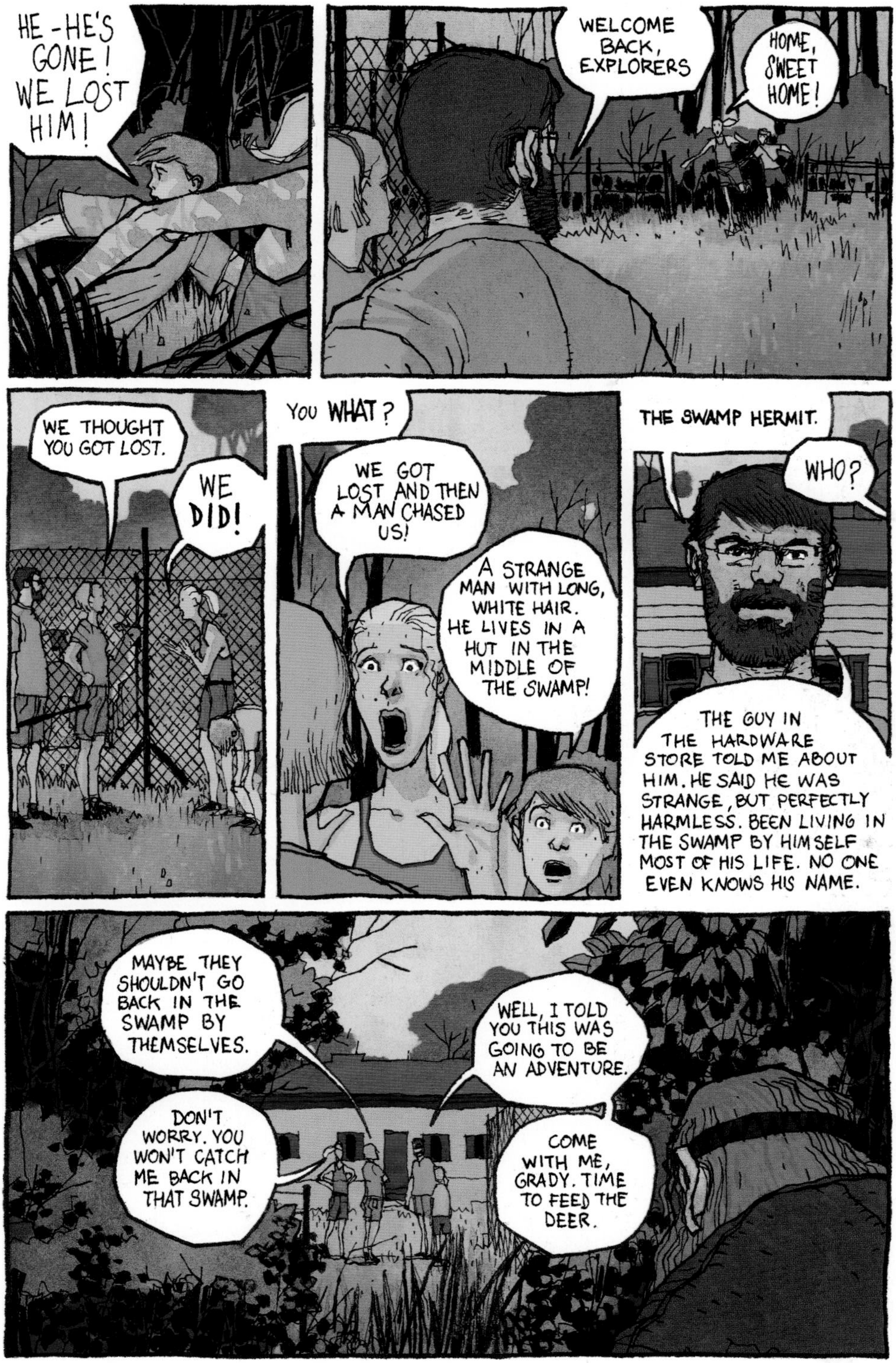
HE-HE'S GONE! WE LOST HIM!
WELCOME BACK, EXPLORERS
HOME, SWEET HOME!
WE THOUGHT YOU GOT LOST.
WE DID!
YOU WHAT?
WE GOT LOST AND THEN A MAN CHASED US!
A STRANGE MAN WITH LONG, WHITE HAIR. HE LIVES IN A HUT IN THE MIDDLE OF THE SWAMP!
THE SWAMP HERMIT.
WHO?
THE GUY IN THE HARDWARE STORE TOLD ME ABOUT HIM. HE SAID HE WAS STRANGE, BUT PERFECTLY HARMLESS. BEEN LIVING IN THE SWAMP BY HIMSELF MOST OF HIS LIFE. NO ONE EVEN KNOWS HIS NAME.
MAYBE THEY SHOULDN'T GO BACK IN THE SWAMP BY THEMSELVES.
DON'T WORRY. YOU WON'T CATCH ME BACK IN THAT SWAMP.
WELL, I TOLD YOU THIS WAS GOING TO BE AN ADVENTURE.
COME WITH ME, GRADY. TIME TO FEED THE DEER.

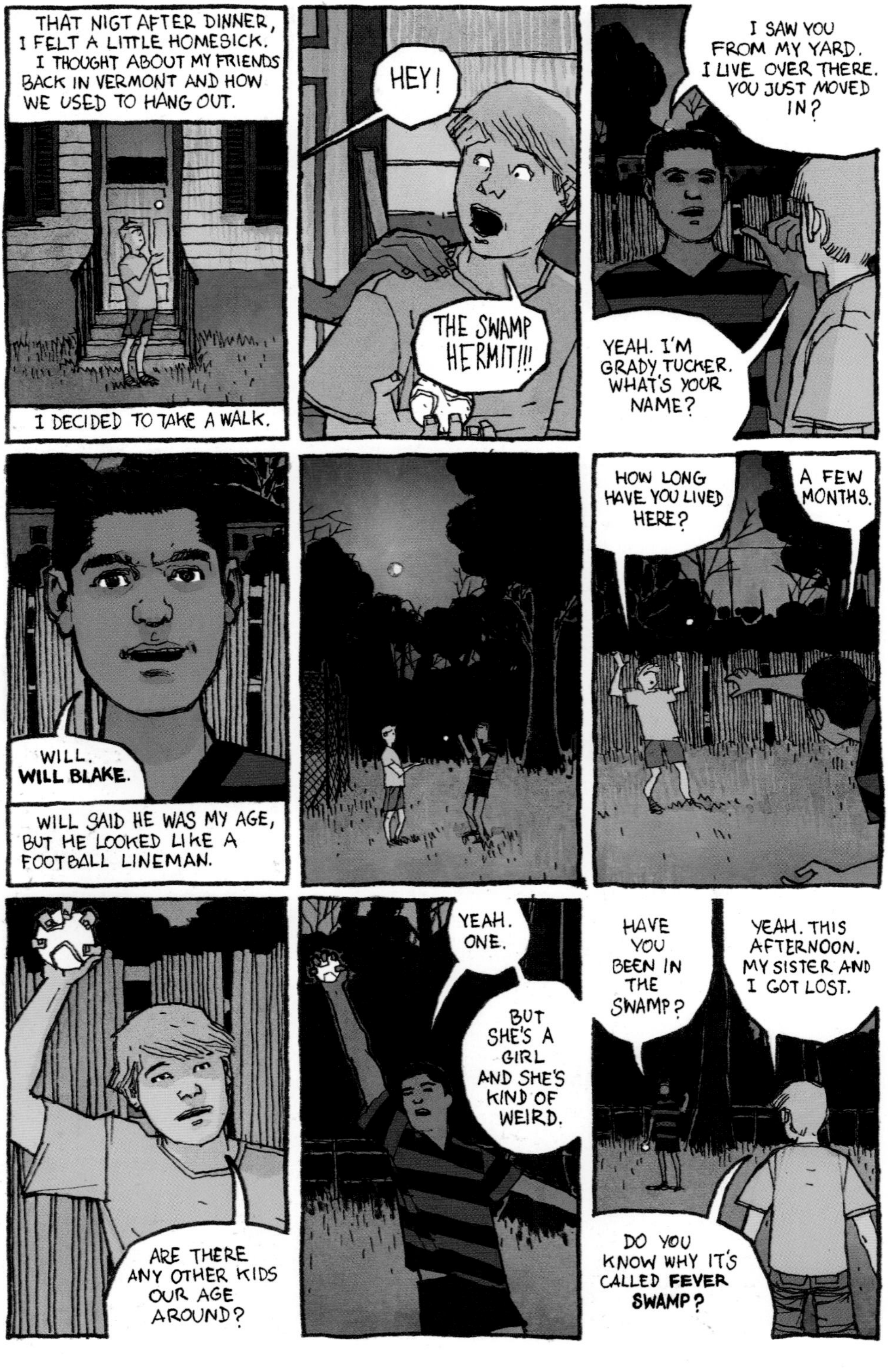
THAT NIGT AFTER DINNER, I FELT A LITTLE HOMESICK. I THOUGHT ABOUT MY FRIENDS BACK IN VERMONT AND HOW WE USED TO HANG OUT.
I DECIDED TO TAKE A WALK.
HEY!
THE SWAMP HERMIT!!!
I SAW YOU FROM MY YARD. I LIVE OVER THERE. YOU JUST MOVED IN?
YEAH. I'M GRADY TUCKER. WHAT'S YOUR NAME?
WILL. **WILL BLAKE.**
WILL SAID HE WAS MY AGE, BUT HE LOOKED LIKE A FOOTBALL LINEMAN.
HOW LONG HAVE YOU LIVED HERE?
A FEW MONTHS.
ARE THERE ANY OTHER KIDS OUR AGE AROUND?
YEAH. ONE.
BUT SHE'S A GIRL AND SHE'S KIND OF WEIRD.
HAVE YOU BEEN IN THE SWAMP?
YEAH. THIS AFTERNOON. MY SISTER AND I GOT LOST.
DO YOU KNOW WHY IT'S CALLED **FEVER SWAMP**?

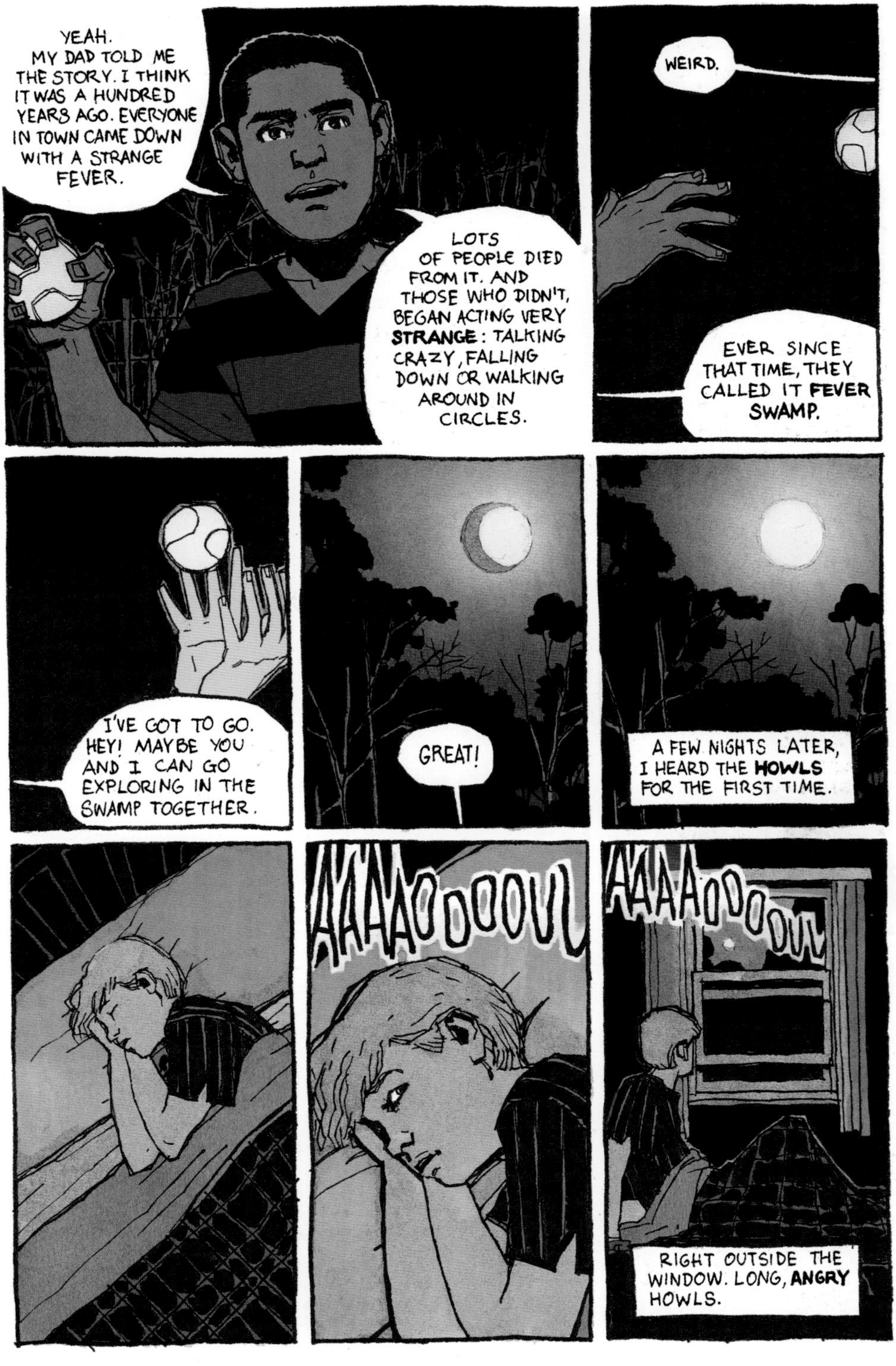
YEAH. MY DAD TOLD ME THE STORY. I THINK IT WAS A HUNDRED YEARS AGO. EVERYONE IN TOWN CAME DOWN WITH A STRANGE FEVER.
LOTS OF PEOPLE DIED FROM IT. AND THOSE WHO DIDN'T, BEGAN ACTING VERY **STRANGE**: TALKING CRAZY, FALLING DOWN OR WALKING AROUND IN CIRCLES.
WEIRD.
EVER SINCE THAT TIME, THEY CALLED IT **FEVER SWAMP.**
I'VE GOT TO GO. HEY! MAYBE YOU AND I CAN GO EXPLORING IN THE SWAMP TOGETHER.
GREAT!
A FEW NIGHTS LATER, I HEARD THE **HOWLS** FOR THE FIRST TIME.
AAAAOOOOUL
AAAAAOOOOUL
RIGHT OUTSIDE THE WINDOW. LONG, **ANGRY** HOWLS.

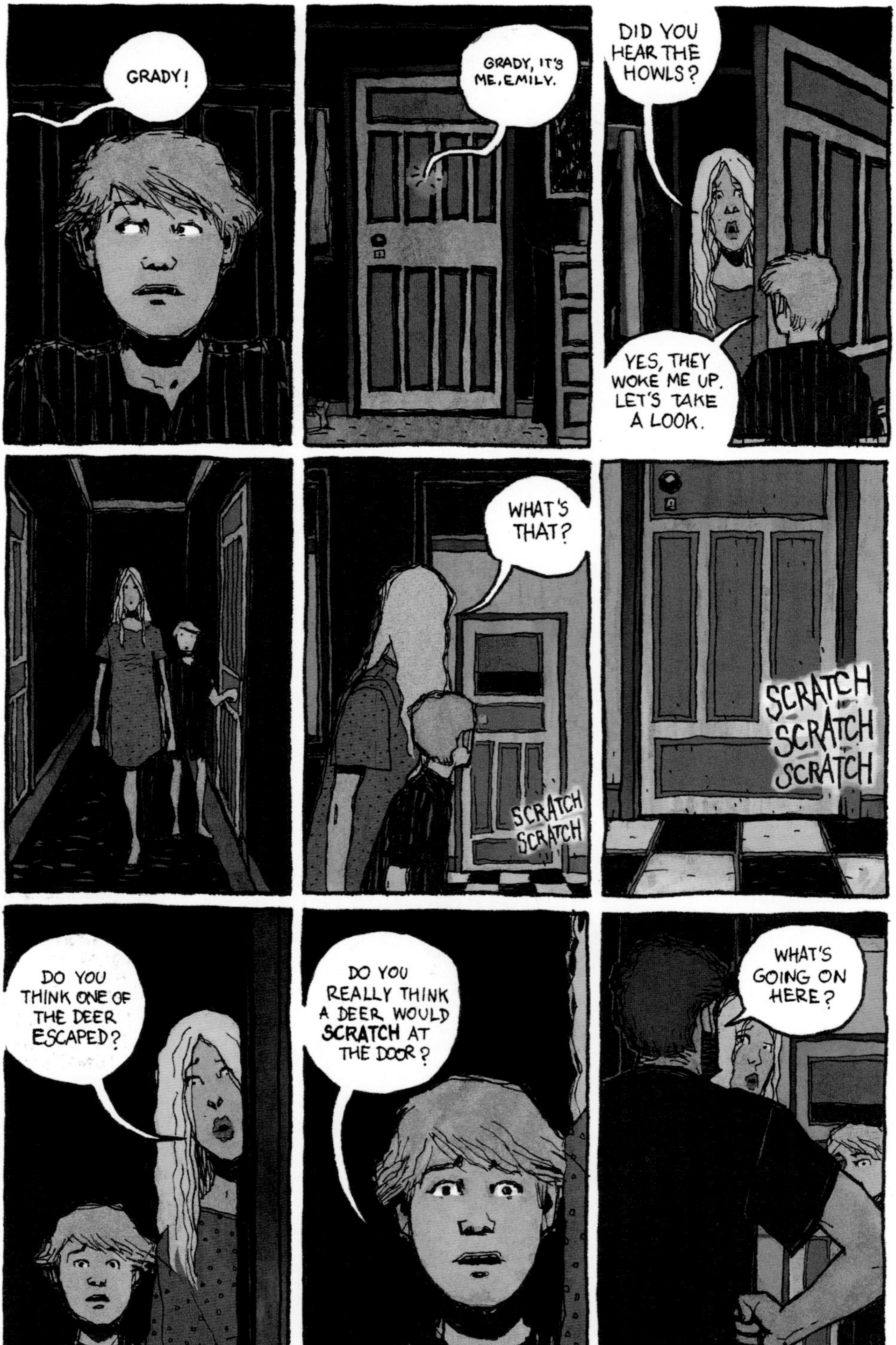
GRADY!
GRADY, IT'S ME, EMILY.
DID YOU HEAR THE HOWLS?
YES, THEY WOKE ME UP. LET'S TAKE A LOOK.
WHAT'S THAT?
SCRATCH SCRATCH
SCRATCH SCRATCH SCRATCH
DO YOU THINK ONE OF THE DEER ESCAPED?
DO YOU REALLY THINK A DEER WOULD **SCRATCH** AT THE DOOR?
WHAT'S GOING ON HERE?

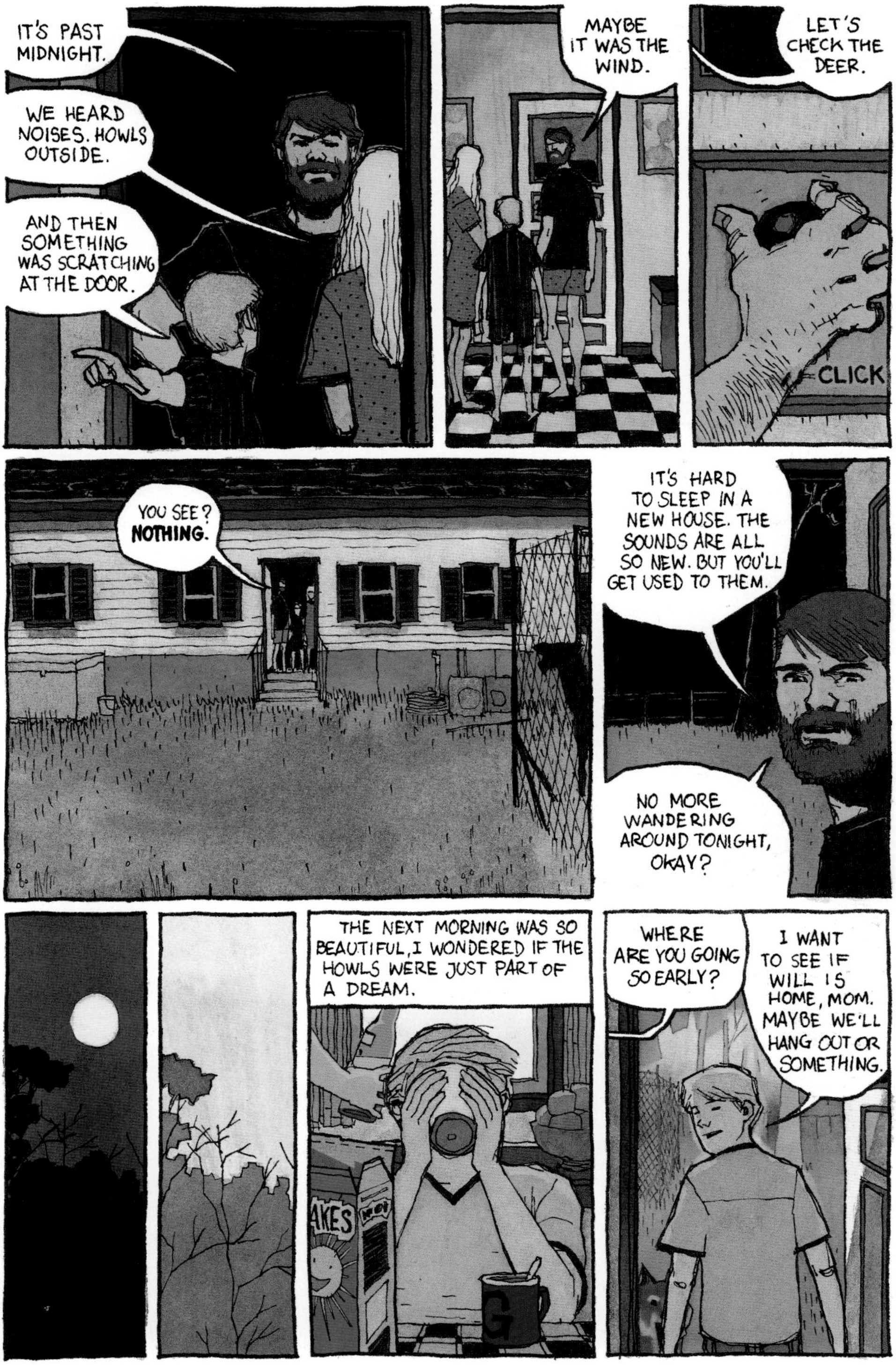
IT'S PAST MIDNIGHT.
WE HEARD NOISES. HOWLS OUTSIDE.
AND THEN SOMETHING WAS SCRATCHING AT THE DOOR.
MAYBE IT WAS THE WIND.
LET'S CHECK THE DEER.
CLICK
YOU SEE? **NOTHING**.
IT'S HARD TO SLEEP IN A NEW HOUSE. THE SOUNDS ARE ALL SO NEW. BUT YOU'LL GET USED TO THEM.
NO MORE WANDERING AROUND TONIGHT, OKAY?
THE NEXT MORNING WAS SO BEAUTIFUL, I WONDERED IF THE HOWLS WERE JUST PART OF A DREAM.
AKES
G
WHERE ARE YOU GOING SO EARLY?
I WANT TO SEE IF WILL IS HOME, MOM. MAYBE WE'LL HANG OUT OR SOMETHING.

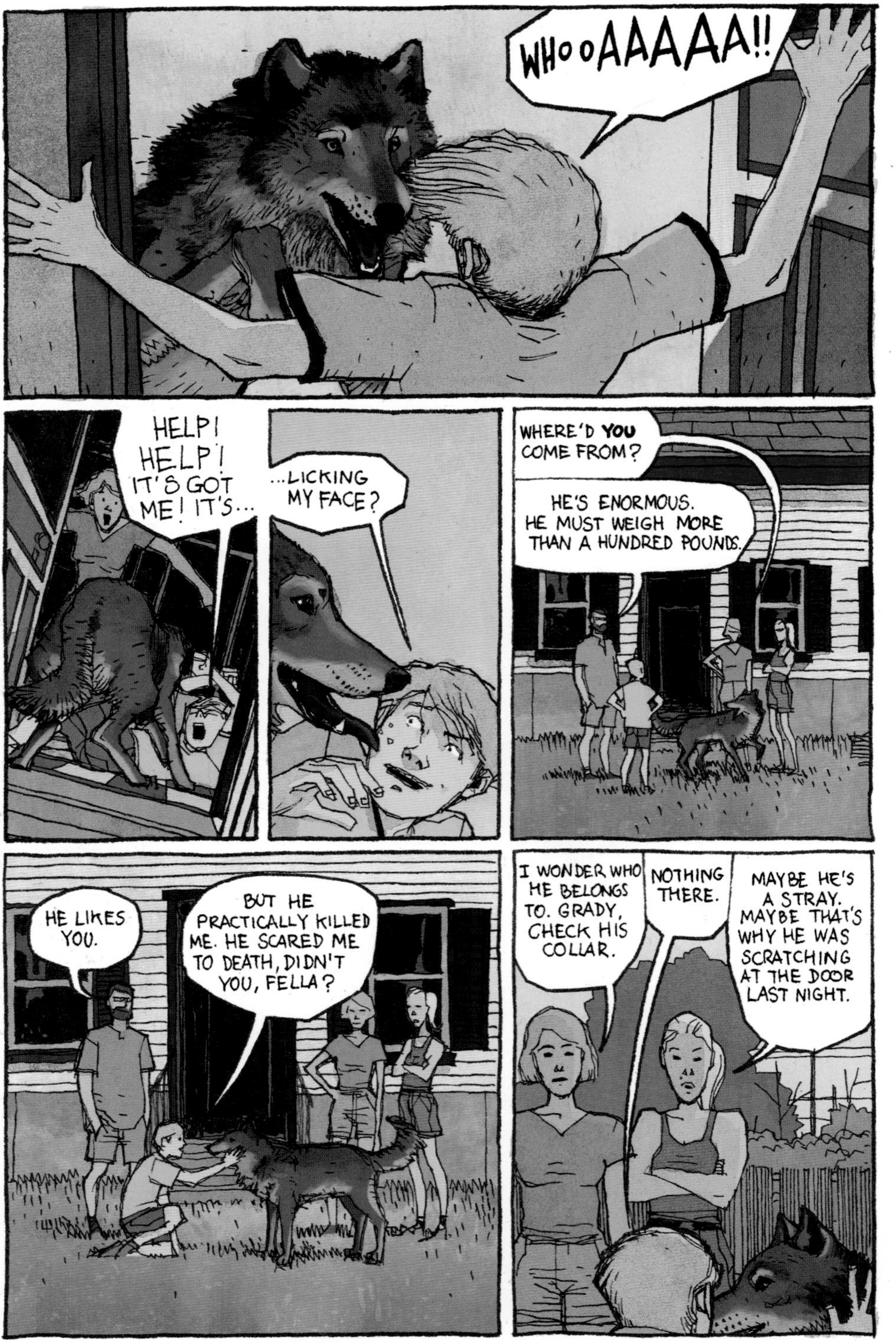
WHOoAAAAA!!
HELP! HELP! IT'S GOT ME! IT'S...
...LICKING MY FACE?
WHERE'D **YOU** COME FROM?
HE'S ENORMOUS. HE MUST WEIGH MORE THAN A HUNDRED POUNDS.
HE LIKES YOU.
BUT HE PRACTICALLY KILLED ME. HE SCARED ME TO DEATH, DIDN'T YOU, FELLA?
I WONDER WHO HE BELONGS TO. GRADY, CHECK HIS COLLAR.
NOTHING THERE.
MAYBE HE'S A STRAY. MAYBE THAT'S WHY HE WAS SCRATCHING AT THE DOOR LAST NIGHT.

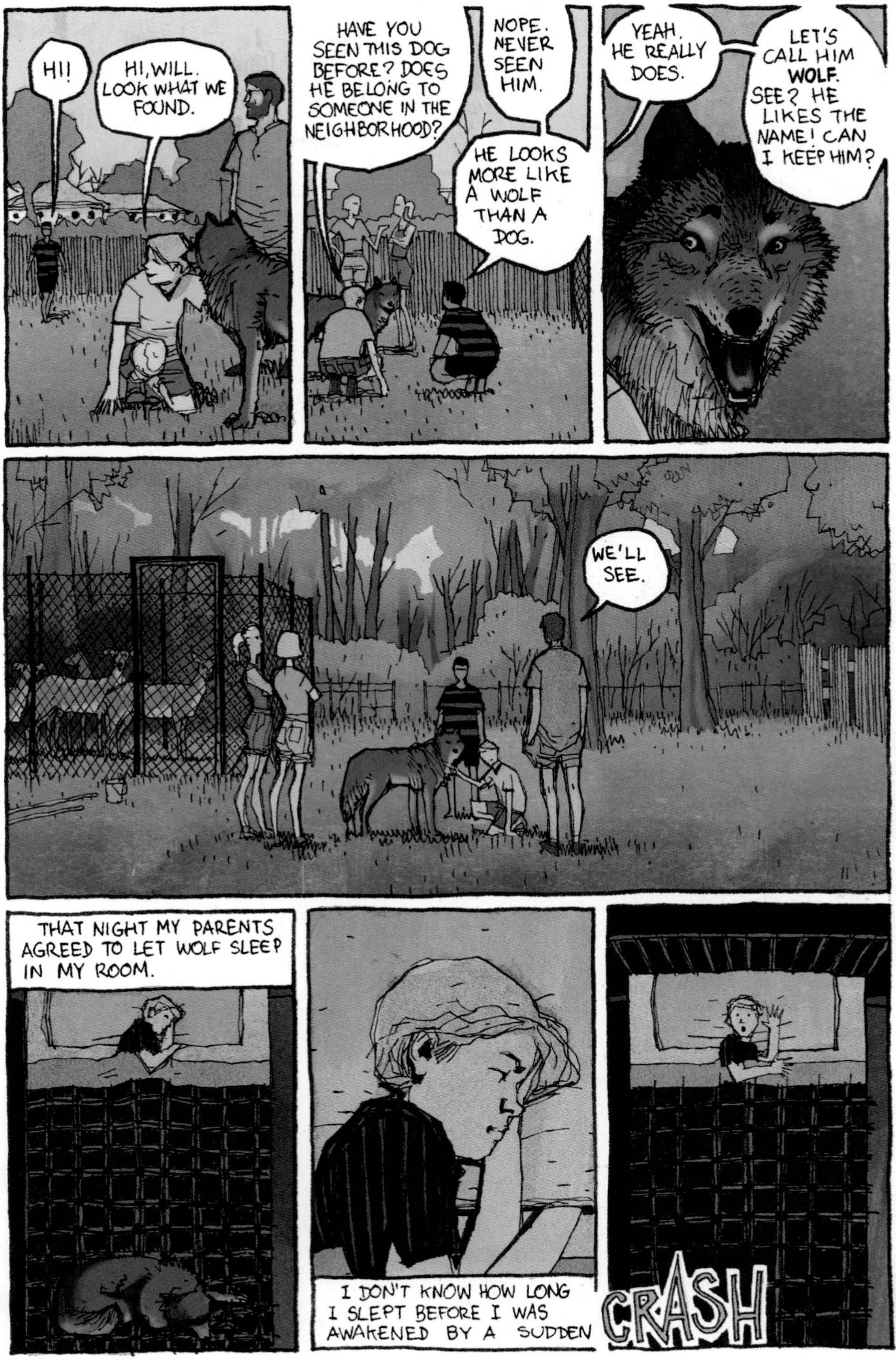
HI!
HI, WILL. LOOK WHAT WE FOUND.
HAVE YOU SEEN THIS DOG BEFORE? DOES HE BELONG TO SOMEONE IN THE NEIGHBORHOOD?
NOPE. NEVER SEEN HIM.
HE LOOKS MORE LIKE A WOLF THAN A DOG.
YEAH. HE REALLY DOES.
LET'S CALL HIM **WOLF**. SEE? HE LIKES THE NAME! CAN I KEEP HIM?
WE'LL SEE.
THAT NIGHT MY PARENTS AGREED TO LET WOLF SLEEP IN MY ROOM.
I DON'T KNOW HOW LONG I SLEPT BEFORE I WAS AWAKENED BY A SUDDEN
CRASH

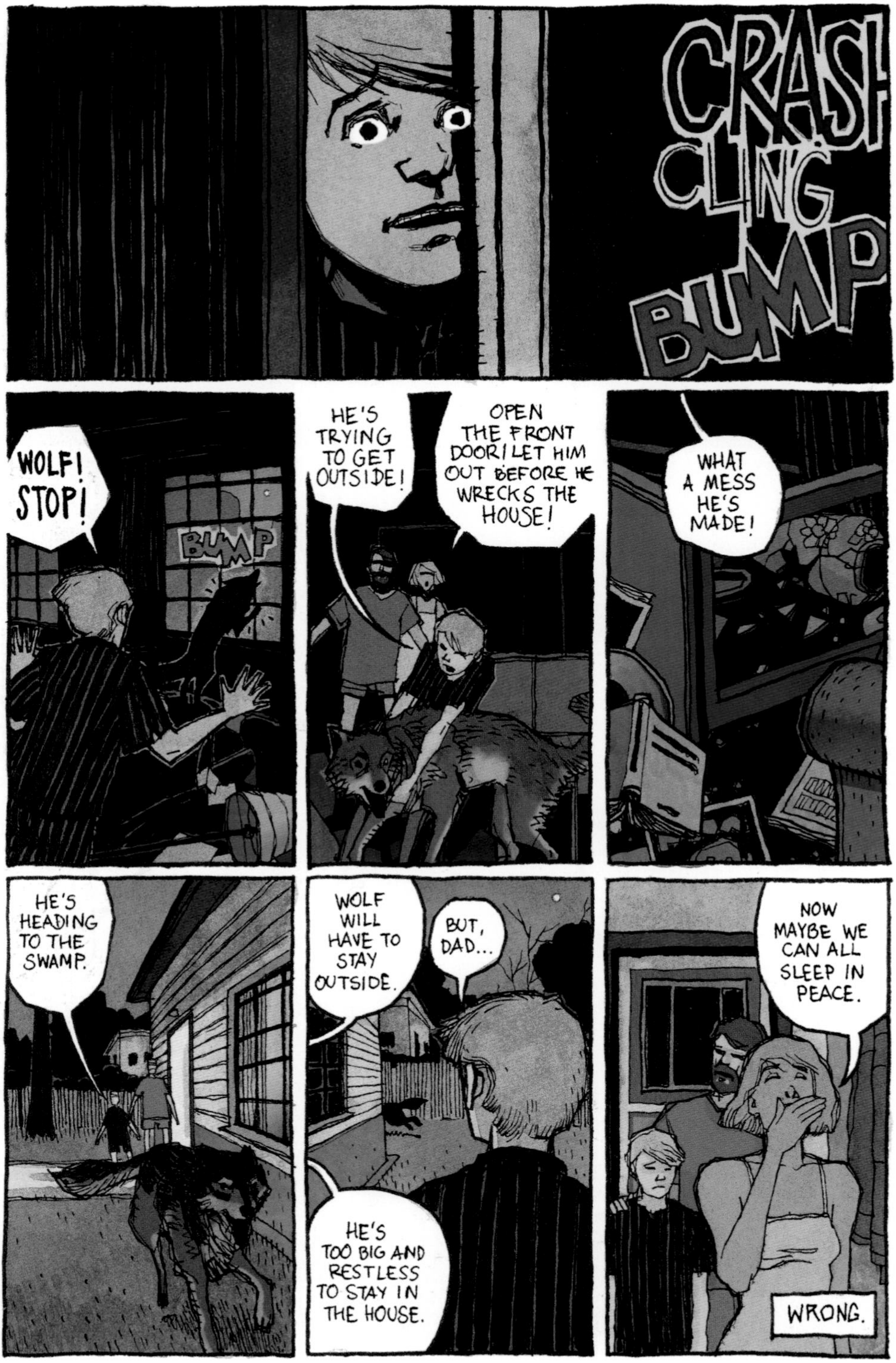
CRASH
CLING
BUMP
WOLF! STOP!
BUMP
HE'S TRYING TO GET OUTSIDE!
OPEN THE FRONT DOOR! LET HIM OUT BEFORE HE WRECKS THE HOUSE!
WHAT A MESS HE'S MADE!
HE'S HEADING TO THE SWAMP.
WOLF WILL HAVE TO STAY OUTSIDE.
BUT, DAD...
HE'S TOO BIG AND RESTLESS TO STAY IN THE HOUSE.
NOW MAYBE WE CAN ALL SLEEP IN PEACE.
WRONG.

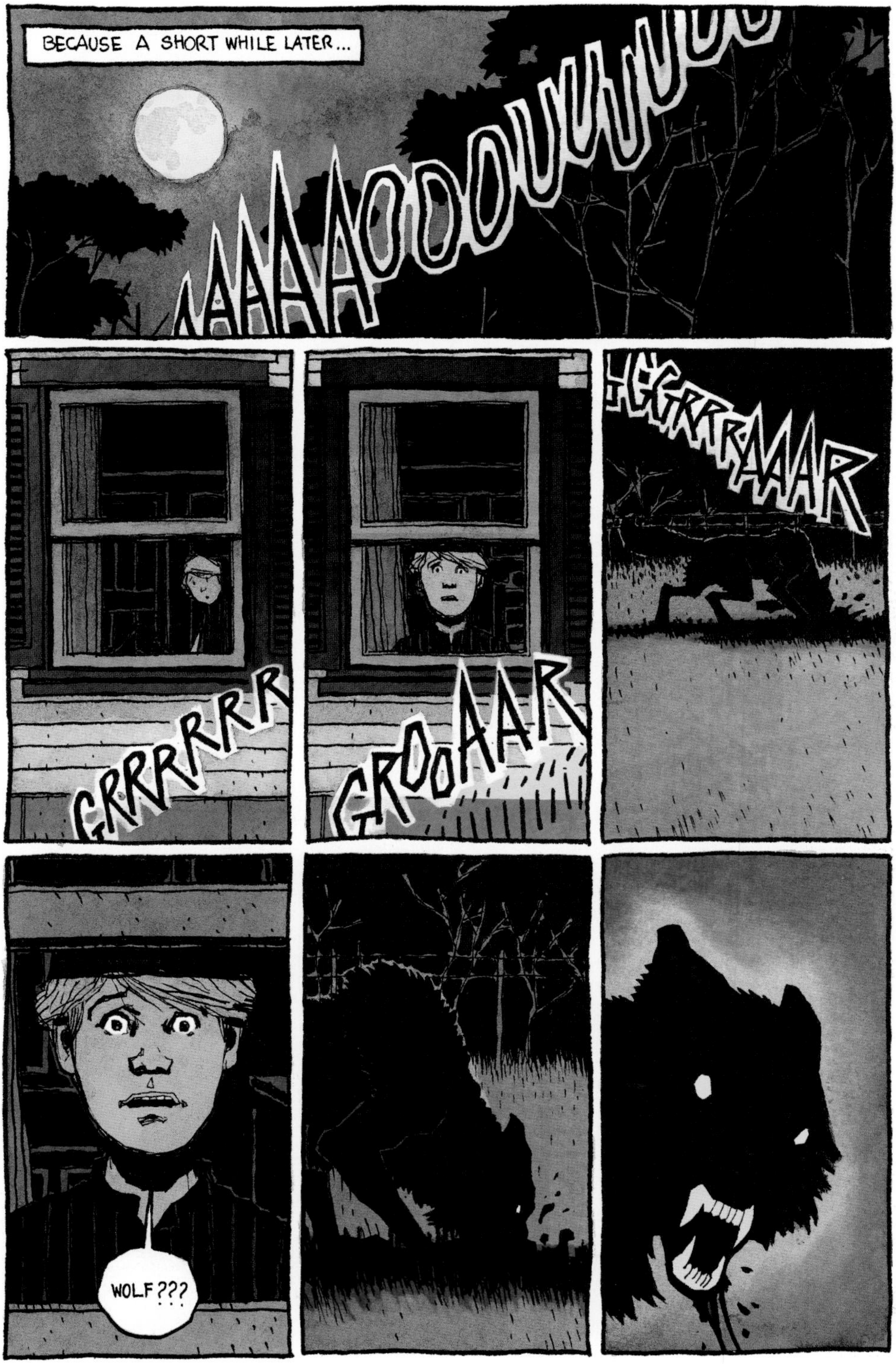
BECAUSE A SHORT WHILE LATER...
AAAAAOOOUUUUOO
GRRRRRR
GROOAAR
GRRRRAAAR
WOLF???

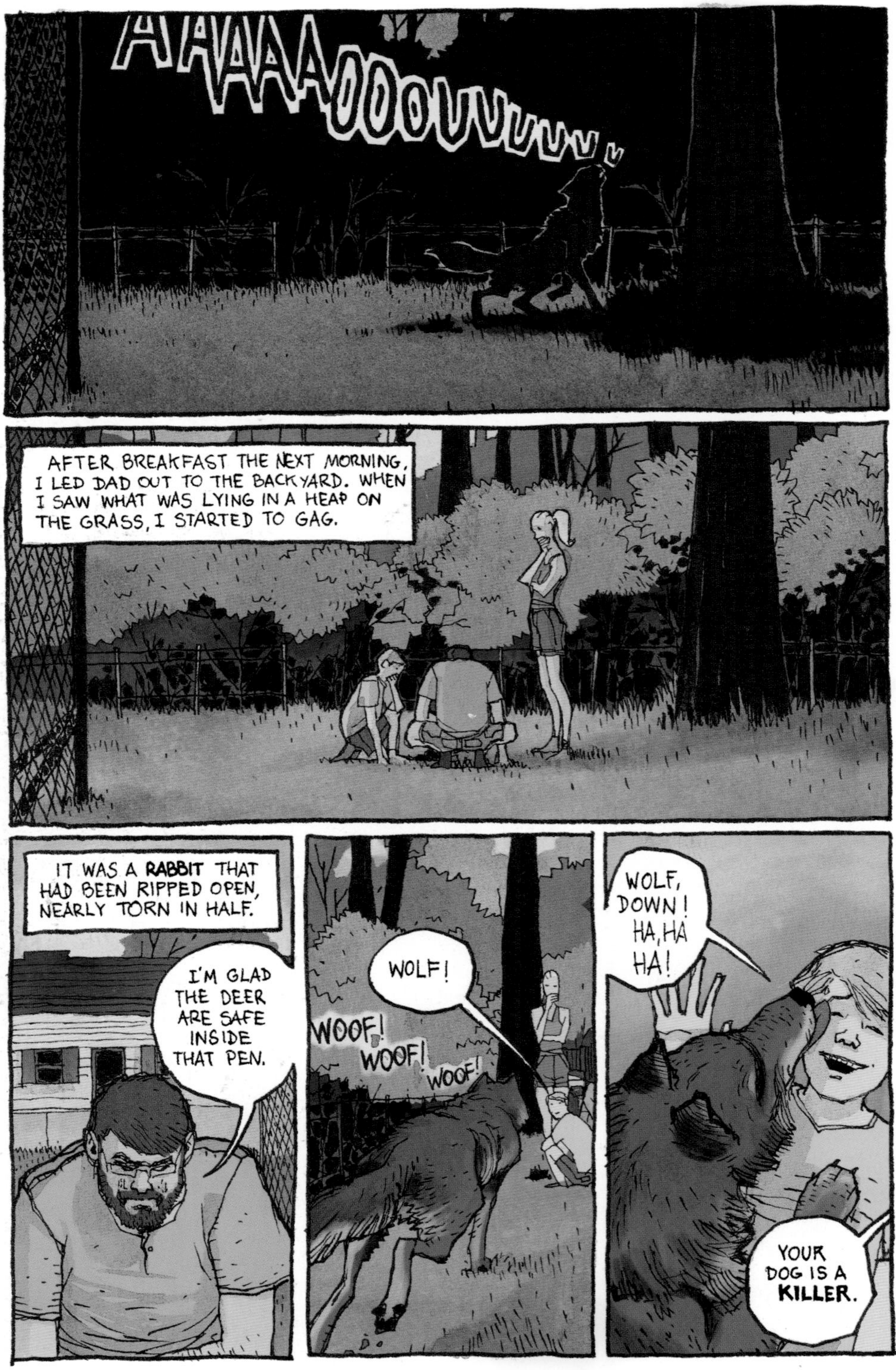
AAAAOOOUUUUUU
AFTER BREAKFAST THE NEXT MORNING, I LED DAD OUT TO THE BACKYARD. WHEN I SAW WHAT WAS LYING IN A HEAP ON THE GRASS, I STARTED TO GAG.
IT WAS A **RABBIT** THAT HAD BEEN RIPPED OPEN, NEARLY TORN IN HALF.
I'M GLAD THE DEER ARE SAFE INSIDE THAT PEN.
WOLF!
WOOF! WOOF! WOOF!
WOLF, DOWN! HA, HA HA!
YOUR DOG IS A **KILLER**.

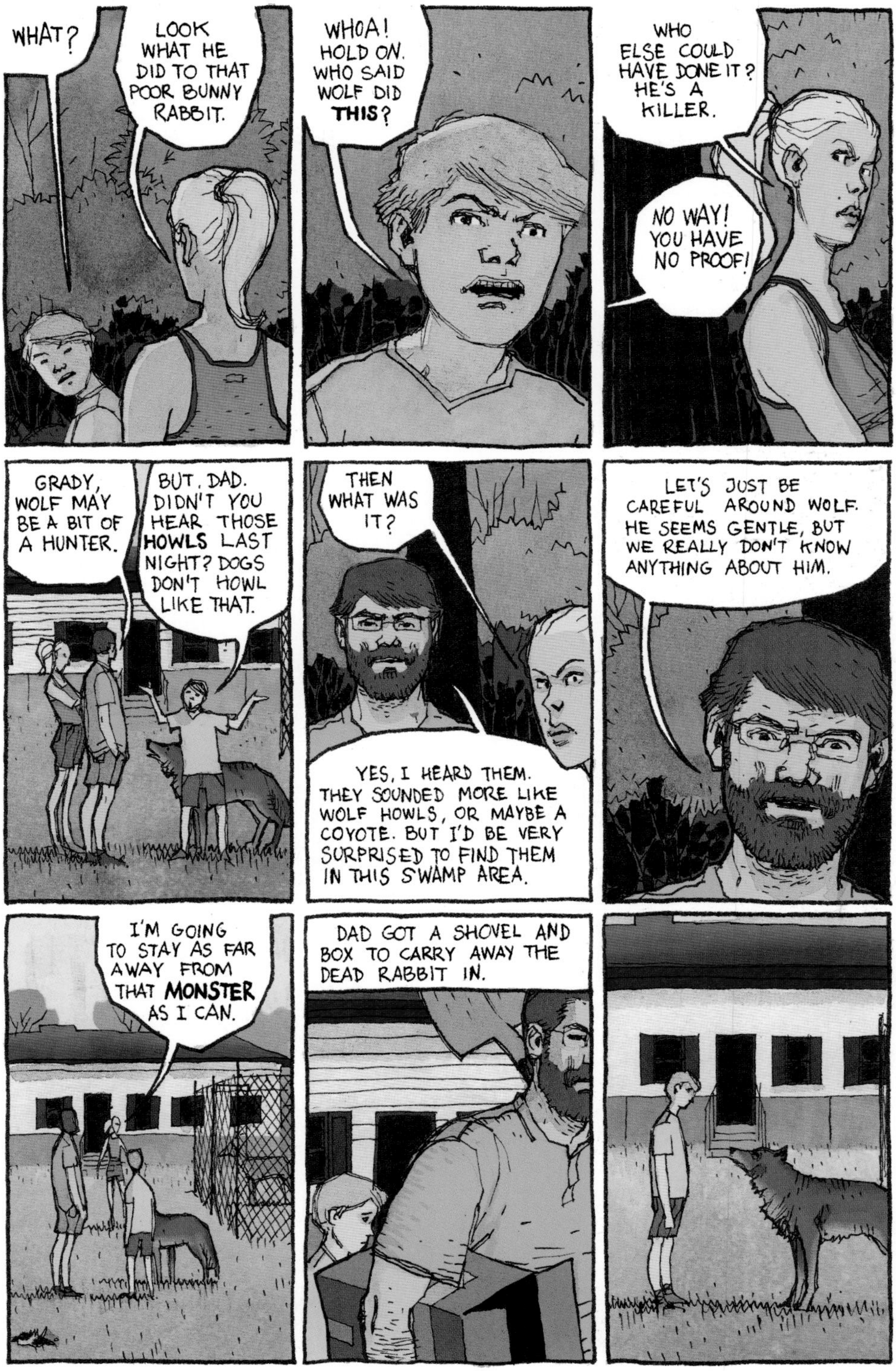
WHAT?
LOOK WHAT HE DID TO THAT POOR BUNNY RABBIT.
WHOA! HOLD ON. WHO SAID WOLF DID **THIS**?
WHO ELSE COULD HAVE DONE IT? HE'S A KILLER.
NO WAY! YOU HAVE NO PROOF!
GRADY, WOLF MAY BE A BIT OF A HUNTER.
BUT, DAD. DIDN'T YOU HEAR THOSE **HOWLS** LAST NIGHT? DOGS DON'T HOWL LIKE THAT.
THEN WHAT WAS IT?
YES, I HEARD THEM. THEY SOUNDED MORE LIKE WOLF HOWLS, OR MAYBE A COYOTE. BUT I'D BE VERY SURPRISED TO FIND THEM IN THIS SWAMP AREA.
LET'S JUST BE CAREFUL AROUND WOLF. HE SEEMS GENTLE, BUT WE REALLY DON'T KNOW ANYTHING ABOUT HIM.
I'M GOING TO STAY AS FAR AWAY FROM THAT **MONSTER** AS I CAN.
DAD GOT A SHOVEL AND BOX TO CARRY AWAY THE DEAD RABBIT IN.

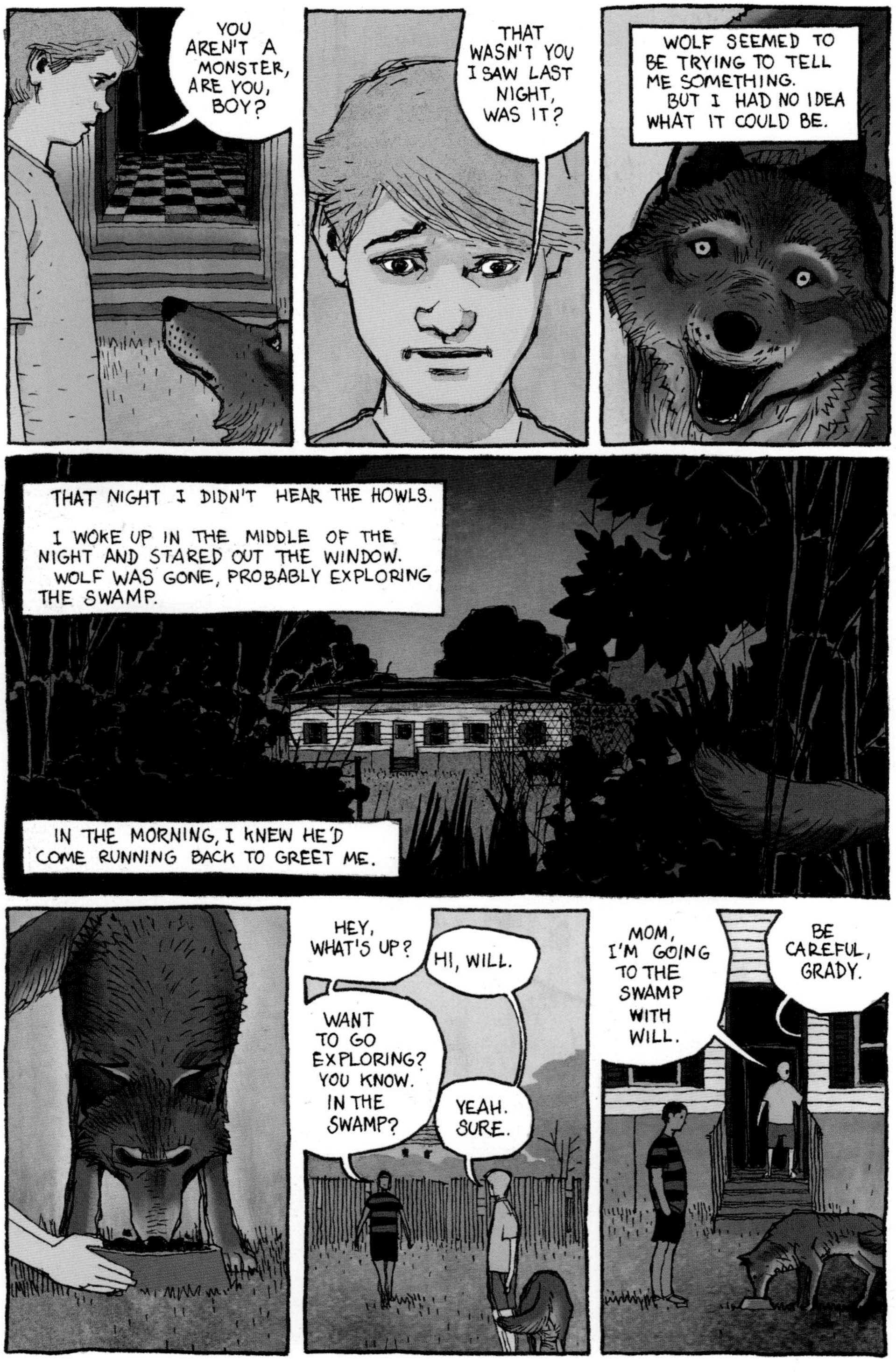
YOU AREN'T A MONSTER, ARE YOU, BOY?
THAT WASN'T YOU I SAW LAST NIGHT, WAS IT?
WOLF SEEMED TO BE TRYING TO TELL ME SOMETHING. BUT I HAD NO IDEA WHAT IT COULD BE.
THAT NIGHT I DIDN'T HEAR THE HOWLS.
I WOKE UP IN THE MIDDLE OF THE NIGHT AND STARED OUT THE WINDOW. WOLF WAS GONE, PROBABLY EXPLORING THE SWAMP.
IN THE MORNING, I KNEW HE'D COME RUNNING BACK TO GREET ME.
HEY, WHAT'S UP?
HI, WILL.
WANT TO GO EXPLORING? YOU KNOW. IN THE SWAMP?
YEAH. SURE.
MOM, I'M GOING TO THE SWAMP WITH WILL.
BE CAREFUL, GRADY.

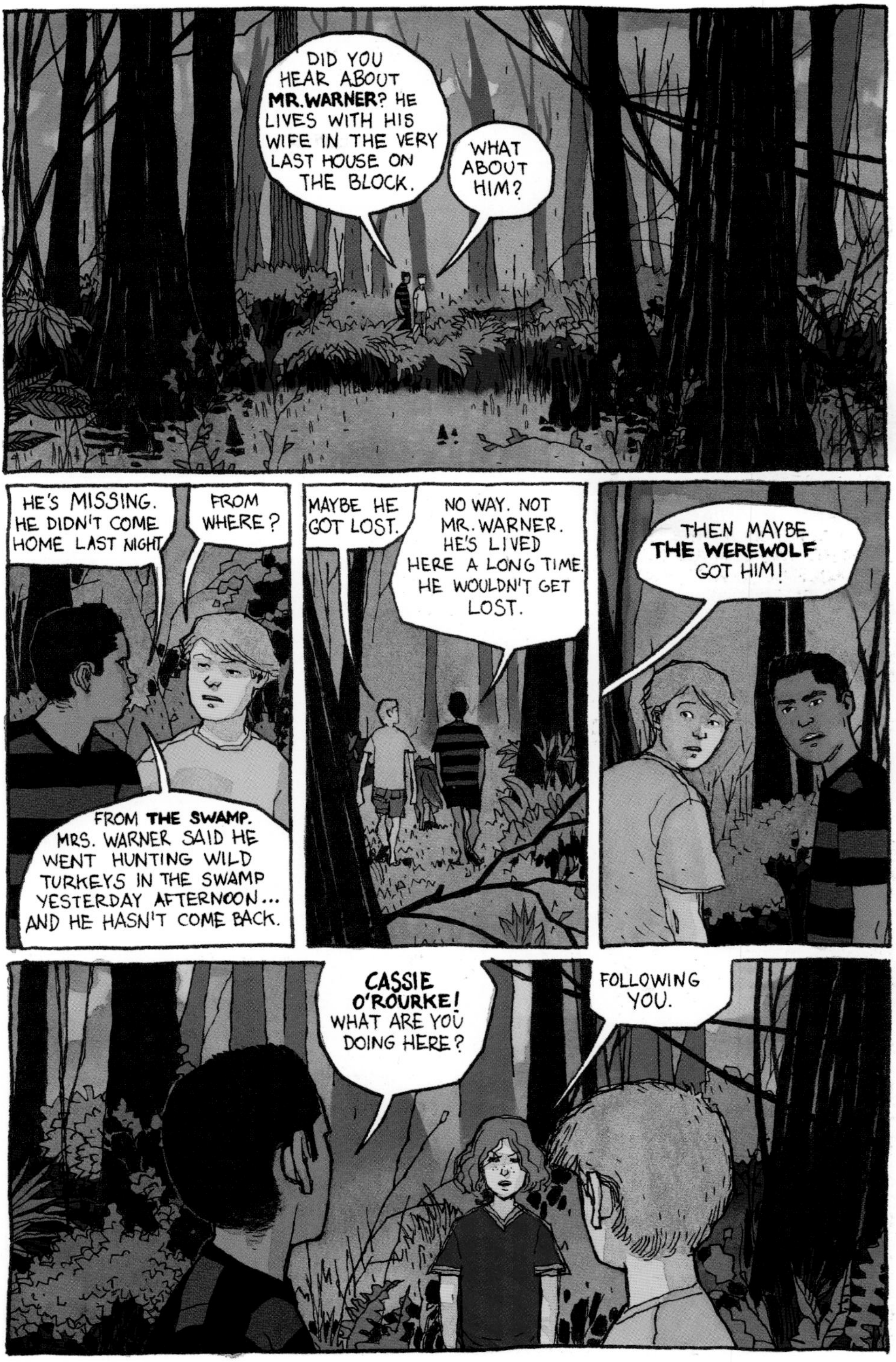

DID YOU HEAR ABOUT **MR. WARNER**? HE LIVES WITH HIS WIFE IN THE VERY LAST HOUSE ON THE BLOCK.
WHAT ABOUT HIM?
HE'S MISSING. HE DIDN'T COME HOME LAST NIGHT
FROM WHERE?
FROM **THE SWAMP.** MRS. WARNER SAID HE WENT HUNTING WILD TURKEYS IN THE SWAMP YESTERDAY AFTERNOON... AND HE HASN'T COME BACK.
MAYBE HE GOT LOST.
NO WAY. NOT MR. WARNER. HE'S LIVED HERE A LONG TIME. HE WOULDN'T GET LOST.
THEN MAYBE **THE WEREWOLF** GOT HIM!
CASSIE O'ROURKE! WHAT ARE YOU DOING HERE?
FOLLOWING YOU.

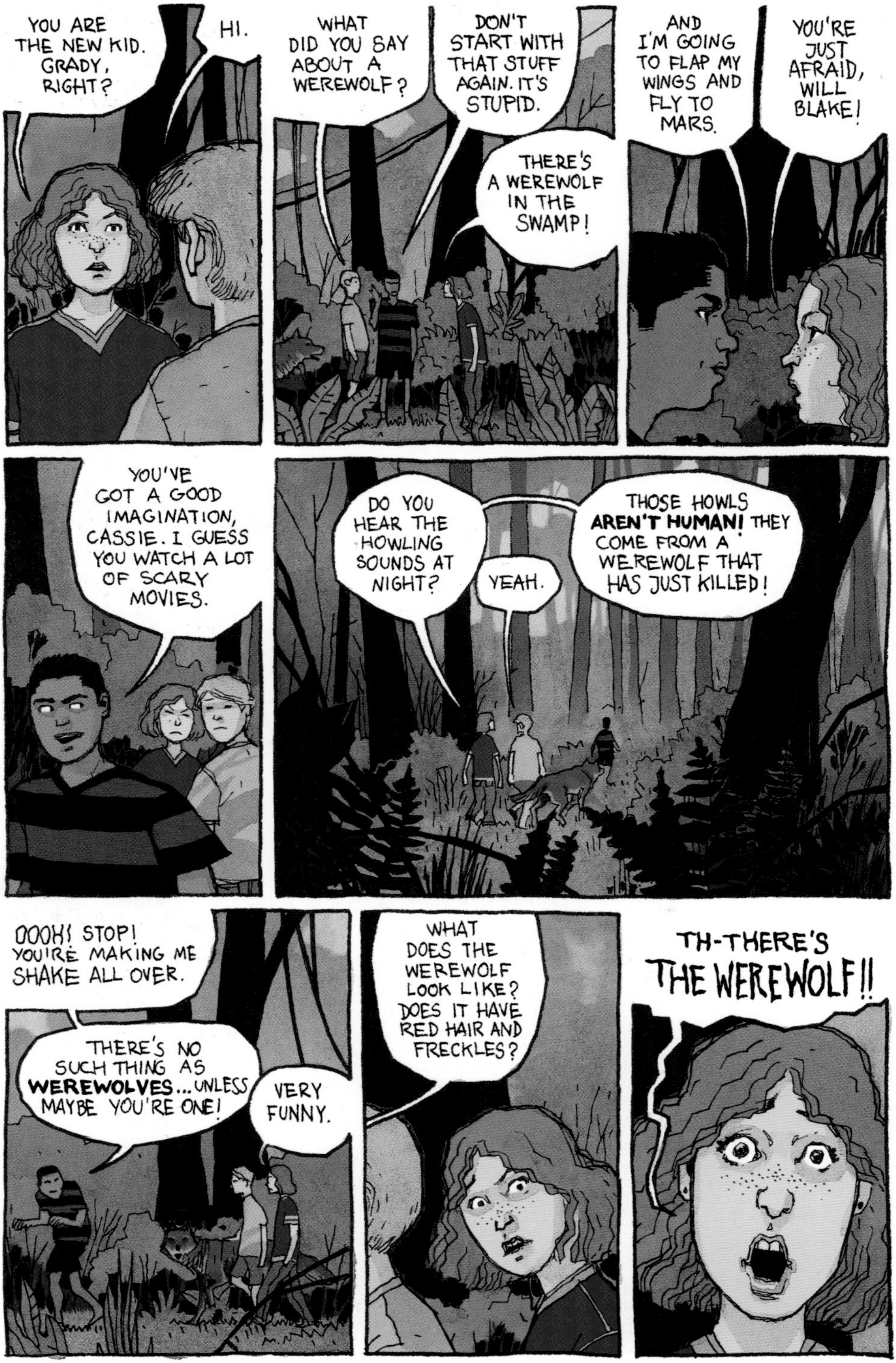
YOU ARE THE NEW KID. GRADY, RIGHT?
HI.
WHAT DID YOU SAY ABOUT A WEREWOLF?
DON'T START WITH THAT STUFF AGAIN. IT'S STUPID.
THERE'S A WEREWOLF IN THE SWAMP!
AND I'M GOING TO FLAP MY WINGS AND FLY TO MARS.
YOU'RE JUST AFRAID, WILL BLAKE!
YOU'VE GOT A GOOD IMAGINATION, CASSIE. I GUESS YOU WATCH A LOT OF SCARY MOVIES.
DO YOU HEAR THE HOWLING SOUNDS AT NIGHT?
YEAH.
THOSE HOWLS AREN'T HUMAN! THEY COME FROM A WEREWOLF THAT HAS JUST KILLED!
OOOH! STOP! YOU'RE MAKING ME SHAKE ALL OVER.
THERE'S NO SUCH THING AS WEREWOLVES... UNLESS MAYBE YOU'RE ONE!
VERY FUNNY.
WHAT DOES THE WEREWOLF LOOK LIKE? DOES IT HAVE RED HAIR AND FRECKLES?
TH-THERE'S THE WEREWOLF!!

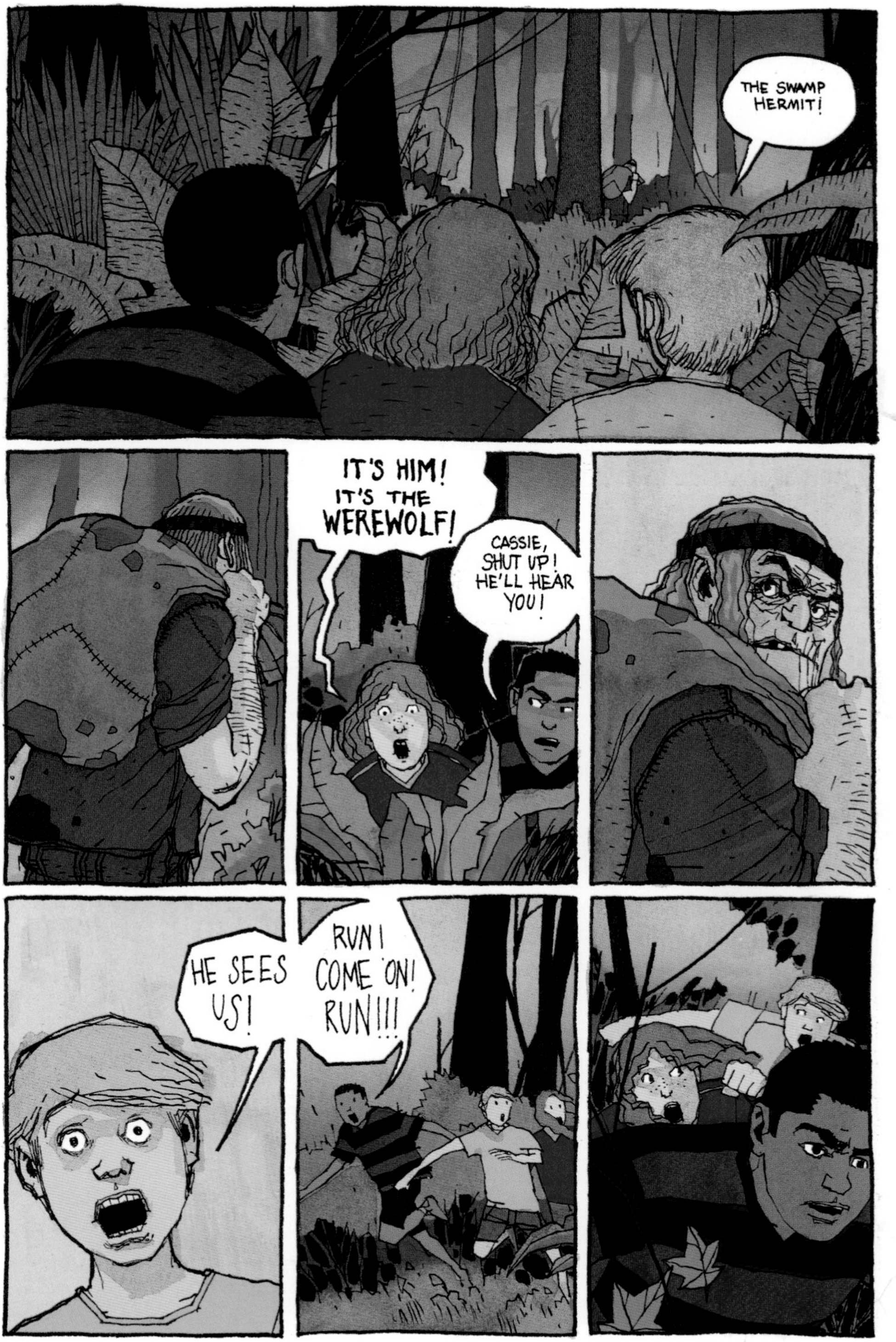
THE SWAMP HERMIT!
IT'S HIM! IT'S THE WEREWOLF!
CASSIE, SHUT UP! HE'LL HEAR YOU!
HE SEES US!
RUN! COME ON! RUN!!!

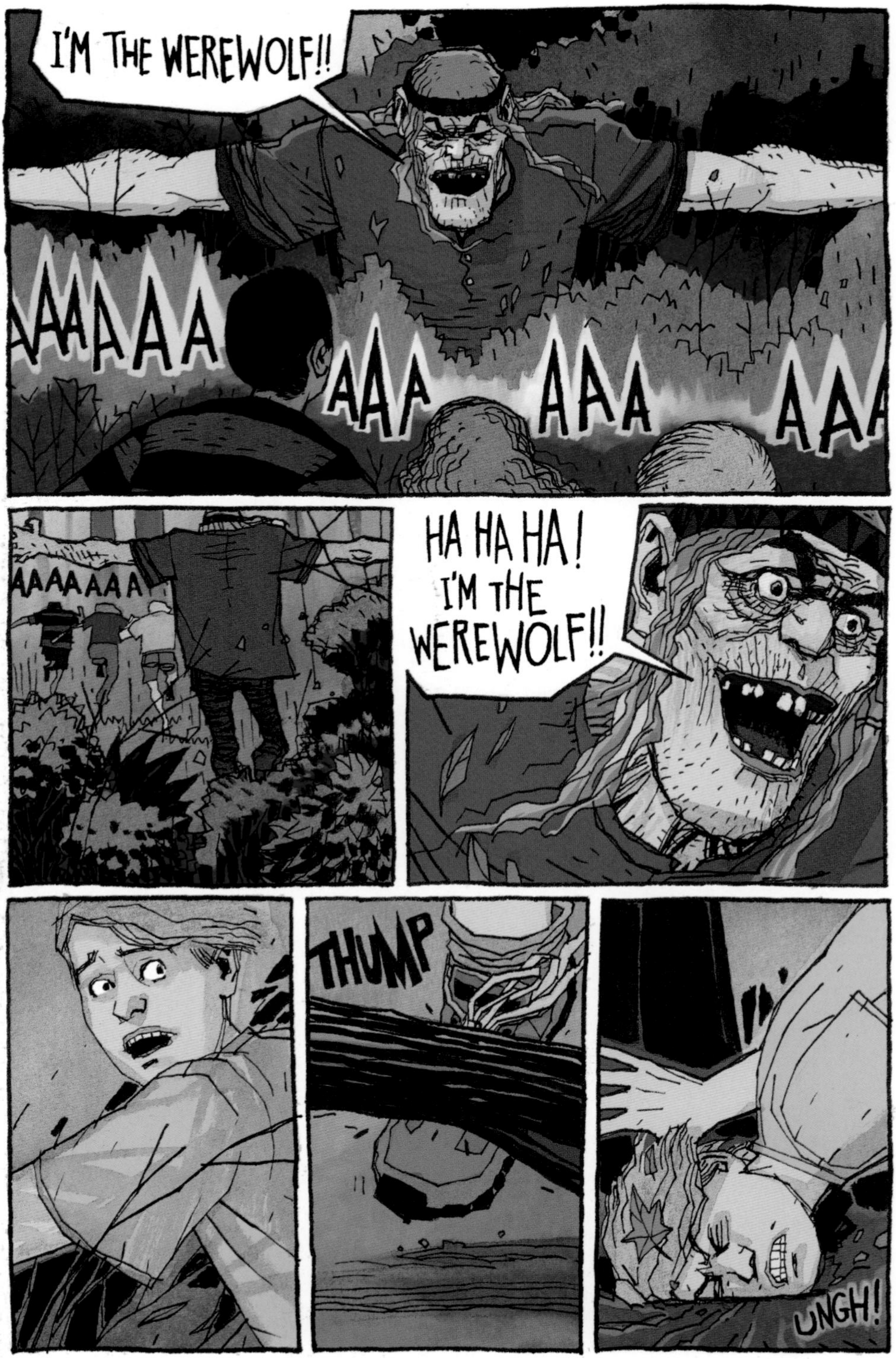
I'M THE WEREWOLF!!
AAAAAAA
AAA AAA AAA
AAAAAAA
HA HA HA! I'M THE WEREWOLF!!
THUMP
UNGH!

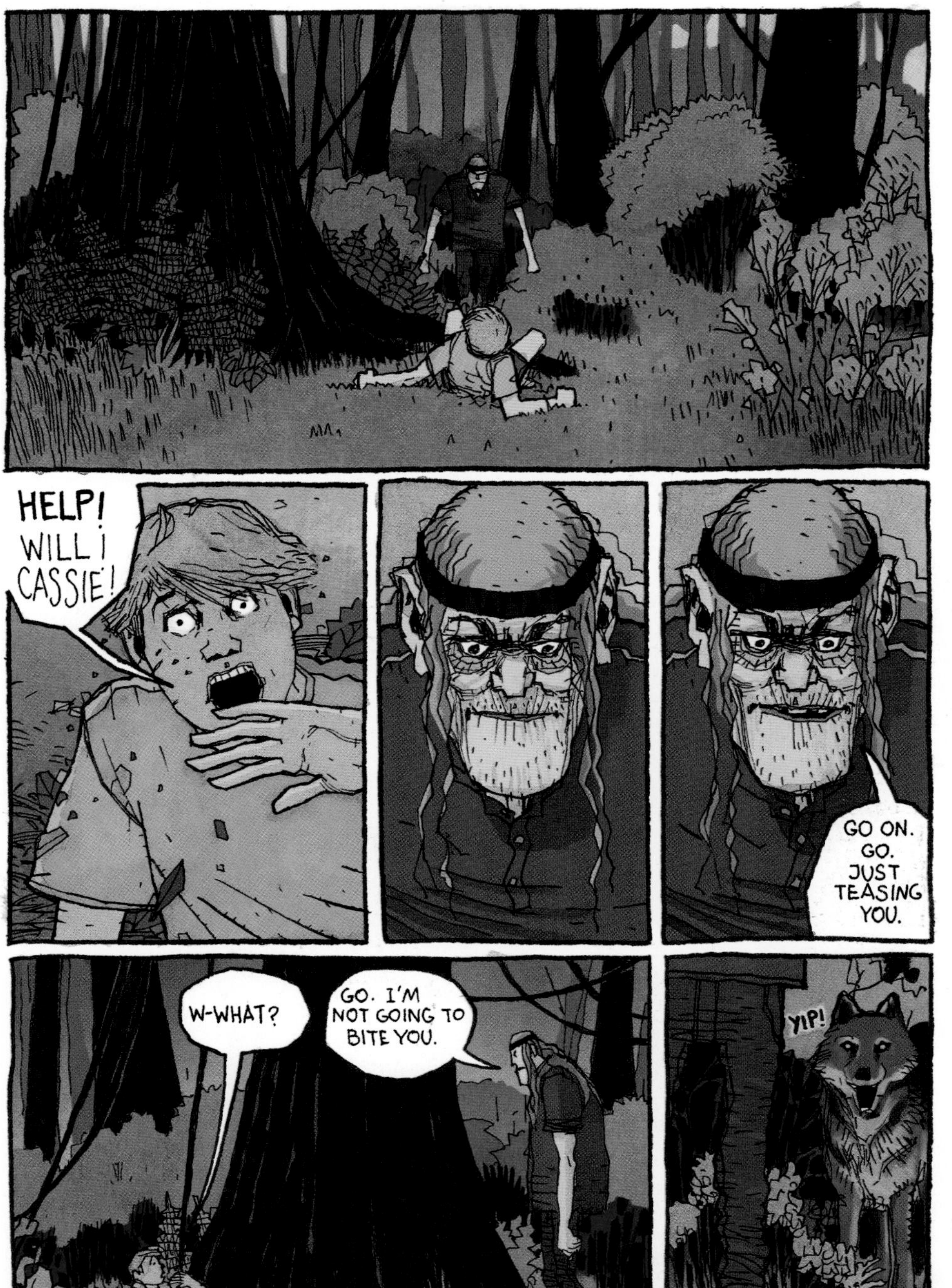
HELP! WILL! CASSIE!
GO ON. GO. JUST TEASING YOU.
W-WHAT?
GO. I'M NOT GOING TO BITE YOU.
YIP!

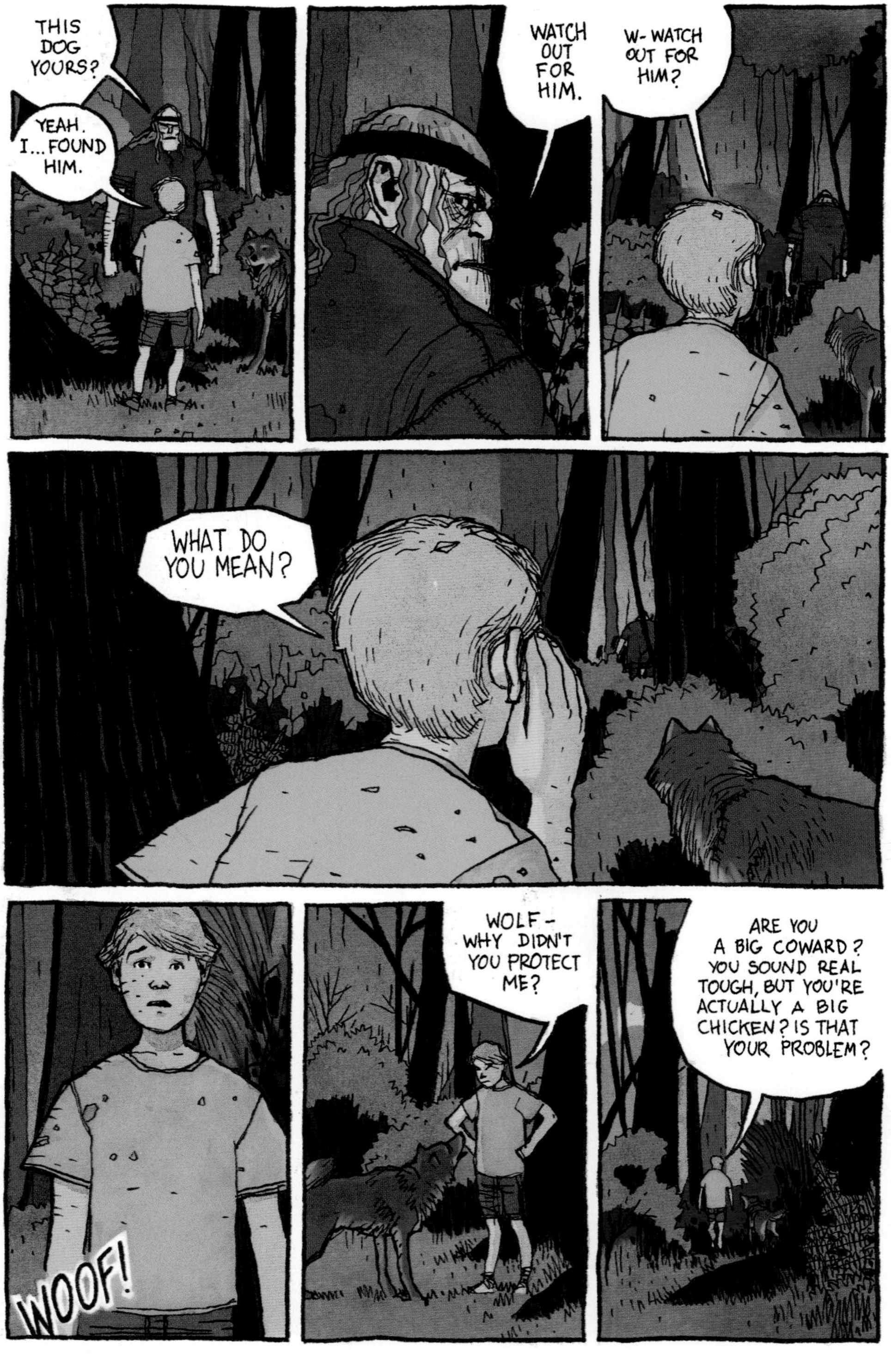

THIS DOG YOURS?
YEAH. I...FOUND HIM.
WATCH OUT FOR HIM.
W- WATCH OUT FOR HIM?
WHAT DO YOU MEAN?
WOOF!
WOLF - WHY DIDN'T YOU PROTECT ME?
ARE YOU A BIG COWARD? YOU SOUND REAL TOUGH, BUT YOU'RE ACTUALLY A BIG CHICKEN? IS THAT YOUR PROBLEM?

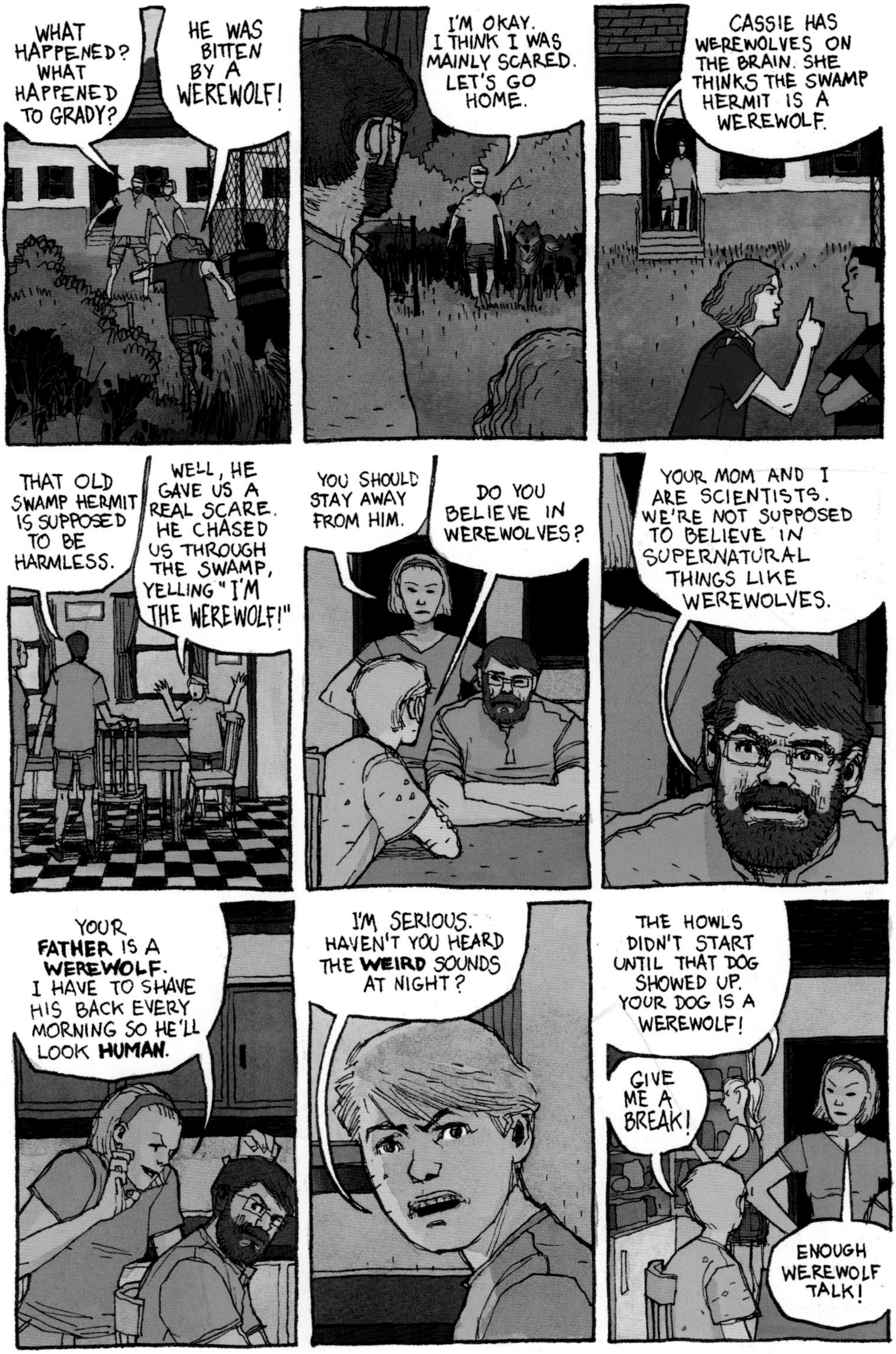
WHAT HAPPENED? WHAT HAPPENED TO GRADY?
HE WAS BITTEN BY A WEREWOLF!
I'M OKAY. I THINK I WAS MAINLY SCARED. LET'S GO HOME.
CASSIE HAS WEREWOLVES ON THE BRAIN. SHE THINKS THE SWAMP HERMIT IS A WEREWOLF.
THAT OLD SWAMP HERMIT IS SUPPOSED TO BE HARMLESS.
WELL, HE GAVE US A REAL SCARE. HE CHASED US THROUGH THE SWAMP, YELLING "I'M THE WEREWOLF!"
YOU SHOULD STAY AWAY FROM HIM.
DO YOU BELIEVE IN WEREWOLVES?
YOUR MOM AND I ARE SCIENTISTS. WE'RE NOT SUPPOSED TO BELIEVE IN SUPERNATURAL THINGS LIKE WEREWOLVES.
YOUR **FATHER** IS A **WEREWOLF**. I HAVE TO SHAVE HIS BACK EVERY MORNING SO HE'LL LOOK **HUMAN**.
I'M SERIOUS. HAVEN'T YOU HEARD THE **WEIRD** SOUNDS AT NIGHT?
THE HOWLS DIDN'T START UNTIL THAT DOG SHOWED UP. YOUR DOG IS A WEREWOLF!
GIVE ME A BREAK!
ENOUGH WEREWOLF TALK!

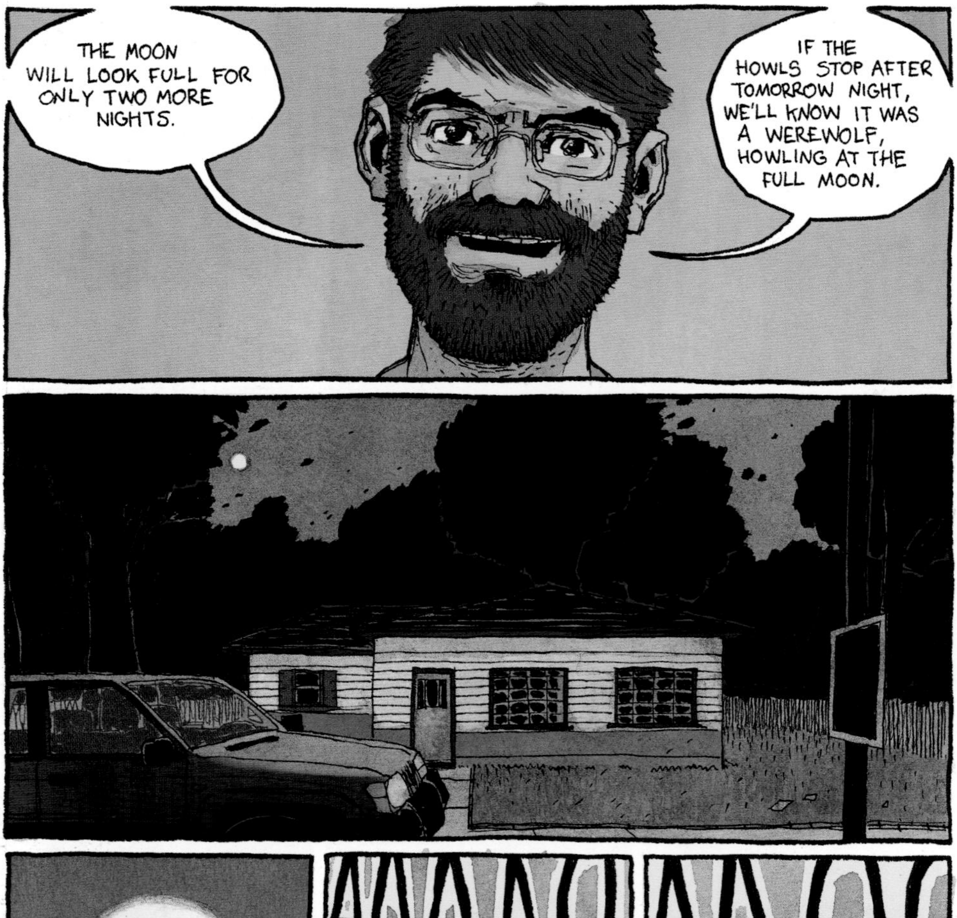
THE MOON WILL LOOK FULL FOR ONLY TWO MORE NIGHTS.
IF THE HOWLS STOP AFTER TOMORROW NIGHT, WE'LL KNOW IT WAS A WEREWOLF, HOWLING AT THE FULL MOON.

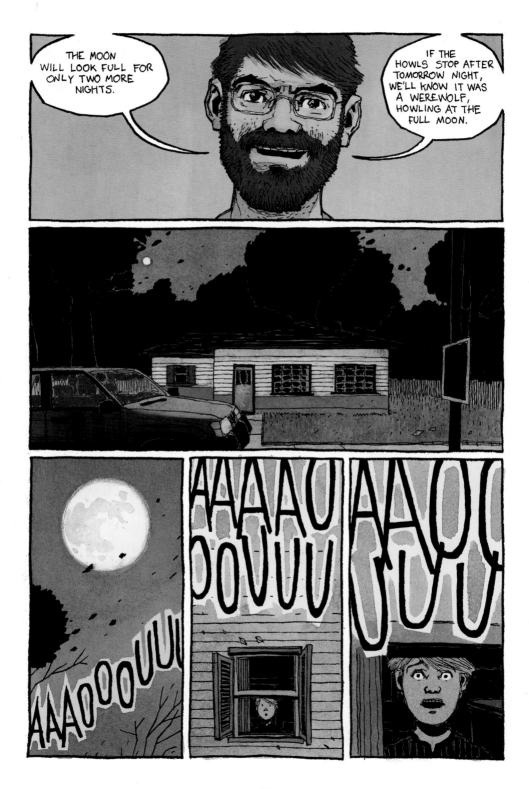

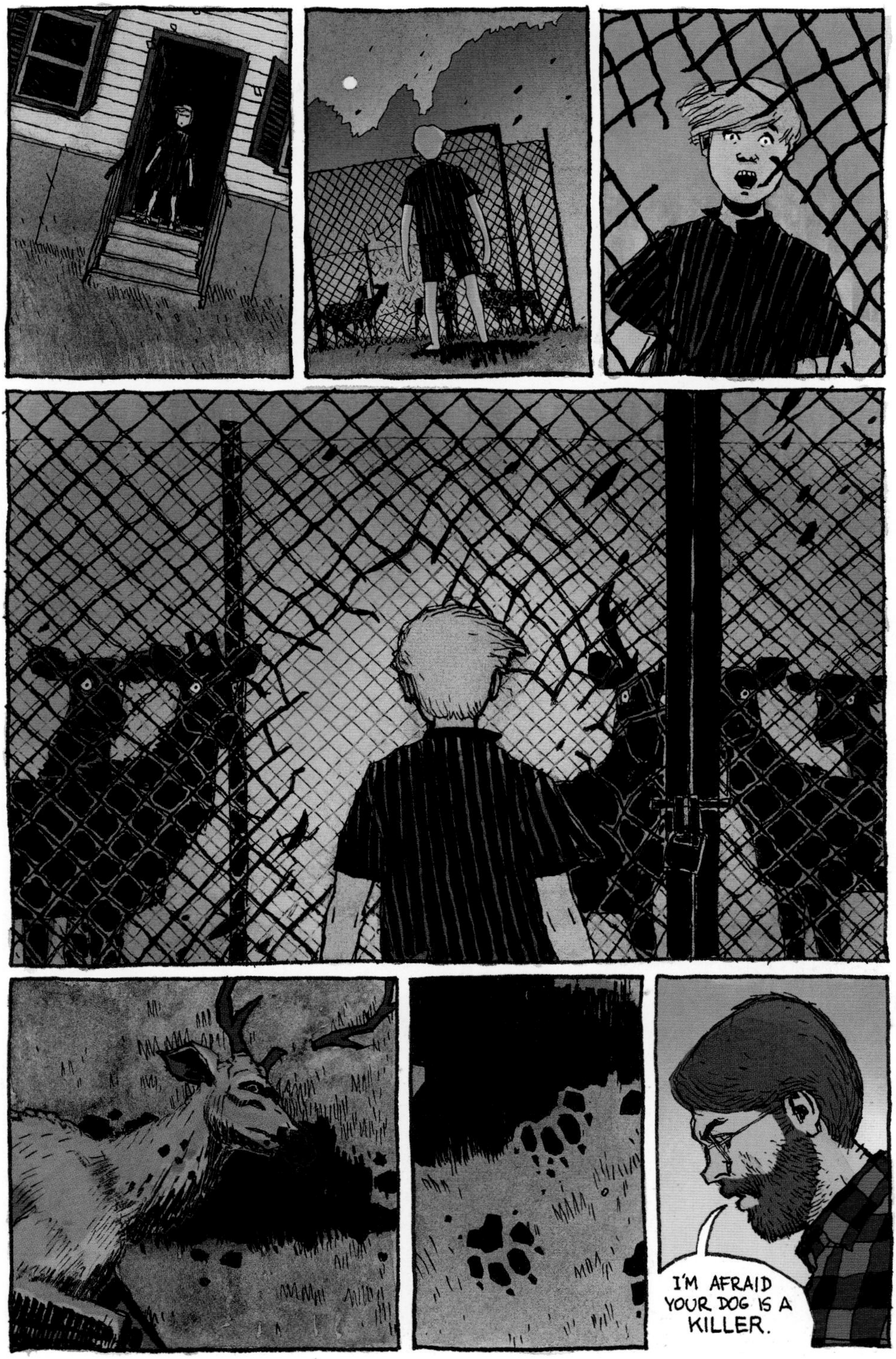
I'M AFRAID YOUR DOG IS A KILLER.

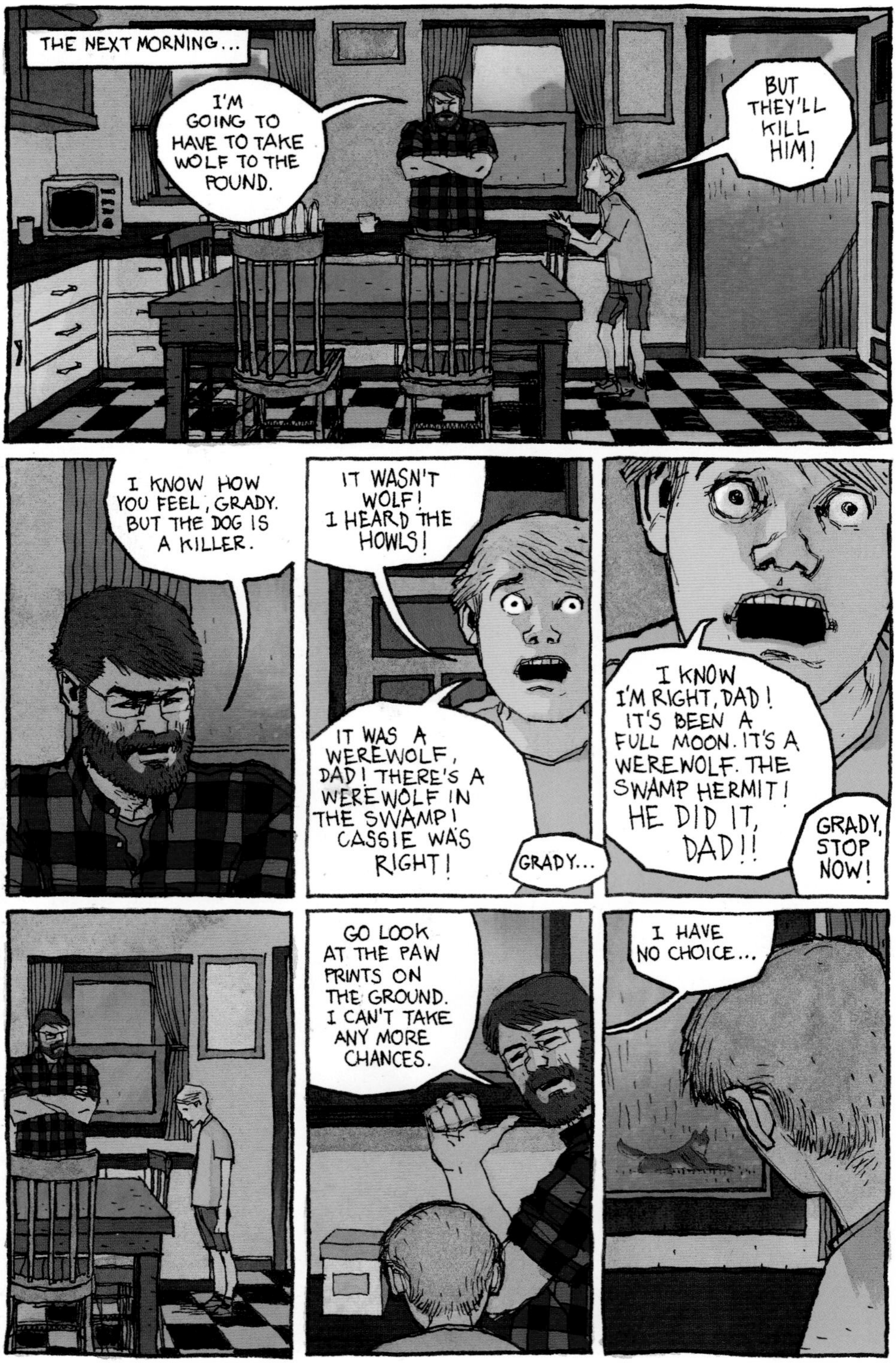
THE NEXT MORNING...
I'M GOING TO HAVE TO TAKE WOLF TO THE POUND.
BUT THEY'LL KILL HIM!
I KNOW HOW YOU FEEL, GRADY. BUT THE DOG IS A KILLER.
IT WASN'T WOLF! I HEARD THE HOWLS!
IT WAS A WEREWOLF, DAD! THERE'S A WEREWOLF IN THE SWAMP! CASSIE WAS RIGHT!
GRADY...
I KNOW I'M RIGHT, DAD! IT'S BEEN A FULL MOON. IT'S A WEREWOLF. THE SWAMP HERMIT! HE DID IT, DAD!!
GRADY, STOP NOW!
GO LOOK AT THE PAW PRINTS ON THE GROUND. I CAN'T TAKE ANY MORE CHANCES.
I HAVE NO CHOICE...

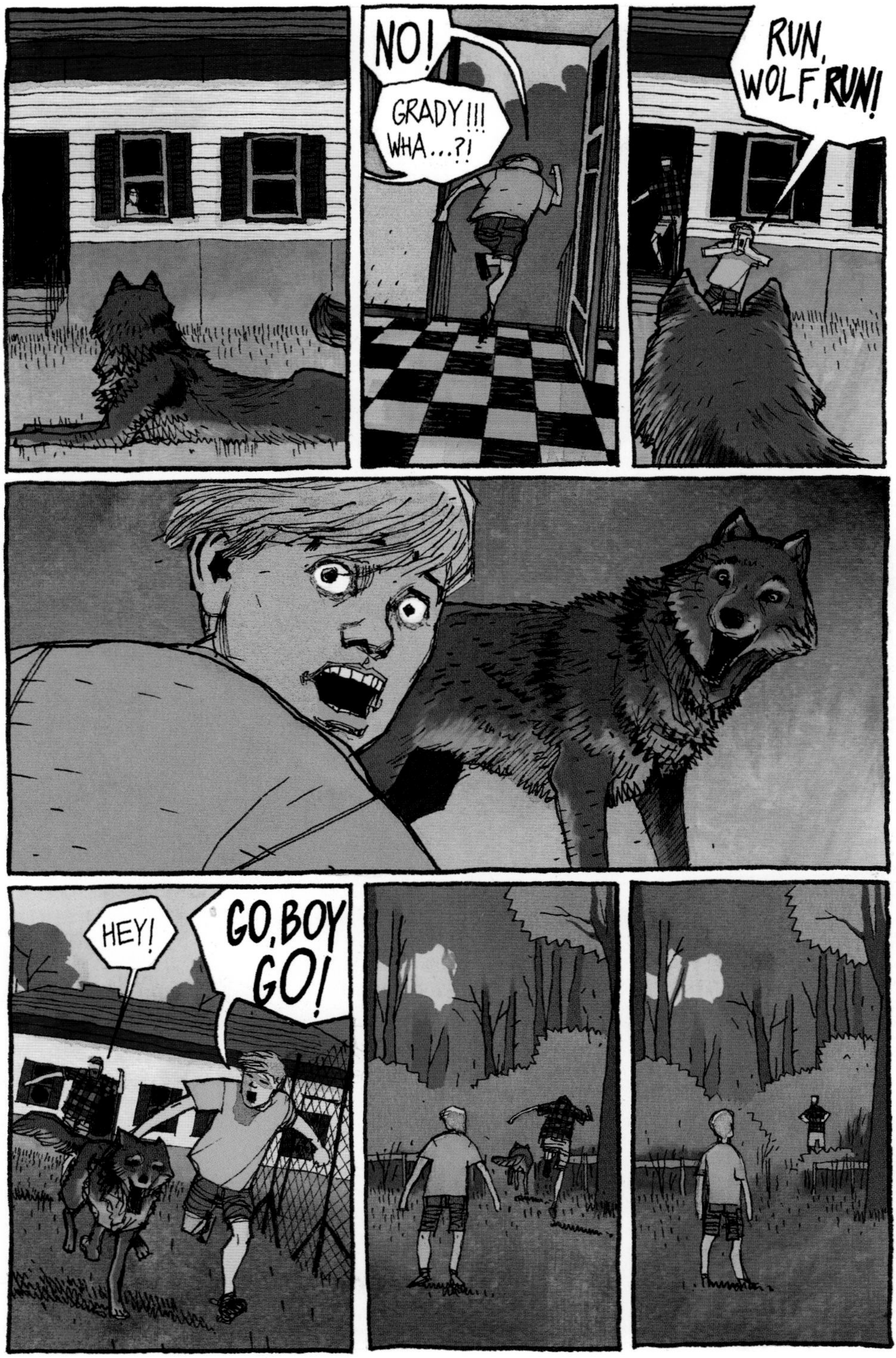
NO!
GRADY!!! WHA...?!
RUN, WOLF, RUN!
HEY!
GO, BOY GO!

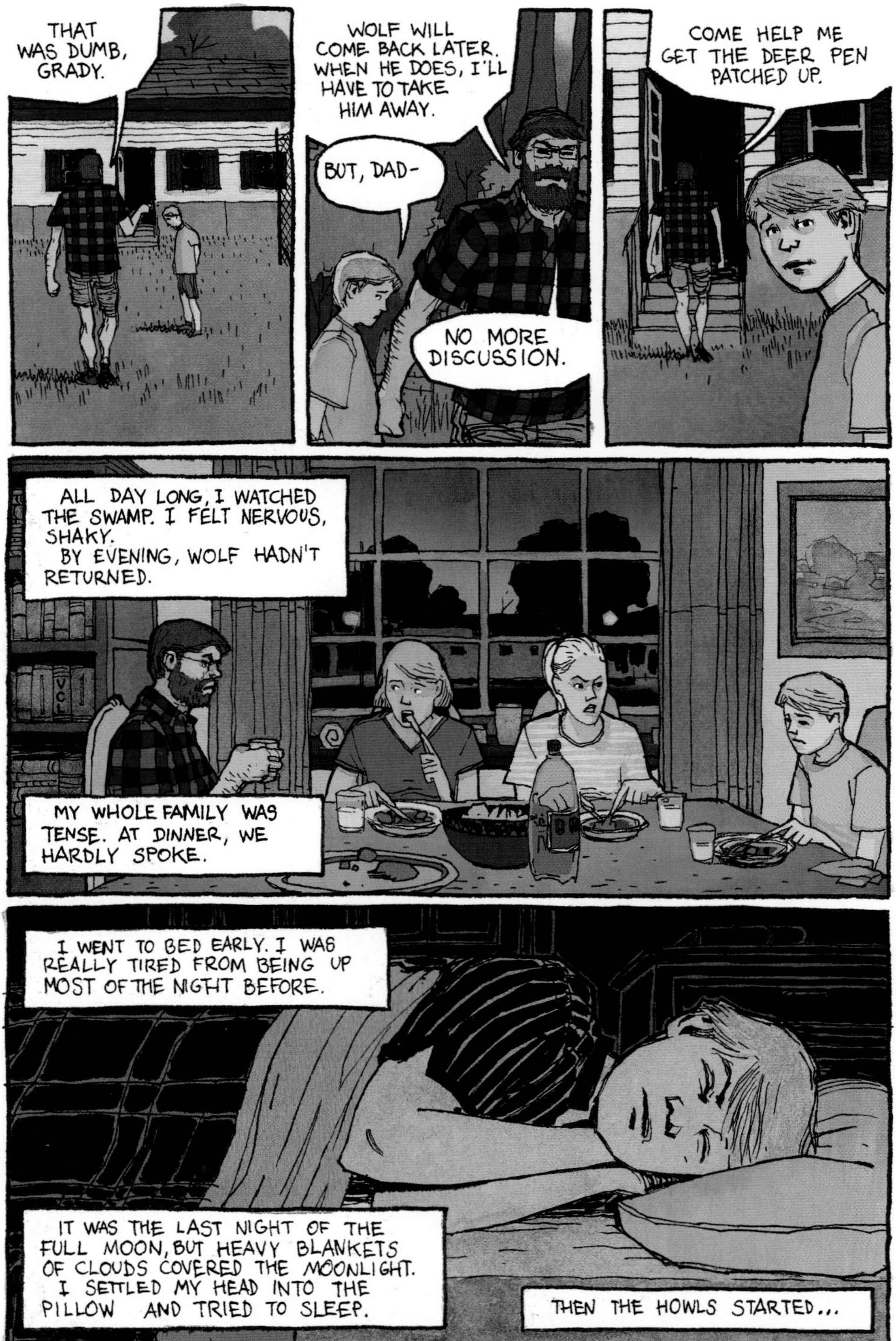
THAT WAS DUMB, GRADY.
WOLF WILL COME BACK LATER. WHEN HE DOES, I'LL HAVE TO TAKE HIM AWAY.
BUT, DAD-
NO MORE DISCUSSION.
COME HELP ME GET THE DEER PEN PATCHED UP.
ALL DAY LONG, I WATCHED THE SWAMP. I FELT NERVOUS, SHAKY.
BY EVENING, WOLF HADN'T RETURNED.
MY WHOLE FAMILY WAS TENSE. AT DINNER, WE HARDLY SPOKE.
I WENT TO BED EARLY. I WAS REALLY TIRED FROM BEING UP MOST OF THE NIGHT BEFORE.
IT WAS THE LAST NIGHT OF THE FULL MOON, BUT HEAVY BLANKETS OF CLOUDS COVERED THE MOONLIGHT.
I SETTLED MY HEAD INTO THE PILLOW AND TRIED TO SLEEP.
THEN THE HOWLS STARTED...

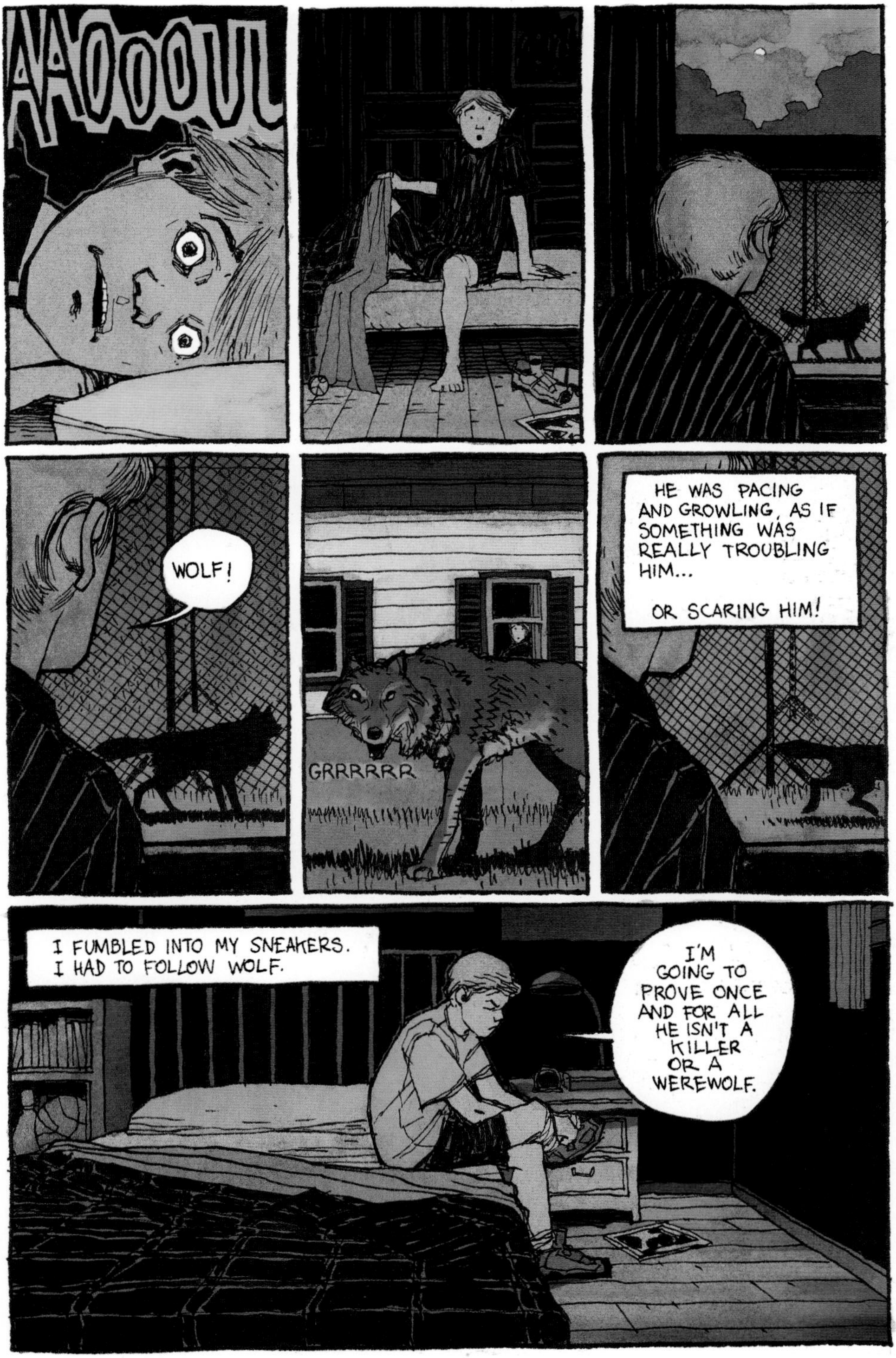
AAOOOUL
WOLF!
GRRRRRR
HE WAS PACING AND GROWLING, AS IF SOMETHING WAS REALLY TROUBLING HIM...
OR SCARING HIM!
I FUMBLED INTO MY SNEAKERS. I HAD TO FOLLOW WOLF.
I'M GOING TO PROVE ONCE AND FOR ALL HE ISN'T A KILLER OR A WEREWOLF.

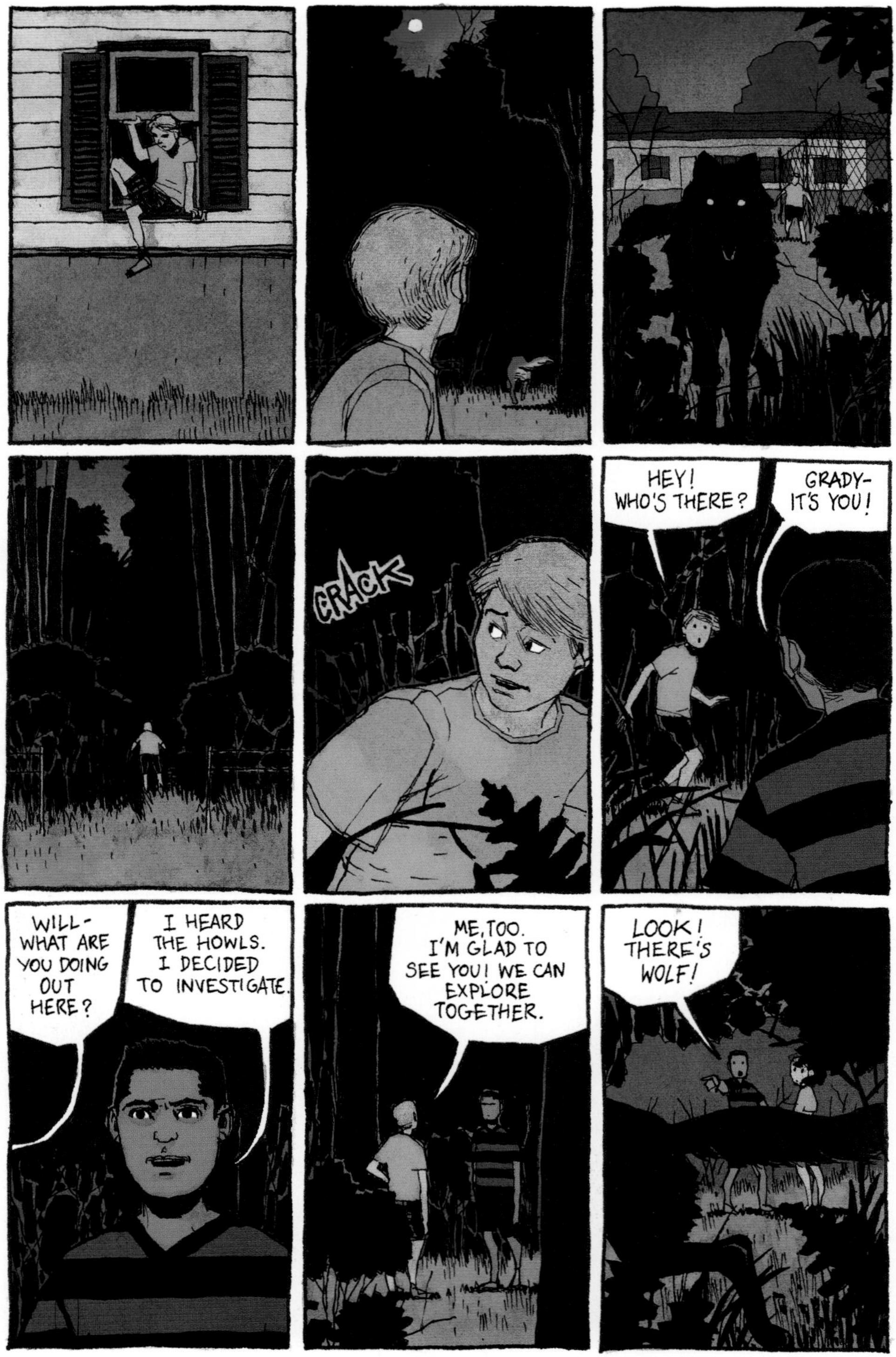
CRACK
HEY! WHO'S THERE?
GRADY- IT'S YOU!
WILL- WHAT ARE YOU DOING OUT HERE?
I HEARD THE HOWLS. I DECIDED TO INVESTIGATE.
ME, TOO. I'M GLAD TO SEE YOU! WE CAN EXPLORE TOGETHER.
LOOK! THERE'S WOLF!

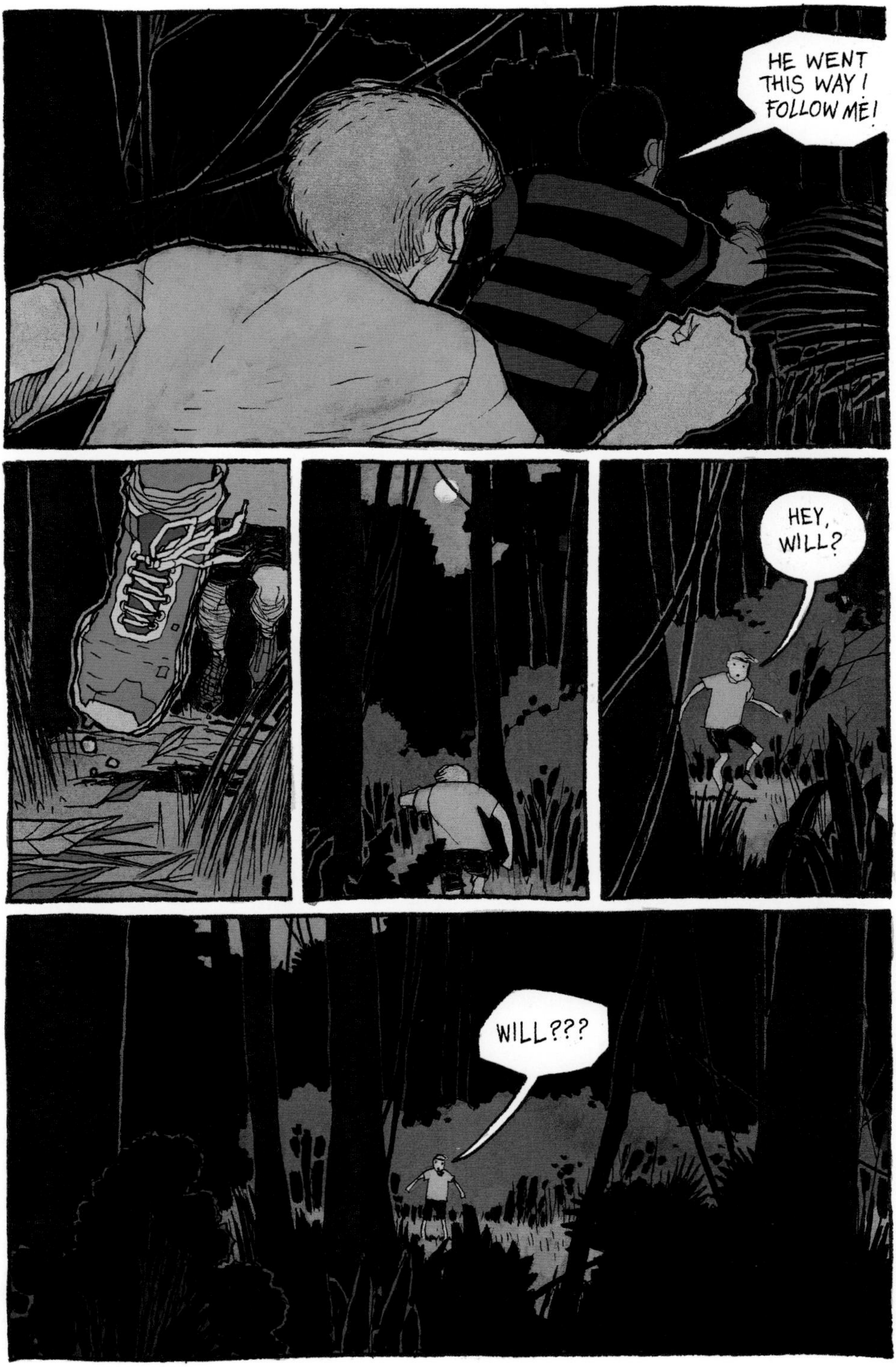
HE WENT THIS WAY! FOLLOW ME!
HEY, WILL?
WILL???

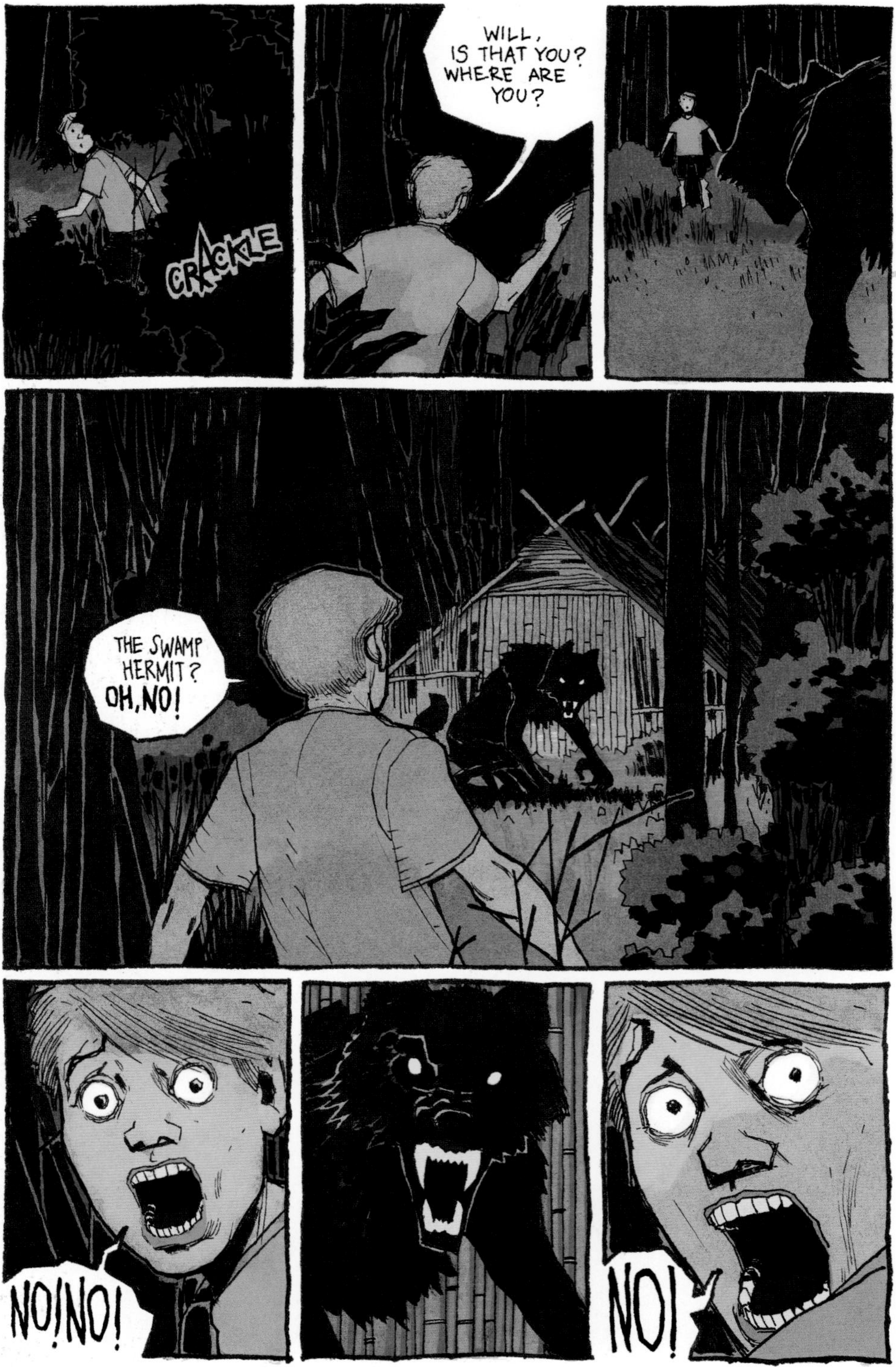
CRACKLE
WILL, IS THAT YOU? WHERE ARE YOU?
THE SWAMP HERMIT? OH, NO!
NO! NO!
NO!

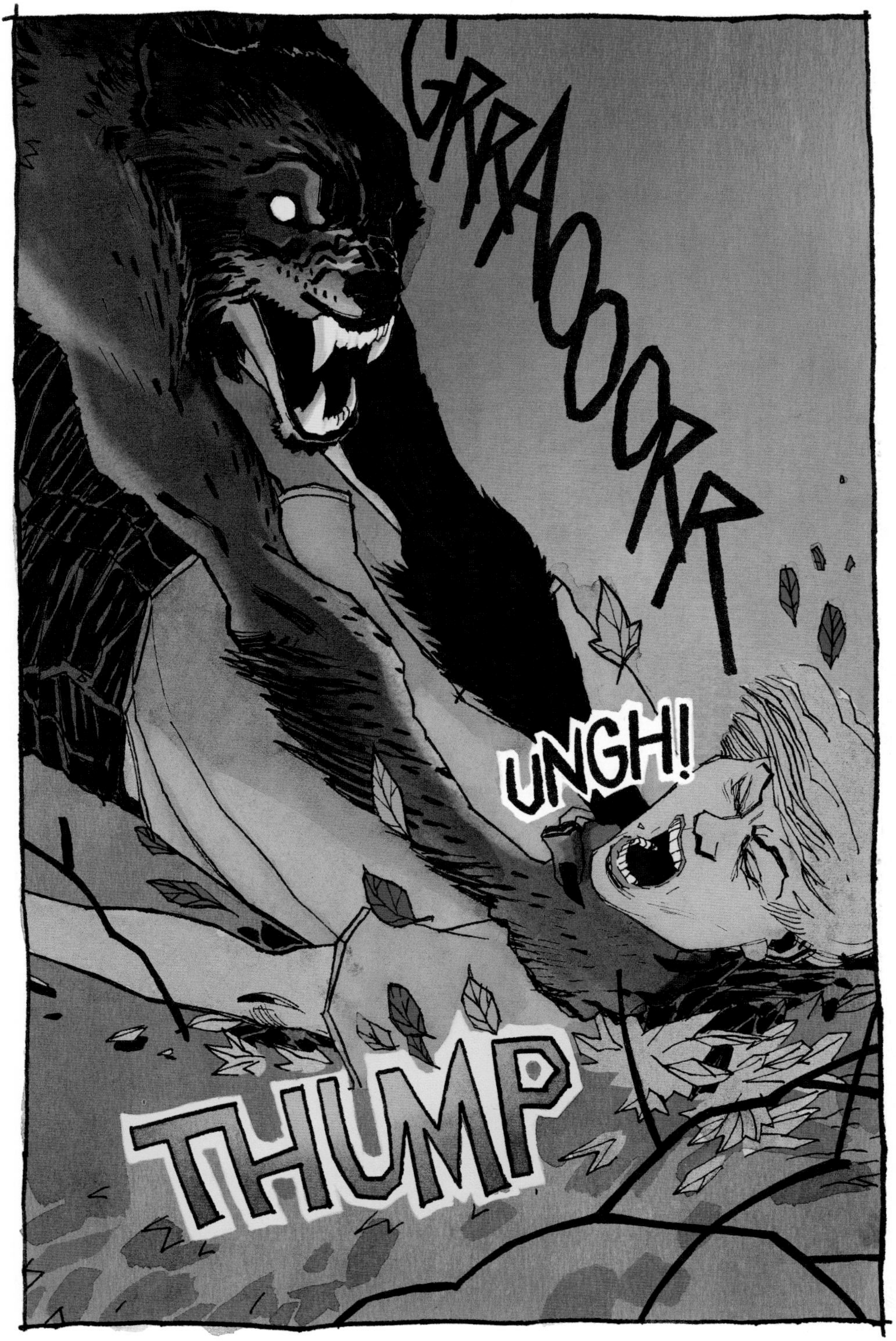
GRRAOOOORR
UNGH!
THUMP

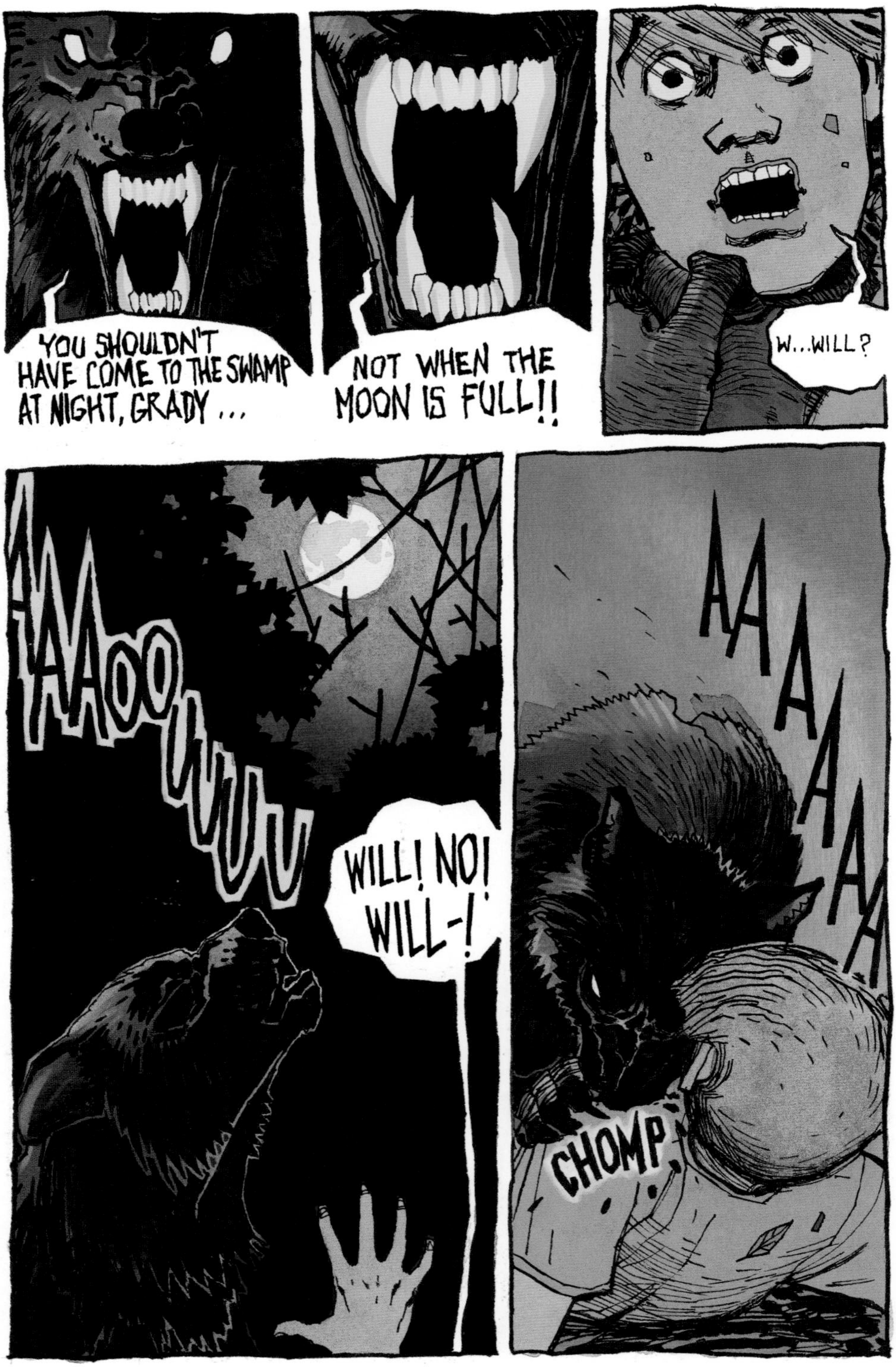
YOU SHOULDN'T HAVE COME TO THE SWAMP AT NIGHT, GRADY ...
NOT WHEN THE MOON IS FULL!!
W...WILL?
AAAOOUUUUU
WILL! NO! WILL-!
AAAAAAA
CHOMP

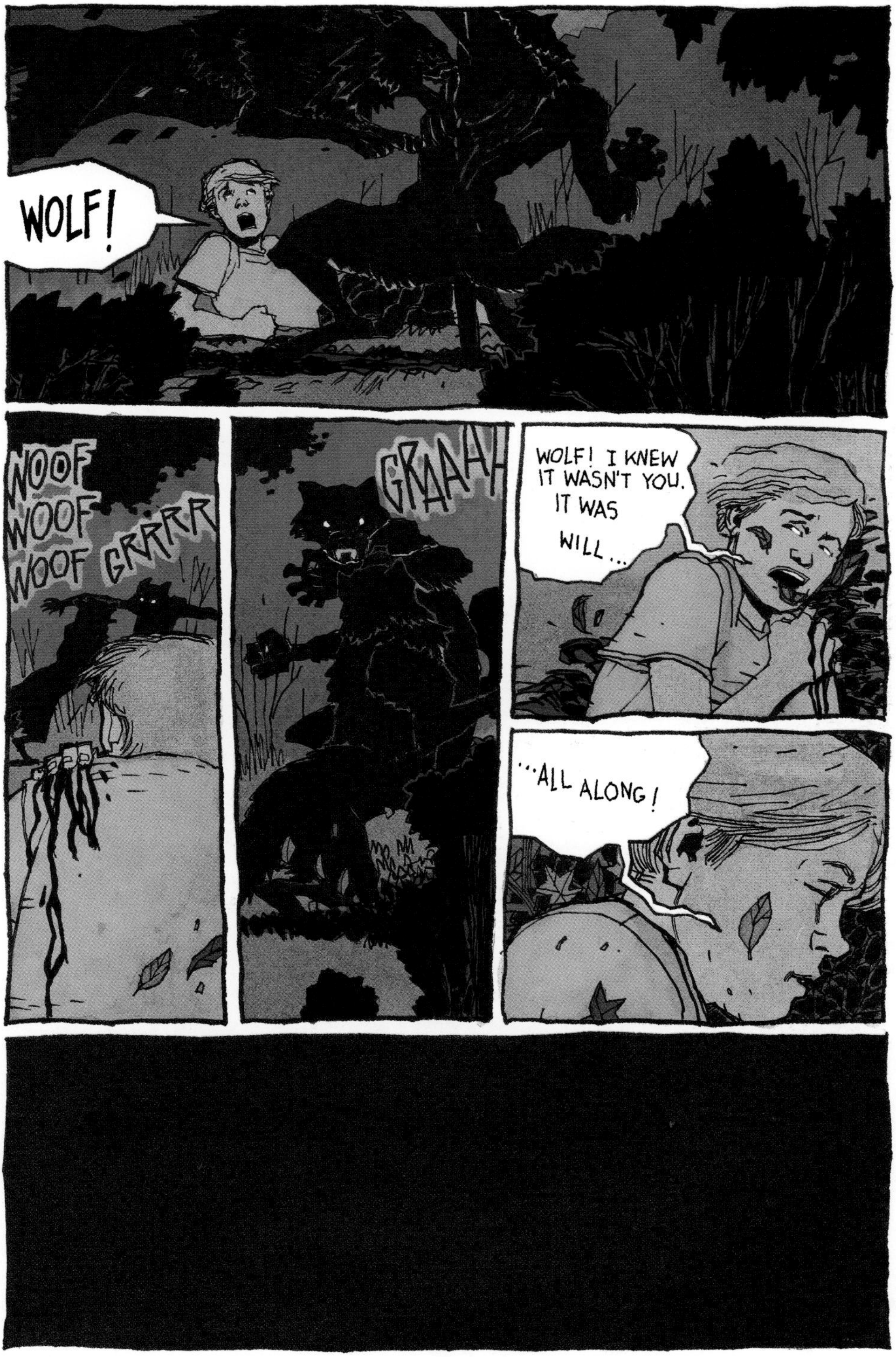
WOLF!
WOOF WOOF WOOF GRRRR
GRAAAH
WOLF! I KNEW IT WASN'T YOU. IT WAS WILL...
...ALL ALONG!

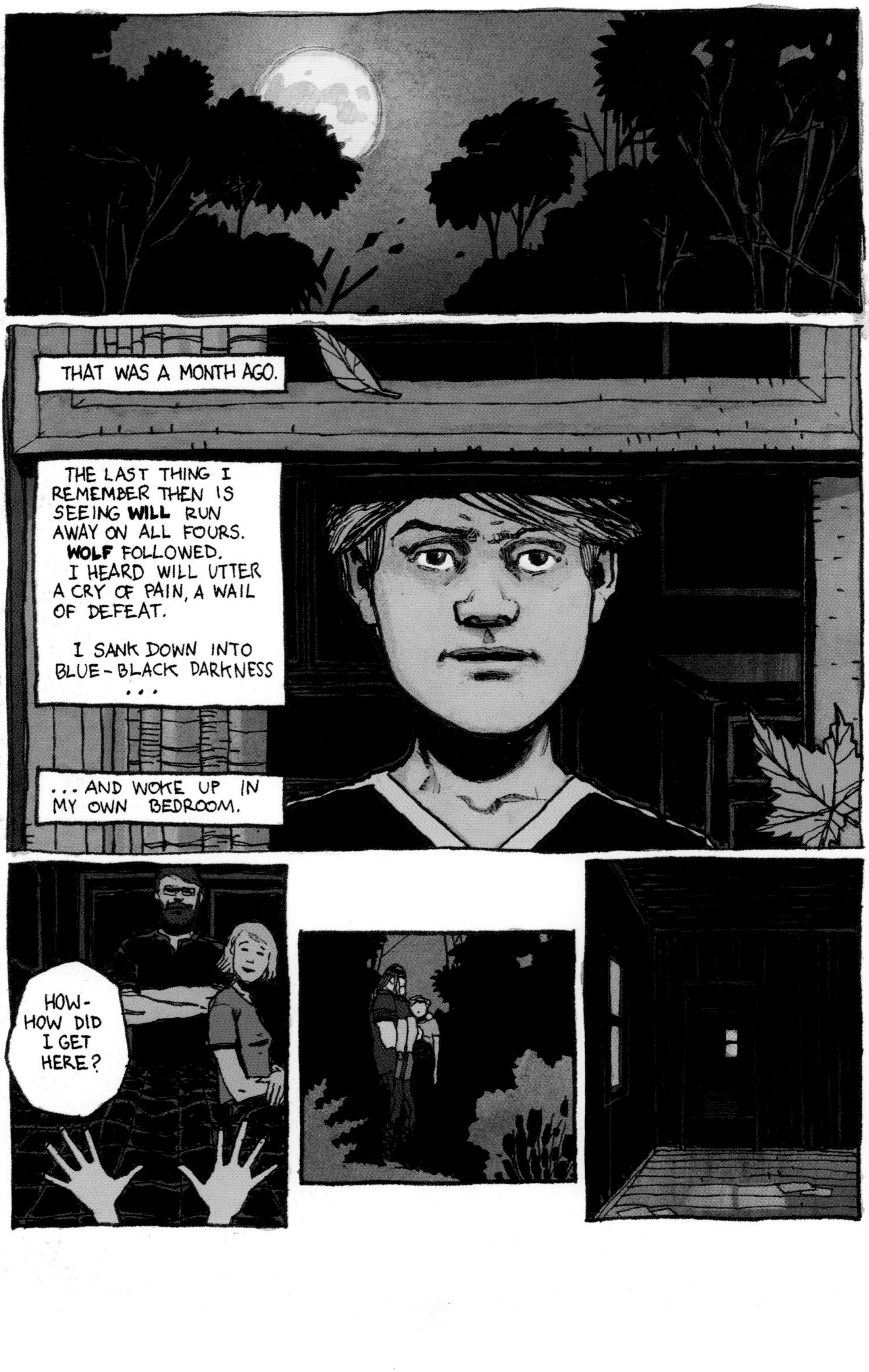
THAT WAS A MONTH AGO.
THE LAST THING I REMEMBER THEN IS SEEING **WILL** RUN AWAY ON ALL FOURS. **WOLF** FOLLOWED. I HEARD WILL UTTER A CRY OF PAIN, A WAIL OF DEFEAT.
I SANK DOWN INTO BLUE-BLACK DARKNESS . . .
. . . AND WOKE UP IN MY OWN BEDROOM.
HOW- HOW DID I GET HERE?

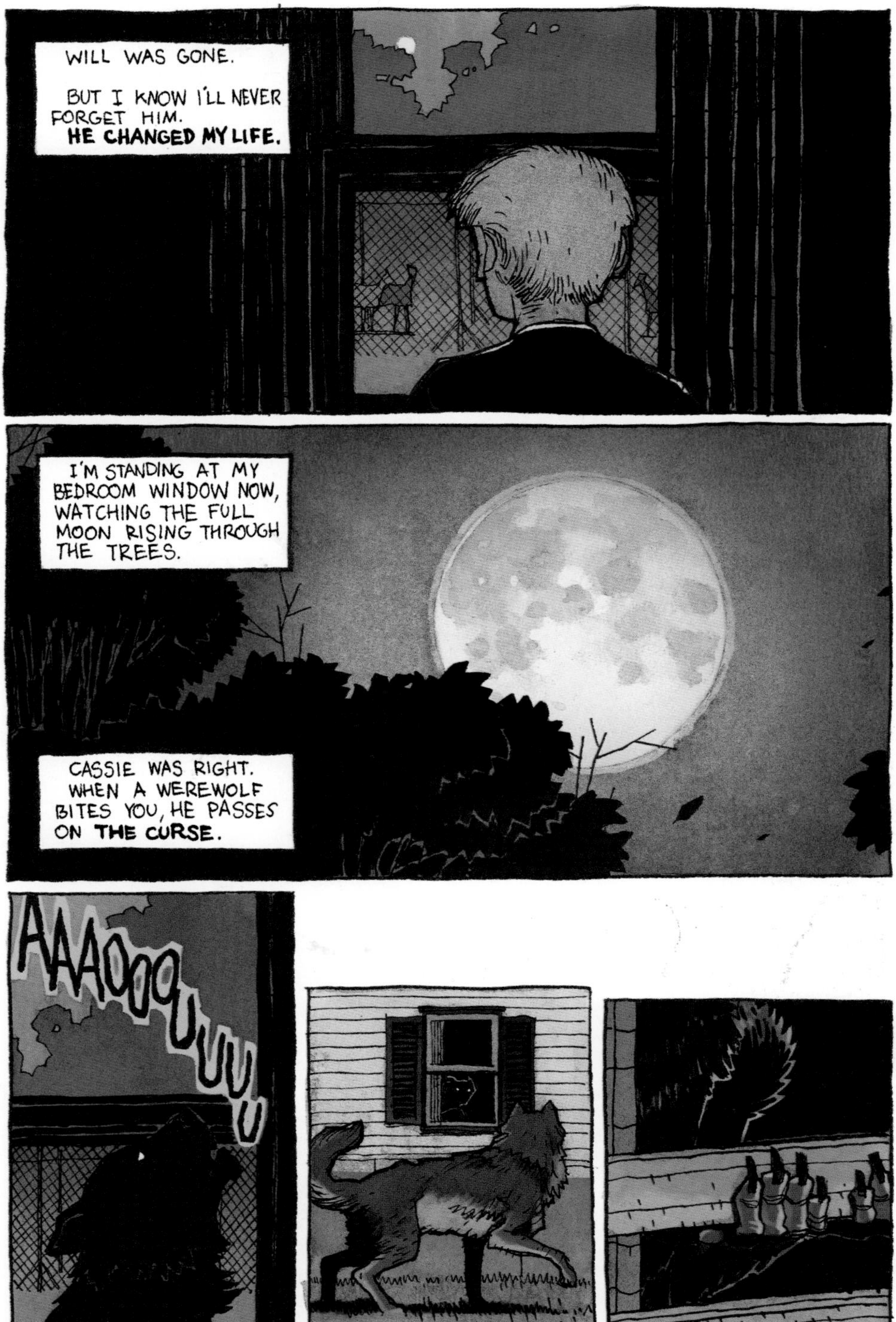
WILL WAS GONE.
BUT I KNOW I'LL NEVER FORGET HIM. **HE CHANGED MY LIFE.**
I'M STANDING AT MY BEDROOM WINDOW NOW, WATCHING THE FULL MOON RISING THROUGH THE TREES.
CASSIE WAS RIGHT. WHEN A WEREWOLF BITES YOU, HE PASSES ON **THE CURSE**.
AAAOOOUUUU

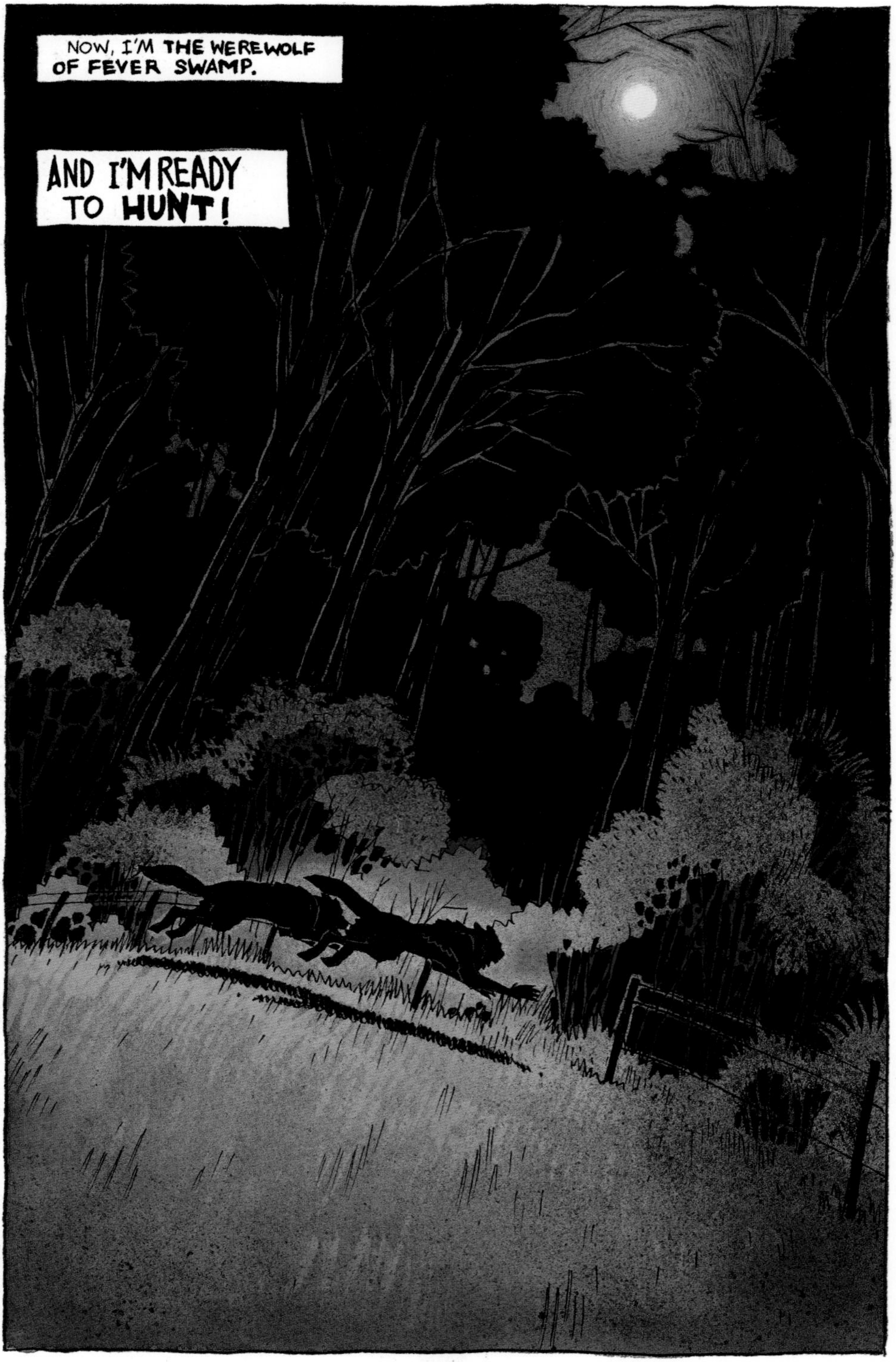
NOW, I'M **THE WEREWOLF OF FEVER SWAMP.**
AND I'M READY TO **HUNT!**

THE END

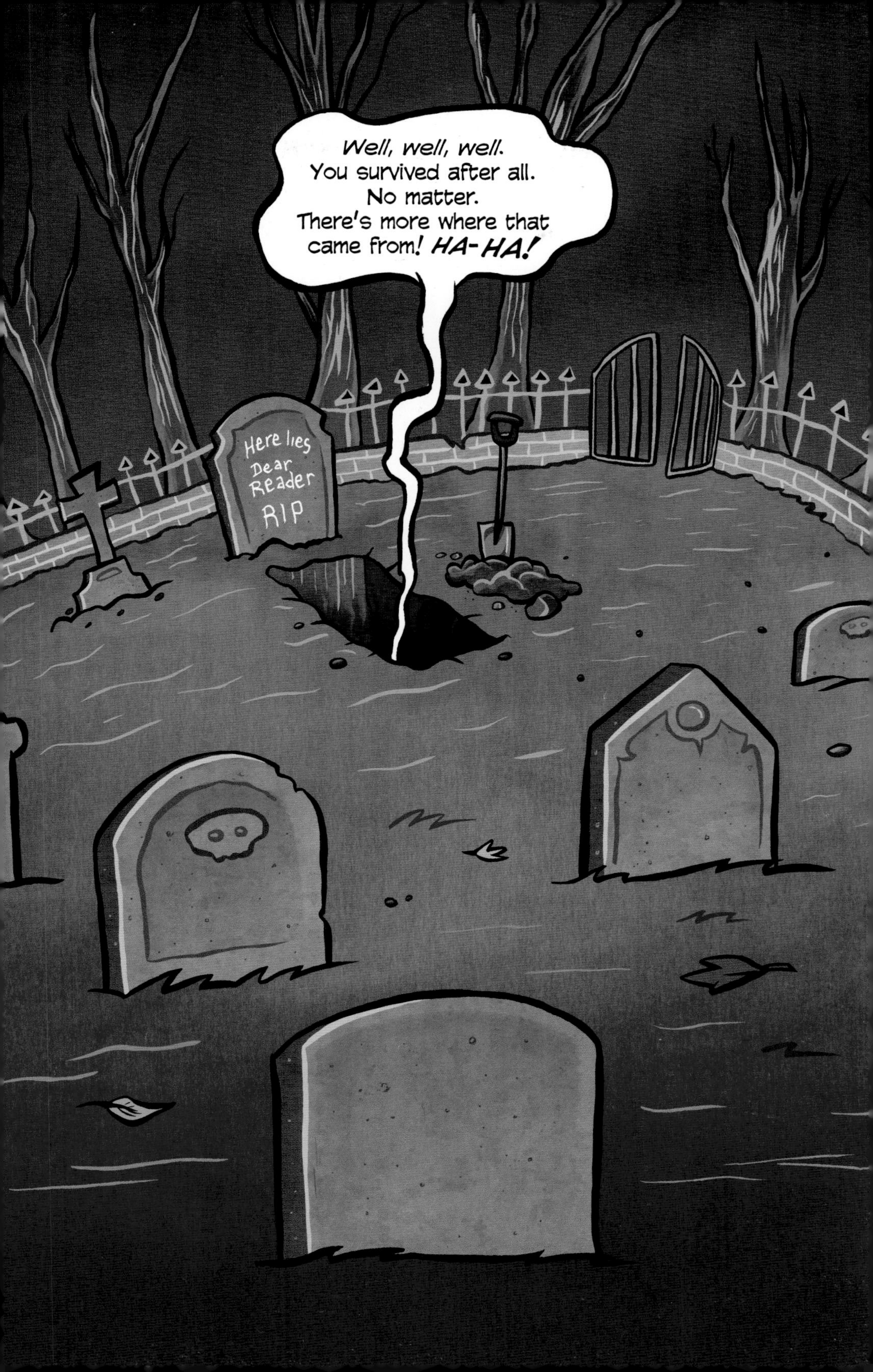
Well, well, well. You survived after all. No matter. There's more where that came from! HA-HA!
Here lies Dear Reader RIP

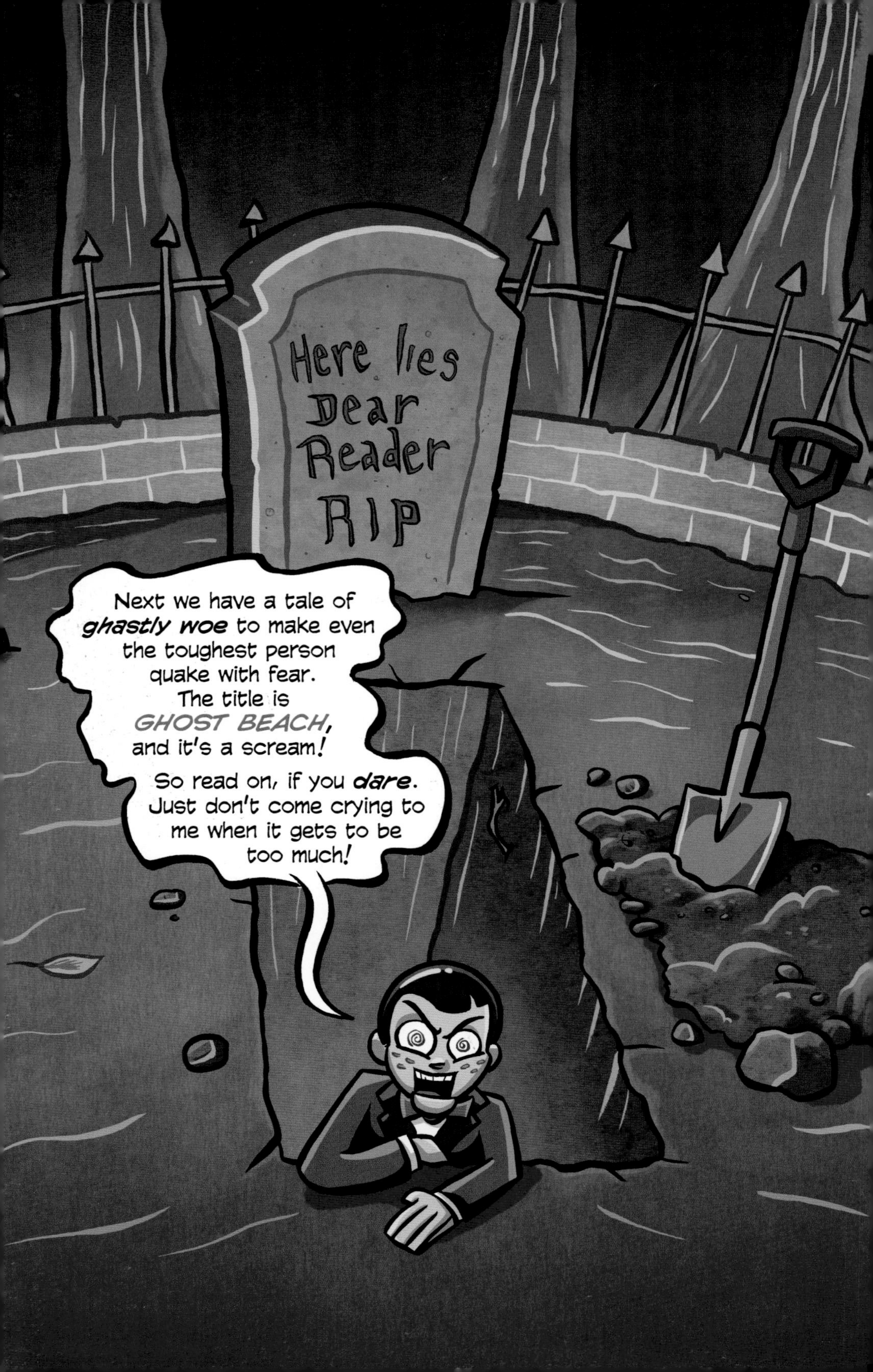
Here lies Dear Reader RIP
Next we have a tale of ghastly woe to make even the toughest person quake with fear. The title is GHOST BEACH, and it's a scream!
So read on, if you dare. Just don't come crying to me when it gets to be too much!

85

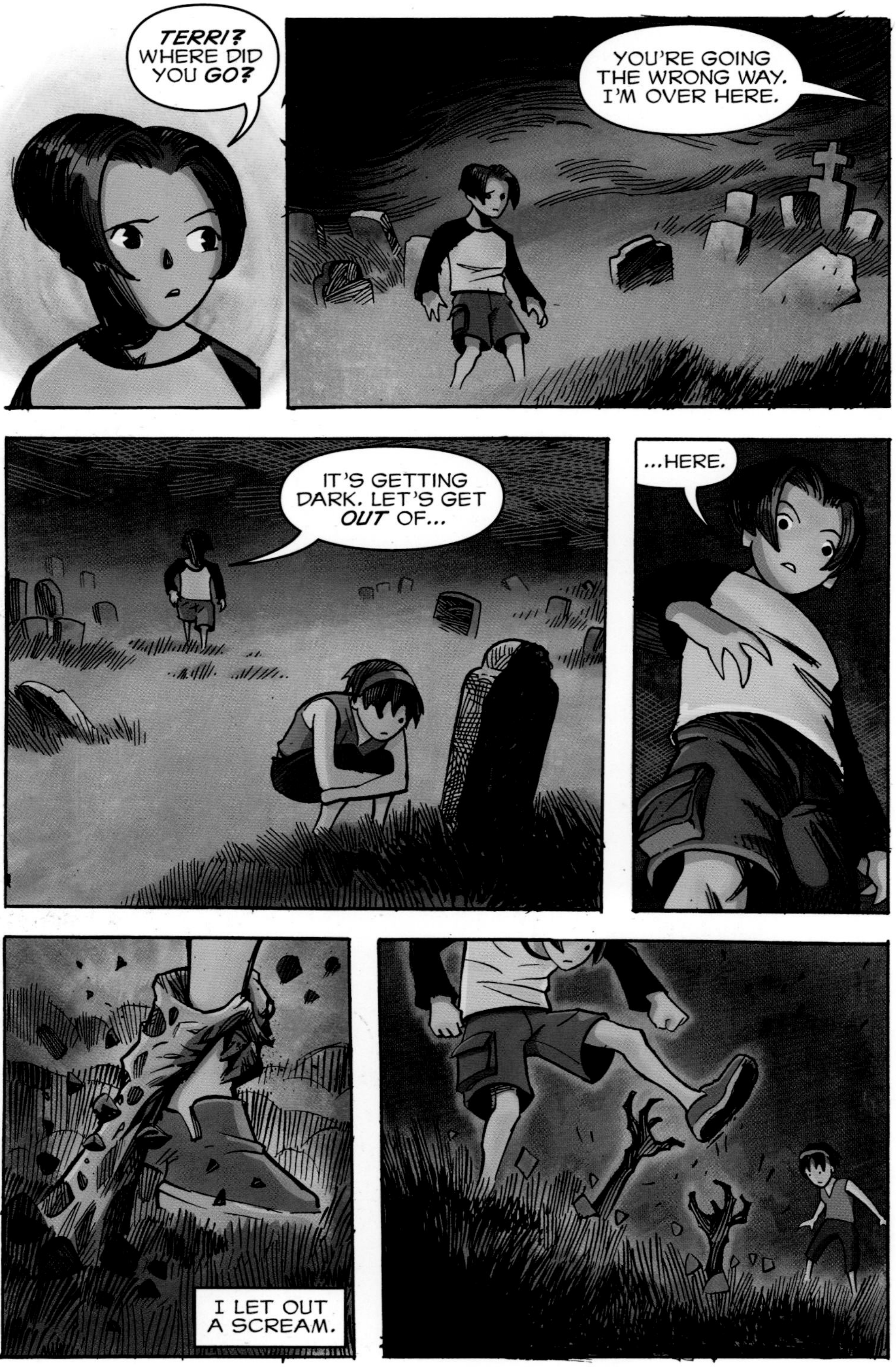
TERRI? WHERE DID YOU GO?
YOU'RE GOING THE WRONG WAY. I'M OVER HERE.
IT'S GETTING DARK. LET'S GET OUT OF...
...HERE.
I LET OUT A SCREAM.

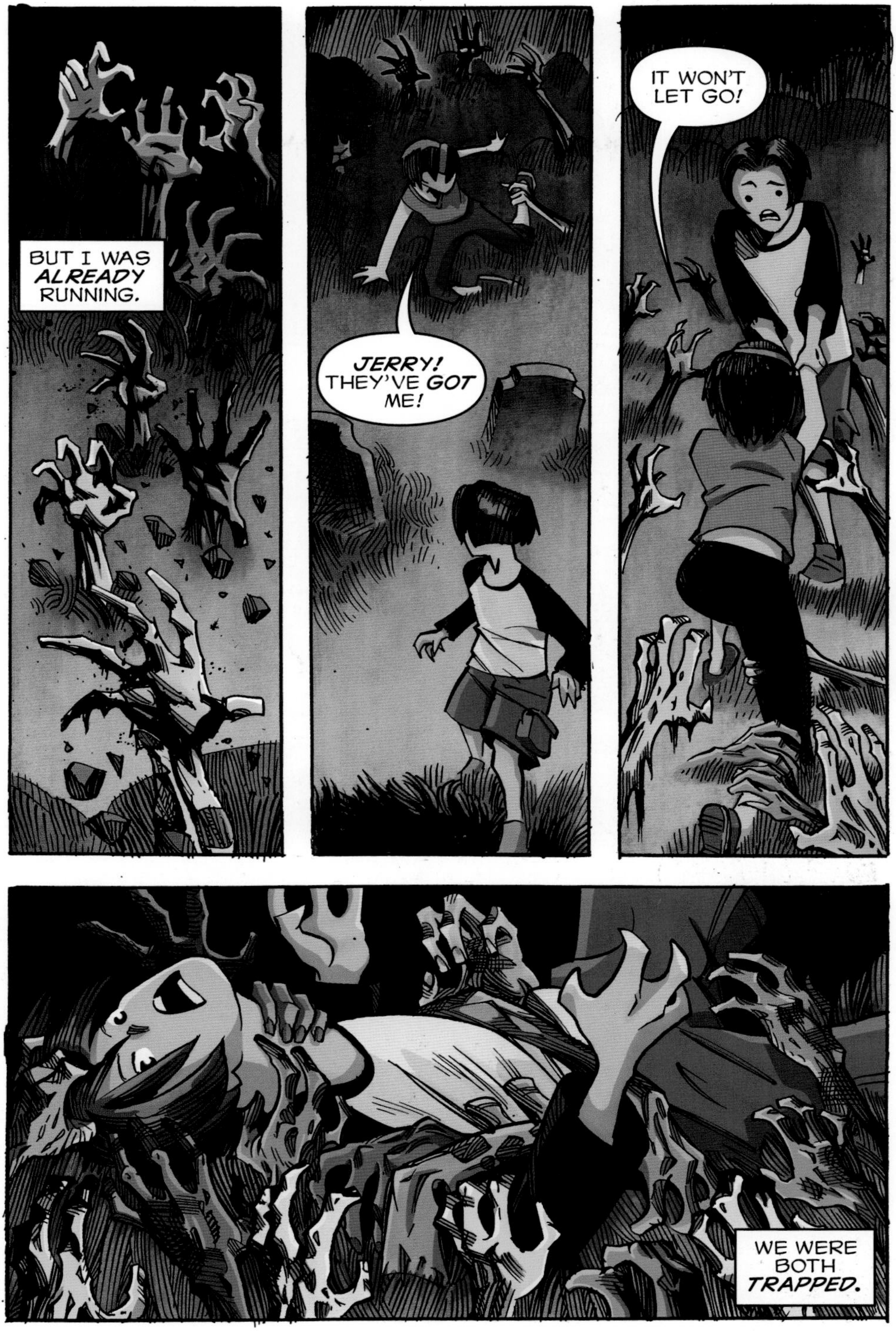
BUT I WAS *ALREADY* RUNNING.
JERRY! THEY'VE *GOT* ME!
IT WON'T LET GO!
WE WERE BOTH *TRAPPED.*

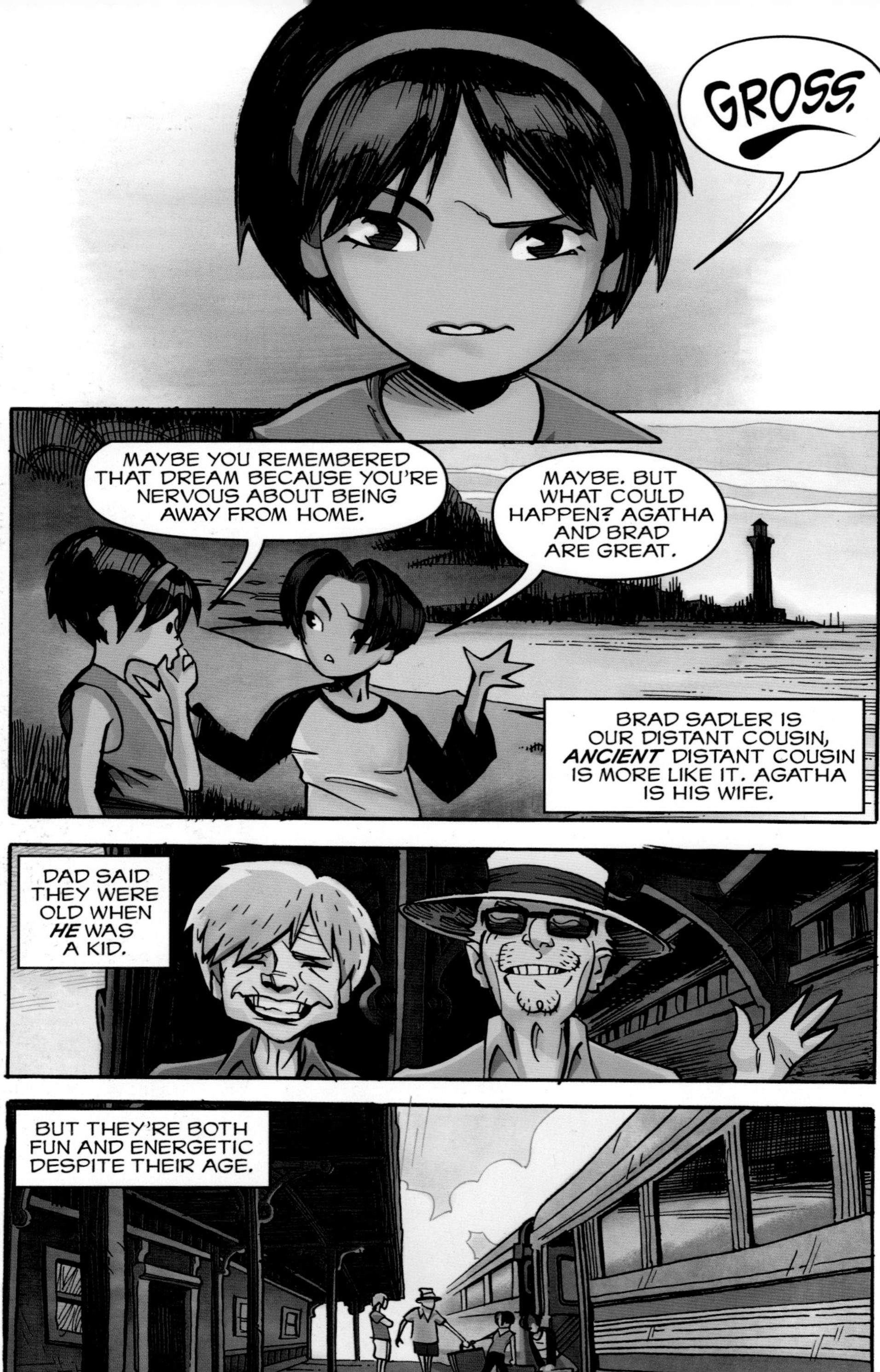
GROSS.
MAYBE YOU REMEMBERED THAT DREAM BECAUSE YOU'RE NERVOUS ABOUT BEING AWAY FROM HOME.
MAYBE. BUT WHAT COULD HAPPEN? AGATHA AND BRAD ARE GREAT.
BRAD SADLER IS OUR DISTANT COUSIN, *ANCIENT* DISTANT COUSIN IS MORE LIKE IT. AGATHA IS HIS WIFE.
DAD SAID THEY WERE OLD WHEN *HE* WAS A KID.
BUT THEY'RE BOTH FUN AND ENERGETIC DESPITE THEIR AGE.

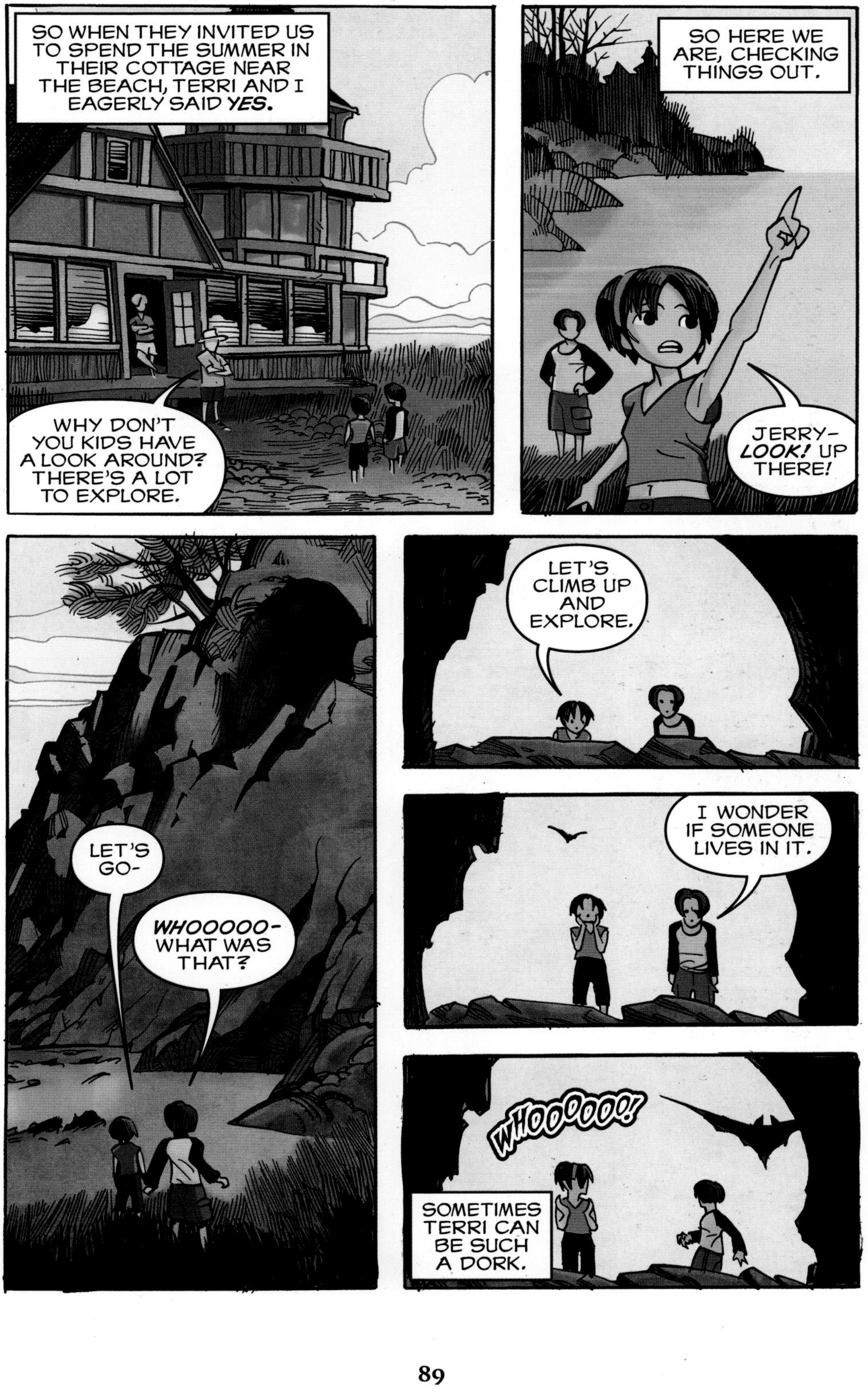
SO WHEN THEY INVITED US TO SPEND THE SUMMER IN THEIR COTTAGE NEAR THE BEACH, TERRI AND I EAGERLY SAID *YES.*
WHY DON'T YOU KIDS HAVE A LOOK AROUND? THERE'S A LOT TO EXPLORE.
SO HERE WE ARE, CHECKING THINGS OUT.
JERRY- *LOOK!* UP THERE!
LET'S GO-
WHOOOOO- WHAT WAS THAT?
LET'S CLIMB UP AND EXPLORE.
I WONDER IF SOMEONE LIVES IN IT.
WHOOOOOO!
SOMETIMES TERRI CAN BE SUCH A DORK.

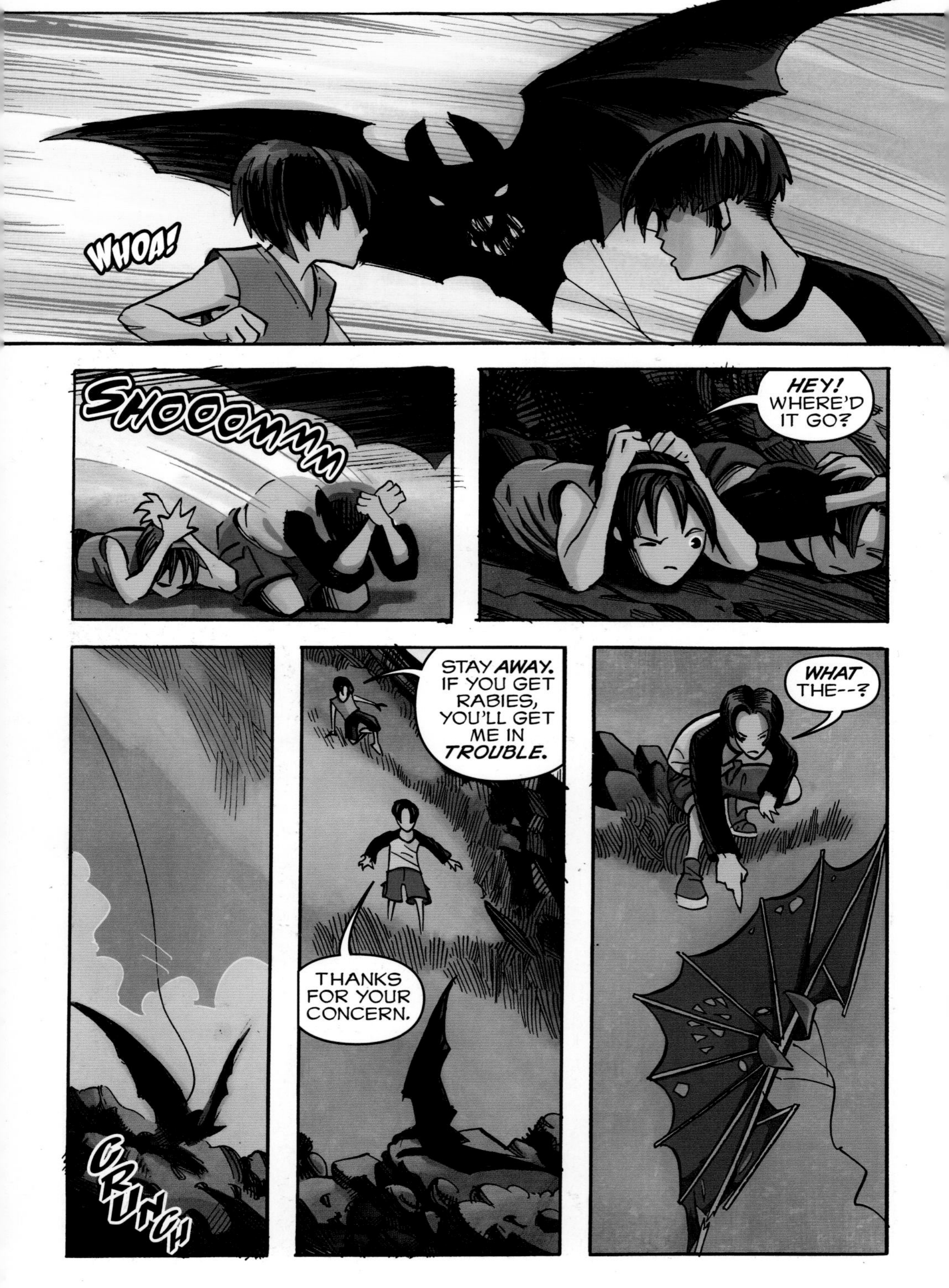
WHOA!
SHOOOMMM
HEY! WHERE'D IT GO?
CRUNCH
STAY AWAY. IF YOU GET RABIES, YOU'LL GET ME IN TROUBLE.
THANKS FOR YOUR CONCERN.
WHAT THE--?

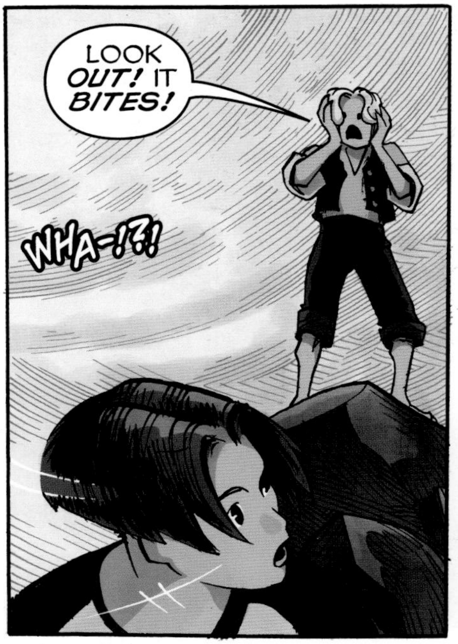
LOOK OUT! IT BITES!
WHA-!?!

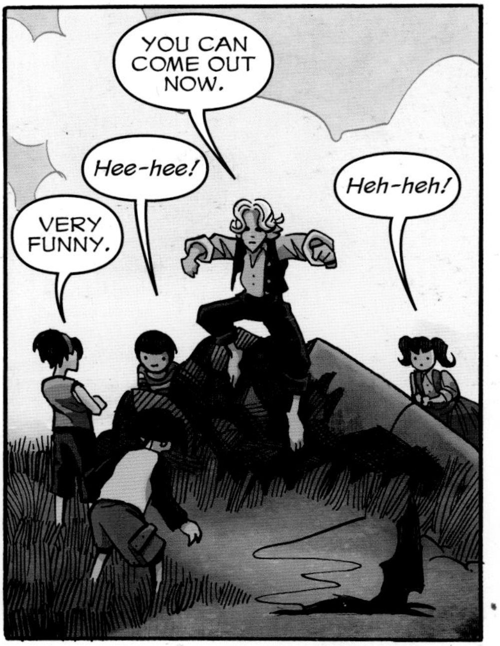
YOU CAN COME OUT NOW.
Hee-hee!
Heh-heh!
VERY FUNNY.

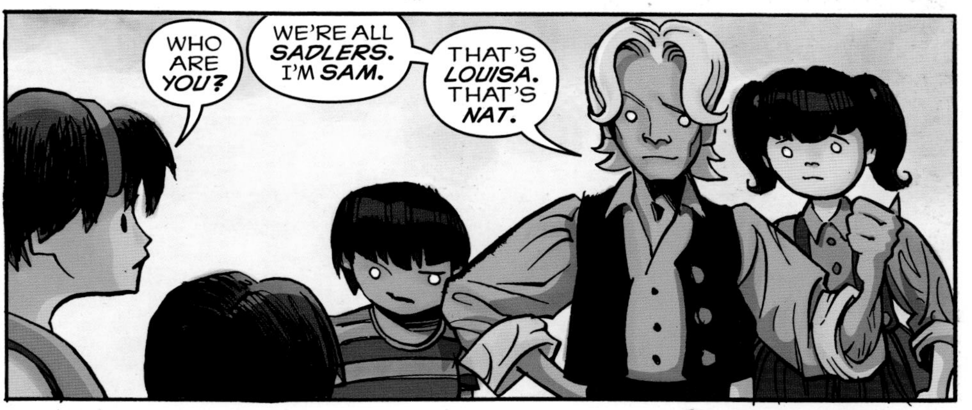
WHO ARE YOU?
WE'RE ALL SADLERS. I'M SAM.
THAT'S LOUISA. THAT'S NAT.

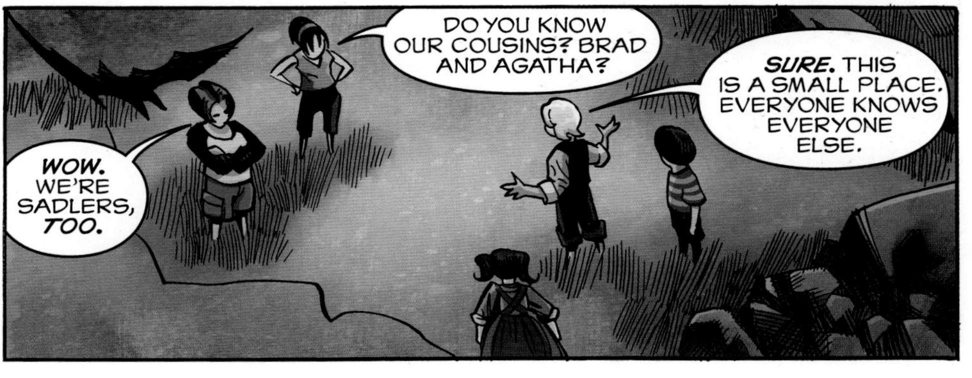
DO YOU KNOW OUR COUSINS? BRAD AND AGATHA?
SURE. THIS IS A SMALL PLACE. EVERYONE KNOWS EVERYONE ELSE.
WOW. WE'RE SADLERS, TOO.

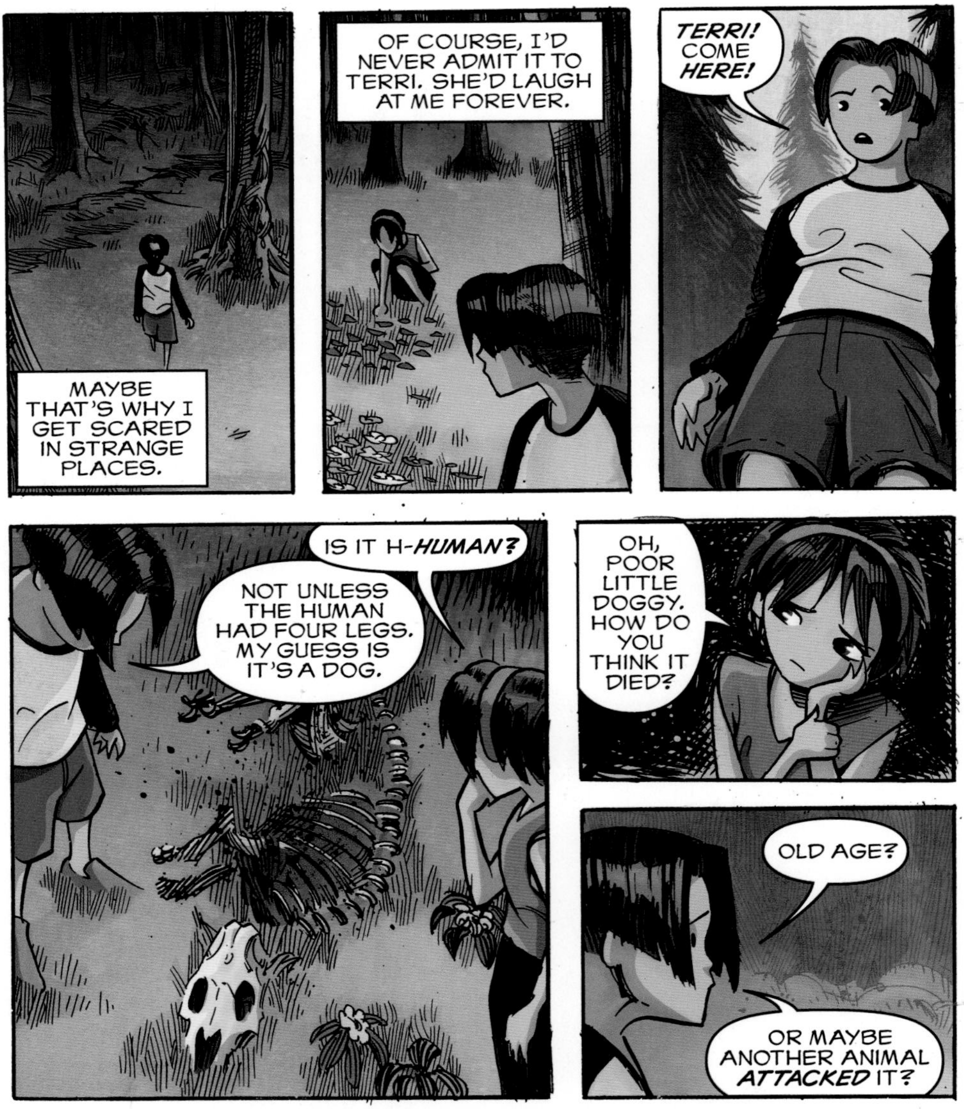
MAYBE THAT'S WHY I GET SCARED IN STRANGE PLACES.
OF COURSE, I'D NEVER ADMIT IT TO TERRI. SHE'D LAUGH AT ME FOREVER.
TERRI! COME *HERE!*
IS IT H-*HUMAN?*
NOT UNLESS THE HUMAN HAD FOUR LEGS. MY GUESS IS IT'S A DOG.
OH, POOR LITTLE DOGGY. HOW DO YOU THINK IT DIED?
OLD AGE?
OR MAYBE ANOTHER ANIMAL *ATTACKED* IT?
ARRR
ROOOOOOOOOOOO!
A SHRILL ANIMAL HOWL FILLED THE FOREST.
WHAT'S *THAT?*
I DIDN'T KNOW.

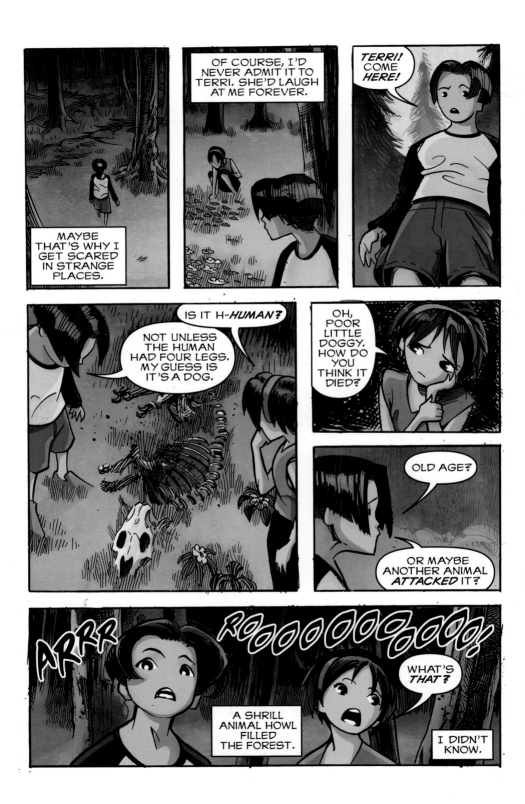

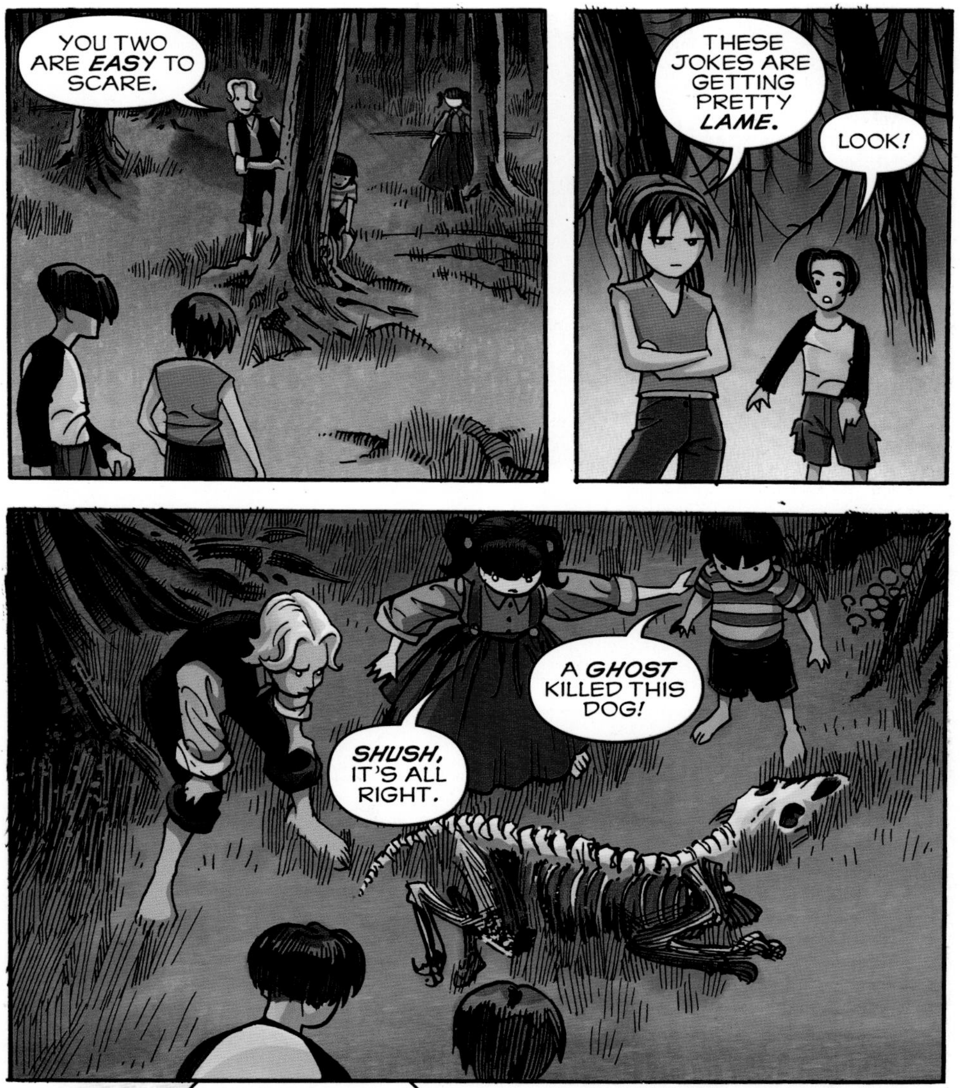
YOU TWO ARE *EASY* TO SCARE.
THESE JOKES ARE GETTING PRETTY *LAME.*
LOOK!
A *GHOST* KILLED THIS DOG!
SHUSH, IT'S ALL RIGHT.
DOGS CAN TELL IF SOMEONE'S A GHOST. THEY ALWAYS BARK WARNINGS.
THERE'S NO SUCH THING AS-
YOU'RE *WRONG.*

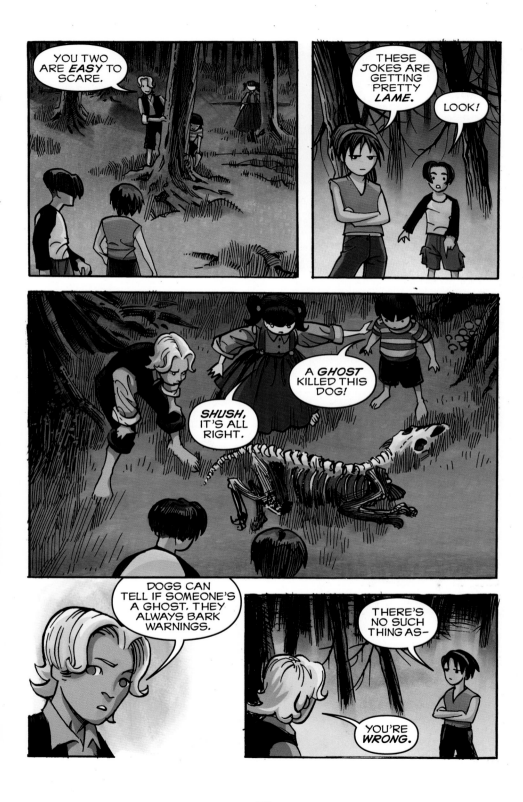

THESE WOODS ARE *FULL* OF SKELETONS, ALL BECAUSE OF THE *GHOST*. HE PICKS THEM CLEAN.

TELL US *MORE*. OR IS THIS ANOTHER ONE OF YOUR FABULOUS JOKES?

MAYBE SOME OTHER TIME.

WAIT! I WANT TO HEAR MORE.

IS THIS THE GHOST IN THE *CAVE?* HAVE YOU *SEEN* IT?

WELL, A FLICKERING LIGHT AND A DOG SKELETON AREN'T ENOUGH TO CONVINCE ME. NICE TRY.

YOU CAN SEE FLICKERING LIGHTS SOMETIMES.

WHAT'D YOU DO *THAT* FOR? I WAS JUST WEASELING SOME *GOOD* STUFF OUT OF THEM.

SOCK

CAN'T YOU *SEE?* IT'S JUST ANOTHER DUMB JOKE.

THERE'S NO GHOST.

DESPITE THE HEAT, A CHILL RAN DOWN MY BACK.

WAS THERE A GHOST?

DID I REALLY WANT TO FIND OUT?

OVER DINNER, WE TOLD AGATHA AND BRAD ABOUT SAM, NAT, AND LOUISA.

THEY SAID THEY KNOW YOU.

YEP. *NEIGHBORS.*

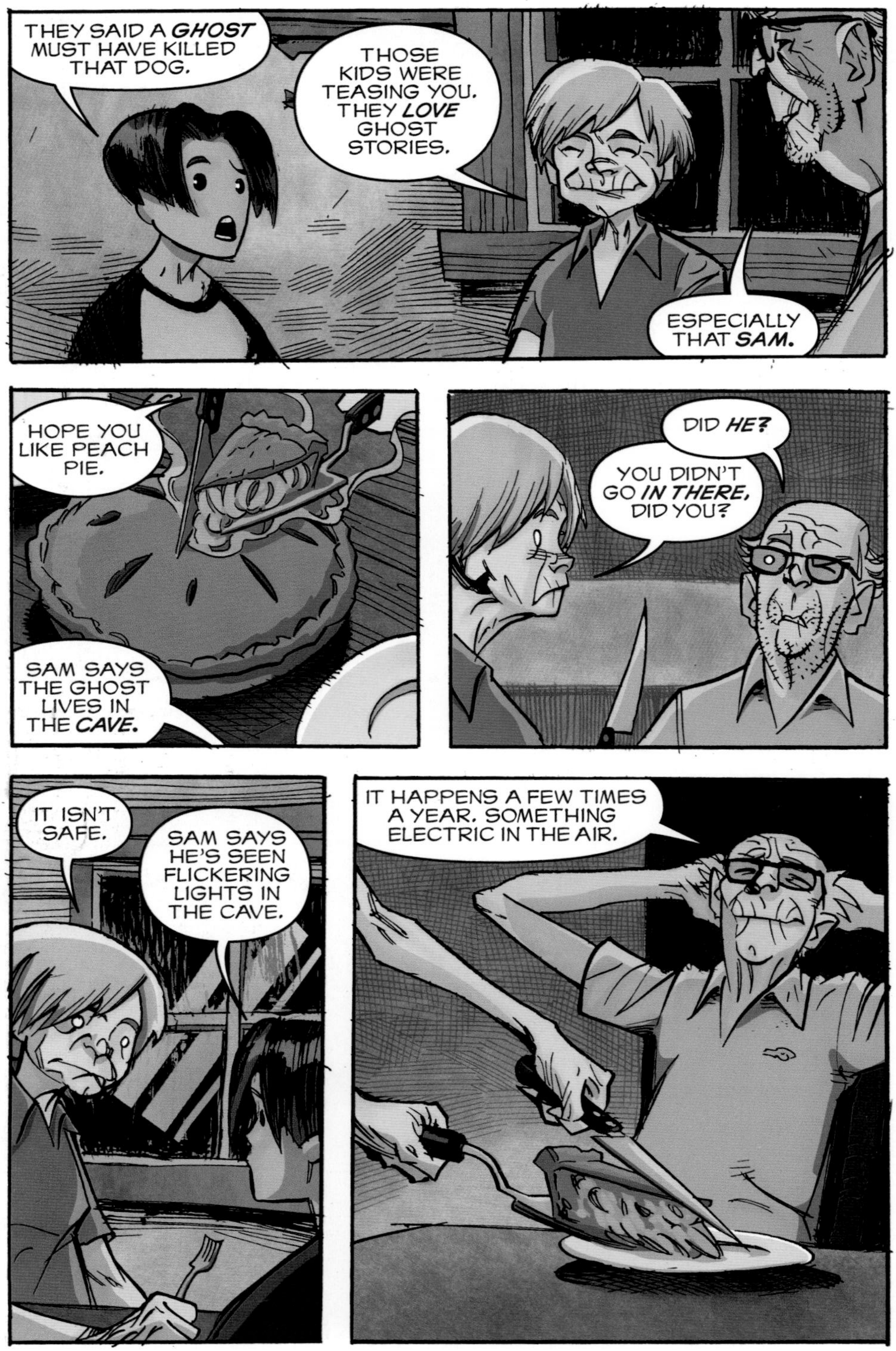
THEY SAID A ***GHOST*** MUST HAVE KILLED THAT DOG.
THOSE KIDS WERE TEASING YOU. THEY ***LOVE*** GHOST STORIES.
ESPECIALLY THAT **SAM.**
HOPE YOU LIKE PEACH PIE.
SAM SAYS THE GHOST LIVES IN THE ***CAVE.***
DID ***HE?***
YOU DIDN'T GO ***IN THERE,*** DID YOU?
IT ISN'T SAFE.
SAM SAYS HE'S SEEN FLICKERING LIGHTS IN THE CAVE.
IT HAPPENS A FEW TIMES A YEAR. SOMETHING ELECTRIC IN THE AIR.

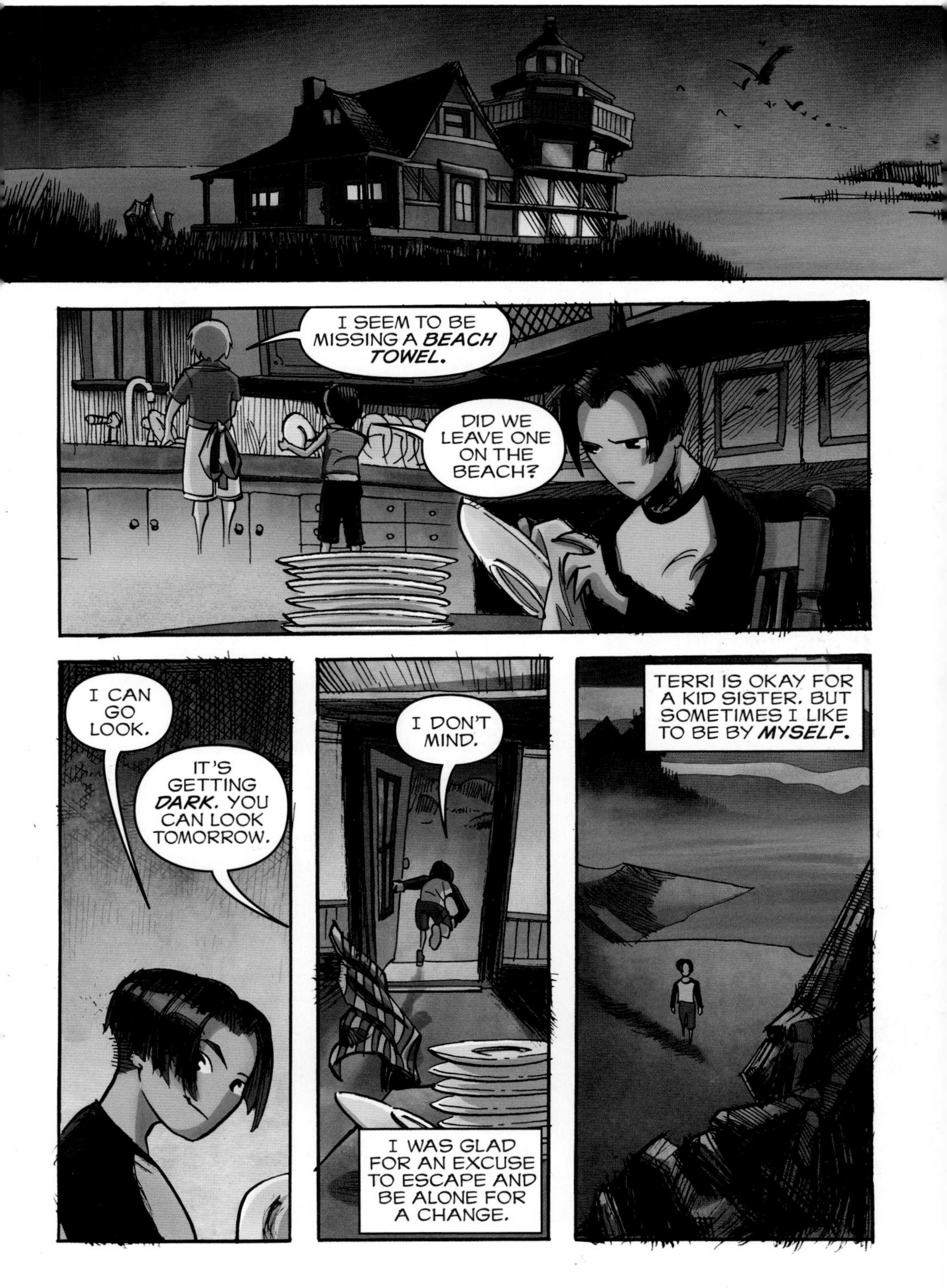

I SEEM TO BE MISSING A *BEACH TOWEL*.
DID WE LEAVE ONE ON THE BEACH?
I CAN GO LOOK.
IT'S GETTING *DARK*. YOU CAN LOOK TOMORROW.
I DON'T MIND.
I WAS GLAD FOR AN EXCUSE TO ESCAPE AND BE ALONE FOR A CHANGE.
TERRI IS OKAY FOR A KID SISTER. BUT SOMETIMES I LIKE TO BE BY *MYSELF*.

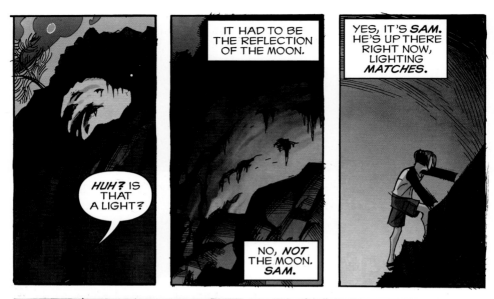

HUH? IS THAT A LIGHT?

IT HAD TO BE THE REFLECTION OF THE MOON.

NO, *NOT* THE MOON. *SAM.*

YES, IT'S *SAM.* HE'S UP THERE RIGHT NOW, LIGHTING *MATCHES.*

WHA!?!

WHAT DO YOU THINK YOU'RE *DOING!*

DO YOU SEE THAT *LIGHT?*

WHAT LIGHT?

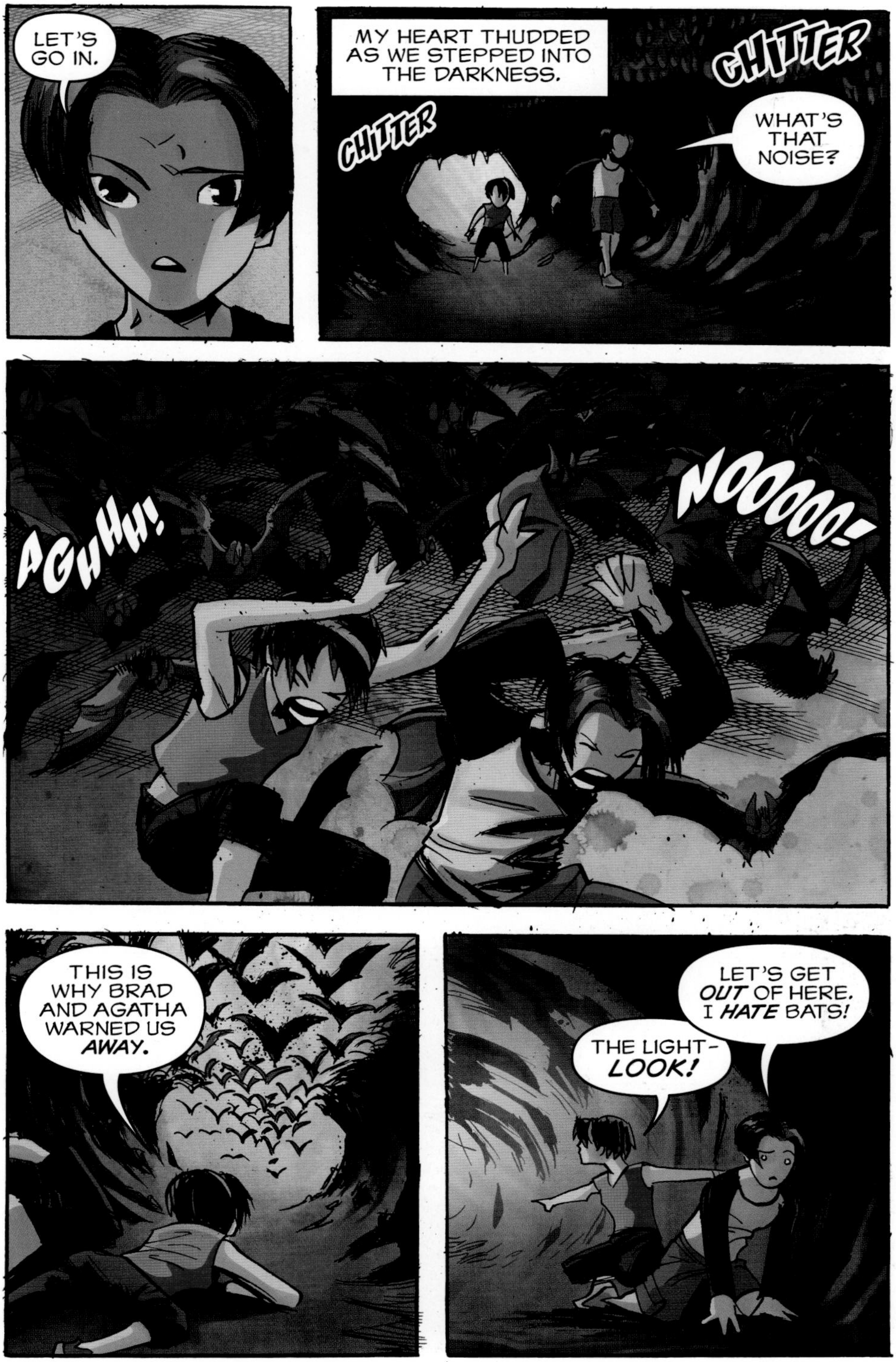
LET'S GO IN.
MY HEART THUDDED AS WE STEPPED INTO THE DARKNESS.
CHITTER
CHITTER
WHAT'S THAT NOISE?
AGHHH!
NOOOOO!
THIS IS WHY BRAD AND AGATHA WARNED US *AWAY*.
LET'S GET *OUT* OF HERE. I *HATE* BATS!
THE LIGHT- *LOOK!*

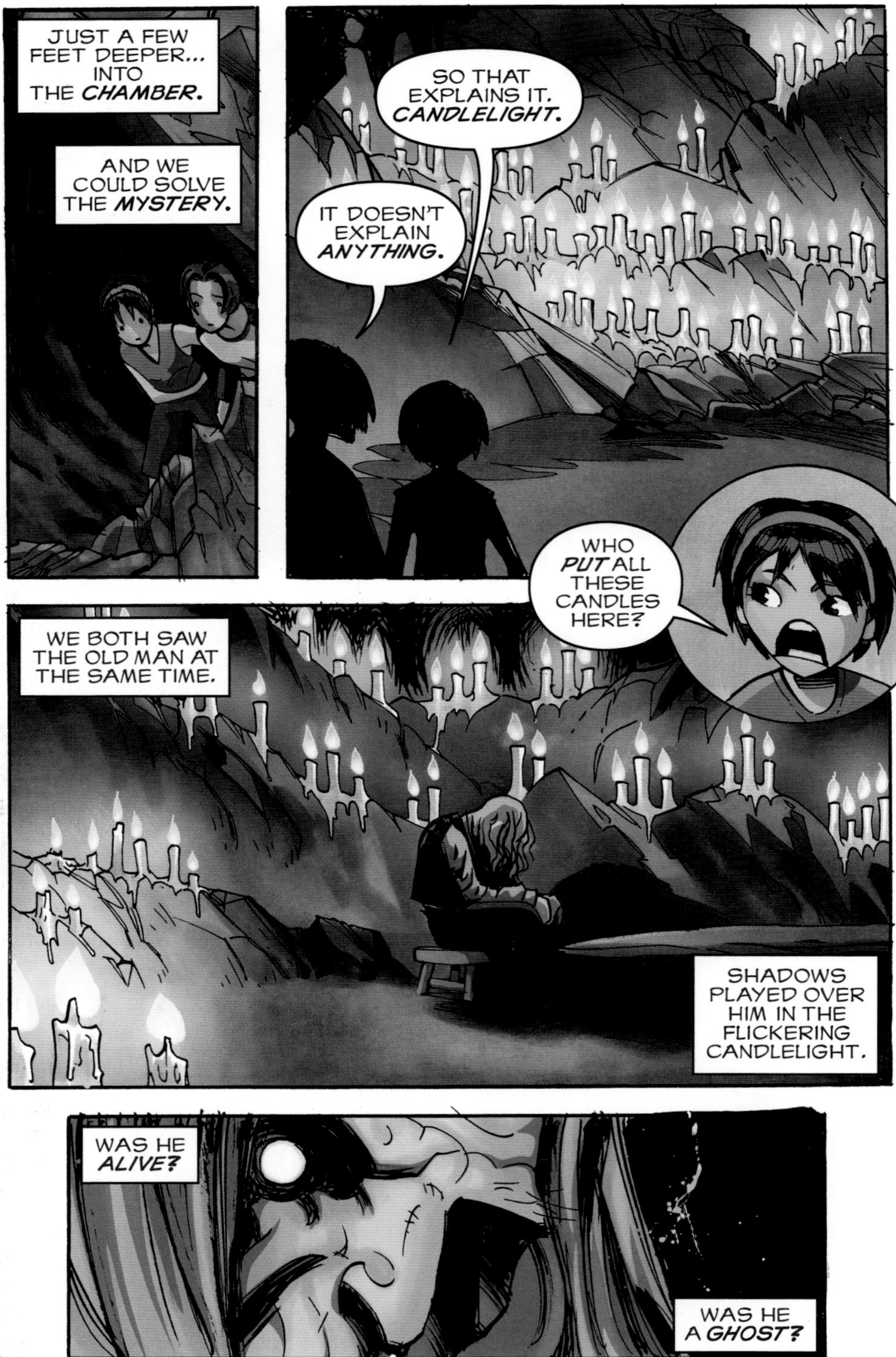
JUST A FEW FEET DEEPER... INTO THE *CHAMBER*.
AND WE COULD SOLVE THE *MYSTERY*.
SO THAT EXPLAINS IT. *CANDLELIGHT*.
IT DOESN'T EXPLAIN *ANYTHING*.
WE BOTH SAW THE OLD MAN AT THE SAME TIME.
WHO *PUT* ALL THESE CANDLES HERE?
SHADOWS PLAYED OVER HIM IN THE FLICKERING CANDLELIGHT.
WAS HE *ALIVE?*
WAS HE A *GHOST?*

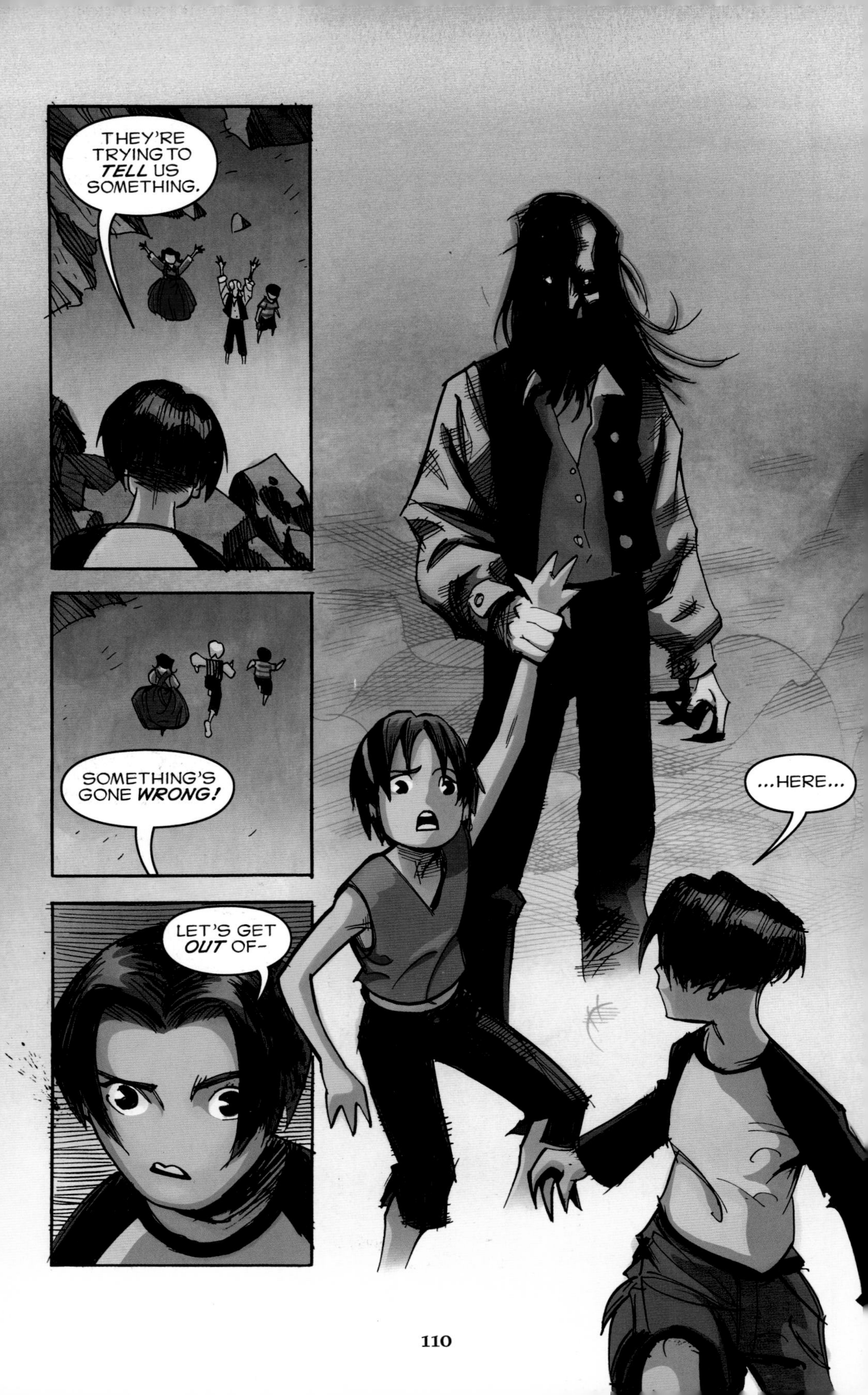
THEY'RE TRYING TO TELL US SOMETHING.
SOMETHING'S GONE WRONG!
LET'S GET OUT OF-
...HERE...

115

116

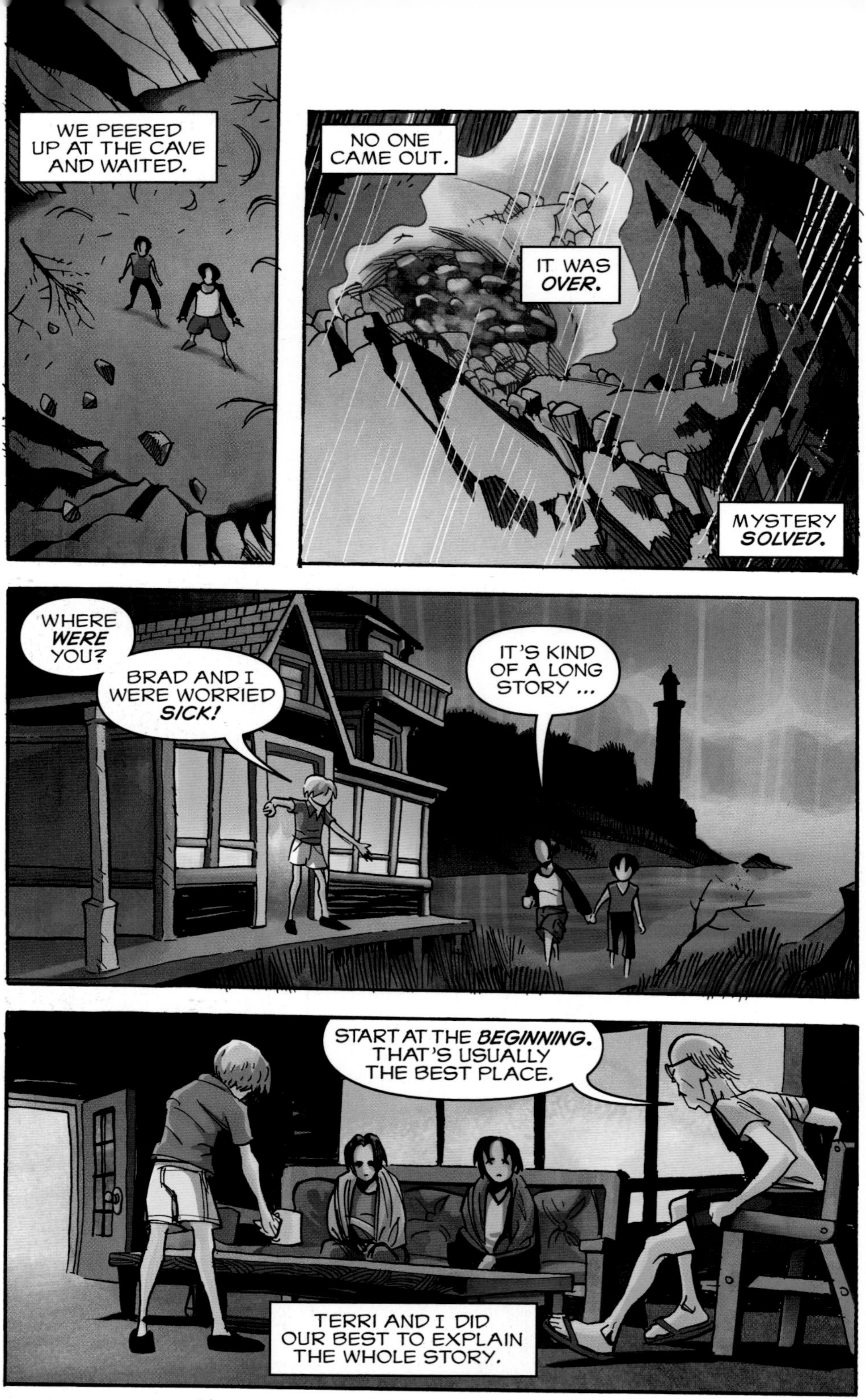
WE PEERED UP AT THE CAVE AND WAITED.
NO ONE CAME OUT.
IT WAS *OVER*.
MYSTERY *SOLVED*.
WHERE *WERE* YOU?
BRAD AND I WERE WORRIED *SICK!*
IT'S KIND OF A LONG STORY ...
START AT THE *BEGINNING*. THAT'S USUALLY THE BEST PLACE.
TERRI AND I DID OUR BEST TO EXPLAIN THE WHOLE STORY.

124

THE END

130

131

132

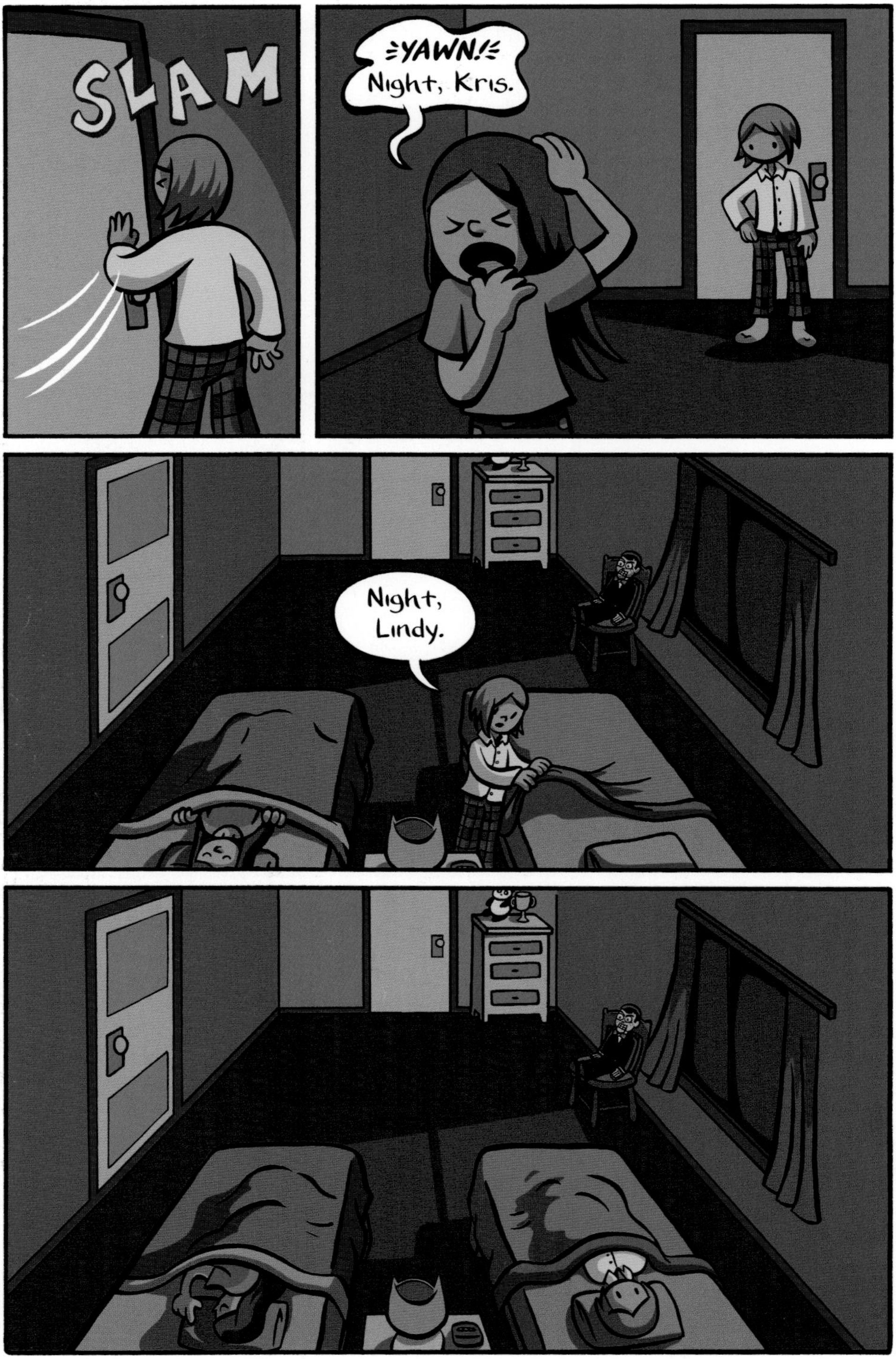
SLAM
YAWN! Night, Kris.
Night, Lindy.

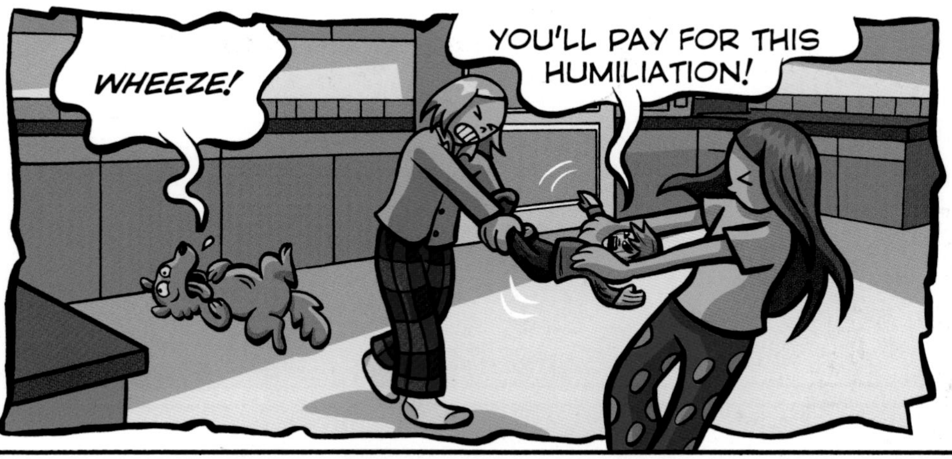
WHEEZE!
YOU'LL PAY FOR THIS HUMILIATION!
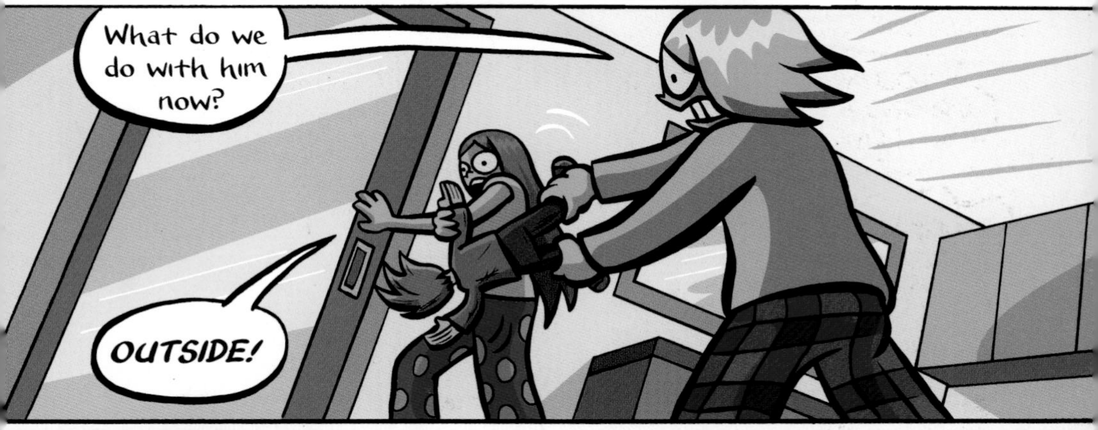
What do we do with him now?
OUTSIDE!
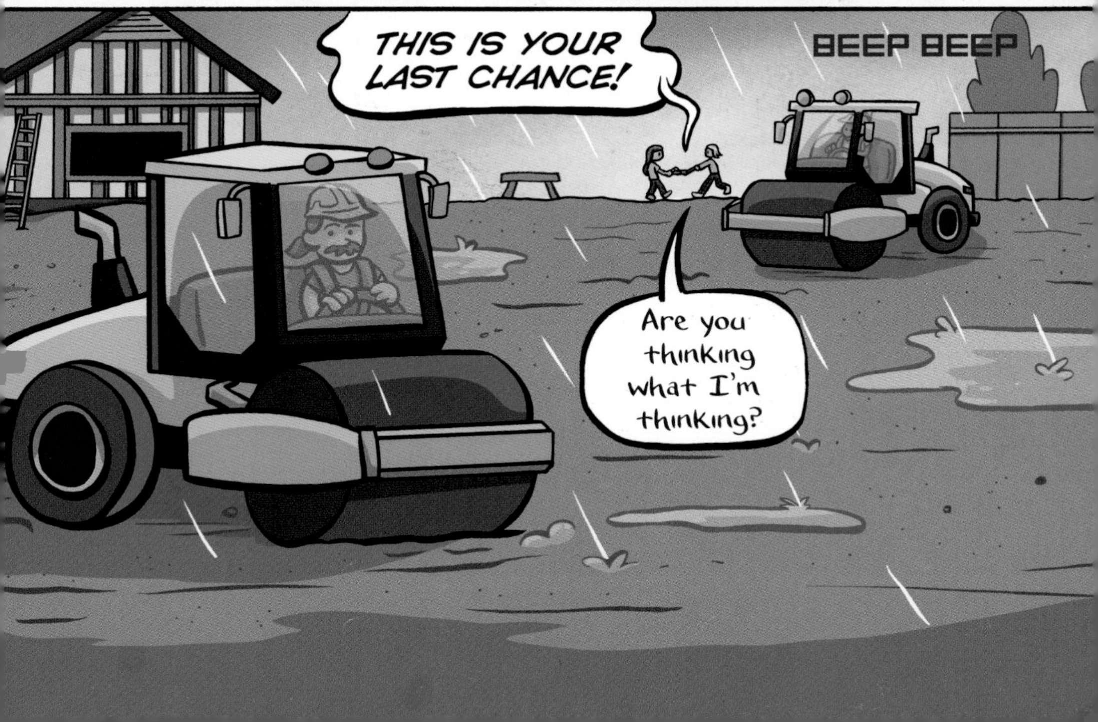
THIS IS YOUR LAST CHANCE!
BEEP BEEP
Are you thinking what I'm thinking?

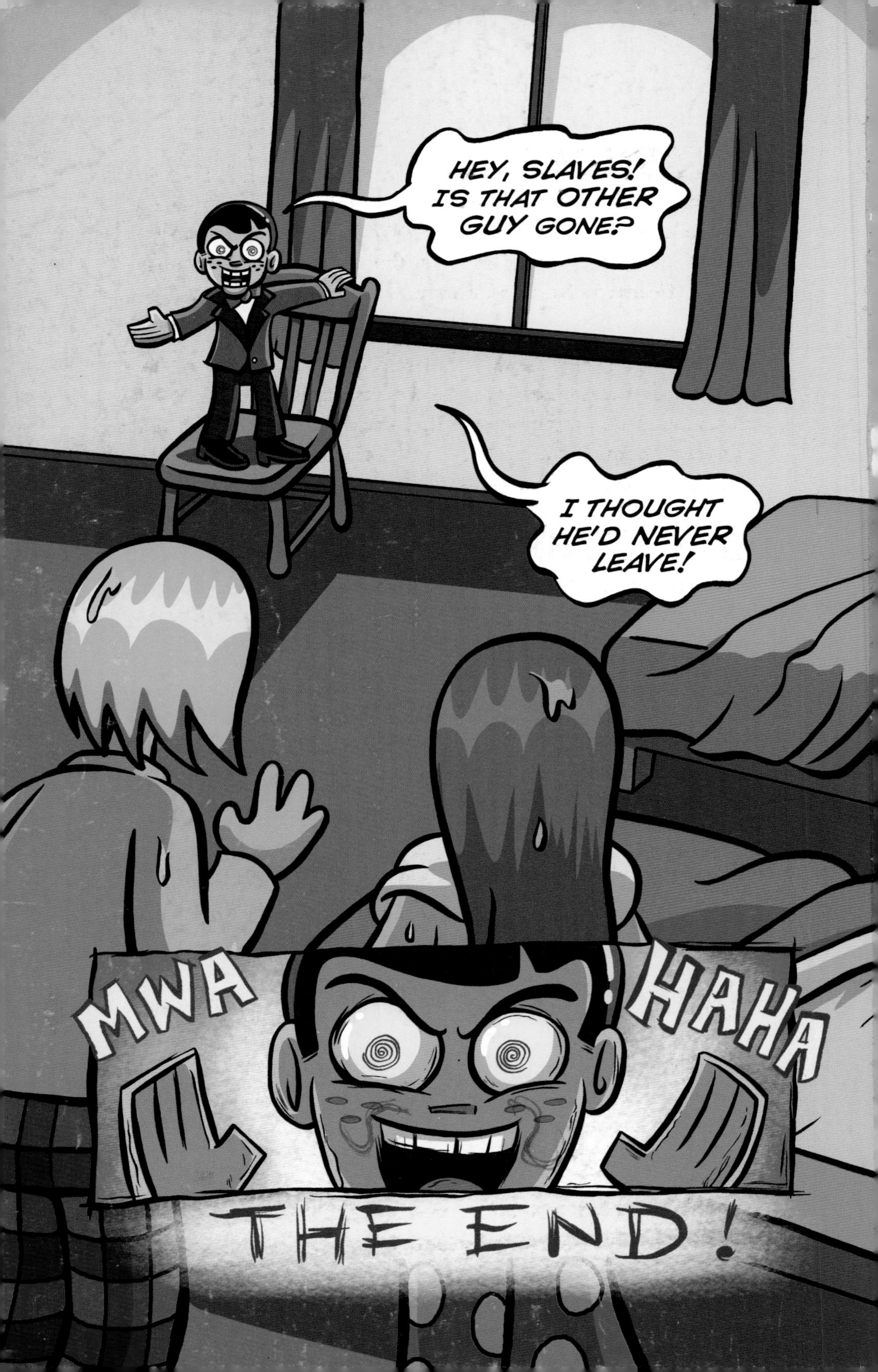
HEY, SLAVES! IS THAT OTHER GUY GONE?
I THOUGHT HE'D NEVER LEAVE!
MWA HAHAHA
THE END!